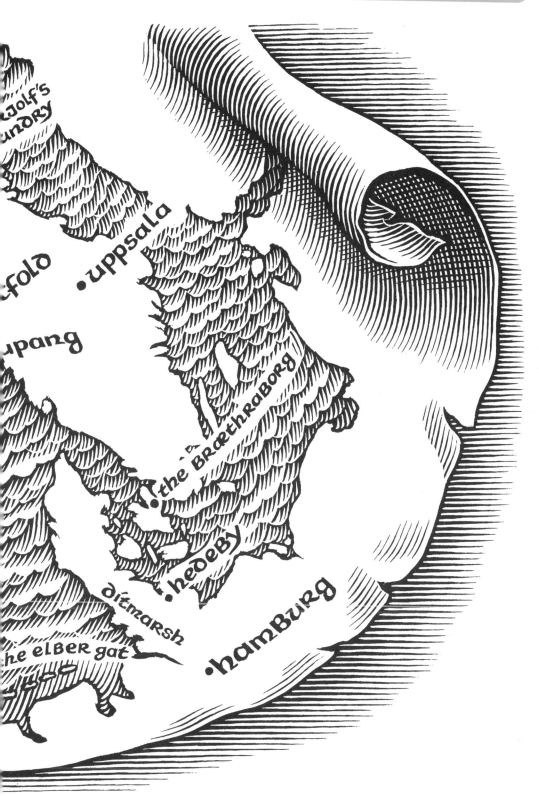

ONE
KING'S
WAY

ONE KING'S WAY

HARRY HARRISON
JOHN HOLM

TOR®

A TOM DOHERTY ASSOCIATES BOOK · NEW YORK

ONE KING'S WAY

Copyright © 1995 by Harry Harrison and John Holm

This book is printed on acid-free paper.

A Tor Book
Published by Tom Doherty Associates, Inc
175 Fifth Avenue
New York, N.Y. 10010

Tor® is a registered trademark of Tom Doherty Associates, Inc.

Interior illustrations by Bill Sanderson

Library of Congress Cataloging-in-Publication Data

Harrison, Harry.
    One king's way : the hammer and the cross / Harry Harrison.
       p.   cm.
    "Book two."
    "A Tom Doherty Associates book."
    ISBN 0-312-85691-1
    1. Great Britain—History—Anglo Saxon period, 449–1066—Fiction.
  2. Vikings—Fiction.   I. Title.   II. Title: Hammer and the
cross.
   PS3558.A667054 1995   94-46358
                                         CIP

First edition: April 1995
Printed in the United States of America

0 9 8 7 6 5 4 3 2 1

ONE
KING'S
WAY

CHAPTER ONE

Frozen in the hard grip of the worst winter in memory, all of England lay under a frigid mantle of snow. The great river Thames was covered with ice from bank to bank. The road leading west to Winchester was a flint-hard, filthy track of frozen hoofprints and caked manure. The horses slipped on the ice, snorting out steaming vapors. Their riders, huddled and chilled, looked up at the dark walls of the great Minster and spurred their tired mounts with little result.

This was the 21st of March of the year of our Lord's Incarnation 867, and a day of greatest portent. A royal union was taking place today. Filling the pews were the military aristocracy of Wessex, every alderman, thane, and high-reeve who could possibly be squeezed within the stone walls, gaping and sweating, a low mutter of explanation and translation continually rising from them, watching intently as the whole elaborate ritual of coronation of a Christian king unrolled its stately dance.

In the right-hand pew at the very front of the nave of the great Minster at Winchester was Shef Sigvarthsson, co-king of the English— and king in his own right of all those parts of it north of the Thames which he could persuade into obedience. He sat uneasily, aware of the many eyes on him.

They saw a man whose age was hard to guess. His thick dark hair and smooth-shaven face made him seem young, too young for the gold circlet of royalty on his brow and the heavy bracelets on both arms. He had the height and the broad shoulders of a warrior in his prime—or of an ironsmith, which was what he had been. Yet for all his youth the dark hair was already streaked with white, and his face showed the betraying grooves of care and pain. His right eye-socket was an empty hollow, and the patch that covered it could not disguise the way the flesh had drawn and fallen in. The whole of England and half of Europe beyond knew how he had been half-blinded on the order of Sigurth Snake-eye, eldest of the sons of Ragnar. And how the smith's apprentice had taken his revenge by killing Sigurth's brother, Ivar the Boneless, Champion of the North, rising from near-thrall to carl of the Viking Great Army, to jarl under the orders of Alfred Atheling. Now to being king and co-ruler with Alfred himself, joint victors over the Frankish Crusade only the year before. Rumors ran everywhere about the meaning of the strange sign he wore round his neck as emblem of the Asgarth Way, an emblem none had worn before him: the *kraki*, the pole-ladder of the mysterious deity Rig.

Shef had no wish to see the coronation, still less the ceremony that would follow. The grooves of pain deepened in his face as he watched. Yet he understood why he had to be there, he and his men: to make a point, to support his co-king. It was Alfred's request, as close to a command as possible, that had brought him here.

"You don't have to take the Mass," Alfred had said firmly to Shef and his supporters. "You don't even have to sing the hymns. But I want you there at the coronation, wearing your pendants, wearing your crown, Shef. Making a show. Pick out your most impressive men, and look rich and powerful. I want everyone to see that I am supported fully by the men of the North, the conquerors of Ivar the Boneless and Charles the Bald. The pagans. Not the wild pagans, the slavers and sacrificers, like the sons of Ragnar: but the men of the Way, the Way of Asgarth, the pendant-folk."

They had at least managed to do that, Shef thought, looking about. Put on their mettle, the two dozen Way-folk selected to sit in the front ranks had responded nobly. Guthmund the Greedy was carrying more gold and silver on his person, in arm-rings, torque, and belt-buckle, than any five thanes of Wessex put together. Of course he had shared in three successive distributions of plunder under Shef, whose fame, though fabulous, was not all exaggeration. Thorvin priest of Thor and his colleague Skaldfinn priest of Njörth, though opposed to worldly display, had nevertheless dressed in shining white and brought with them their signs of office, the short hammer for Thorvin and the seaman's boat for Skaldfinn. Cwicca, Osmod and the other English freedmen now veterans of Shef's campaigns, though hopelessly unimpressive in person from youthful hunger, had managed to dress themselves in the unheard-of luxury of silken tunics. They also carried carefully sloped the tools of their trade: halberds, crossbows, and catapult-winders. Shef suspected that the mere sight of men so obviously English, so obviously low-born, and so obviously rich beyond the dreams of the average Wessex thane, let alone churl, was the most powerful silent argument for Alfred's success that could be found.

The ceremony had begun hours before with the forming of a great procession from the king's residence to the Minster itself—a walk of barely a hundred yards, but every yard of them seeming to demand some special observance. Then the high mass in the Minster, the nobles of the realm crowding up to take communion, not so much out of reverence as out of an earnest desire not to miss any luck or blessing that might be granted to others. Among them, Shef had noted, had been many seemingly incongruous figures, the undersized frames and rough clothes of slaves that Alfred had freed and churls he had promoted. They were now here to take the word back to their towns and villages: the word that there was no doubt, no doubt at all that Alfred Atheling was now Alfred King of the West Saxons and of the Mark, by all the laws of man and of the Christian God.

Also in the first row, towering over those around him, sat the Marshal of Wessex, the man chosen by custom as the most notable warrior of the kingdom hand-to-hand. The Marshal, Wigheard, was indeed an imposing sight, nearer seven foot than six and twenty English stone if an ounce in weight; he carried the king's state sword at arm's length as effortlessly as a twig, and had already shown uncanny ability to fence with a halberd as if it were a willow-wand.

There was one man in Shef's group, sitting immediately to his left, who had difficulty following the ceremony, who glanced again and again at the Champion. This was the giant Brand, himself champion of the men of Halogaland, still wasted and shrunken from the belly-wound he had taken in his duel on the gangplank with Ivar the Boneless, but slowly regaining strength. Brand, shrunken as he was, still seemed the bigger man of the two. His bones were almost too big for his skin, with knuckles like rocks, and ridges jutting out over his eyebrows like armor. Brand's fists, Shef had once noted by careful comparison, were bigger than a pint pot: not just huge, but disproportionate even to the rest of him. "Men grow big where I come from," was all that Brand would ever say.

The noise of the congregation died as Alfred, now thoroughly blessed and prayed over, turned to face them to take his oaths. For the first time Latin was abandoned and the service broke into English as

Alfred's senior alderman asked the solemn question: "Do you grant us
our rightful laws and customs to be held, and do you swear after your
power to grant rightful dooms and defend the rights of your people
against every enemy?"

"I do." Alfred looked round the packed Minster. "I have done so,
and I will do so again." A rumble of assent.

Now a trickier moment, Shef thought as the alderman stepped back
and the senior bishop stepped forward. For one thing the bishop was
startlingly young—and for good reason. After Alfred's dispossession
of the Church, his excommunication by the Pope, the Crusade against
him and his final declaration of non-communion with Rome, every
senior cleric in his kingdom had left. From the Archbishops of York
and Canterbury down to the least bishop and abbot. Alfred's response
was to promote ten of the best remaining junior priests and tell them
the Church in England was in their hands. Now one of them, Eanfrith
Bishop of Winchester, six months before priest of a village no-one had
heard of, came forward to ask his question.

"Lord King, we ask you to grant to us protection for Holy Church
and due law and rightfulness for all those who are members of it."

Eanfrith and Alfred had been days working out the new formula,
Shef recalled. The traditional one had asked for confirmation of all
rights and privileges, tithes and taxes, ownerships and possessions—
all of which Alfred had in fact taken away.

"I grant protection and due law," Alfred replied. Again he looked
round, again added words beyond tradition. "Protection to those
within the Church and without it. Due law to members of it and to
others."

The highly trained choristers of Winchester, choirmonks and
choirboys together, burst into the anthem of Zadok the Priest,
Unxerunt Salomonem Zadok sacerdos, as the bishops prepared for the
solemn moment of blessing with the holy oil, after which Alfred would
be literally the Lord's Anointed, against whom rebellion was also
sacrilege.

Shortly, thought Shef, would come the difficult moment for him. It
had been explained to him very carefully that Wessex, ever since
Queen Eadburh of wicked memory, never had a Queen, and that the
King's wife could have no separate coronation. Nevertheless, Alfred
had said, he was insistent that his new wife should be accepted by him
in front of the people, in honor of her courage in the defeat of the
Franks. So, he had said, after the donning of the regalia, sword, ring
and scepter, he meant his wife to come forward and be named before

the congregation, not as Queen, but as the Lady of Wessex. And who better to lead her to the altar than her brother, Shef, also his co-king?

Who might have to yield his kingdom to the child of Alfred and the Lady, if he had no child himself.

This would be the second time he had given her away, Shef thought bitterly. Once again he must forget the love, the passion that had once bound them. The first had been to a man they both hated, and in punishment for that, it seemed, he must now hand her over to a man they both loved. As Thorvin nudged him with a mighty elbow, to tell him the time had come to step forward and lead the Lady Godive with her train of maidens to the altar, Shef met her eyes—her triumphant eyes—and felt his heart turn to ice.

Alfred might now be a king, he though numbly. He himself was not. He did not have the right, or the strength.

As the choir broke into the *Benedicat* he decided that he would do it. Do the thing he wanted to, not just what he felt was his duty. He would take out the fleet, the new navy of the co-kings, to work out his inner anger on the enemies of the realm: the pirates of the North, the fleets of the Franks, the slavers of Ireland or Spain, anyone. Let Alfred and Godive find their own happiness at home. He would find peace in drowned men and shattered ships.

Earlier this same day, far to the north in the land of the Danes, a simpler and more terrifying ceremony had taken place.

It had begun before dawn. The bound man lifted from where he lay on the floor of the guard-hut had long since ceased to struggle, though he was neither a coward nor a weakling. Two days before, when the emissaries of the Snake-eye had marched into the slave-pen, he had known what would be in store for the man they chose. When they picked him from the others, he had known also that the least chance of escape was to be seized, and he had seized it: secretly gathered the slack in his wrist-chains as they marched him off, waited till the guards were hustling him over the wooden bridge that led to the inner heart of the Braethraborg, the stronghold of the three last sons of Ragnar. Then struck suddenly to his right with the chain, and hurled himself for the rail and the swift river beneath it—at the best to swim for freedom, at the worst to die his own man.

His guards had seen many such desperate attempts. One snatched at his ankle as he lunged for the rail, two others had him pinned before he could recover. They had beaten him systematically with their spear-shafts, not in malice, but to ensure he would be too stiff and

battered to move swiftly again. Then taken off the chains and replaced
them with rawhide thongs, twisting and wetting them with sea-water
to dry even tighter. If the bound man could have seen his fingers in the
dark, they would have been blue-black, swollen like a corpse's. Even if
some god intervened to save his life, it would be too late now to save
his hands.

But neither god nor man would intervene. The guards had ceased to
acknowledge his existence when they talked among themselves. He
was not dead, because for what he had to do a man was needed with
the breath, and especially the blood, still in him. But that was all.
There was no need for anything else.

Now, at the end of the long night, his guards carried him out of the
longhouse where the great fresh-tarred flagship lay, and down the long
row of rollers that led down the slipway to the sea.

"Here will do. This one here," grunted the burly middle-aged
warrior in charge.

"How do we do it?" asked one of the others, a young man without
the campaign-marks, the scars and silver arm-rings of the others.
"I've never seen this done before."

"So watch and you'll learn. First, cut that rawhide round his wrists.
No, don't worry," as the younger man hesitated, looked round
automatically for any slightest glimpse of an escape, "he's a goner,
look at him, couldn't even crawl if we let him go. Don't let him go,
mind. Just cut his wrists free, right."

A few minutes of sawing, and the bound man staggered as the
lashings freed, stared a moment in the pale but growing light at the
hands in front of him.

"Now lay him out flat on that roller. Belly down. Feet together.
Now see here, young Hrani, because this is the important bit. The
thrall has to have his back upwards, for why you'll see very shortly. He
can't have his hands behind him, same reason, and he mustn't be able
to move. But he mustn't be able to stop himself moving either.

"So what I do is this." The middle-aged leader pressed his
captive's face down on to the solid pine trunk he lay on, seized both
arms and dragged them forward above his head, till the victim looked
like a man diving. He pulled a hammer and two short iron spikes from
his belt.

"We used to tie them, but I think you get a better roll like this. I saw
something like it once in one of the Christers' churches. Course, they
put the nail in the wrong place. Half-wits."

Grunting with effort, the veteran began to hammer a spike carefully
through the junction of wrist and hand. Behind him, there came a

rustle of many men moving. Against the dawn-light of the east, dark shapes began to show. Spears and helmets silhouetted against the sky where the sun would soon show its first glimmer on this, the first day of the warriors' new year, when day and night were the same length.

"He's taking it well," said the young man as his instructor started to hammer in the second spike. "More like a warrior than a thrall. Who was he, anyway?"

"Him? Just some fisherman we picked up on the way back last year. And he's not taking it well, he can't feel a thing, his hands have been dead for hours.

"Soon over now," he added to the man now firmly nailed to the log, patting his cheek. "Speak well of me in the next world. This could go a lot worse if I bungled it. But I haven't. Just lash his legs down, you two, no need for another spike. Feet together. He's got to turn when the moment comes."

The little group got to their feet, leaving their victim stretched out along the pine-trunk.

"Ready, Vestmar?" said a voice behind them.

"Ready, lord."

The space behind them had filled up while they worked. At the rear, away from the shore and the long sea inlet, lay hump after hump of dark shapes, slave-pens, workshops, boathouses, and in dimly-sensed ranks the rows of regular barracks that housed the trusted troops of the sea-kings, the sons of Ragnar—once four, now three. From the barracks the men had come streaming, all men, no women, no youths, to see the solemn spectacle: the launch of the first ship, the start of the annual campaigning season that once again was to bring terror and ruin to the Christians and their allies of the South.

Yet the warriors hung back, ranking themselves round the inlet's shore in a deep semi-circle. Pacing down to the very shore itself came only three men, all tall and powerful, men in their prime, the three remaining sons of Ragnar Hairy-Breeks: Ubbi the grizzled, despoiler of women, Halvdan the redbeard, the fanatical dueller and champion, dedicated to the warrior's life and code. Before even them, Sigurth the Snake-eye, so called for the whites that surrounded every part of his eye-pupils like the gaze of a snake: the man who meant to make himself King of all the lands of the North.

All faces were turning now to the east, to see if the first glimpse of the sun's disk could be seen on the horizon. Most years, here in Denmark in the month the Christians called March, only cloud. Today, good omen, clear sky, with just the light haze already turned pink by the still-invisible sun. A slight murmur came from the watchers as the readers of omens came forward, a stooped and aged band, clutching their holy bags, their knives and knucklebones and sheep's shoulder-blades, the instruments of divination. Sigurth watched them coldly. They were necessary, for the men. But he had no fear of a bad divination, a poor set of omens. Augurs who augured badly could find themselves on the sacrifice-stone as well as any other.

In the dead, intent silence, the man stretched out on the pine-log found his voice. Pinned and lashed as he was, he could not move his body. He strained his head back, and called out in a choked voice, aiming it at the midmost of the three men by the shore.

"Why can you do this, Sigurth? I was no enemy of yours. I am no Christian, nor man of the Way. I am a Dane and a freeman like yourself. What right have you to take my life?"

A roar from the crowd drowned his last words. A line of light showed in the east, the sun poking up over the near-flat horizon of Sjaelland, eastmost of the Danish islands. The Snake-eye turned, threw back his cape, waved to the men in the boathouse above him.

Instantly a creaking of ropes, a simultaneous grunt of effort, fifty men, the picked champions of the Ragnarsson army, throwing their mighty weight on the ropes attached to the spiked rowlocks. Out from the boathouse loomed the dragon-prow of the Snake-eye's own ship, the *Frani Ormr* itself, the *Shining Worm*. Grinding forward along the flat on the greased rollers prepared for it, ten tons of weight on a fifty-foot keel made of the stoutest oak-tree in Denmark.

It reached the top of the slipway. The pinned man craned his neck sideways to see his fate looming against the sky, and clamped his mouth shut to avoid the scream welling from inside him. One thing only he could avoid giving his tormentors, and that was the joy of a good omen, a year launched in fear and despair and shrieks of pain.

The men heaved at the ropes together, the prow tipped and began to slide down, thumping over each roller in turn. As it ground down towards him, as the projecting prow reached over him, the sacrifice called out again, meaning it in defiance: "Where is your right, Sigurth? What made you a king?"

The keel struck him accurately in the small of the back, rode over him and crushed down with its immense weight. Involuntarily, the breath pressed from his lungs in a weird cry, turning into a shriek as pain overcame any possible self-control. As the ship roared over him, its haulers running now to keep up, the roller to which he was nailed whirled round. The blood of his crushed heart and lungs spurted up, driven out by the massive rounded keel.

It splashed upwards on to the flaring bow planks above him. The augurs watching intently, crouched low so as not to miss any detail, whooped and whirled their fringed sleeves in delight.

"Blood! Blood on the planks for the sea-king's launch!"

"And a cry! A death-cry for the lord of warriors!"

The ship surged on into the calm water of the Braethraborg fjord. As it did so the sun's disc rose fully above the line of the horizon, sending a long flat ray beneath the haze. Throwing aside his cape, the Snake-eye seized his spear by the butt and lifted it up above the shadow of the boathouse and the slipway. The sun caught it and turned its eighteen-inch triangular blade to fire.

"Red light and a red spear for the new year," roared the watching army, drowning out the augurs' shrilling.

"What made me a king?" shouted the Snake-eye to the passing spirit. "The blood I have shed, and the blood in my veins! For I am the god-born, the son of Ragnar, the son of Völsi, the seed of the immortals. And the sons of men are logs beneath my keel."

Behind him his army ran, crew by crew, towards their waiting ships, to take their turn by the stronghold's crowded slipways.

The same chill winter that held fast to England had fallen also on the other side of the channel. In the cold city of Cologne, on this same day, as Alfred was being crowned, eleven men met in a bare unheated room of a great church hundreds of miles to the south of the Braethraborg and its human sacrifice. Five of them wore the purple and white of archbishops' rank—none, as yet, the scarlet of a Cardinal. Slightly behind and to the right of each of the five sat a second man, each of these dressed in the plain black robe of a canon of the Order of Saint Hrodegang. Each was his archbishop's confessor, chaplain and counselor—of no rank, but of immense influence, with the best hope also of succeeding to the dignity of a Prince of the Church.

The eleventh man also wore the black robe, this time of a mere deacon. He looked covertly from side to side at the assembled gathering, recognizing and respecting power, but unsure of his own place at the table. He was Erkenbert, once deacon of the great Minster at York and servant of Archbishop Wulfhere. But the Minster was no more, sacked by the enraged heathen of the North the previous year. And Wulfhere, Archbishop though he remained, was a mere pensioner of his fellow-archbishops, an object of contemptuous charity like his co-Primate of Canterbury. The Church in England was no more: no lands, no rents, no power.

Erkenbert did not know why he had been called to this meeting.

He did know that he was in deadly danger. The room was not bare because the great Prince-Archbishop of Cologne could not afford furniture. It was bare because he wished to have no cover for any possible eavesdropper or spy. Words had been said here that would mean death for all present if repeated.

The group had eventually, slowly, cautiously, come to a decision, feeling each other out. Now, the decision made, tension slackened.

"He has to go, then," repeated Archbishop Gunther, the host of the meeting in Cologne.

A circuit of silent nods around the table.

"His failure is too great to overlook," confirmed Theutgard of Trier. "Not only did the Crusade he sent against the province of the English meet defeat in battle . . . "

"Though that itself is a sign of the divine disfavor," agreed the notoriously pious Hincmar of Rheims.

" . . . but he allowed a seed to be planted. A seed worse than defeat for one king or another king. A seed of apostasy."

The word created a momentary silence. All knew what had happened the year before. How under pressure from both the Vikings of the North and his own bishops at home the youthful King Alfred of the West Saxons had made common cause with some pagan sect— called, so they heard, the Way. Had then successively defeated the dreaded Ivar Ragnarsson of the Vikings, followed by Charles the Bald, Christian king of the Franks and deputy of the Pope himself. Now Alfred ruled unchallenged in England, though sharing his dominions with some heathen jarl whose name seemed almost a joke. But it was no joke that in retaliation for the Crusade sent against him by Pope Nicholas Alfred had declared the Church in England out of communion with the Catholic and Apostolic Church of Rome itself. Even less of one that he had stripped the Church in England of its lands and wealth, allowing Christ to be preached and served only by those who were prepared to earn their own livings by free offerings, or even—it was said—through supporting themselves by trade.

"For that defeat, and that apostasy, he must go," repeated Gunther. He looked round the table. "I say, Pope Nicholas must go to God. He is an old man, but not old enough. We must hasten his departure."

Now that the words had been spoken aloud a silence fell; it was not easy for princes of the Church to talk of killing the Pope. Meinhard, Archbishop of Mainz, a fierce, hard man, spoke in a loud voice. "Have we any way to do that?" he queried

The priest to Gunther's right stirred and spoke. "There will be no difficulty. There are men we can trust in the Pope's entourage at Rome.

Men who have not forgotten that they are Germans like ourselves. I do not recommend poison. A pillow in the night. When he does not waken his office can be declared vacant without scandal."

"Good," said Gunther, "for though I wish his death, I take my oath before God that I wish Pope Nicholas no harm."

The group looked at him with faint signs of scepticism. All knew that only ten years before Pope Nicholas had deposed Gunther and deprived him of his see as a penalty for disobedience. As he had done also to Theutgard of Trier, while he had further rebuked and overruled even the pious Hincmar over a dispute with a mere bishop.

"He was a great man, who did his duty as he saw it. I do not blame him even for launching King Charles on his ill-fated Crusade. No, there is no harm in Crusades. But he made a mistake. Tell them, Arno," he added to his confessor. "Tell them our appreciation of the situation." He sank back, lifting the gold goblet of Rhenish wine on which so much of his archbishopric's revenue depended.

The younger man pulled his stool forward to the table, his sharp face gleaming with enthusiasm beneath close-cropped blond stubble. "Here in Cologne," he began, "we have made careful study of the arts of war. Not merely on the field of battle itself, but also in its wider context. We try to think not merely like a *tacticus*"—he used the Latin word, though up till then all had spoken the Low German of Saxony and the North—"but like a *strategos* of the old Greeks. And if we think *strategice*"—Hincmar at least winced at the strange medley of Greek and Latin—"we see that Pope Nicholas made a critical error.

"He failed to see what we here call the *punctum gravissimum*, that is, the heavy point, the point of main weight, of an enemy's attack. He did not see at once that the real danger, the real danger to the whole Church, lay not in the schisms of the East, or in the struggles of Pope against Emperor, or in the naval raids of the followers of Mahound, but in the little-known kingdoms of the poor province of Britannia. Because only in Britannia did the Church find more than an enemy: a rival, a supplanter."

"He is an Easterner," said Meinhard contemptuously.

"Just so. He thinks that what happens here in the West, here in the North-West of Europe, in Germany and Frankland and the Low Countries, is of minor importance. But we know that here lies destiny. The destiny of the Church. The destiny of the world. I dare to say it, if Pope Nicholas does not: the new chosen people, the only true bulwark against the barbarians."

He ceased, his fair face already flushing with pride.

"You will find no arguments on that score here, Arno," Gunther remarked. "So, once Nicholas is dead, he must be replaced. I know"—he raised a hand—"the Cardinals will not elect anyone to Pope who has any more sensible opinion, and we cannot expect to sway the Italians to sense. But we can sway them to nonsense. I think we are all agreed that we will use our revenues and our influence to ensure the election of someone we can count on to be popular with the Romans, well-born among the Italians, and a complete nonentity. I believe he has already chosen his papal name: Adrian II, they tell me.

"More serious is what must be done closer to home. Not only Nicholas must go. King Charles too. He also has been defeated, and by a rabble of peasants."

"Gone already," said Hincmar decisively. "His barons will not forgive humiliation. Those who did not share it with him cannot believe that Frankish lancers could be defeated by slingers and bowmen. Those who did are anxious not to share his disgrace. There will be a rope round his neck or a knife in his ribs without us stirring a hand. But who is to replace *him*?"

"Your pardon," said Erkenbert quietly. He had been listening with the greatest care, and slowly the conviction had come to him that these men, unlike the pompous and inefficient clerics of the English Church he had served all his life, actually respected intelligence more than rank. Juniors spoke without rebuke. They put forward their own ideas, and had them accepted. Or if they were rejected, it was with reason given, and after careful thought. Among these men, the only sin was to fail in logic, or in imagination. The excitement of abstract thought worked on Erkenbert more than the fumes of the wine in his goblet. He felt that at last he was among equals. Above all, he wished to have them accept him too as an equal.

"I understand Low German, for it is like my own English. But allow me to speak in Latin for the moment. I do not understand how King Charles the Bald of Francia can be replaced. Or what advantage any successor would be to this group. He has two sons, am I correct? Louis and Charles. He had three brothers, Ludwig and Pepin and Lothaire, of whom only Ludwig is still alive, and—is it seven living nephews, Louis and Charles and Lothaire . . ."

". . . and Pepin and Carloman and Ludwig and Charles," completed Gunther. He laughed briefly. "And what our English friend is too polite to say is that not one of them can be told from another. Charles the Bald. Charles the Fat. Ludwig the Saxon. Pepin the Younger. Which is which and what does it matter? So I will put it this way in his place.

"The seed of the Emperor, the great Charles, Charlemagne himself, has failed. The virtue is gone out of it. As we find a new Pope in Rome, so we must find a new king here. A new king's line.''

The men round the table looked cautiously at each other, less cautiously as each realized that the unthinkable was being thought. Gunther smiled briefly at the effect of his words.

Greatly daring again, Erkenbert spoke. "It is possible. In my own country kings' lines have been deposed. And in yours—did not the great Charlemagne himself come to power through the deeds of his ancestors, who deposed the god-born to whom they had been servants? Deposed them and shore their hair in public, to show they were no longer holy? It could be done. What is it, after all, that makes a king?''

One man during the whole discussion had not spoken, though he had nodded in assent from time to time: the immensely-respected Archbishop of Hamburg and Bremen in the far North, the disciple and successor of Saint Ansgar, Archbishop Rimbert, famous for his personal courage in fanatical missions to and against the pagans of the North. As he stirred, all eyes turned to him.

"You are right, brothers. The line of Charles has failed. And you are wrong. Wrong in many ways. You speak of this and that, of strategy and the *punctum gravissimum* and the West and the East, and in the world of men what you say may have a meaning.

"But we do not live only in the world of men. I say to you that Pope Nicholas and King Charles had a worse failing than any you have seen. I pray only that we may not fall into it ourselves. I say to you, they did not believe! And without belief, all their weapons and their plans were straw and chaff, to be blown away on the wind of God's displeasure.

"So I will tell you that we do not need a new king, nor a new king's line. No. What we must have now is an Emperor! An *Imperator Romanorum*. For we, comrades—we Germans are the new Rome. We must have an *imperator* to mark it.''

The others stared at him in silence, a new vision slowly forming in their minds. It was the blond-cropped Arno, Gunther's counselor, who broke it.

"And how is the new Emperor to be chosen?'' he asked cautiously. "And where is such a one to be found?''

"Listen,'' said Rimbert, "and I will tell you. And I will tell you also the secret of Charlemagne, the last true Emperor of Rome in the West. I will tell you what it is that makes the true king.''

CHAPTER TWO

The strong smell of sawdust and wood chips filled the air as Shef and his companions, rested now from the long ride from Winchester, strolled down to the keelyard. Although the sun had not long cleared the eastern horizon, hundreds of men were already working—leading up great carts loaded with wood and drawn by patient oxen, clustered round forges, bustling in and out of rope-walks. The noise of hammers and saws came from all directions, mixed with the furious voices of gang foremen: but no whip-cracks, no cries of pain, no iron slave-collars.

Brand whistled slowly and shook his head as he surveyed the scene. Only just released from his sick-bed, he was still carefully watched by his physician, the diminutive Hund. Until now he had seen none of what had been achieved over the long winter. And indeed, even Shef, who had driven the work on in person or by deputy every single day, found it hard to credit. It was as if he had released a torrent of energy rather than creating it. Again and again over the winter he had found his wishes anticipated.

After the fighting had ceased last year he had found himself with the resources and wealth of a kingdom to command. His first and most urgent task had been to ensure the defense of his precarious realm. He issued the orders and his commanders applied themselves eagerly—building war machines and training their users, recruiting troops, mixing his potentially refractory groups of freed slaves, Vikings of the Way, and English thanes performing military service in return for their leases of land. This accomplished he had set himself to his second task; to ensure the royal revenues. The job of recording all details of land and tolls, debts and taxes, till then carried on by custom and memory, he had passed on to the priest Boniface. With instructions to do in all the counties Shef now controlled what he had begun in Norfolk alone. It would take time and skill, but the results had already become visible.

The third task, though, was Shef's alone: and that was to build a navy. If there was one thing that was clear, it was that all the battles of the previous two years had been fought on English soil and paid for with English lives. The way to ensure defense, Shef had seen, was to stop the attackers, and especially the Vikings outside the Way, in the place where they reigned supreme: at sea. Supported by the accumulated wealth and taxes of East Anglia and East Mercia as well, Shef had started immediately to build a fleet.

He had had much help and experience to draw on. The Vikings of the Way contained many skilled shipwrights, quite ready to pass on their knowledge and skills if properly rewarded. Thorvin and his fellow-priests of the Way, immensely interested, had plunged into the work as if they had asked nothing better all their lives—as indeed was true. Conforming to their code of forever seeking for new knowledge and supporting themselves and their religion by their working skills alone. Smiths, carpenters, hauliers, poured from all over eastern England to the site Shef had chosen for his dock, on the north bank of the Thames. It lay within his own dominions but facing those of King Alfred, poised to guard—or to threaten—both the Channel and the North Sea, a short distance downriver from the commercial port of London, at the tiny hamlet of Creekmouth.

The problem had been direction. Holding all these skilled and experienced men to the plan Shef had formed, but which directly contradicted much of their life-times' collective experience. At first Shef had asked Thorvin to direct the site, but he had refused, saying he must be free to leave at any time if the demands of his faith required it. Then he had thought of Udd, the ex-slave who had, almost single-handed, invented the crossbow and made safe the torsion catapult. Thus—to some eyes—defeating both Ivar Ragnarsson, Champion of the North, and weeks later Charles the Bald, King of the Franks, at what men were coming to call the Battle of Hastings, 866.

Udd had been a disaster, soon replaced. Left to himself it transpired that the little man was only capable of taking an interest in things made of metal. He also could not direct so much as the boy who blew the bellows, from constitutional shyness. He had been removed and set to the much more congenial task of finding out everything that could be discovered about steel.

As confusion grew, Shef had had to think over his true needs: a man used to the sea and ships, used to organizing the work of others, but not so independent as to alter Shef's orders or so conservative as to fail to understand them. Shef knew few people. The only one of those who seemed even possible was the fisherman-reeve of Bridlington, Ordlaf, whose capture of Ragnar Hairy-Breeks two summers before had unleashed the fury on England. He it was, now, who turned to greet Shef's party.

Shef waited for him to kneel and rise. Early attempts to do away with the formal code of respect had foundered on the looks of hurt and uncertainty of Shef's thanes.

"I brought someone to see the work, Ordlaf. This is my friend and one-time captain, Viga-Brand. He comes from Halogaland, far, far in the North, and has sailed more miles than most men. I want his opinion of the new ships."

Ordlaf grinned. "He'll see much to stretch his eyes at, lord, however far he's sailed. Things no-one has seen before."

"Truth—right there is a thing that I have not seen before," said Brand. He waved at a pit a few yards off. Inside it was a man pulling one end of a six-foot saw. Another stood on the huge log above pulling on the other. Ready hands held the plank as they sawed it from the log.

"How does it work? I have only ever seen planks hewed out with adzes."

"Me too, till I came here," said Ordlaf. "The secret lies in two things. Better teeth on the saws—that is the work of Master Udd. And teaching these blockheads here"—the men looked up grinning—"not to push the saw, just *take turns pulling it*. Saves a lot of wood and a lot of work," he added in a normal voice. The plank eased to the ground, caught by helpers and the two sawyers changed places, the one beneath shaking dust and shavings from his hair. Shef noticed as they changed over that one wore round his neck the Hammer of Thor, as did most of the workmen on the site, the other an almost indistinguishable Christian cross.

"But that's nothing, sir," Ordlaf went on to Brand. "What the king really wants you to see are his pride and joy, the ten ships we're building to his design. And one of them, lord, now ready for your inspection, finished while you were in Winchester. Come and see."

He led them through the gate of a stout palisade to a ring of jetties projecting out into a still backwater of the river. There in front of them lay ten ships, men working on all of them, but one, the nearest, evidently complete.

"Now, sir Brand. Did you ever see anything like that this side of Halogaland?"

Brand stared, considering. Slowly he shook his head. "It is a big one, right enough. They say the biggest ocean-going ship in the world is Sigurth Snake-eye's own *Frani Ormr,* the *Shining Worm,* that rows fifty oars. This is as big. All these ships are as big."

Doubt clouded his eyes. "What are the keels made of? Have you taken two trunks and joined them? If you have, well, maybe on a river or off the coast in fair weather, but for deep sea or long voyage—"

"All single trunks," said Ordlaf. "What you may be forgetting, sir, if you don't mind me saying so, is that up there in the North where you come from you have to work with the wood you can get. And while I can see men grow big enough up there, it isn't the same for trees. What we got here is English oak. And say what they like, I've never seen better wood or bigger wood."

Brand stared again, shook his head again. "Well and good. But what in Hel have you done to the mast? You've—you've put it in the wrong place. And raked forward like a—like an eighteen-year-old's prick! How is that going to shift a ship that size?'' Honest pain filled his voice.

Both Shef and Ordlaf grinned broadly. This time Shef took up the tale.

''The whole idea of these ships, Brand, is that they have only one purpose. Not crossing the ocean, not carrying men with spears and swords, not carrying cargo.

''These are ships for battle. Ships to battle other ships. Not by coming alongside and having their crews board each other. Not even by doing what Father Boniface tells me the ancient Rome-folk did, by ramming. No: by sinking the other ship and its crew along with it, and doing it from a distance. Now there's only one thing we know that can do that.

''You remember the pull-throwers I first made at Crowland that winter? What do you think of them?''

Brand shrugged. ''Good against people. Wouldn't like to have one of those rocks fall into my ship. But as you know, you have to be the right distance to get a hit. Two ships, both moving . . .''

''Right, no chance. Now what of the twist-shooters we used against King Charles's lancers?''

''Might kill the crew, one man at a time. Couldn't sink a ship. The arrow they shoot would plug its own hole.''

''That leaves us with the last weapon, the one that Erkenbert the deacon made for Ivar. Guthmund used them to knock down the palisade at the camp above Hastings. The thing the Rome-folk called the *onager*—the wild ass. We call it the mule.''

At a signal deck-hands dragged tarred canvas away from a squat, square object mounted in the exact center of the nearest ship's undecked hull.

''What do you say to a hit from one of those?''

Brand shook his head slowly. He had seen the onagers shoot only once, and then from a distance, but he remembered seeing carts fly in pieces, whole files of oxen smashed to the ground. ''No ship in the world could survive it. One hit, and the whole frame would go to pieces. But the reason you call it the mule is . . .''

''Because of the kick. Come and see what we've done.''

The men walked up the gangplank to stare at the new weapon close up. ''See,'' Shef explained. ''These weigh a ton and a quarter. They have to. You see how it works? Stout rope down at the base, with two handles. You twist the rope both sides. It holds this bar''—he patted a five-foot beam standing upright, a heavy leather sling dangling from a peg at its top. "You force the bar down on to the deck, held by an iron clamp, and keep twisting. When it's at greatest strain you release the clamp. Bar shoots up with a rock in the sling, sling whirls round . . . "

"Bar hits the crosspiece." Ordlaf patted a thick beam on a massive frame, padded both sides with heavy sandbags.

"The bar stops, the sling releases, the rock keeps going. It throws flat and hard, anything up to half a mile. But you see the problem. We have to build it heavy, to take the kick. We have to have it dead over the center-line, so we can fix the frame down on to the keel. And because it weighs so much, we have to have it centered fore and aft as well."

"But that's where the mast should be," objected Brand.

"So we had to move the mast. That's where Ordlaf showed us something."

"You see, sir Brand," Ordlaf explained, "where I come from we have boats like yours, double-ended and clinker-built and all. But because we're in it for fish, not for far voyaging, we rig them different. We step the mast forward of center, and we rake it forward too. And then, you can see, we cut the sail different. Not square, like yours, but on a slant."

Brand grunted. "I know. So if you take your hands off the steering oar she turns head into wind and rides the waves. Fisherman's trick. Safe enough. But slow. Especially with all this weight to shift. How fast is she?"

Shef and Ordlaf exchanged glances. "Not fast at all," Shef conceded. "Guthmund ran a trial against one of his boats before we put the mule in this one, and even without that weight, well— Guthmund sailed rings round her.

"But you see, Brand, we aren't trying to catch anyone! If we meet a fleet in the open sea, and they come to fight us, we'll sink them! If they sail away, the coastline has been defended. If they get past us, we'll follow and sink them wherever they go. This isn't a transport, Brand. It's a ship for battle."

"A battleship," added Ordlaf approvingly.

"Can you train it round?" asked Brand. "The mule, I mean. Can you point it different directions? You could with your dart-throwers."

"We're working on it," said Shef. "We tried putting the whole thing on a cartwheel, putting the cartwheel on an axle, and bedding the other end of the axle in a hole bored in the keel. But it was all too heavy to turn, and the kick kept breaking the axle. Udd has some idea of putting the whole thing on an iron ball, but . . . No. It will only shoot directly on the beam. But what we have done is fit two bars, two ropes, two sets of handles and so on, one either side. Only one crosspiece, naturally. But that means we can shoot to either beam."

Brand shook his head again. As they stood he had been feeling the ship heave gently beneath him, even in the Thames backwater, trying to estimate how she would feel in the open sea. A ton and a quarter of weight, much of it high up so that the machine stood higher than the gunwales. Sail pressure way off center-line. A wide yard so they could spread plenty of sail, he noticed. But tricky to handle. He had no doubt the fisherman knew his business. And there was no question what a hit from one of those rocks would do. Remembering the fragile frame of every boat he had ever sailed, their planks not even nailed to the ribs, but lashed with sinew, Brand could see the whole construction springing apart in a moment, leaving an entire crew struggling in the sea. And not even Sigurth Snake-eye's own fifty champions could fight against that.

"What are you going to call her," he asked suddenly. "For luck." His hand shot automatically to the hammer pendant on his chest. Ordlaf copied his gesture, fishing from under his tunic the silver boat of Njörth.

"We've got ten of the battleships," said Shef. "I wanted to call them after the gods of the Way, *Thor*, *Frey*, *Rig*, and so on, but Thorvin would not allow it. He said it would be bad luck if we had to say 'Heimdall is aground,' or 'Thor is stuck on the sandbank.' So we changed our minds. We decided to call each ship after one of the counties in my realm, and as far as we can we will crew her from that county. So this is the *Norfolk*, over there the *Suffolk*, the *Lincoln*, the *Isle of Ely*, the *Buckingham*, and all the others. What do you think?"

Brand hesitated. Like all sailors, he had deep respect for luck, and no wish to say the ill word that might bring down bad luck on the enterprise of his friend. "I think that once again you have brought a new thing to the world. It may be that your 'Counties' will sweep the seas. Certainly I would not care to encounter one, and men do not call me the timidest of the Norsemen. It may be that the kings of England will be the sea-kings in the future, and not the kings of the North.

"Tell me," he went on, "where do you mean to make your first cruise?"

"Across to the Dutch shore," said Shef. "Then up along the coast past the Frisian islands and into Danish waters. That is the main route the pirates come. We will sink every pirate ship we see. From then on any who wish to invade us must take the long sea-crossing from

Denmark. But in the end we will destroy their bases, seek them out in their own home-ports."

"The Frisian islands," muttered Brand. "The mouths of the Rhine, the Ems, the Elbe, the Eider. Well, I will tell you one thing, young man. All that is pilot water. You understand what I mean? You will need a pilot who knows the channels and the landmarks, so he can find his way by smell and hearing if he needs to."

Ordlaf looked stubborn. "I've found my way all my life with no more than lead, lookout and log-line. Nor do I feel my luck has got any the worse since I left the monks who were my masters and found the gods of the Way."

Brand grunted. "I say nothing against the gods of the Way." Again, both he and Ordlaf touched their protecting pendants, and this time Shef, with a self-conscious gesture, reached also to pull out his strange ladder-like charm, the token of his patron Rig. "No, the gods may be well enough. But as for lead, lookout and log-line—you'll need more than that off Bremen! I say it, I, Brand, Champion of the men of Halogaland."

The listening workmen shifted and muttered. Some of those new to the yards nudged each other, pointing at the unfamiliar pendant of Rig.

Sun slanted through the high windows of the great library in the cathedral of Cologne, to fall on the open pages of several books spread across the massive lectern. Erkenbert the deacon, his short frame barely able to see its upper edges, stood lost in thought. He was alone. The *librarius*, knowing he had the archbishop's favor, and approving the intentness of his research, had left him to himself, even with the great and precious Bible, written on the skins of eighty calves.

Erkenbert was comparing texts. Could the fantastic tale that the archbishop Rimbert had told them days before possibly be true? It had convinced everyone else at the meeting, archbishops and counselors alike. But then it had flattered their pride, appealed to their sense of themselves as a nation, and as a nation continually rejected and undervalued by the power of Rome. Erkenbert did not share that feeling—or at least not yet. The English nation, remembering its conversion by the blessed Pope Gregory, had long boasted its loyalty to the Popes and to Rome. But what had Rome sent in return? If what Rimbert said was true, then maybe it was time to be loyal . . . elsewhere.

The texts, now. First among them was one that Erkenbert knew

well, could have recited in his sleep. Nevertheless, important to look
again. The four gospellers' accounts of the crucifixion of Christ all told
slightly different tales—proof of their truth, of course, for who does
not know that four men seeing the same thing will pick different parts
of it to repeat? But John—John said more than the others. Turning the
great, stiff pages, Erkenbert found the passage he wanted and read it,
whispering the Latin words softly to himself and mentally translating
them into his native English.

". . . *sed unus militum lancea latus eius aperuit.* But one of the
soldiers pierced his side with a lance." With a lance, thought
Erkenbert. With a Roman soldier's lance.

Erkenbert knew better than most men what Roman soldiers'
weapons looked like. At what had once been his home at the great
Minster of York, there had still remained standing much of what was
formerly the headquarters building of the Sixth Legion of *Eboracum.*
The legion had left York and Britain four hundred years before, called
away to fight a civil war on mainland Europe, but much of its arsenal
had remained behind, and much of what had not been stolen or used
still lay in the vaults. The imperishable bronze fittings for the catapults
Erkenbert had made for the heathen Ivar had been genuine old work,
as good as the day they were made. Iron rusted, but for all that
Erkenbert had seen on its stand, kept cleaned and polished as a
trophy, the full panoply of a Roman legionary, helmet, cuirass,
short-sword, greaves, shield and of course the iron-shafted Roman
javelin, the *pilum.* Also called a *lancea.*

Yes, thought Erkenbert, that could have happened. And no question but that the lance, the Holy Lance, the lance that had pierced the
side of the Son of God himself, could have survived physically. He had
himself seen and handled weapons that might be as old.

But who might have thought to preserve such a thing? It would have
had to be someone who recognized its importance at the very moment
of its use. Otherwise the weapon would have gone back to the
barracks, been mixed with a thousand others. Who could have set
aside such a weapon? Not, thought Erkenbert, for all the archbishop
had said, the pious Jew Joseph of Arimathea, whom John the gospeller
mentioned four verses later. Such a man, if a disciple of Jesus, might
well have been able to beg the body from Pilate, and to preserve the
holy chalice in which Jesus had celebrated the Last Supper—though
John said nothing of that. He would not have been able to gain
possession of an infantry issue weapon from the Romans.

But the centurion, now. Erkenbert turned the pages of the Bible
thoughtfully, moving from one Gospel account to the next. The

centurion was mentioned in three out of four, and in all three he said almost the same words: Luke, "truly this was a righteous man," Mark, "truly this man was the Son of God," Matthew, "truly this was the Son of God." And in the fourth, in John, might the writer not have meant the centurion by "one of the soldiers"? If the centurion pierced the side of Jesus, as was his duty, and had seen or felt the miracle—what easier than for him to keep and treasure his own lance?

Now where did the centurion go after the Crucifixion? Erkenbert turned to another book, small, shabby, untitled, a book it seemed of letters, one after another, prattling of land and loans and debts, written by many authors, the kind of thing many efficient *librarii* would have sent to be scraped and re-used. Erkenbert fixed on the one of which Rimbert had told him. It seemed plain enough. A letter from Roman times, written in Latin—not good Latin, Erkenbert noted with interest, the Latin of a man who knew only the words of command, and to whom grammar was a mystery—and said at the top to be from one Gaius Cassius Longinus, centurion of Legio XXX Victrix. Describing in admiring terms the crucifixion at Jerusalem of a troublemaker, and now sent to the centurion's home at—Erkenbert could not read the name, but certainly something German, Bingen or Zobingen maybe.

Erkenbert pulled at his lower lip. A forgery? The letter had clearly been copied several times, but that was natural over the centuries. If the copier had been concerned to stress its importance, would he have made such a shabby copy, with such inferior penmanship? As for the tale itself, Erkenbert had no doubt that a centurion in Jerusalem in the Year of Our Lord 33 might well have been from the Rhineland. Or from England for that matter. Had the great Constantine, who had made Christianity the religion of the Empire, not himself been proclaimed Emperor on the very site of Erkenbert's own Minster at York?

The critical text was the third, a modern work, written no more than thirty years before, or so Erkenbert judged from its style. It was an account of the life and the death of the great Emperor Charlemagne, whose degenerate descendants, in Archbishop Gunther's view, now incompetently ruled the West. Much of it was familiar to Erkenbert already—the Emperor's campaigns, his fostering of learning. As Erkenbert never for a moment forgot, Charlemagne had called Alcuin, another man of York, another humble deacon like himself, from the English minster to control the destiny and the scholarship of the whole of Europe. Alcuin had been a man of great learning, true.

But in literature, not in the practical arts. He was not an *arithmeticus*, as Erkenbert was. There was nothing to say an *arithmeticus* might not be as great a man as a poet.

But in this Charlemagne chronicle there was something Erkenbert had indeed never heard, till Rimbert had told them all of it. Not how the Emperor died, for that was known, but the portents that announced it. Erkenbert shifted the book into full sunlight and read intently.

The emperor, aged seventy, was returning, it said, from his forty-seventh victorious campaign, against the Saxons, in full majesty and power. But then across the evening sky a comet had flashed. *Cometa*, thought Erkenbert. What we call the long-haired star. Long hair is the sign of the sacred king. That is why Charlemagne's ancestors had the kings they deposed shorn in public. The hairy star fell. And as it fell, the chronicle asserted, the emperor's horse shied and threw him. It threw him so violently that his sword-belt was torn off. And the lance he was carrying in his left hand flew from it and landed many yards away. At the same time, at the emperor's chapel in Aachen, the word "Princeps," or "Prince," had faded from an inscription the emperor had erected for himself, and never returned. The king had died weeks later, the chronicle said, insisting to the last that these portents did not mean that God had taken his authority from him. Yet of them all the greatest was the emperor's dropping of the lance, which previously he had carried everywhere with him—for that lance, the book insisted, was the *beata lancea* itself, the Lance of the German centurion Longinus, taken from its hiding-place in Cologne by Charlemagne in youth, and never leaving his side again in all his many campaigns and victories.

He who holds this Lance, the chronicle said, sways the destiny of the world. But no scholar knows where it is, for Charlemagne's counts diced for it after his death, and revealed only to each other who had been the winner.

And according to Rimbert no man knows now, thought Erkenbert, straightening up from his books. For by his account the Holy Lance was taken by Count Reginbald to Hamburg and treasured as a relic, inlaid with gold and precious stones. But since the heathens of the North sacked Hamburg twelve years ago, it has not been seen. Stolen away by some chieftain or kinglet. Destroyed maybe.

But no. For if it is the holy relic, God would guard it. And if it was made marvelous with gold and gems, even the heathen would respect it.

Does that mean that some petty chief among the church-despoilers shall be the overlord of Europe, the new Charlemagne? Remembering Ragnar Hairy-Breeks, whom he himself had put to the serpent-pit, and his sons, Ubbi, Halvdan, Ivar the Boneless and worst of all, the Snake-eye, Erkenbert felt his spine cringe in fear.

That could not be allowed. If the relic were in the hands of the heathen, it would have to be rescued, as Rimbert had urged so passionately. Rescued and transferred to the new emperor, whoever he might be, to unite Christendom once again. But what guarantee was there that this whole story, of lance and crucifixion and German centurion, was not just a fable? A forgery?

Leaving the books, Erkenbert strolled to the window and stared out at the peaceful spring scene. He had come to the library to check the documents, and check them he had. They seemed reliable. The story they told held together. Furthermore, he realized, it was a *good* story. He wanted to believe it. And he knew why he wanted to believe it.

All his life, Erkenbert reflected, he had been in the hands of bunglers. Incompetent archbishops like Wulfhere, incompetent kings like Ella and the fool Osbert before him, stupid thanes and illiterate priestlings, in their posts only because of some kinship with the great. England was a land where all his tools had been made of straw.

It was different here, in the land of the German Prince-Archbishops. Orders were carried out. Counselors were picked for their brains and their learning. Practical matters were attended to promptly, and those who understood them appreciated. Resources were far greater. Erkenbert knew that he had come to the great Gunther's attention simply because he had recognized the high quality of the Archbishop's silver currency, and asked how it was maintained. From the new mines, they had told him, in the Harz mountains. But a man who knows how to purify silver and separate out the lead is always welcome.

Yes, thought Erkenbert. He admired these people. He wanted them to accept him. But would they? He could sense their fierce pride in their own race and language, and knew that he was to that an outsider. He was short and dark as well, and knew how much they valued strength and the fair hair they thought a mark of their origin. Could his personal destiny ever be here? He needed a sign.

The rays of the sun had been moving all afternoon steadily westwards, across the lectern and the shelf of books beside it. As Erkenbert turned from the window it shone on an open page. Gold glittered from the massive illuminated capital on it, done with fantastic art in interlaced serpent-bodies, shining with silver and ruby patterns.

That is English art, thought Erkenbert. He looked again at the great

Bible whose pages he had been turning, intent only on what they said, not on their art or origin. Certainly English work, and from Northumbria at that. Not York maybe, but Wearmouth or the *scriptorium* of the great Bede at Jarrow, from the time before the Vikings came. How did it get here?

How did Christianity get here? Hamburg and Bremen were pagan towns to Charlemagne. It was brought here by the English missionaries, by the men of my own blood, by the blessed Willibrord and Wynfrith and Willebald the breaker of idols. My ancestors brought them a great gift, Erkenbert told himself with a flush of pride. The Christian religion and the learning with which to understand it. If any check me with my foreignness, I will remind them of that.

Carefully, Erkenbert replaced the precious books on their shelves and let himself out. Arno, the archbishop's counselor, sat on a bench in the square outside. He rose as he saw the little deacon emerging.

"Well, brother? Are you satisfied?"

Erkenbert smiled with total confidence and enthusiasm. "Completely satisfied, brother Arno. You may be sure that the holy Rimbert has made his first convert of alien race. I bless the day he told me of this greatest of relics."

Arno grinned down, momentary tension relieved. He had come to respect the little Englishman for his learning and his foresight. And after all—were the English not only some other kind of Saxon?

"Well, then, brother. Shall we be about God's work? The finding of the Holy Lance."

"Yes," said Erkenbert fervently. "And after that, brother, the work it was sent for. The finding of the true king, the emperor of New Rome in the West."

Shef lay stretched on his back, drifting in and out of sleep. The fleet was due to sail next morning, and from all that Brand had said about the hardships of life at sea, it was important to sleep while one could. But it had been a trying evening. Shef had been obliged to host all his captains, the ten English skippers he had with difficulty found to command his "battleships," and the forty or more Way-Vikings who skippered his conventional craft. It had needed much drinking of toasts, with both groups anxious not to be outdone.

Then, when he had got rid of them and hoped for a confidential talk with Brand, his convalescent friend had been in sour mood. He had refused to accompany Shef in the *Norfolk*, saying he preferred his own ship and crew. He had insisted that it was bad luck to sail with so many men in the fleet who did not know the *haf*-words, the elaborate taboo-language by which sailors avoided mentioning directly such unlucky things as women, cats or priests. Finding that dismissed even by Thorvin, who did intend to sail in the *Norfolk*, he had fallen back on telling depressing tales from his homeland, tales mostly of the unknown creatures of the sea, the mermaids and marbendills, men who had angered the skerry-elves and been turned into whales, eventually one of a scoffer and scorner whose boat had last been seen being drawn under water by a long arm covered in gray hair. At that, Shef had broken off the conversation. Now he lay, afraid of what his dreams would show him.

When the dream came, Shef knew immediately—for once—exactly where he was. He was in Asgarth, home of the gods, and moreover he was standing exactly outside the greatest of the halls of Asgarth, Valhalla, Othin's home of the heroes. In the distance, though still inside Asgarth, he could see a vast plain, with what looked like a confused battle taking place on it: a battle with no battle-lines, where every man struck everyone else, falling and bleeding at random.

As the day wore on, men fell and did not rise. The battle resolved itself into a string of duels between single men. The losers fell, the winners fought again. In the end only one man was left, hideously wounded, leaning on a great bloody axe. Shef heard a dim and distant cheering: Hermoth, Hermoth.

The dead began to rise, their severed limbs reuniting, the gashes in their sides healing up. They helped each other up, the men who had killed each other laughing and showing how things had gone. Slowly they formed into ranks and began to march back to the great hall, twelve abreast, a column thousands long, the figure with the great axe at their head. They marched round the building a few feet from Shef's unnoticed person, wheeled left and tramped without breaking their ranks or their stride through the double doors of the hall, now flung wide. The doors slammed. Light even in Asgarth began to fade. Sounds of revelry rose from inside.

Now up to the door came limping a poor man, roughly dressed. As Shef looked at him he knew that only in Asgarth could such a creature remain alive. His back was broken in two, so that his upper half lurched along seemingly without connection to his legs. His ribs were splayed wide, his middle crushed flat as if by the stamp of some mighty animal. Burst entrails projected from his coat.

He reached the gate of Valhalla and stared at it. A voice came from inside, one of the mighty voices Shef had often heard before: not the amused and cynical voice of his own patron—or maybe his own father—the god Rig, fomenter of skills and trickery. No, a cold and gravelly voice. This is the owner of the hall, thought Shef. This is Othin the mighty himself.

"Who sent you, mannikin?" said the voice.

Shef could not hear the low reply, but the voice could.

"Ah," it said. "Well I know his mark. There will be a place for him here among my heroes. When the time comes."

The crushed man spoke again, still inaudible.

"You?" said the mighty voice. "There is no place here for the likes of you. Who are you to stand in line against the Fenris-brood, when I have need of men? Away with you. Go round the back, to my kitchen-men. Maybe my chamberlain Thjalfi has need of another trencher-licker."

The crushed man turned and hobbled away, round the building in the opposite direction to that from which the marching host had come. On his face, Shef saw as he passed, was an expression of such desolate despair as he hoped never to see again.

That is a man for whom even death has brought no peace, he thought. Are even the gods allowed to do such harm? What need is it that drives them to such evil?

CHAPTER THREE

From his vantage-point in the stern of the leading ship, Shef looked back at the long, trailing line. The *Bedfordshire*, fourth ship from the van, was sagging out of line again, as she had done ever since, by trial and error, they had picked on their present formation. All ten of the English "battle-ships," as Ordlaf insisted on calling them, were heading due east with the south-west wind behind them and on the beam, as easy a point of sailing as could be imagined, certainly far easier than their awkward sail up the first part of the Dutch coast from the Rhine mouth with the wind almost directly behind them. Just the same the *Bedfordshire* was wallowing slowly out to sea again.

No point in shouting to the ship behind, to pass on a message mouth to mouth till it reached the *Bedfordshire*'s skipper. He knew the importance of keeping in line, he had had it shouted at him time and time again by all the other skippers in turn every time they camped for the night. There was some error in his ship's construction. For some reason or other she made more of this "leeway" that Ordlaf was always complaining about. They would get it fixed when they returned to dock. Meanwhile the *Bedfordshire* would do what she always did: wallow out to sea till she was a hundred yards out of line, and then brace her sail round and awkwardly maneuver back into place. Where the others sailed along more or less straight, her progress was a string of shallow zig-zags, like the patterns on a welded sword.

It did no harm, at least for the moment, Shef concluded. He had realized one thing, though, and realized it some days before, almost as soon as he and the rest of the landsmen had stopped retching over the side. That was that the reason the Vikings ruled the seas, and could descend at any spot in the Western world regardless of the precautions and the guards of the Christian kings, was that they were very very good at something quite unexpectedly complex and difficult: sailing boats.

The seamen and skippers Shef had recruited from the English coastal ports were good enough sailors in their way, but it was not the Viking way. Fishermen almost to a man, what they were good at was coming back alive. Like Ordlaf, if the children's bellies had to be filled, they would put to sea in almost any weather. They had no interest, though, in getting anywhere unless it were to another likely bank or shoal, and certainly no interest in going anywhere fast or unexpectedly. As for the crewmen from the inland counties, aboard to man the mules and shoot the crossbows, every detail of life at sea was a burden to them. At least six of them had fallen overboard already while trying to attend to their natural functions, though it was true that they had all been recovered from the calm and shallow sea. The main reason Shef insisted on camping every night instead of pressing on was that he dreaded the results of trying to cook afloat.

Shef turned from the problems of the *Bedfordshire* to the low, sullen, sandy shore slipping by to the right—or to "steerboard" as the sailors called it, the side of the ship which had the long steering-oar mounted. Shef unrolled the long scroll of parchment on which he was attempting, following his earlier experience, to draw a chart of these unfamiliar lands. The natives on the coastal islands they had passed had told him a great deal—they were, of course, Frisians, and the Frisians felt strong kinship both with the English to whom they were related, and to the men of the Way, whose religion and order had been founded by their own Duke Radbod a hundred and fifty years before. But, more important, the Frisians of the islands were the poorest of the poor. On the desolate sandbanks on which they lived, sometimes twenty miles long but never more than a mile across, no hut, no flock of sheep was ever more than ten minutes from a Viking marauder. The islanders lived with little and stood ready to abandon that any moment.

That did not mean they were not happy to strike back. Once the news had spread up along the islands that the strange fleet was an English one, come to fight the Vikings, men had drifted in to every camp fire, eager to speak for a mug of ale or a good silver penny of the new coinage.

The picture they gave was clear. As one rounded the Ijsselmeer the chain of islands began, running like the coast they sheltered slightly north of east. The islands' names seemed to become more familiar as one went further along. The Texel, Vlieland, Terschelling, which they had passed three days before—Shef did not know what those names meant. But then they had passed Schiermonnikoog, and further along a string of similar names, Langeoog, Spiekeroog, and Norderney. All these were easy to understand, for -oog was just the hoarse Frisian way of saying "ey," an island, an eyot, and -koog was the familiar Norfolk "key," a sandbank.

And all these islands *were* just sandbanks, drifts piled up over centuries by the rivers that flowed into the sea and that continually threatened to choke themselves with silt. The first slight break in the chain had been the Ems. Further up, the twin estuaries of the Jade and the Weser, with somewhere inside them the guarded bishop's town of Bremen. Just ahead, past Wangeroog, the last of the long Frisian island-chain now slipping past to starboard, lay the greater flow of the Elbe, with on it the port and stronghold of Hamburg under its powerful archbishop. Hamburg, famously sacked by the Vikings a dozen years before, so Brand said, who had taken part, but once again recovering, the very spear-point of the Empire of Christendom leveled at Denmark and Scandinavia beyond.

There would be a time to look into Hamburg and Bremen. But not now. Now the plan was to push ahead across the estuary of the Elbe, to the spot where the coastline turned north to the North Frisian islands, to Jutland, to the South Danes. And—so some of the seamen said—to the flatlands from which the English had come in their turn, centuries before, to the sack of Britannia and the overthrow of the Rome-folk. Shef felt a slight stirring of excitement. Who was to say that up there, there might not still be Englishmen left, who could be called to the defeat of what surely must be their Danish oppressors? But it would be enough if he could reach there—reach there and return, having tried his ships and given their crews confidence.

What he really needed, Shef reflected, still staring at the markings on his map, was a chart of what lay *inside* the island chain, between the islands and the main shore. If they could sail along there, his ships could defy wind and weather and water-shortage, cruise along as easily as on the Ouse or the Stour at home. Lurk inside shelter to pounce out on Viking fleets.

But Ordlaf had refused flatly to take the ships inshore, and Brand had backed him utterly. Pilot water, he had repeated. Don't try it without a man born and bred there and one you can trust. Shoals, banks, currents, tides. You can wreck a ship on sand or on chesil as easily as you can on Flamborough Head. Easier, Ordlaf had added. At least you can see Flamborough Head.

Shef wondered obstinately how much of that was the Viking contempt for English seamanship. It had grown steadily during the days of their cruise, the Viking jokes getting continually more barbed till Shef had had to restrain the crew of the *Norfolk* from manning the mule and sending a few of the loudest laughers to the bottom. Since then they had evolved their current formation: the ten battleships cruising inshore and using all their efforts to keep up a decent speed, while the forty accompanying craft—all Viking-manned, all built on the shores of the Kattegat or the Norway fjords, but all bearing the Hammer and Cross of the Way kingdoms stitched to their sails— swept their contemptuous arcs far ahead and out to sea. Though never out of sight. Always one sail remained on the horizon, keeping a keen eye on the English lubbering along behind, itself watched keenly by the sharpest eyes in Brand's small fleet a further horizon away.

They can laugh, thought Shef. And they can sail too, I admit it. But this is like the sack of York, a new kind of battle. My men don't have to be the best sailors since Noah. They just have to be at sea. If the Ragnarssons want to get past us, or any other damned pirates out of the North, they must come in range. Then we sink them. The best sailors in the world can do nothing on shattered planks.

He rolled up his scroll, thrust it in its waxed leather bag, and walked forward to pat the comforting bulk of the mule. Cwicca, now senior catapult-captain of the fleet, grinned gap-toothed at the gesture. He had won forty well-stocked acres and a young bride for his part in last year's successes, wealth literally unimaginable for one who had been a slave of the monks of Crowland, owning nothing but a bone-and-bladder bagpipe. Yet he had left it all, his silk tunic apart, for this cruise. Hard to tell whether he hoped for more riches or more marvels.

"Sail turning this way," yelled the lookout suddenly from his uncomfortable stance on the single yard fifteen feet above Shef's head. "And more behind, I can see them! All coming straight for us."

The *Norfolk* heeled instantly as the more excitable crew-members rushed over to the left side, the backboard, to see for themselves. Moments of confusion as the boatswain and his mates kicked them back. Ordlaf shinning deftly up the knotted rope that led to the yard, following the lookout's pointing finger. Sliding back down again, face tense, to report.

"It's Brand, lord. All his ships tearing along together, fast as they can go, wind on the beam. They've seen something right enough.

They'll tack and be alongside—'' he pointed at the sky—''when the sun's gone so far.''

"Couldn't be better," said Shef. "A still morning and a long afternoon to fight in. Nowhere for the pirates to hide. Serve the men their noon-meal early." He clutched his pendant, the silver pole-ladder. "May my father send us victory. And if Othin wants heroes for Valhalla," he added, remembering his dream, "let him take them from the other side."

"Well now, what do we make of that?" asked Sigurth the Snake-eye. He spoke to his two brothers, flanking him in the prow of the *Frani Ormr*. "A fleet in front, steering to meet us, and then suddenly they all spin round and take off as if they'd heard their wives were offering it free to all comers back home."

A voice behind him, the skipper of the *Ormr*, Vestmar. "Pardon, lord. Hrani here, the lookout, he wants to say something."

Sigurth turned, looked at the young man now being thrust forward. A young man, where almost everyone else on the ship, Sigurth's fifty picked champions, was in his prime. A poor man, too, without a gleam of gold on him, and a plain bone hilt to his sword. Picked out by Vestmar and added to the crew, Sigurth remembered, for his sharp sight. Sigurth did not bother to speak, merely raised an eyebrow.

Staring into the famous snakes' eyes with their white-bordered pupils, Hrani flushed and stammered. Then collected himself, swallowed, and began. "Lord. Before they turned I got a good look at the lead ship. There was a man standing in the prow, like you are, lord, looking at us." He hesitated. "I think it was Brand. Viga-Brand."

"You've seen him before?" asked Sigurth.

The young man nodded.

"Now, think carefully. Are you sure it was him?"

Hrani hesitated again. If he were wrong—Sigurth had a fearsome reputation for vengeances, and every man in the fleet knew of his and his brothers' consuming desire. To find and kill the men responsible for the death of their mad brother Ivar, Skjef the Englishman and Viga-Brand, Brand the Killer. If the brothers were disappointed . . . Yet on the other hand to lie to them, or to hide what one saw, both were equally dangerous. Hrani considered for a moment what he had actually seen, as the leading enemy ship rose on a wave. No, he had no real doubt. The figure he had seen was too big for any other man.

"Yes, lord. In the prow of the lead ship stood Viga-Brand."

Sigurth held his gaze for a moment, then slowly stripped a gold bracelet from his own arm, handed it over. "Good news, Hrani. Take this for your sharp eyes. Now tell me one more thing. Why do you think Brand turned away?''

Another gulp as the young man hefted the weight of the bracelet, hardly able to believe his luck. Turn away? Why would anyone turn away? "Lord, he must have recognized the *Frani Ormr*, and feared to meet us. Feared to meet you," he corrected hastily.

Sigurth waved a hand in dismissal, turned back to his brothers.

"Well," he remarked. "You heard what the idiot thinks. Now what do we think?''

Halvdan stared at the waves, felt the wind on his cheek, watched the faint dots of sail on the horizon. "Scouting ahead," he observed. "Fallen back on reinforcements. Trying to lead us on."

"Lead us on to what?" asked Ubbi. "There were forty of them. That's about what we expected, of our own folk known to be—" he spat over the side "—with the Waymen."

"More Wayfolk might have sailed south," suggested Halvdan. "Their priests have been stirring them up."

"We'd have heard, if there'd been any great number of them."

"So if the reinforcements are there," concluded the Snake-eye, "they must be from England. Englishmen in ships. A new thing. And where there is a new thing . . .''

"There you find the Sigvarthsson," completed Ubbi, his teeth showing in a snarl.

"Up to something," said Sigurth. "Up to something, or he wouldn't dare to challenge us, not at sea. Look, the Waymen are tacking, turning in to the land. Well, we'll take their dare. Let's see how good their surprise is. And maybe we can surprise them too."

He turned to Vestmar, standing a careful few paces to the rear. "Vestmar, pass the word. All ships ready for battle. Reef sail, rig the oars. But don't step the masts. Leave the yards up."

Vestmar goggled for a moment. He had been at a dozen sea battles round the coasts of Britain and Denmark, Norway and Sweden and Ireland too. Masts and yards were always stepped and stowed, to decrease the top-hamper, give the ships every yard of speed under oars that they could make. In close-quarter battle there were no men free to trim sails, and no wish for anything that would block a man's sight of arrow or javelin.

He caught himself, nodded, turned back, bellowing orders to his own crew and the ships nearest to him, orders to be passed on along and back to the hundred and twenty longships cruising behind and aside. Quickly, skillfully, the Ragnarsson fleet prepared for action.

*   *   *

Shef leaned over the backboard as Brand's ship, the *Walrus*, ranged easily alongside at the end of the long turn that had brought it and the rest of the Wayman fleet back into line with his own ten.

"The Snake-eye?" he shouted.

"Yes. It's the *Frani Ormr* in the lead right enough. They outnumber us three to one. Have to fight them now. If you tried to get away they'd sail you down before the sun started to sink."

"That's what we came for," called Shef. "You know the plan?"

Brand nodded, stepped back, pulled from round his neck a long red silken scarf. Stepping to the leeward side he let it stream in the breeze.

Instantly the ships behind him lowered the sails they had half-reefed and began to surge ahead, spreading into line abreast as they did so. A volley of orders from Ordlaf and the *Norfolk* began to check her already sluggish pace, while her consorts also began to range up on her, not moving abreast, but forming a close line, so close that the prow of each battleship almost overlapped the stern of the one ahead. Steersmen watched with anxious care as the clumsy craft edged up on each other.

At a wave from Cwicca, the catapult-crews lowered their throwing bars to the deck, fixed them with the well-greased sliding bolts, began to throw their weight on to the winding-handles to bring the stout ropes to maximum torsion. "Wind both sides," called Cwicca, looking at his master. "We might get a shot either way, God be good to us. I mean Thor be good to us." He pulled his hammer-pendant out to swing free.

Slowly the Wayman fleet edged into its agreed battle-formation, like an inverted T thrusting at the enemy. In front, lined up abreast, Brand's forty ships, sails now furled and masts stepped, moving forward at easy pace under oars alone—Shef could hear the men grunting as they put their weight into the easy swell of the waves. Behind their center, in line ahead and still under sail, the ten English battleships.

As the formation took shape, Shef felt the familiar sense of relief. All battles to him, he realized, had come to feel the same. Terrible, gnawing anxiety before they started, while he thought of the hundred and one things that could go wrong with a plan—skippers not understanding, crews not moving fast enough, the enemy coming up unexpectedly, before they were ready. Then the relief, followed instantly by a desperate curiosity. Would it work? Could there be something he had forgotten?

Brand was bellowing from the stern of his ship, breaking off to point forward urgently at the Ragnarsson fleet, now a bare half-mile off and closing quickly, oars threshing. What was he shouting? Shef heard the words and realized for himself at the same moment. The enemy were coming on to battle just as predicted. But their masts were still standing, though the sails were furled.

". . . he's smelled a rat!" came the tail-end of Brand's bellow.

Smell it or no, thought Shef. The rat is in range now. Now all it has to do is bite. From his neck he pulled a long blue scarf—Godive's gift, he remembered with a pang, given him the day she had told him she would marry Alfred. He streamed it to leeward, saw the faces turning as the lookouts saw it. Not a good luck memory, he thought. He loosed his grip on the silk, let the wind carry it into the yellow turbid sea.

Sigurth Ragnarsson, standing in the prow of his ship, noted the strangely-cut sails at the rear of Brand's thin line, Noted, too, the giant figure of Brand standing directly opposite him, waving an axe in ironic salute. Up to something, he thought again. Only one way to find out what it is. With elaborate care he stripped off his long scarlet cape, turned, threw it into the bottom of the boat. At the same instant a man stationed by the mast jerked a rope. From the top of the mast, above the yard, there flew free suddenly a great banner, with on it a black raven: the Raven Banner of the sons of Ragnar, woven it was said all in one night, with magic in its weft for victory. No man had seen it fly since the death of Ivar.

As the watching fleet saw it break out, each oarsman put his back into five mighty heaves, then simultaneously tossed oars upright and hurled them clattering into the longships' wells. Over the din, they gave one short cheer and seized up shields and weapons. Each steersman swung his suddenly accelerated boat so as to close on its next neighbor, boatswains swinging grapnels so as to lash them fast. As was always the custom, the fleet would gain momentum and then drift down on its enemies lashed together, to lock prows with the opposing fleet and there fight it out with spears and swords over the half-decked forecastles, till one side or other gave way and tried— usually unsuccessfully—to break free.

Brand saw the banner fly, saw the men bracing themselves for their last sudden spurt. Even as the oars bent under the first fierce stroke, he bellowed, in a voice fit to carry over an Atlantic gale: "Back oars and turn!"

The Wayman front line, carefully rehearsed, split instantly in the center. Brand's ship and all those to seaward of it swung hard to port, starboard oars pulling madly, port oars backing water. All those to shoreward swung hard the other way. Then, as the helmsmen struggled to keep from running foul of their fellows, the oars swung again, the fast maneuverable boats leapt away.

Shef, standing by the mast of the *Norfolk*, saw Brand's ships swerve away to left and right with the unanimity of two flocks of migrating birds. With a stab of fear—not fear for himself but for his plan—he realized the Ragnarsson fleet was closer than he expected and coming on fast. If those veteran warriors laid aboard him there could be only one ending. In the same moment he felt the *Norfolk* surge forward as Ordlaf spread sail to its fullest extent. Slowly the battleship swung round to port, presenting her starboard beam to the dragon prows not a hundred yards off. Behind her, her nine consorts swung round in close line ahead. Again the *Norfolk* picked up a yard or two of speed as the wind came more directly over her stern.

Shef heard Ordlaf shouting encouragingly: "The wind's rising! We'll get round in time."

Maybe, thought Shef. But just the same, they were too close. Time to check them. He nodded to Cwicca, crouched expectantly by the release.

Cwicca hesitated for only an instant. He knew the plan was to sink the lead center ship, the one with the great gilded snake's head on its prow. But his mule was still not bearing directly on it. Impossible to train it round. Waiting a split second for the heel of the waves, he jerked free the release bolt.

A flash of motion, a violent thud against the padded beam, a thud that shook the whole ship and seemed for an instant to check her way. The black streak that was a thirty-pound boulder lashing across the water. A streak that ended just behind the prow of the ship immediately to port of the *Frani Ormr*.

For a second or two the advancing line of ships seemed to roll on as if nothing had happened, sending Shef's heart leaping into his mouth. Then tiredly, irresistibly, the ship fell apart. The flying rock had smashed the stem-post to matchwood. The planks carefully fitted into it sprang from their notches. Below the waterline the sea rushed in, forced on by the ship's own motion. As it shot through the well the sinews holding planks to ribs and ribs to keel sprang apart. The mast, its keelson pulled from under it, swayed forward, held for an instant by its stays, then swung wearily to one side. Like a giant's club it scythed through the gaping crew of the ship next alongside.

To the watchers in the English line it seemed as if the ship had suddenly vanished, been pulled under by one of the water-hags of Brand's stories. For a moment or two they could see men apparently standing on the water, then fighting for their footing on loose planks,

then down in the sea, or struggling for a hand-hold on the gunwales of
the ships alongside.

And then the *Suffolk* too brought her mule to bear. Another streak
flashed into the heart of the Ragnarsson fleet. And another as the third
ship in line swung round.

Suddenly, as Shef gaped, noise seemed to be added to the battle.
All at once he was aware of the snap of the crossbows, the song of the
rope as Cwicca's handlers frantically wound their machine, the crash
of rock on wood and waves of cheering as Brand's ships swung round
to come in on the Ragnarsson flanks. At the same time Shef felt a
sudden lash of rain and the ships opposite blurred for a moment. A
rain shower passing over the sea. Would it soak the ropes and at this
worst moment take his artillery out of action?

Out of the blur came three dragon prows, shockingly close. Not the
snake's head of the enemy flagship, now a hundred yards behind
them, but some other alert enemy skipper, who had cast his grapnels
free and re-manned his oars, realizing his foe had no intention of
closing to fight fair. If they managed to lay alongside . . .

Cwicca raised a thumb. Shef nodded. The bone-jarring thud again,
the streak of movement that ended this time almost before it had
begun, at the very base of the center ship's mast. Again, suddenly, no
ship, just a flurry of planks and men gasping in the water.

The other two were still coming on, only yards away now, men in
each prow with grapnels swinging, fierce bearded faces staring over
their shields, a simultaneous deep grunt as the oarsmen took one last
stroke to drive themselves over the gap.

A storm of cheering almost in Shef's ear and a great bulk like a
whale shouldering past only feet in front of the *Norfolk*'s bow. One of
Brand's ships driving in under oars to intercept. Its prow swept along
the starboard side of the Ragnarsson ship at a closing speed of twenty
miles an hour, snapping the oars, hurling their butt-ends back to cave
in the ribs and shatter the spines of the rowers. As the two ships
ground past each other Shef saw the Wayman rowers rising from their
benches to pour a storm of javelins over the side at point-blank range.
The third Ragnarsson ship saw the carnage, swung away past the
Norfolk's stern, picking up speed for the open sea.

Shef caught Ordlaf by the shoulder, pointed across a half-mile of
sea filled with shattered ships, drowning men, and desperate combats
of single ships and groups. Through the showers of rain and spray
picked up by the rising wind he could see the Raven banner still flying.
But already turned and moving east. The *Frani Ormr*, masterfully
handled, had swerved its way unscathed through the English line,

swung about and was already in full flight. As the two men watched her sail swept down from the yard, bellied out, and began to glide easily to safety.

"Follow," said Shef.

"She sails two yards to our one."

"Cut her off from the open sea while you have a chance. Drive her inshore."

"But that's the Elber Gat," protested Ordlaf.

Shef's fingers tightened commandingly on his shoulder.

CHAPTER FOUR

Sigurth Ragnarsson stared thoughtfully over his ship's port quarter. Significantly, he had not picked up his long scarlet cape, but had left his arms free for action. He braced himself against the *Ormr*'s heel on a long spear, iron-shafted, with a heavy triangular head. His brothers stood with their backs to him, also seeming relaxed but with weapons drawn. Discipline was savage in the Ragnarsson fleet. But the men in it were savage too, and these were picked veterans. They had no liking for turning from a battle, were already imagining what men might say about them later. Wondering if the Snake-eye had gone soft.

No point in trying to explain. Just keep them wondering a little while longer.

"What do you make of our friend behind?" said Sigurth to Vestmar, indicating the *Norfolk* laboring a long mile in their rear.

"It's a clumsy rig, but he can sail it," replied Vestmar briefly. "One thing, though. He doesn't know his way. See the lookout on the yard, and the skipper leaning over the prow looking for shoal water?"

"Plenty of that around," said Sigurth. He turned to look inland. A coast nearly featureless. The two small islands of Neuwark and the Scharhorn already passed. The silty current of the Elbe stirring beneath the keel, and then nothing till the base of Jutland and the fought-over lands between Denmark and the Empire of the Germans.

"All right. Strike sail. Get the men to the oars. And get someone in the bow with a lead-line."

Vestmar gaped, almost voicing a protest. A lead-line, he thought.

But I know the Elber Gat like I know my wife's backside. And if we strike sail those bastards back there will be hurling their *iötunn*-rocks at us while we break our backs to get away. He swallowed the words and turned on his heel, calling hoarsely.

"We're gaining on them," called Shef. "Cwicca, stand by the mule!"

Ordlaf did not reply. He looked tensely at the sky, looked again at the ship they were pursuing, took the lead which his crewman in the bow had passed to him. Sniffed the mud sticking still to the wax at the end of the lead cylinder on the five-fathom rope. Stuck a tongue out, tasted it.

"What are you doing that for?"

"Don't know," muttered Ordlaf. "Sometimes you can tell if there's shellfish, what kind of sand it is . . . If there's a shoal coming up."

"Look," snarled Shef. "He doesn't know where he is either, he's had a man in the bow swinging the lead this last two miles, just like you. Keep behind him, and if he doesn't run aground you won't."

Not as easy as that, young lord, thought Ordlaf, not as easy as that. There's other things, like the current—see him sliding through it like a snake while it grips our keel. And the wind, and these blasted squalls of rain coming down. And the tide. Is it still making? Now if I was at home in Yorkshire I'd feel it in my bones when we got to the full. But here in foreign parts who's to know when it turns? Can't be far off.

"Another quarter-mile and we're close enough for a shot," called Shef. "Get the oars out bow and stern. Just leave space clear round the mule."

As the grinning men heaved awkwardly in the short chop of the waves, the *Norfolk* picked up another trifle of speed, began visibly to close on the long dragon-shape ahead. Shef stared, estimating range and bearing.

"Right, that'll do. Take a good aim, Cwicca. Ordlaf, swing her to the right, no, to starboard, so we can shoot."

As the *Norfolk* swung to the steering-oar, the sail canted round. Yells of rage from Cwicca as its lower edge blocked his view. A scurry of sailors hastily heaving the ropes to brail up. Ordlaf cursing furiously as the oarsmen faltered in their stroke and the prow swung further, steadied, lurched back. As the sail finally jerked up out of their way Shef and Cwicca gaped for a moment, wondering where their quarry had gone.

"There!" In the instants of confusion the *Frani Ormr* had jinked like a hare, spun to port, and was now directly stern on to them, moving away at a frantic speed, oars flashing like the last moments of a race.

"Too far for a shot now," yelled Cwicca into Shef's ear, beside himself with excitement.

"They can't keep that up for long. Ordlaf, take us in after her."

Ordlaf hesitated, eying the long ripples of shoal water either side of the fleeing Viking. Shoal water half a mile wide between two long banks just showing. Beyond that, a waste of unknown banks and channels leading for miles to the featureless German shore.

The memory of the other skipper's lead-line reassured him. Dangerous water, but he doesn't know it either. If anyone strikes, he'll strike first. The *Norfolk* heeled round, bringing the wind on to her other beam, spread sail again and headed for the narrow channel in her enemy's wake.

That'll do, thought Sigurth, feeling the faintest grate of sand under his keel. We're through, at the very top of the tide. He caught a glint of relief in Vestmar's eyes as well, hastily dropped. One of the rowers blew out his cheeks and, greatly daring, raised an eyebrow at the helmsman. They had felt the pull of the sand under their blades these last minutes, had rowed shallow automatically like the seamen they were. Now they could feel the water deepening again. Maybe the Snake-eye had not lost all his luck. Maybe . . .

Behind them Sigurth could see the English ship still coming on, the hammer and cross half-visible on her sail. And behind her a squall blowing across the flat open estuary, a squall that would catch up with her . . . Now.

As the rain drummed down with sudden April fury Ordlaf peered tensely over the bow. The leadsman's voice in his ear rose to a shriek: "Two fathom now, skipper, two fathom and I can see the shoal!"

"In oars," bellowed Ordlaf in the same moment, "furl sail, stand by to back off."

Too late. As he shouted, one of the oarsmen, swinging stoutly but unskillfully, felt his oar turn under him, twist and throw him bodily off his bench, half over the side. Jammed in the sand, the stout ash wood held the weight of the driving ship for an instant, dragged her over, snapped into splinters. As the ship heeled, more oars caught, throwing the rowers this way and that. The last gust of the squall caught the sail, drove the keel on to the crest of a wave. Dropped her with a grinding thud on the sand. For seconds there was total confusion as Ordlaf and his mates, yelling frenziedly, kicked men out of their way, heaved ropes, seized oars, tried first to boom the ship off the bank on to which she had run, then to prop her at least on an even keel. Slowly the noise died, the landsmen, their king included, huddled nervously in the center of the boat. Shef found himself facing a pair of reproachful eyes.

"We didn't ought to have done it. Run aground right on top of the tide. Look—" Ordlaf pointed over the gunwale at the sandbanks already appearing to either side, as the sea started its long six-hour ebb.

"Are we in any danger?" asked Shef, remembering the way Ragnar's two knorrs had run aground and gone to pieces before both of them two long springs before.

"No, not danger of breaking up. It's soft sand, and we hit fairly slow. But they took us in proper." Ordlaf shook his head with rueful admiration. "I bet that skipper there knew where he was to the inch. Swinging away with that old lead-line, and just drawing us on. And now a mile off and making his way back to sea."

Shef looked round sharply, suddenly conscious of what might happen if the Snake-eye and his picked crew came wading across the shallows. But they were nowhere to be seen. He stepped to the prow and looked slowly and carefully right round the flat gray horizon, looking for the mast, the Raven banner that had been flying in front of them not ten minutes before. Nothing to be seen. In some inlet or creek the *Frani Ormr* was lurking like a poison snake, waiting for the tide and clear passage out. Shef sighed deeply, tension released, and turned back to Ordlaf and the silent crew.

"Can we get off before nightfall?"

Ordlaf shrugged. "We can try and kedge her off. Keep everyone busy."

Hours later, the mood round the stranded ship had lightened, lifted by hard work, sweat and a growing feeling that at least the battle had been won, even if some of the enemy had got away.

The dropping tide—fifteen feet of drop in these parts—had revealed to everyone what the *Norfolk* had done. She lay now half a mile from the main Elbe channel, in a shallow valley between two long sandbanks, with runnels and streamlets stretching in all directions through the rounded hillocks of the shoals, broken here and there only by planks and ribs from long-forgotten wrecks. At first Ordlaf had had the crew over the side, digging round and under the keel with the intention of dragging the boat bodily backward the way she had come. As the tide fell and the distance to the main channel became clear, they had abandoned that idea. Not more than sixty or seventy feet ahead there lay another deep-water channel, still ten feet or more deep

even with the tide almost out. Clearly the Ragnarsson skipper had
reached it, knowing well it was there, and then swung right or left
while his enemy's attention was distracted. Inland towards Hamburg
and the main channel, or out to sea by some unknown route, it made
no difference now. Now the business of the *Norfolk*'s crew was to drag
their ship the few feet needed to get her over the almost imperceptible
crest of the shoal, and then down and into deep water. Already they
had dug the sand away in front of her so that her bows now pointed
definitely if gently down. But to shift her before the night-time tide,
they needed a purchase.

Ordlaf had rigged one rope already, fixed at one end to the ship's
anchor firmly planted in hard sand, passed round the base of the mast,
and then handed to thirty men hauling together. The ship had stirred,
groaned. Remained motionless.

"We need another rope," said Ordlaf. "With a straighter pull if we
can get it, and room for the rest of the lads to heave. Best if we could fix
it over there." He pointed to the sandbank the other side of the
channel in front of them, maybe thirty yards wide.

"Have you got one long enough?" asked Shef.

"Yes. And we've fixed up another anchor out of halberd-heads. We
just got to get it over there."

Shef heard a silent appeal. The *Norfolk*, big as she was in comparison with other vessels of her day, was far too small to carry even a
dinghy in the cramped space that had to hold everything, crew and
provisions. She had instead a tiny craft made of skin over a pole frame,
more a coracle than a canoe, hard to steer and easy to capsize. Ordlaf
or any of his Norfolk fishermen could handle it, but they were busy at
skilled tasks. Any of the landsmen who made up the rowers and
mule-team would certainly capsize it and drown.

Shef sighed. An hour before he had drawn out the last of the ship's
scanty, daily-renewed store of firewood, and told Cwicca to light a fire
on the sand, rig the ship's great iron kettle, and make what he could
out of the hard rations: flour, salt fish and barley meal. To a hungry
man the smell beginning to rise from the kettle was tempting. He
looked at the sun already sinking down the sky, considered a night
spent struggling in rising water, and gave in.

"All right. I suppose I was a fenman before they made me a jarl or a
king. I'll do it."

"Can you handle it?"

"Watch me. If I didn't have the anchor to carry I could swim over
in a dozen strokes anyway."

Ordlaf's boatswain loaded the anchor carefully in the bottom of the coracle, keeping sharp edges away from the hide, made certain the rope attached ran freely. Shef looked again at the kettle, calculated the distance and the chances of an upset, and removed the gold circle he wore as a sign of rank. He handed it to Hwithelm, a handsome youth of noble family and impenetrable stupidity who had been forced upon him as his ceremonial swordbearer, and who was already carrying his swordbelt.

"Hold that till I come back."

Hwithelm frowned at the casualness of the gesture, but slowly accepted its sense. "And your bracelets, lord?"

Shef thought for a moment, then slowly pushed the gold bracelet he wore on each bicep down and over his wrists, passed them to Hwithelm. They were unlikely to fall off, but if the coracle tipped over, as was likely enough, who knew what might happen?

He strolled to the edge of the channel, settled himself in the coracle, accepted the paddle, and shoved off. A difficult craft to steer with only one paddle and an awkward weight in it that brought the sea to within three inches of the gunwale. The trick lay in a twist of the paddle to straighten her up with every stroke. Cautiously Shef navigated across, tormented all the while by the smell of food, splashed ashore, dug the anchor in to cries of direction from Ordlaf. Then, with more haste as he heard the sounds of pottery bowls being served out, scrambled back in for the return crossing.

The rope was stretched across the channel. Easier than paddling was to sit with his back to the ship and haul himself along the rope, hand over hand.

Slowly Shef realized that the shouting from the ship had changed its tone, become urgent, frantic. He turned to the left, as he always did with his one eye, to see what was happening. Nothing visible, but Ordlaf with a look of horror on his face gesturing and pointing. Pointing to the right.

Shef swung hastily the other way, almost overturning the coracle with the jerk. For a moment all he could see was a black bulk throwing white water, almost on top of him. Then his mind took in what it saw.

The *Frani Ormr* bearing down on top of him, oars flashing, bow-wave curling to either side of the narrow channel. With mast stepped and snake-prow and dragon-tail removed she had lain concealed, no higher than a war-canoe, behind some nameless and invisible bank, watching her opportunity. Now she had seen it and was coming down as if to ram and trample her frail enemy under. In the same instant that he recognized the boat Shef saw a scarlet-caped warrior leaning over the prow, a mighty spear balanced in his hand.

His teeth showed in a grimace of hate and concentration. In that instant Shef knew that there was no chance such a man would miss his throw. The arm went back, the spear poised.

Shef hurled himself instantly over the side, down into the water, plunging desperately for depth. A great surge in the water pressed him further down till he felt the sand grate on his chest, for a moment he felt as if he would be caught between keel and sea-bottom, he scrabbled furiously up and away. Something struck him a glancing blow on the side of the head, an oar digging deep, and he dived again. Then his lungs would bear no more, he had to surface and breathe, but the surface was not there, he fought his way up with frantic strokes . . .

Shef shot gasping into the air a few yards behind the *Ormr*'s stern, stared wildly round him, struck out for the nearest shore. Found himself back on the sandbank where he had sunk the anchor. On the opposite bank someone had turned over the kettle, swords and halberds were being thrown to men clustered round their ship, a line of helmets showed over its gunwale as the dozen crossbowmen wound their weapons. Ordlaf was shouting directions, preparing to fight off an assault over the sand. No chance of bringing the mule to bear as the *Norfolk* lay, bows on to the channel and in any case tilted half over on one side.

The *Frani Ormr* was turning in her own length in the narrow channel, port oars pulling, starboard reversing. Turning not towards the *Norfolk*, but towards Shef, standing isolated on the wrong side of the deep water. Shef contemplated a plunge and a dozen strokes back to his friends, hesitated, imagining the harpoon plunging into his back as he swam. Too late. The prowless *Ormr* was stroking steadily towards him, a handful of men clustered by the side watching him intently.

Shef backed away, further up the sandbank, out of easy javelin range, wondering what came now. He was weaponless and alone. A cry and the oars stopped their beat, remained jutting out from the rowlocks. A man stepped over the side, on to one, walked down it in sailor's goat-skin shoes, jumped the last feet on to the hard sand. A young man, Shef saw watching warily a dozen yards away. But tall and strong, with a gold bracelet round one biceps.

A rush of air overhead, and another. Crossbow bolts from the *Norfolk*, trying to help. But a long carry from stranded ship to channel and then across the channel, and the bulk of the *Ormr* in the way. Shef backed further as the young man drew his sword. Three more men stepped on to oars and made their way towards him. Shef, sparing just one glance from his nearest enemy, recognized all three: Halvdan

Ragnarsson, who had umpired his holmgang at York, Ubbi Ragnarsson the grizzled, and between them Sigurth, who had taken Shef's eye at Bedricsward. As if remembering, Shef's empty eye-socket suddenly gushed salt water. The Ragnarssons held axe, sword and spear. All three wore mail. The young man closest to Shef did not.

Shef turned and began to run down the sandbank. It took him away from the *Norfolk*, but that could not be helped. If he stayed where he was, they would kill him, if he ran across the bank he would be floundering in water again in a few strides. Mistake, he realized an instant later. He was running the same way as the *Ormr* was facing, and she was keeping easy pace with him on his right, shielding his pursuers from the crossbows and with men ready for a shot with bow or javelin. He veered to the left, hearing feet pounding on the sand behind him. The bank came to an end. He hurled himself straight out into the water in a flat dive, took three, four, powerful strokes, felt the sand under his belly again and scrambled to his feet once more.

A dozen strides and he risked a look over his shoulder. The young man had hesitated on the edge of the water, but was splashing through it, no more than waist-deep. The Ragnarssons were behind, older men and weighed down by their mail, but spreading out to cross the little channel yards apart and cut off any break back. In front of him, and on both sides, there lay nothing but a confusion of rounded banks, with pools and shallow runnels draining to the main channels. Every now and then one of the runnels was a deep one. That was where they might catch him, still swimming as Sigurth aimed his spear or the young man caught his heel. But if he got enough of a lead he could swim one of them and get away. Men in mail would not be anxious to try a deep channel, and would lose sight of him if they did.

Shef turned as the young man reached shore, and ran again. Ran just a little slower than his best, swerving and glancing over his shoulder every dozen yards, as if terrified. Fifty yards and splash through a shallow pool. Fifty more and round a steeper bank. The *Ormr* a furlong away now and powerless to intervene, the Ragnarssons spread out and calling to each other to keep him in sight. The tall young man's panting easy to hear as he closed the gap, raising his sword every few strides as if hoping to strike.

Vikings were poor runners, Shef remembered grimly. He swerved through another knee-deep rivulet, leapt up the other side on to firm sand, and swung round.

The young man paused in the water, then grinned exultantly and leapt forward, sword up for a forehand cut. Shef sprang inside the blow, both hands grabbing the right wrist, and backheeled his enemy's legs from under him. Both went down with a thud on the sand, the sword bouncing away.

No time to grab it, and too risky to grapple. All the Viking had to do was hold him till the Ragnarssons got there. Shef stepped back, arms spread in the wrestler's stance. The young man faced him, still panting, still grinning.

"My name is Hrani," he said. "I am the best wrestler in Ebeltoft."

He closed, reaching out for a collar-and-elbow grip. Shef ducked and snatched for the knife at Hrani's belt. As Hrani dropped a hand to cover it, he straightened up, swinging his left arm backhand under Hrani's neck and thrusting a hip behind him. Off balance, the tall man fell backwards. On to a knee braced to catch his spine. In the same instant Shef heaved down with both arms and all the smithy-trained strength in his body.

A snap of spine, and Hrani looking upwards with terror in his eyes. Still holding him over one knee, Shef patted his cheek gently.

"You are still the best wrestler in Ebeltoft," he said. "It was a foul throw."

He pulled the knife from Hrani's belt and stabbed upwards, deep under the ribcage. Rolled the body aside and straightened, retrieving the sword with its plain bone handle.

A deeper channel just a few yards away. Shef trotted to it, hurled the sword thirty feet to the other side, plunged in and stroked swiftly across. Turned and stood on the shore to face the Ragnarssons, trotting up together, breathing hard. He ducked his head for a moment to let his empty eye drain, then looked across and met the Snake-eye's gaze.

"Come over," he called. "There are three of you, all great warriors. So was your brother Ivar. I killed him in the water too."

Halvdan strode into the water, sword raised. His brother Ubbi caught him by the shoulder.

"He would cut you down before you had your feet under you."

Shef grinned, deliberately exaggerating it, hoping to provoke a charge. If one man came across, he would try to kill him while the water still hampered his movements. If two or three crossed together, he would run again, confident that if nothing else he could outdistance them. He had the initiative now. This was a puzzle they had to solve. For they did not know he had made up his mind to run. If they all crossed together, the odds were that they would kill him, but he would get at least one blow in first. They might think, seeing the body of their henchman, that he was full of the fighting madness and would take their dare.

Without warning or backlift Sigurth's javelin came darting at his belly, launched without as much as a flicker of expression. Shef saw the flash, leapt with the reactions of youth into the air, kicking his legs wide. The shaft tapped him agonizingly in the groin as it flew through. Shef landed in a crouch on the sand, bit his lip to conceal the pain.

"At least your brother Ivar fought fair, standing on the same plank as I did," he called. "Did anyone tell you how he died?" His testicles crushed in my grasp, he thought, and his face cut to ribbons where I butted him with the edge of my helmet. I hope that was not the story they heard. For if he fought fair I certainly did not.

The Snake-eye turned away, not even bothering to draw his sword. He muttered something to his brothers and they turned too, stepping back towards the body of Hrani. Shef saw Sigurth stoop and retrieve the gold bracelet from Hrani's arm. Then the three began to make their way together back to their ship. They had not taken the dare.

Sigurth is a clever man, thought Shef. He turned and fled from the sea-battle rather than fight according to my plan. Now he has done the same again. I must remember, that does not mean that he has given up.

He looked round, assessing his own situation.

He was cut off from the *Norfolk*. It might or might not be attacked by Sigurth and his crew, might or might not win the duel. But in any case he did not dare to try to rejoin it. Impossible to say what ambushes Sigurth might lay in the sandbanks. He would have to go the other way, towards the unknown shore, across maybe a quarter-mile yet of sandbanks.

He had the clothes he stood up in, a flint and steel tied to his belt, and a poorly made iron sword with a bone handle. His stomach reminded him that he had not eaten since the noon-meal. He was already starting to shiver uncontrollably in his soaked woolen breeches and tunic. The salt water was irritating his empty eye, so that by some freak the other one wept continually. The sun was a bare hand's breadth above the flat horizon. And he could not stay where he was. The tide was rising. Soon he would be faced with a long swim rather than a walk.

He felt less of a king than ever. But then, he told himself, he had never felt truly a king at all. At least now that he was a man he had no master or stepfather to beat him.

Turning towards the German shore on the north bank of the Elbe, he thought to pick up the javelin Sigurth had hurled at him. A fine weapon, as was to be expected, iron-shafted for a foot below its long triangular head. The head itself of excellent steel, without marks of use. No silver inlay or decoration. The Snake-eye, sensible man, wasted no money on what he meant to throw at his enemies. Yet there were marks on the steel, runes. Tutored carefully by Thorvin, Shef managed to read them: "Gungnir," they said.

So, the Snake-eye thought it no desecration to imitate Othin himself. It was no heirloom or ancient weapon. Shef's smithcraft told him that this was new-forged. Thoughtfully, Shef sloped the spear over one shoulder, tucked Hrani's sword into his belt, and set out wearily and cautiously for the north bank of the Elbe across its guardian sands, just visible in the twilight.

Far to the north of the sandbanks of the Elbe, north even of the Ragnarssons' stronghold in Danish Sjaelland, the great college of the Way in far-off Kaupang lay still under deep snow on the Norwegian shore. Thick ice bridged the fjords from one bank to the other. Men out in the open moved hurriedly to the next place of shelter.

Yet between the rapid shapes of skiers one figure came to a halt, stood motionless in the snow: Vigleik of the many visions, most respected of the priests of the Way. Where he stood, birds began to flutter out of the sky, land around him, forming a circle. As the flock grew thicker, men pointed, called others to watch. Slowly a circle of men, priests and their apprentices and servants, formed outside the ring of birds, keeping a decorous fifty yards away.

One of the birds, a small redbreast, flew up from the throng, perched on Vigleik's shoulder, twittered loud and long. Vigleik stood unmoving in the snow, his head cocked as if paying attention. Finally he nodded courteously, and the bird flew off.

A second bird came, sat on his gloved hand where it clutched the pole of his skis. This time it was a tiny wren, its tail cocked up like a rider's spur. It too sang a long song, and waited. "Thank you, sister," the watching priests heard Vigleik say.

Then all the birds flew hastily up and off to safety in the branches. The newcomer was a great black crow, which did not sit by Vigleik but paced up and down in front of him, calling from time to time in harsh and challenging caws. It sounded as if it were jeering. Still Vigleik stood silent. In the end the bird lifted its tail, squirted a stream of droppings on to the grass, and in its turn flew off.

After a while Vigleik raised his eyes and stared into the far distance. When he dropped them, his face had changed back to its normal expression. Knowing the vision had passed from him, his colleagues ventured to approach. In the lead was Valgrim, admitted head of the College, and priest of Othin All-Father—there were few who cared to take such responsibility.

"What news, brother?" he said at last.

"News of the death of tyrants. And worse news. My brother the redbreast told me that Pope Nikulaus is dead in Rome-burg, smothered under a pillow by his own servants. He paid the price not for sending his men against us, but for losing."

Valgrim nodded his head, a smile of pleasure creasing his beard.

"My sister the wren told me that in Frankland King Karl the Bald is also dead. One of his counts told the story of how Karl's ancestors had the long-haired kings shaven to show that they were kings no more, and said that God had sent baldness to Karl to show he should never have been king. When Karl told men to lay hands on the count, the other counts rose and slew him instead."

Valgrim smiled again. "And the crow?" he prompted finally.

"That was the worse news. He told me there is a tyrant still living, though close to death today, Sigurth Ragnarsson."

"Tyrant he may be," said Valgrim. "Yet he is the favorite of Othin for all that. If the Way could win him to its side, it would gain a mighty champion."

"That may be too," said Vigleik. "Yet his creature the crow treats us as his enemies, the murderers of his brother. It threatened me, threatened all of us, with his vengeance. And yet the crow was not telling all the truth, I know. He was keeping something back."

"What?"

Vigleik shook his head slowly. "That is still hidden from me. Yet for all you say, Valgrim, I do not think the road to victory at Ragnarök lies through the likes of Sigurth Ragnarsson, with his sacrifices and his cruelty. It is not great champions alone that will overcome Loki and the Fenris-brood. Nor is it blood that will bring Balder back from the dead. Not blood, but tears."

Valgrim's face flushed even in the cold at the challenge to his authority, and the mention of unlucky names and deeds. Controlling himself, he asked finally, "And at the end, when you seemed to look far away?"

"Then I saw eagles in the distance. First one mounted above the other, and then the lower one flew higher again. I could not see which would win in the end."

CHAPTER FIVE

Erkenbert the deacon sat in the sunlight behind a stout table, ink and parchment in front of him. It had been a long day's work, almost over now. But a deeply satisfying one. Erkenbert felt confidence, respect, almost awe creeping over him as he shuffled the thick pile of parchment sheets, filled with row after row of names: each one an application to join the ranks of the new Order which the archbishops of the West had proclaimed: the Order of the Lance, or in their tongue the *Lanzenorden*.

During their slow journey north from Cologne to Hamburg, Erkenbert had realized that there were special factors favoring the establishment of an order of warrior-monks here, in the German lands. In his native Northumbria, as indeed over the whole of family-conscious England, the thanes who formed the backbone of any army were good at one thing alone: establishing themselves comfortably on the estates granted them by the king. And then moving heaven and earth to see that not only did they hold on to them, however old, fat or unfitted for military service they became, but also that the estates were passed on in due form to their children. Sometimes they sent sons to perform service for them, sometimes they worked their way into royal or monastic favor by enforcing the king's dooms, or the abbot's, and witnessing any charter that needed a voice to swear one way or the other. However they did it, even if they had to send their daughters to tempt some magnate's lust, it was rare in England to find a parcel of land without some noble's son who thought he had a claim on it, or a noble's son who would prove in the end to be disappointed.

Not so in Germany. The warrior-class there had not been allowed to settle in and make itself comfortable. Service had to be performed. If it was not, a better replacement was found immediately. A middle-aged warrior had better have seen to his own security by the time his sword-arm stiffened, for his lord would feel no obligation to do it for him. As for the sons of warriors, there were many with little prospects, no assured future. In a sense, thought Erkenbert very quietly to himself, for all their concern with noble blood, they were more like peasants or churls than nobles, for they might be dispossessed at any moment. To such men, warlike though they were, to be allowed to enroll in an Order which would provide them a home and comradeship till the day they died, as if they were black monks, might well have unexpected appeal.

Yet he and his colleagues would not have had so much success in recruiting their serf-soldiers if it had not been for the oratory of Archbishop Rimbert. A dozen times as they made their way north from Cologne to Hamburg, Erkenbert had heard him call together the masses in whichever town they had chosen for their halt, and had heard him preach.

Always he took as his text the words of Saint Mark, "I will send you forth as sheep in the midst of wolves." He reminded his hearers how Jesus had forbidden Saint Peter to resist the soldiers when they came for him in the garden of Gethsemane, how he had urged his disciples to turn the other cheek, and if a man compelled them to go with him one mile, to go with him voluntarily for two. He would pursue the theme till he saw the looks of doubt, or disgust, on the faces of his warlike listeners.

And then he would say to them that what Jesus said was no doubt true. But what if a man compelled you to carry his pack for a mile, and you carried it from good will for two—and then instead of thanking you, he cursed you and told you to carry it another two, another ten, another twenty? What if you turned the other cheek and your enemy struck it again, and again, using his heaviest dogwhip? As his listeners stirred and muttered angrily, he would ask them why they felt anger. For were these things that he put to them not far less, not a hundred times less, than the insults and injuries they had had to endure from the pagans of the North? And then he talked to them of what he, Rimbert, had seen in his many years as the apostle to the North: daughters and wives ravished, men taken away and left to die in

slavery, Christians on their knees in the snow, wailing as they waited
to be sacrificed to the heathen gods at Odense or Kaupang or, worst of
all, Swedish Uppsala. Wherever he could, he would tell each particular
audience of what had happened to men or women from that town or
that district—he seemed to have an inexhaustible stock of heart-
rending stories, as who would not, Erkenbert reflected, if he had spent
thirty years on the pointless and hopeless task of preaching to the
heathen.

And when his audience's anger was at its height, when the
serf-knights among them scowled and wrung their hands and swept
off their leather caps in passion, then Rimbert would tell them his text:
"I will send you forth as sheep in the midst of wolves. Yes," he would
say, "the good priests of my missions, not one in ten of whom ever
returns to his home, they have been sheep—and sheep they will
remain. But from now on—and as he said this, his voice would rise to
an iron clangor—when I send out my sheep, I will see that with each
sheep there goes, not another sheep, not a wolf, no. But a great dog, a
great mastiff of the German breed, with a good spiked collar round his
neck, and twenty other wolfhounds running with him. Then we will
see how the wolves of the North listen to the sheep's preaching! Maybe
they will listen closely to his bleat in the future."

And Rimbert would condescend to joke and play with words,
sometimes even imitating the noise of a sheep to set his audience
laughing uproariously in the relief of its tension and anger. And then
Rimbert would tell them, slowly and quietly, of his plan. To send
mission after mission into the North, through the friendlier of the
chiefs and kings of the heathen, each mission centered on a learned
and pious priest, as had always been the custom, but each mission
containing also a new and strong bodyguard for that priest: men of
noble birth and knightly station, men without wives or children or
ties, men expert with sword and lance and mace, men who could ride
a war-stallion with shield on one arm and lance in the other,
controlling it with knees and fingertips alone—men whom even the
pirates of the North would walk carefully around, fearing to antagonize
them.

And then, when he had their full attention, Rimbert would tell
them of the Holy Lance, and of how, when it came back to the Empire,
the spirit of Charlemagne would come again and lead Christendom
once more to triumph over all its enemies. And he would invite
suitable applicants to present themselves to his servants, to see if they
were worthy of a place in the *Lanzenorden*.

Which was why Erkenbert now had the thick piles of parchment in his hand, covered with row after row of names: the applicants' names, their claims to noble birth—for no peasants or peasants' sons would be admitted under any circumstances—the lists of the worldly wealth they could bring to the order, and the details of their personal arms and equipment. In due course some names would be crossed out, some would be accepted. Most would be crossed out. And most of those not for failure in wealth or nobility, but because they could not pass the tests devised for them by the archbishop's *Waffenmeister*, his master-at-arms. Which, as Erkenbert ceased his writing, were going on in this place or that all over the wide exercise field outside the wooden stockade of much-sacked Hamburg. Men cutting at each other with blunted sword and shield. Men riding horses along a complex course of jumps and figures to strike down with a lance. Men grappling with each other, hand to hand, in the ring. And everywhere the grizzled *Waffenmeister* or the sergeants of his staff, noting, comparing, repeating names.

Erkenbert looked across at Arno, the counselor of Gunther, sent along with Erkenbert into Rimbert's archdiocese to watch, assist and report. They grinned at each other with the curious fellow-feeling that had grown between them, the small dark one and the tall fair one, each recognizing the other's delight in efficiency, in the exercise of pure intelligence.

"The Archbishop will get his first hundred easily," offered Erkenbert.

Before Arno could reply, another voice cut in. "He will only need ninety-nine now," it said.

Deacon and priest stared up from their stools at the newcomer.

He was not a tall man, Erkenbert noted, ever sensitive on this point. But his shoulders were extraordinarily broad, made to seem even more so by a pinched, narrow waist like a girl's. He was wearing a padded leather jacket such as horsemen wore under their mail. Erkenbert saw that extra strips had been sewn in to widen the upper body, neatly, but without any attempt to match colors. Beneath the jacket there seemed to be only a fustian tunic of the cheapest kind, and well-worn woolen breeches.

The eyes staring down were a bright, penetrating blue, the hair as fair as Arno's, but sticking up like the bristles of a brush. He had seen dangerous faces, and crazy faces, Erkenbert reflected, remembering Ivar the Boneless. He could not remember ever seeing a harder one. It seemed to have been chiseled out of rock, the skin stretched taut over prominent bones. Set on a neck as thick as a bulldog's, the head seemed almost small.

Erkenbert found his voice. "What do you mean?"

"Well, fellow, the archbishop wants one hundred, I make one, one less than one hundred—have you heard of the art of arithmetic?—that makes ninety-nine."

Erkenbert flushed at the jibe. "I have heard of arithmetic. But you have not yet been selected. First we need to know your name, and your parents' names, and many other things. And you would have to go before the *Waffenmeister*. In any case you are too late for today."

He felt a hand laid on his arm, Arno speaking softly and carefully. "Colleague, you are correct, but I feel in this case we may make an exception. The young *herra* here is known to me, to us all. He is Bruno, son of Reginbald, the Count of the Marches. There can of course be no doubt as to his suitability on the score of ancestry."

Erkenbert reached irritably for the parchment. "Very well. If we are to do this in proper form we must then proceed to the questions of wealth and the contributions the applicant can bring to the order." He began to write. "The name is Bruno, the son of a count must naturally be Bruno of? . . ."

"Bruno von nowhere," said the soft voice. Erkenbert felt his writing hand enclosed in a vast, irresistible grip, gentle but with metal cables stirring beneath it. "I am the Count's third son, with no estate. I own nothing but my arms and armor and my good horse. But let me ask a few questions of you, little man with the paper. You speak *teutsch* well, but I can tell you are not one of us. I have heard nothing also of your noble family. I ask myself, who is this who has the right to say who shall and who shall not be a *Ritter* of a noble order? No offense, I hope."

Arno cut in hastily. "The learned deacon is an Englishman, Bruno. He fought in the Pope's army that was beaten and came to tell us the story. He saw also the deaths of the famous Vikings, Ivar Boneless and Ragnar of the Hairy Breeches. He has told us a great deal of value, and is heart and soul for our cause."

The grip round Erkenbert's hand released, the blond man stepped back, interest showing on his craggy face.

"Good," he said, "good. I am prepared to accept an Englishman as a comrade. And there is one thing the little Englishman has said— take no offense, friend, each of us has his strengths—one thing that is true. I must certainly pass the *Waffenmeister*." His voice rose to a shout. "Dankwart! Where are you, you old villain. Set me a test. No, do not trouble. I will set them myself."

During the talk with Erkenbert, activity had ceased on the field. The *Waffenmeister*, his sergeants, the so-far successful applicants had quit their various tasks and come to cluster round the newcomer. They cleared a lane for Bruno as he stepped away from the table.

In four bounds he had reached the great black horse standing untethered close by. He sprang into the saddle without touching stirrup or pommel, snatched a lance stuck in the ground, and was already in motion towards the circuit of jumps and quintains. As his horse rose to the first hurdle Erkenbert realized the blond man had tucked his left arm theatrically behind his back, to make up for the fact that he carried no shield. His reins were dropped, he was controlling the stallion by knees and thighs alone. An overarm stab at the first quintain, an instant twist and leap. As dust rose from the field Erkenbert could make out only the crash of tumbling targets and a black centaur rising every few seconds over fence after fence. The more expert watchers had started to cheer every stroke. In what seemed moments the horse was back, the rider swinging again to the ground, breathing hard and grinning broadly.

"Did I pass that part, Dankwart? Tell the man with the paper, then, it doesn't count if he doesn't mark me down. But now, Dankwart, we have an expert watching, one who has seen real battles and seen great champions fight. I want to show him something and have his opinion. Who is the best man here today with sword and shield?"

The grizzled *Waffenmeister* pointed impassively to one of the applicants who had been sparring with his sergeants. A tall young man in a white surcoat over mail. "That one there, Bruno. He's good."

Bruno walked towards his proposed adversary, took one hand between his two, looked up at him with a curious tenderness, like a lady to her lover. "You agree?" he asked.

The tall man nodded. Sergeants handed each of them a shield, a heavy kite-shaped one of the horseman's pattern. Then a heavy sword, edges blunted, point carefully rounded. The two men stepped back, began to circle each other warily, each moving to the right, away from his opponent's sword.

Erkenbert, no expert, saw only a blur of motion, three repeated clashes as the tall man struck, low, high, backhand, whirling the sword as if it were weightless. Three solid determined parries from Bruno, twisting his wrist each time to take the blow at right angles on his own blade, ignoring the shield. Then as the fourth blow came he had stepped inside it, jerking the edge of his shield up to catch the descending sword just above its guard. As the tall man stepped back to recover his balance, Bruno's sword was in the air. It seemed for an instant as if three swords were striking at once, the tall man parrying desperately in all directions. Then his shield was down, his sword was up, he was in a half-crouch to parry a blow not struck. Bruno seemed even to pause for an instant, to weigh what was needed.

Then his sword swept through the gap too fast for sight. A thud, a gasp, and the tall man was sprawling on his back. Erkenbert realized a second after the blow that he had seen the count's son deliberately rolling his wrists at the moment of impact, to soften the blow. He had had no need to exercise his full force.

Bruno had already dropped sword and shield, was helping his opponent up with the same curious tenderness. He patted his cheek, looked closely into the other man's eyes, waving a hand in front of them to see if the other could focus. Relief crossed his face, he stepped back, grinning. "A good bout, young knight. I am glad we shall be comrades of the Order. Another time I will show you the trick of that feint, it is easy to learn." He looked round, acknowledging the applause of the circle of watchers, waving so that his opponent should be included in it.

Another thing about these Germans, thought Erkenbert, remembering the prickly, awkward insistence on rank and precedence of his homeland. They work together very easily. They like to form clubs and groups and companionships and all share their food and their beer. Yet they will still accept a leader who insists on being one of the men. Is that a strength or a weakness?

Bruno was approaching the table again, eyes shining with a kind of manic glee. "Now," he said, "will you write me down?"

As Arno reached for the pen and the parchment he laughed, bent over, collected Erkenbert's gaze and said with sudden gravity: "Now, comrade. They say you have seen the great champions, Ivar Boneless and maybe the warrior they call Killer-Brand. Tell me, how do you think one such as myself would compare with them? Tell me the truth, now, I take no offense."

Erkenbert hesitated. He had seen Ivar fight in battle against the champions of Mercia, though only from a fair distance behind. At closer quarters he had seen the duel on the gangplank between Ivar and Brand. He remembered Ivar's snake-like speed, the unexpected power in his relatively slender frame. Thought of what he had just seen, measuring the strength and leverage of the broad shoulders in front of him.

"Ivar was very quick," he said at last. "He could dodge a blow rather than block it, and still remain poised to strike back. I think if you had an open space to fight him in you might have worn him down, for you would be the stronger. But Ivar is dead."

Bruno nodded, face intent. "So what of Killer-Brand, the one who killed him?"

"It was not Brand who killed him. Ivar was too quick for Brand, mighty man though he is. No." The hatred in Erkenbert's heart welled up. "It was another who killed Ivar. The son of a churl, devil-possessed. He had only a dog's name to call himself, Shef, and he did not know his father. In fair fight you would defeat a hundred like him. And now they call him a king!"

The blue eyes were thoughtful. "Yet he killed a great champion, you say, fair fight or no. These things do not happen by accident. Such a man should never be despised. The greatest gift a king can have, some say, is luck."

By the time Shef reached solid ground he was chilled through, his teeth chattering uncontrollably. The rising tide had forced him to swim twice, no great distance but soaking him through each time. There was no sun to dry him. A fringe of seaweed marked the edge of tidal sand, with just beyond it a shallow dyke, obviously man-made. Shef scrambled to the top of it and turned to look out to sea, hoping against hope that he would see the *Norfolk* standing in to rescue him, and that in an hour or so he could count on dry clothes and a blanket, a hunk of bread and cheese, maybe a fire on the sand while someone else stood guard. At that moment he could imagine no greater reward for being a king.

There was nothing to be seen. The gray twilight made everything out on the flats seem the same, gray sea, gray sky, gray sandbanks slowly yielding to the water. He had not heard the clash of battle behind him as he made his way to the shore, but that did not mean anything. The *Norfolk* might have been carried by boarders. Or she might have been refloated and be continuing her single-ship duel with the *Frani Ormr*. Or both ships might long have sailed out once more to the open sea. There was no hope in that direction.

Shef turned the other way and contemplated the drab landscape in front of him. Plowed fields with shoots of green barley showing. Somewhere a few hundred yards off in the dimness black bulks that might well be grazing cows. All that showed a certain confidence here on the edge of the pirate sea. Were the men of this land great warriors? Or slaves of the Vikings? Or did they rely on the dangerous shoals to keep them safe? Whichever was true, their land was no great prize: flat as a man's hand, kept from the tide only by a six-foot dyke, muddy, sodden and featureless.

More to the point, there was no prospect of warmth in it anywhere. In a wooded country Shef might have thought to find a fallen tree to break the wind, boughs to pile under and over him to keep him out of the wet, maybe a drift of decaying leaves to rake over himself. Here there was nothing but mud and wet grass. Yet the cows and the plowed fields showed there was a village not too far away. Men never plowed more than a couple of miles from their homes and byres: the time it took an ox to travel that distance, morning and evening, was the most that any sensible man would add on to his day. So there must be a house, and with a house a fire, somewhere all but in sight.

Shef looked round for a gleam of light. Nothing. That was only to be expected. Anyone who had light and fire would have the sense to shut it in. Shef turned to his left, for no reason than that it was away from the land of the Christians and Hamburg further down the Elbe, and began to walk briskly along the dyke. If he had to, he decided, he would walk all night. His clothes were bound to dry on him in the end. He would be ravenously hungry by dawn, his body's resources used up by keeping out the cold, but that could be borne. He had fed well all the months he had been a king, and a jarl before that. Now was the time to use some of that up. But if he lay down in the fields, he would be dead by morning.

After only a few minutes of stumbling, Shef realized that he was crossing a track. He paused. Should he follow it? If the natives were hostile he could be dead well before morning. The patter of rain on his shoulders made his mind up for him. He moved cautiously down the track, his one eye probing the darkness.

The village was no more than a cluster of longhouses, their low walls showing just slightly darker than the sky. Shef reflected. No hall for a lord, no church for a priest. That was good. The longhouses were different sizes, some long, some short. One of the shortest ones was the closest to him. In the winter these folk, like the poor people of Norfolk, would bring their beasts in the house with them, for warmth. A small house meant few cows. Was it not true that charity was likeliest among the poor? He moved cautiously towards the door of the nearest house, the smallest. A chink of light through the wooden shutters.

He planted the Snake-eye's spear butt-down in the ground, pulled the sword from his belt and held it by the blade. With his right hand he pounded on the ill-fitting door. A scurrying inside, muttered words. It creaked open.

Shef stepped forwards into the ill-lit doorway, his sword balanced across both hands in token of submission. Without a pause he found himself lying on his back, staring up at the sky. He had felt no blow, had no idea what had happened. His arms and legs seemed to pay no attention to his insistent commands to them to move.

He felt a fist gripping the neck of his tunic, hauling him half upright, a voice in his ear muttering in a thick dialect, but comprehensibly, "All right, come along, get your feet under you, let's get you inside and have a look at you."

His legs sprawling, Shef staggered inside, his arm round someone's shoulder, and sank on to a stool by a meager fire.

For long moments he could pay no attention to anything but the warmth, holding his hands out to it, crouching over it. As the steam started to rise from his clothes he shook his head, rose unsteadily to his feet, and looked round. Facing him was a stocky man, hands on hips, with a mop of curly hair and an expression on his face of irrepressible good humor. From the thinness of his beard Shef realized that he was even younger than himself. In the background stood two older folk, a man and a woman, looking at him with alarm and distrust.

Shef tried to speak, realized his jaw was stiff and sore. An exploring hand found a growing lump on the right-hand side.

"What did you do?" he asked.

The stocky man grinned even more broadly than before, made swift darting movements with his hands and body. "Gave you a bit of a dunt," he replied. "You walked right into it."

Shef cast his mind back, amazed. In England, and among the Vikings, men hit each other with their fists often enough, but wrestling was the warrior's sport. By the time someone had raised his fist and swung it, even a grandfather should be able to duck out of the way. Even walking into a dark room, he would have expected to see a swing coming and at least react to it. Nor would you expect a swing to knock a man down. Fighting with fists was an affair of prolonged and clumsy bludgeoning, which was why the warriors despised it. Yet Shef had seen nothing and felt nothing till he was on the ground.

"Do not be surprised," said the old man in the background. "Our Karli does that to everyone. He is a champion. But you had better tell us who you are, or he will strike you again."

"I got separated from my ship," said Shef. "Had to walk and swim across the sandbanks."

"Are you one of the Vikings? You speak more like one of us."

"I am an Englishman. But I have been much among Norsemen, and can understand their speech. I have spoken with Frisians as well. You speak most like them. Are you Frisians? The free Frisians," Shef added, remembering how they liked to describe themselves.

Even the old woman laughed. "The free Frisians," said the stocky youth. "Living on sandbanks and running for their lives every time they see a sail. No, we are Germans."

"The archbishop's men?" inquired Shef cautiously. He could see his sword now, standing in a corner where they must have put it. If the answer were wrong, he would lunge for it and try to kill the stocky youth at once.

Again they laughed. "No. Some of us are Christians, some follow the old gods, some none. But none of us has any wish to pay tithes or kneel to a lord. We are the folk of the Ditmarsh," the youth ended proudly.

Shef had never heard the name from anyone before. He nodded. "I am cold and wet. And hungry," he added. "May I sleep inside your house tonight?"

"Sleep by the fire and welcome," said the older man, who Shef realized must be the father of the stocky one, the master of the house. "As for hunger, we have plenty of that ourselves. But you can dry yourself here rather than die out on the marsh. Tomorrow you must go before the village for a doom."

I have gone into a doom-ring before, thought Shef. But maybe the Ditmarshers' doom will be kinder than the Great Army's. Feeling his swollen jaw again, he moved to the side of the fire while the family of the house prepared itself for sleep.

CHAPTER SIX

hef woke in the morning feeling strangely calm and rested. For a few moments he lay on the packed earth floor and wondered why. The fire was out, and he had kept from shivering in the night only by curling into a ball and gripping knees with arms. His clothes had dried from body heat, but dried stiff and harsh from salt water. His belly was pinched with hunger. And he was alone and without resources in a strange and probably hostile land. So why did he not seem more anxious?

Shef got to his feet, stretched luxuriously, and pushed open the wooden shutter, letting in the sunlight and the fresh air smelling of grass and blossom. He knew the answer. It was because his cares and responsibilities had fallen from him. For the first time for many months he did not have to think about other people's needs: how to feed them, how to persuade them, how to praise them to make them do his will. His childhood had made him used to cold and hunger. And to blows and the threat of slavery as well. But now he was no child, but a man in his prime. If anyone struck him he could strike back. Shef's one eye noted the weapons he had leant against the corner of the hut. Hrani's sword and Sigurth's spear. They were the only possessions he now had, apart from the pendant round his neck and the flint and eating-knife slung from his belt. They would have to do.

Out of the corner of his eye Shef saw that the older couple had emerged from their box-bed. The man went straight out of the door. That could be ominous. The woman pulled a quern from under their rough table, scooped grain from a barrel into it, and began to grind it with a hand-pestle. The sound brought Shef's childhood back even more strongly. As long as he could remember, every day had started the same way, with the sound of women grinding grain into flour. Only jarls and kings could live far enough away from daily necessity not to hear it. It was the task warriors hated most, though on campaign even they had to do it. Perhaps women hated it too, Shef reflected. At least it showed these people had food. His belly cramped in response to the thought, and Shef glanced again towards his weapons.

A touch on his arm. The young man with the curly hair stood there, grinning as always. He held out a hunk of black bread in a dirty fist, strong-smelling yellow cheese on top of it. As Shef took it, his mouth running instantly with saliva, he produced an onion, divided it in his palm with a crude knife, and passed Shef half.

The two squatted on the floor and began to eat. The bread was hard, old, full of bran and gritty with stone from the hand-quern. Shef tore it with his teeth, relishing every mouthful.

After a while, his stomach relaxing in its demands, he remembered the soreness in his jaw, the strange events of last night. As his hand went up to explore the swelling, he caught the young man—what had the woman called him? Our Karli?—grinning at the gesture.

"What did you hit me for?" he asked.

Karli seemed surprised at the question. "I didn't know who you were. Simplest way to deal with you. Simplest way to deal with everybody."

Shef felt a certain irritation rising. He swallowed the last lump of cheese, rose to his feet, spreading his arms and flexing the muscles in his back. He remembered the man he had killed yesterday, the young Viking from Ebeltoft. He had been a bigger man even than Shef, and Shef out-topped Karli by a head.

"You would not have done it if it had not been for the dark."

Karli was on his feet too, a look of glee on his face. He started to circle Shef in a strange shuffle, not like a wrestler's planted stance. His fists were doubled, his head sunk below his shoulders. Impatiently Shef stepped forward, hands grabbing for a wrist-hold. A fist jabbed at his face, he brushed it aside. Something struck him below the ribs on his right side. For an instant Shef ignored it, tried again to grapple. Then pain shot up from his liver, he felt his breath leave him, and his hands dropped automatically to guard the spot. Instantly his head snapped back and Shef found himself staggering back against the wall. As he straightened, blood ran down into his mouth, his teeth felt loosened.

A surge of anger drove Shef forward with lightning speed, aiming to body-check, trip and go for a bonebreaker hold. The body was not there, and as he whirled to reach the darting figure now behind him, he felt another blow in the back, a stab of agony from a kidney. Again he blocked a blow at the face, this time remembering instantly to swipe downwards to thwart the liver-punch that followed. Still no grip, and another blow high up on the cheekbone as he hesitated. But the circling had brought Shef into easy reach of the spear propped against the wall. How would that grin look? . . .

Shef stood up straight, spread his arms wide in token of defenselessness. "All right," he said, looking at Karli's grin. "All right. You would have knocked me down even if it had not been dark. I can see you know something I do not. Maybe many things."

Karli grinned even more broadly than before, and dropped his hands. "I expect you know some things too—a seafarer like you, with a spear and a sword as well. I have never been outside the Ditmarsh—hardly ever outside this village. How about a trade? I will show you what I know, and you show me what you know. I could soon teach you how to strike and guard with your fists, like we do here in the Ditmarsh. You move very fast. Too fast for most of these ploughboys."

"A trade," Shef agreed. He spat on his palm and looked at Karli to see if he understood the gesture. The other grinned, and spat too. The pair slapped palms violently to seal the bargain.

As Shef wiped the blood from his nose with the back of his sleeve, they resumed their companionable squat.

"Now listen," said Karli. "You've more important things to learn right now than fist-fighting. My old man has gone out to tell the village you're here. They'll assemble outside, make the ring, and decide what to do with you."

"What are their choices?"

"First off, someone will say you're a slave. That'll be Nikko. He's the richest man in the village. Wants to be a lord. But silver is short in the Ditmarsh, and we never make slaves of each other. Having someone to sell in the market at Hedeby is what he thinks about all the time."

"Hedeby is a Danish town," said Shef.

Karli shrugged. "Danish, German, Frisian, we don't care. No-one tries any tricks on the Ditmarsh. They couldn't find the path through the fens. And anyway, they know there's no silver here. Lot to lose for a tax-collector, nothing much to gain."

"If I don't want to be a slave, what's the other choice?"

"You could be a guest-friend." Karli looked at him sideways. "Like with me. That means exchanging gifts."

Shef felt his biceps, regretting the last-minute decision yesterday to strip the gold bracelets from them. One of those would have bought him hospitality for a year. Or a knife in the back. "What do I have, then? A spear. A sword. And this." He pulled the silver pole-ladder of Rig from under his tunic, and glanced across at Karli to see if he recognized the sign. No interest there. But Karli had glanced more than once at the weapons propped in the corner.

Shef stepped over to them, picked them up for a closer look. The spear with the 'Gungnir' runes: excellent steel, glinting new-forged, a beautiful balance in the hand. The sword: serviceable enough, but a little too heavy, the blade mere sharpened iron without a specially welded edge, beginning already to pock slightly with rust. Swords were more valuable than spears, the mark of the professional warrior besides. Still . . .

Shef held out the sword. "Take this, Karli." He noted the way the young man took it, the way he held the blade slightly off the square, disastrous for a parry. "And I will give you two more things. One, I will show you how to use the sword. Two, if ever we stay by a forge, I will forge it again for you to make it a better weapon."

The freckled face flushed with pleasure as the door opened. Karli's father came in, jerked a thumb over his shoulder.

"Come, stranger," he said. "The doom-ring is outside."

Some forty men stood outside in a rough circle, their wives and children forming a larger circle outside them. All the men were armed, but not well—spears and axes, but no mail or helmets. A few had shields on their shoulders, but not strapped on ready for use.

What the Ditmarshers saw emerging from the hut was a tall warrior, his calling unmistakable from his bearing: straight back, wide shoulders, no sign of the stoop or the cramped muscles of the peasant who had to follow a plow or bend every day over hoe or sickle. Yet he bore no gold or silver on him, carried only the long spear in his right hand. He was scarred as well, with one eyelid drooping over a sunken socket, and the whole side of his face seeming drawn in. Unnoticed blood smeared his face, and his plain tunic and breeches were dirtier than a peasant's. The circle stared at him, unsure how to read these signals. There was a low mutter of comment as Karli emerged behind him, gripping in inexpert hands the sword he had been given.

Shef looked round, trying to appraise the situation. The waking feeling of calm and confidence was still with him, unshaken by the brush with Karli. Thoughtfully he pulled the silver Rig-pendant up on its chain so that it hung outside his tunic. Another mutter of comment, men peering closer to try to identify the sign. Some of the men watching, maybe a quarter of those present, similarly hitched pendants into view: hammers, boats, phalluses. None like Shef's.

The man directly facing Shef stepped forward, a bulky man in middle-age with a red face.

"You came from the ships," he said. "You are a Viking, one of the robbers of the North. Even such as you should know better than to set foot on the Ditmarsh, where the free men live. We will enslave you and sell you to your kin at Hedeby. Or to the bishop's men at Hamburg. Unless there is someone who will pay to have you back—not likely, from the look of you."

Some instinct drove Shef forward across the ring, sauntering slowly till he came face to face with his accuser. He looked at him, tilting his head back to accentuate his greater height.

"If you know I came from the ships," he said, "you know there were two ships fighting. One was a Viking. It was the *Frani Ormr*, the great ship of Sigurth Ragnarsson. Did you not see the Raven Banner? The other one was mine, and Sigurth was running from it. Get me back to it and I'll give you a man's price in silver."

"What kind of ships chase Viking ships?" said the burly man.

"English ships."

The listening crowd made noises of surprise, disbelief. "It's true the first ship was a Viking," said a voice. "But he wasn't running. He was leading on. And he fooled the other skipper proper. If that second ship was English they must all be fools. Mast and sail all wrong, too."

"Take me back to it," repeated Shef.

Karli's voice came from behind him. "He couldn't do it if he wanted to, stranger. No boats. We Ditmarshers are bold enough in the marsh, but half a mile out to sea and that's pirate water."

The burly man flushed and glanced angrily round. "That's as may be. But if you've nothing else to say, one-eye, then what I said stands. You're my slave till I find a buyer. Hand over that spear."

Shef tossed the spear in the air, caught it at its point of balance, and feinted a lunge. He grinned broadly as the other man jumped clumsily away, then turned his back on him, ignoring the threatening axe. He began to stroll round the circle, looking into face after face, and addressing his words directly to the pendant-wearers in the circle. They were just like the Norfolk farmers whose disputes he had so often judged as a jarl, he decided. Get their interest and exploit their village divisions.

"A strange thing," he remarked. "Man gets washed up on the shore, might be alive, might be dead, what do you do with him? Where

I come from, the fishermen, if they have the cash, put a silver ring in their ears. You know what that's for. So if they drown and their bodies come to shore, the folk are paid for burying them. The folk would bury them anyway, in duty, but they don't like the idea of taking a last service for nothing.

"Now here I am, no ring in my ear, but not dead either. Why should I get worse treatment? Have I done any harm? I've made a gift to your Karli there, and in exchange he's knocked me down, bloodied my nose, loosened my teeth, and given me a sore jaw—so we're all good friends."

A rumble of amusement. As Shef had guessed, Karli was something between an object of admiration and a standing joke.

"Now what surprises me is our friend behind me." Shef jerked a thumb over his shoulder at the burly man. "He says I'm a slave. Well, maybe. Says I'm *his* slave. Did I go to his house? Did he capture me single-handed in peril of his life? Maybe you all decided that anything that fell off a ship belonged to him. Is that right?"

This time a definite rumble of rejection, and what sounded like a loud breaking of wind from Karli.

"So what I suggest is this." Shef had almost completed his circuit now, and was coming back face to face with the burly man. "If you want to make a slave of me, Nikko, then take me along to Hedeby and put me in the sale-ring. If you can make a sale, well and good. But then you must share the money with the village. Till you get to Hedeby, though, I stay free: no bonds, no collar. And I keep my spear. Sure, you can guard me as much as you like. Finally, till we get there I'll work for my keep." Shef tapped his pendant. "I have a skill. I'm a smith. Give me a forge and tools and I'll work at whatever you need."

"Sounds fair enough," called one voice. "I have a plowshare with its edge coming away, needs careful work."

"He don't talk like a Viking," called another. "More like a Frisian, only without the cold in his head."

"Did you hear the bit about sharing out?" called a third.

Shef spat on his palm and waited. Slowly, with hate in his eyes, the burly Nikko spat too. They slapped palms perfunctorily. As the tension slackened, Shef turned and walked back to Karli.

"I want you to come to Hedeby too," he said. "See the world. But we both have much to learn before we get there."

Forty miles out to sea, within sight of the Holy Island, the English fleet rocked on the waves, sails furled, like a flock of giant sea-birds. At the center four ships were lashed together for conference: the *Norfolk*, escaped from the muddy channels of the Elber Gat, the *Suffolk*, commanded by the senior English skipper Hardred, Brand's *Walrus* and the *Seamew* of Guthmund the Greedy, to represent the Viking Waymen. Feelings were running high, and strong voices carried over the water to the listening fleet.

"I can't believe you just left him on the Thor-forsaken sandbank," said Brand at a pitch just short of a bellow.

Ordlaf's face remained mulish. "Nothing else to do. He'd vanished out of sight, tide coming in, night coming on, no knowing if Sigurth and his picked champions weren't going to appear from the next sandbank. We had to get out of there."

"Do you think he lived?" asked Thorvin, flanked on either side by fellow-priests of the Way called from their ships.

"I saw four men go after him. Three came back. They didn't look pleased. That's all I can say."

"So the chances are he's stuck in the Ditmarsh somewhere," concluded Brand. "All those bastards have webbed feet."

"They tell me he's a fenman too," said Ordlaf. "If he's there, he's probably all right. Why don't we just go after him? It's daylight now, and we can pick our tide."

This time it was Brand's turn to look mulish. "Not a good idea. First off, no-one lands in the Ditmarsh, not even for water or an evening's *strandhögg*. Too many crews have vanished. Second, like I told you weeks ago, all this is pilot water. And you said you could find your way with lead and lookout! You got stranded, and you could again, maybe in a worse place next time.

"Third thing, though, is we still have the Ragnarssons around. They started off with a long hundred of ships, a hundred and twenty, the way you count. How many do you think we sank or captured?"

Hardred replied. "We captured six. The catapults sank at least a dozen more."

"Which leaves them a hundred, to our fifty. Less than fifty, since they boarded the *Buckinghamshire* and cut a hole in her bottom, and I have half a dozen ships too weakly manned now to be useful. And we won't take them by surprise again."

"So what do we do?" asked Ordlaf.

There was a long silence. Finally Hardred broke it, his careful Anglo-Saxon contrasting oddly with the camp-patois brewed from Norse and English of the others.

"If we are unable to rescue the king," he said, "as I am told we are, then I see it as my duty to return the rest of the fleet to English waters, to take instructions from King Alfred. He is my master, but the agreement between himself and King Shef''—he hesitated before coming out with the words—''was that one should succeed to all the rights of the other, if the other should pre-decease him. As may now be the case.''

He waited for the storm of protests to die down, then went on, his voice gaining firmness. ''After all, this fleet is now the main shield and protection of English shores. We know we can sink the pirates if they appear, and we will. That was the main aim and goal of King Shef, as of King Alfred: to have a peaceful coastline and a peaceful land behind it. If he were here he would tell us to do what I suggest.''

''You can go,'' shouted Cwicca, the freed slave. ''Go back to your master. Our master is the one who took the collars from our necks, and we won't leave him to have some webfoot half-breed put one on his.''

''How are you going to get there?'' said Hardred. ''Swim? Brand won't take you. Ordlaf daren't, not on his own.''

''We can't just sail away,'' pleaded Cwicca.

Thorvin's deep voice broke in. ''No. But it is in my mind that we can sail on. Or some of us can. Something tells me that it is not Shef Sigvarthsson's fate to die silently, or to vanish. Someone may have him for ransom. Or for sale. If we go to a major port, where news is gathered, we will hear something of him. I suggest we go on to Kaupang, some of us.''

''Kaupang,'' said Brand. ''To the College of the Way.''

''I have reasons of my own for going there, it's true,'' said Thorvin. ''But the Way has many followers, and many resources, and the college is deeply concerned about Shef. If we go there we will get help.''

''I won't,'' declared Hardred flatly. ''Too far, too risky, hostile waters all the way, and we know now the 'Counties' aren't fit for a deep-sea crossing.'' Ordlaf nodded in glum agreement.

''Some go back, some go on,'' said Thorvin.

''Most go back, I think,'' said Brand. ''Forty ships, even fifty ships, aren't enough to get through all the fleets of Norway and Denmark— the Ragnarssons, King Halvdan, the Hlathir jarls, King Gamli, King Hrorik, and all the others. They'd best turn back, to guard the Way in England. There are plenty who'd be glad to stamp it out.

''I'll take the *Walrus*. Go out deep sea, not hug the coast. I'll get through. I'll take you, Thorvin, and your fellows, to Kaupang and to the college. Who else? How about you, Guthmund?''

''Take us!'' Cwicca was on his feet, face red with rage. ''We aren't turning back. Take me and my mates, and our catapult too, we can unship it from the *Norfolk* if that Yorkshire fart won't risk his skin.

Cowpang, Ditfen, we'll take them all if we got to." A hubbub of agreement from the waist of the ship showed that the freed slaves of the catapult crews had been listening.

"Me too," said an almost inaudible voice from a small figure lurking behind the mast. Brand looked in several directions till he realized it came from Udd, the steelmaster, allowed on the cruise only in his former role of catapult crew spare hand.

"What do you want to go to Norway for?"

"For knowledge," said Udd. "I have heard men speak of Jarnberaland. Iron-bearing Land," he added, translating.

Another slight figure appeared to stand unspeaking by him. Hund, the leech, Shef's childhood friend, now with the silver apple of Ithun round his neck.

"Very well," said Brand decisively. "I'll take my own crew and the *Seamew* as consort. I'll have space for no more than ten volunteers. You Hund, you Udd, and you, Cwicca. Cast lots for the rest."

"And us as passengers," said Thorvin, nodding to his two fellow-priests. "Till we reach the college."

CHAPTER SEVEN

hef stepped back a pace, his feet sinking into the soft mire. He twirled the peeled branch in his hand and eyed Karli carefully. The short man had lost his grin and gained a look of anxious determination. At least he had learnt to hold his sword right: edge and guard absolutely parallel with the line of his forearm, so that cut or parry would not be deflected. Shef moved in, swung forehand, backhand, thrust and sidestep, as Brand had taught him months before in the camps outside York. Karli parried easily, not quite managing to catch the light wood with his heavier blade, but well into line every time—the speed of his reactions was excellent. Still the same old problem, though.

Shef accelerated slightly, feinted low and rapped Karli briskly over the sword-arm. He stepped back and lowered his stick.

"You've got to remember, Karli," he said. "You aren't cutting brushwood. What you've got there is a two-edged sword, not a one-edged billhook. What do you think the second edge is for? It's not for your main stroke, because you always slash with the same edge, to get your full force into it."

"It's for the back-flick," said Karli, repeating his lesson. "I know, I know. I just can't make my muscles do it unless I think about it, and if I think about it, it's too late. So tell me, what would happen if I tried to face a real swordsman, a Viking from the ships?"

Shef stretched out a hand for the sword he had reforged, looked at its edges critically. It was not a bad weapon, not now. But with what he had had by him at the forge in the Ditmarsh village, he had not dared to do too much. The weapon was still all of one metal, without the blends of soft and hard that gave a superior sword its flexibility and strength. Nor had he been able to weld on the hardened steel edges that were the sign of a master-weapon—no good metal, and a forge that would not get iron to more than red heat. So, now that they had left the village, every time he had fenced with Karli using his 'Gungnir' spear like a halberd, the iron edges of the cheap sword showed notches, to be taken out with hammer and file. Yet you could learn from the notches. If they were at right angles to the blade, Karli was fencing properly. A bungled parry showed cuts and shirrs of metal at odd angles. None this time.

Shef passed it back. "If you faced a real champion, like the man who taught me, you'd be dead," he said. "So would I. But there are plenty of farmers' sons in Viking armies. You might meet one of those. And don't forget," he added, "if you're facing a real champion, you don't have to fight fair."

"You've done that," guessed Karli.

Shef nodded.

"You've done a lot you don't tell me about, Shef."

"You wouldn't believe me if I told you."

Karli pushed his sword back into the wooden, wool-lined scabbard they had made for it, the only thing that would keep out the rust in the everlasting damp of the Ditmarsh. The two men turned and started back to the makeshift camp in the clearing thirty yards away, smoke trailing sullenly from the cooking fires into the misty air.

"And you don't tell me what you're going to do, either," Karli went on. "Are you just going to walk into the slave-ring and let Nikko sell you, like you say?"

"I'll walk into the slave-ring at Hedeby right enough," said Shef. "After that, things will go as they will. But I don't reckon to end up as a slave. Tell me, Karli, how am I coming along?"

He referred to the hours Karli had spent, in exchange for the fencing lessons, teaching him how to make a fist, how to strike straight forward instead of with the usual round-arm swing, how to step forward and put the weight of the body into a hooked punch, how to block with the hands and weave the head.

Karli's habitual grin spread across his face once more. "Just like me, I guess. If you met a real champion, a fist-fighter from the marsh, he'd be all over you. But you can knock a man down well enough, if he stands still."

Shef nodded thoughtfully. That at least was a skill worth knowing. Strange that they should have so specialized in one fighting art, here in this unvisited corner of the world. Perhaps it was because they did so little trade and had so little metal that they fought by choice empty-handed.

Only Nikko bothered to look up as they rejoined the campsite, giving the pair of them an angry glare.

"We reach Hedeby tomorrow," he said. "Then your prancing will have to stop. I say, your prancing will have to stop," he repeated, voice rising to a shout as Shef ignored him. "The master you'll find in Hedeby won't let you fool around pretending to be a swordmaster. It'll be work all day and the leather across your back if you shirk! You've felt it before, I've seen you stripped! You're no warrior out of luck, just a runaway!"

Karli lobbed a handful of mud neatly into Nikko's campfire and the shouting died into exasperated mutters.

"It is our last night," said Karli in a low voice. "I've got an idea. See, we're coming out of the Ditmarsh. Be on the high road tomorrow, and the dry land, where the Danes live. You can talk to them then, but I'm not so good at it. But there's a village half a mile off, where the girls still speak good marsh-talk, like me—and you too, you still talk like a Frisian, but they'll understand you. So why don't we just slip off and see if there isn't anyone in the village who feels like a bit of a change from whichever mudfoot she's attached to?"

Shef looked at Karli with a mixture of irritation and affection. During the week he had stayed in the Ditmarsh village by the sea, he had realized that Karli, cheerful, open and thoughtless, was one of those men whom women invariably liked. They responded to his humor, his lack of care. He seemed to have tried his luck with every woman in his home village, and usually successfully. Some husbands and fathers knew, some turned a blind eye, all were careful about giving Karli an excuse to use his fists. But there had been general approval of Karli going off with Nikko and the others on their trading trip to Hedeby, whether they managed to include Shef as merchandise or not. Their last night in the hut Karli shared with his parents had been broken by continual scratching on the shutters and stealthy disappearances into the bushes outside.

They were not Shef's women, so he had no cause for complaint. Yet Karli made him anxious at some deeper level. In his youth, working at the forge at Emneth in the fen, and traveling round the neighboring villages on work-errands, Shef had several lusty encounters with girls—churls' daughters, even thralls' daughters, not young ladies whose virginity was prized and guarded, but ready enough to educate his ignorance. It was true they had never sought him out as they did

Karli, perhaps put off by his unsmiling concern for the future, perhaps sensing his inner obsessions, but at least he had had no need to think he was lacking, or abnormal.

Then had come the sack of Emneth by the Vikings, the crippling of his foster-father, the capture and then the rescue of Godive. The moment in the little hut in the copse that summer morning, when he had become Godive's "first-man," and thought he had reached the summit of his ambition. And since then Shef had had no dealings with any woman, not even Godive after he had won her back, not even after they had put the gold circle of kingship on his head and half the trulls in England had been his for the taking. Shef wondered sometimes whether the threat of Ivar to castrate him had worked on his mind. He knew he was still a whole man—but then so had Ivar been, or so Hund had insisted, and he had been called "the Boneless," just the same. Could he have caught impotence from the man he had killed? Had his half-brother, Godive's husband, put a curse on him before he was hanged?

It was something in the mind, Shef knew, not in the body. Something to do with the way he had used the woman he loved as bait and as bribe, an inner agreement with her rejection of him and her marriage to Alfred, the most truthful man Shef had ever met. Whatever the case, he did not know the cure. Going with Karli might lead only to humiliation. Tomorrow he would be in the slave-ring, and the day after he could be facing the gelders.

"Do you think I stand a chance?" he asked, patting his ruined eye and face.

Karli's face creased with delight. "Of course! Great tall fellow like you, muscles like a blacksmith. Foreign accent, air of mystery. What you got to remember, these girls out here, they're *bored*. Nothing ever happens. They aren't allowed out near the road where anyone could grab them. No-one ever comes into the marsh. They see the same faces from the day they're born till the day they die. I tell you . . ." Karli expanded in fancies as to how the girls of the Ditmarsh had to amuse themselves for want of handsome strangers—or ugly strangers for that matter—while Shef stirred the stewpot and twisted strips of dough round twigs to toast in the fire. He did not think Karli's plan would work, or not for him at any rate. But he had gone on the naval expedition in the first place for one reason only: to shake off the black mood of Alfred and Godive's marriage. He would take any opportunity to break the spell upon him. But without any expectations. It would take more than a marshwife to remove his memories.

* * *

Hours later, walking back to camp through the marsh in the black night, Shef wondered again at his own lack of concern. Things had gone much as he had foreseen: the arrival in the village at the hour when folk left their doors and strolled round, the casual conversation with the menfolk to pass on news, Karli's meaningful looks and quick words with one listening girl and then another, while Shef held the attention of their male protectors. Then the ostentatious leaving at dusk, followed by the stealthy circuit back to a willow copse hanging over stagnant water. The arrival of the girls, panting, fearful and excited.

Shef's had been a pleasant plump girl with a pouting face. At first she had been flirtatious. Then scornful. Then, finally, as she realized that Shef himself had no hope or anxiety concerning his own failure, worried. She had stroked his ruined face, felt the scars on his back beneath the tunic. "You have had hard times?" she had said, half-questioning. "Harder than those scars show," he had replied. "Things are hard for us women too, you know," she had told him. Shef thought of what he had seen at the sack of York and in the ruin of Emneth, thought of his mother and her life story, of Godive and Alfgar and the bloody birch, of the stories of Ivar the Boneless and his dealings with women: remembered finally the slave-girls' bones, buried alive with their backs broken, which he had stumbled over in the old king's howe, and said nothing. Then for a while they had lain without speaking till the urgent noises coming from Karli and his mate had ceased once and then again. "I won't tell anyone," she had whispered as the other pair finally emerged damp and muddy from their hollow. He would never see her again.

It ought to worry him, Shef reflected, not to be a whole man. Somehow it did not. He paused, tested the footing of the stretch ahead with the butt-spike of his spear. In the darkness of the marsh something gurgled and plopped, and Karli drew his sword with a gasp.

"It was just an otter," Shef remarked.

"Maybe. Don't you know there are other things in the marsh?"

"Like what?"

Karli hesitated. "We call them thurses."

"Yes, so do we. Great big things that live in the mud and catch children who play too close. Giant women with green teeth. Arms covered in long gray hair that reach up and turn over a fowler's boat," Shef added, embroidering on one of the stories he had heard from Brand. "Merlings that sit and feast on the . . ."

Karli grabbed his arm. "Enough! Don't say it. They might hear themselves called and come."

"There are no such things," said Shef, confident again of his bearings and moving off on the slightly firmer ground between two sloughs. "People just make up the stories to explain why people don't come back. In marshes like this you don't need a thurs to make you vanish. Look, there's the camp through these alders."

Karli looked up at him as they reached the edge of the camp clearing, men already wrapped motionless in their blankets. "I don't understand you," he said. "You're always sure you know best. But you act like a sleepwalker. Are you sent by the gods?"

Shef noticed Nikko, awake and seated silently observing from the shadows. "If I am," he said, "I hope they have some help for me tomorrow."

In his dream that night he felt as if the nape of his neck were gripped in steely fingers, forcing him to look this way and then that.

The first sight he saw was somewhere on a desolate plain. A young warrior stood, holding himself upright with difficulty. Black blood covered his armor, and more ran down his legs from under the mail shirt. He clutched a broken sword in his hand and another warrior lay at his feet. From somewhere far off Shef heard a voice chanting:

Sixteen wounds I have, slit is my armor,
Closed my eyes, I cannot see to walk.
Angantyr's sword sliced me to the heart
The sharp blood-pourer, poison-hardened.

You can't harden swords in poison, thought Shef. Hardening is a matter of great heat and sudden cooling. Why is water not sudden enough? Maybe it is the steam that comes from it. What is steam anyway?

The fingers at his neck tweaked him suddenly, as if to make him pay attention. Across the plain Shef saw birds of prey flying, and the chanting voice said again:

The hungry raven roves from the South,
The white-tailed carrion-fowl follows his brother.
It is the last time I lay for them a table.
It is my blood now the battle-beasts feast on.

Behind the birds Shef thought for a moment he could see women, female shapes riding on the wind, and behind even them the dim sight of great doors opening: doors he had seen before, the doors of Valhalla.

So the heroes die, said another voice, not the chanting one. Even in the

*paralysis of his dream Shef felt a chill as he recognized the grim ironic tones
of his protector, the god Rig, whose ladder-sign he wore round his neck.
That is the death of Hjalmar the Magnanimous, the voice went on. Picked a
fight with a Swedish berserk, provided two recruits for my father Othin.*

*The scene vanished, Shef felt his eyes twisted supernaturally elsewhere.
A moment, and then another vision came into focus. Shef was looking down
at a narrow pallet laid on an earth floor. It was somewhere aside from
main rooms, maybe a blind passageway somewhere out of the way of
passing feet, but cold and comfortless. On it an old woman was stretching
herself out, carefully and painfully. Shef knew that she had just been told
that she was bound to die, by a leech or a cunning man or a beast-doctor.
Not from the lung-sickness that usually carried off the old folk in the
winter, but from some growth or evil inside her. It hurt her terribly, but she
dared not speak of it. She had no relatives left, if she had had a man or sons
of her own, they were dead or gone, she lived now on the doubtful tolerance
of those not her blood. If she gave trouble of any kind even her pallet and
her bread would be withdrawn. She was a person of no importance.*

*She was the girl he had left in the marsh, come to the end of her life. Or
she could be. There were others she could be: Shef thought of Godive's
mother, the Irish slave whom Wulfgar his foster father had taken as a
lemman and then sold away from her child when his wife grew jealous. But
there were others, many many others. The world was full of desperate old
women, and old men too, trying with the last of their strength to die quietly
and not attract attention. Then they could creep into their graves and
vanish from mind. They had been young once.*

*From the scene Shef felt such a wave of hopelessness as he had never
imagined before. And yet there was something strange about it. This slow
dying might be years in the future, as he had first thought when he seemed
to recognize the woman. Or it might be years in the past. But for a moment
Shef seemed to know one thing: the old woman praying for an unnoticed
death on the pallet bed was him. Or had he been her?*

Shef snapped awake with a jerk and a sense of relief. Round him the
camp lay quiet in its blankets. He let his inhaled breath out slowly and
relaxed his tensed muscles one at a time.

They came out of the marsh the next morning almost in a stride. One
moment they were plodding forward through the black pools and
across the shallow streams that seemed to flow in no direction, in a
thin cold mist. Then the ground was rising beneath their feet, the mist
cleared away, and barely a mile off across bare turf, Shef could see the
Army Road marching along the skyline, with on it a continual
to-and-fro of travelers. He looked back and saw that the Ditmarsh was

invisible beneath a blanket of fog. It would clear in the sun and reform again at nightfall. No wonder that the Ditmarshers lived hand to mouth, and knew no invaders.

Shef was amused also to see how his companions changed as they came out on to the road. In the marsh they had been secure, confident, ready to sneer at the outside world and their neighbors. Here they seemed to put their heads down and hope to escape without attention. Shef found himself standing straight and looking round him, while the others stooped and closed up together.

Shortly a party on horseback caught up with them, ten or a dozen men riding together with pack animals, a salt-train heading north up the Jutland peninsula. As they rode past the Ditmarshers they called to each other in Norse.

"Here, see the mudfeet out of the fen. What have they come out for? Look, there's a tall one, must have been mother's little adventure. Hey, marshman, what are you looking for? Is it a cure for your spotted bellies?"

Shef grinned at the loudest laugher, and called back, in the fluent Norse he had learnt from Thorvin and then from Brand and his crew.

"What would you know about it, Jutlander?" He exaggerated the hoarse gutturals of the Ribe dialect they spoke. "Is that Norse you are speaking, or is it a disease of the throat? Try stirring honey in your beer and maybe you can cough it up."

The traders checked their horses and stared at him. "You are no Ditmarsher," said one of them. "You do not sound like a Dane either. Where are you from?"

"*Enzkr em*," said Shef firmly. "I am an Englishman."

"You sound like a Norwegian, and one from the back end of nowhere at that. I have heard voices like yours trading furs."

"I am an Englishman," Shef repeated. "And it is not furs I am trading. These folk and I are going to the slave-ring at Hedeby, where they hope to sell me." He pulled his ladder pendant into view, turned his face full on to the Danes, and winked his one eye solemnly. "No need to keep it a secret. After all, I have to find a buyer."

The Danes looked at each other and rode on, leaving Shef well content. An Englishman, with one eye, and a silver pole-ladder round his neck. It only needed one friend of Brand, or of the Way, or even one of his skippers from last year's campaign gone home to retire to hear that, and Shef should at least have enough credit to get passage back to England: though he did not want to take ship from Hedeby on the Baltic shore.

Nikko scowled at him, feeling that the situation was slipping beyond his grasp. "I'll have that spear of yours before we reach the market."

Shef used it to point to the wooden stockade round Hedeby coming into view.

As he shuffled slowly forward in the line of merchandise for sale the next day, Shef felt his heart beating faster. He still had the inner calm—or was it indifference?—which had never left him since he woke up, king no more, in Karli's hut. Yet though he knew what he planned to do, he could not know how it would be taken. It depended on what a man's rights were. In the slave-market at Hedeby, what he and his friends could enforce, likely enough.

The market itself was no more than a cleared space on the shore, with a central knoll a few feet high to display the goods to the buyers. Behind it the tideless Baltic lapped gently on a thin strip of sand. To one side wooden piers ran out far into the shallow water, to enable the broad-hulled knorrs to come in and out with cargo. Around the whole ran a stout stockade of logs, flimsy enough in comparison with the Roman walls of York far away, but in good repair and heavily manned. Shef had heard little of the deeds of King Hrorik, who ruled in Hedeby and from it to the Dane-dyke thirty miles to the south. But his revenues depended entirely on the tolls he took from traders in the port, and he both guarded it and ruled it with a prompt and heavy hand. Shef glanced from time to time at the gallows erected in plain sight on the outermost jetty, a half-dozen bearded corpses dangling from it. Hrorik was anxious to show traders their rights would be protected. One of the many things Shef could not know was whether his plan might be taken as a discouragement to trade. But in any case, as the morning drew on and the line moved forward, his mood grew grimmer.

The lot being put up this time consisted only of women: six of them, pushed forward by a group of grinning Vikings. His man held each of them by the arm while their leader walked round the knoll shouting their merits out. All young girls, Shef could see. At a word, their mantles were pulled away and each stood in a short tunic, bare-legged to above the knee, the white skin drawing all eyes in the sunlight. Whoops filled the air, lewd suggestions shouted across the crowd.

"Where are they from?" Shef asked the armed guard standing near the slave-line. The man eyed Shef's build and bearing curiously, grunted a reply.

"Wends. See the white skin and the red hair. They catch them on the south shore of the Baltic."

"And who are the buyers?" Shef could see, now, a group of dark men in strange clothing pressing forward to inspect the women more closely. They wore head-cloths instead of standing helmeted or bare-headed, and the curved daggers in their belts glittered with precious metal. Some of them at all times faced outward, as if expecting surprise attack.

"Men from the Southlands. They worship some god who is a rival to the Christ-god. Great buyers of women, and they pay in gold. Have to pay high this year."

"Why is that?"

The guard looked at him curiously again. "You speak Norse, but don't you know anything? The woman-price went up as soon as the English market turned nasty. Used to get good girls from England."

The Cordovan Arabs were asking questions now, through an interpreter. A bystander relayed them to the crowd.

"He wants to know if they're all virgins."

Roars of laughter and a great bull voice crying, "I know the tall one isn't, Alfr, I saw you trying her out yesterday outside your booth."

The leader of the sellers looked round angrily, trying to scowl the barrackers into silence. The Arabs called to their interpreter, huddled together. Finally, a bid. Expostulation, rejection. But no counter-bids. A deal struck—Shef saw the flash of money as it was paid out, and drew in his breath at the sight, not of silver, but of gold dinars. A toll paid to the auctioneer, another to the jarl of King Hrorik, watching with careful eye, and the women were wrapped and hustled away.

Next to go forward was a strange figure, a middle-aged man in the remains of a black robe. He appeared to be bald, but a slight black fuzz grew on his scalp. A Christian priest, Shef realized, with a tonsure that had not been shaved recently. As he came out, another man pushed his way out of the crowd and seemed to go to embrace him: another priest, another black robe, but this time with fresh tonsure. A guard thrust him back, another called for bids.

Instant response, from a party of tall men, heavily-built and swathed in furs even in the spring sunlight. Swedes, Shef thought, remembering the accent of Guthmund the Greedy and some of the others he had met in the ranks of the Ragnarssons' Great Army. They were offering eight ounces of silver. One of them pulled a purse from his belt and threw it on the ground to back the offer up.

The priest who had been pushed away was back again, dodging the guards, spreading out his arms and shouting passionately.

"What's he say?" muttered the guard by Shef.

"He's trying to forbid the sale," Shef answered, catching some part of the gabble of Norse and Low German that the priest was using. "Says they have no right to sell a priest of the true God."

"They'll sell him too if he doesn't shut up," said the guard.

Indeed, the Swedes had thrown another purse on the ground, exchanged words with the auctioneer, were walking forward towards both men, satisfaction on their faces.

Another man stepped from the crowd and the satisfaction faded, replaced by looks of wary calculation. Shef, used to judging warriors, could see immediately why.

The newcomer was not a tall man, shorter than the shortest of the Swedes. But he was immensely broad across the shoulders. More, he moved with an easy confidence that set men back. He wore a padded leather jacket, worn and with different strips let into it here and there. His left hand rested on the pommel of a long horseman's sword. His hair stood up like a stiff, blond brush, over a face tight-drawn, clean-shaven, as hard as stone. But it was smiling.

The blond man put a toe under one of the purses, flicked it back to the Swedes, flicked back the other.

"You can't have him," he said in stilted Norse, his voice carrying in the sudden silence. "Neither of them. They are priests of Christ, and they are under my protection. The protection of the *Lanzenorden*." He called suddenly in a louder voice, and swept his arm around. Shef realized there were a dozen men mailed and armed close to the ring. They outnumbered the Swedes. But there were two hundred Norsemen watching, all armed as well. If they made common cause against the Christians . . . Or if King Hrorik's men decided to protect their trade and market . . .

"We'll pay for one of them," called the blond man conciliatingly. "Eight ounces. Christian money is as good as heathen."

"Ten ounces," said the leader of the Swedes.

The auctioneer looked questioningly at the blond man.

"Twelve ounces," he said in a slow, deliberate voice. "Twelve ounces and I will forget to ask how one of you comes to have a Christian priest—and what you others want Christian priests for. Twelve ounces and think you are lucky."

The Swede slipped his hand further down the handle of his axe, spat on the ground.

"Twelve ounces," he said. "And the money of Othin rings better than the money of any smoothface gelding of a Christian."

Shef felt the guard beside him start to move, saw Hrorik's jarl also

begin to step forward. As he finished speaking the Swede threw his axe
up to grip it in striking position. But before any of them had completed
his movement there was a streak in the air, a thud, a gasp. The Swede
was gaping down at a brass hilt protruding from the center of his body.
Shef realized that the blond man had never attempted to draw sword,
but had instead flicked a heavy knife from his belt and thrown it
underhand. Before the thought had formed, the blond man had
already taken three steps forward, drawn, and was standing with the
point of his long sword resting exactly on the throat-ball of the seller.

"Do we have a sale?" he called, looking for an instant sideways at
the hesitating jarl.

The seller, slowly and cautiously, nodded.

The blond man flicked the sword away. "Just a private disagree-
ment," he remarked to the jarl. "Doesn't affect the market. Happy to
settle with his friends anywhere outside the town."

The jarl hesitated, then nodded too, ignoring the shouts of the
Swedes bent over the body of their leader.

"Pay the money and take your man away. And hold that noise, the
rest of you. If you call men names you'd better learn to be quicker. If
you have a grudge you're welcome to fight it out. But not here. Bad for
business. Come on, somebody, get the next lot up here."

As the Christian priests embraced and the blond man rejoined his
knot of mailed supporters, bristling with weapons, Shef found himself
thrust forward on to the knoll. For a moment panic seized him, like an
actor forgetting his lines on an unexpected cue. Then as Nikko bustled
forward, and he saw the worried face of Karli just behind him, he
remembered what he had to do.

Slowly he started to pull off his grubby woolen tunic.

"What's this?" said the auctioneer. "Strong young man, able to do
simple smith-work, offered for sale by—some webfoot, who cares."

Shef threw the tunic to the ground, adjusted the silver pendant of
Rig in the center of his chest, flexed his muscles in a parody of the
behavior of farmhands at a hiring fair. The sunlight showed the old
scars of flogging across his back, flogging he had received from the
hands of his stepfather years before.

"Is he tractable?" shouted a voice. "He sure doesn't look it."

"You can make a slave tractable," shouted Nikko, standing next to
the auctioneer.

Shef nodded thoughtfully, stepped over to the pair of them. As he
did so he carefully spread the fingers of his left hand and then curled
them into a tight fist, thumb outside the second joint, as Karli had
shown him. He had to make this dramatic. Not a shove, not a scuffle.

Stepping forward on to the left foot according to Karli's demonstra-
tions, he swung his left arm in a short arc, putting all the weight of his
body behind it, and aiming as if to end with his fist behind his right
shoulder. The left hook connected not with Nikko's jaw—Karli had
advised against that for beginners—but with his right temple. The
burly man, completely unprepared, dropped instantly to his knees.

Instantly Shef had him by the collar, jerked him to his feet, turned
to face the crowd.

"One webfoot," he shouted in Norse. "Talks a lot. No good at
anything. What am I bid?"

"I thought he was selling you," shouted a voice.

Shef shrugged. "I changed my mind." He stared round at the
crowd, trying to overbear them with his one eye. What made a thrall?
In the end, there must be consent. A thrall who simply disobeyed,
simply fought back, could be killed, but was worth nothing. On the
edge of the ring he realized there was a minor fracas going on, as
Nikko's son and nephew came forward to his assistance, only to find
Karli barring their path, fists raised.

"All right, all right," snarled the jarl almost in Shef's ear. "I can see
the pair of you are unsaleable. But I'll tell you this—you still owe an
auction fee, and if you can't pay it I'll take it out of both of you."

Shef looked round. A dangerous moment. He had hoped to see a
friendly face before this, if the Danes met on the road had spread the
word. Now he would have to settle with the toll-jarl on his own. He
had only two possessions left. One hand closed round the silver
pendant—that was his last resort. The other?

The 'Gungnir' spear thumped into the turf at his feet. Karli,
beaming and rubbing his knuckles, waved cheerfully at him. Shef
started to pull the spear out, to show the rune-marks on it to the
contemptuous jarl, to try to strike a deal.

"If he's for sale, the one-eye," called a voice, "I'll buy him. I know
someone who wants him bad."

With a feeling of doom at his heart, Shef turned to face the voice.
He had hoped a friend would recognize him. He had not forgotten the
chance that it would be an enemy, but had gambled that all the
followers of the Ragnarssons, the survivors of the men he had known
in the Great Army, would be with the Ragnarsson fleet at sea on the
other side of Denmark. He had reckoned without the loose alliances,
the continuous joinings and defections, of the Viking world.

It was Skuli the Bald, who had commanded a tower in Shef's scaling
of the York walls the year before, but had then thrown in his lot with

the Ragnarssons who had betrayed them. He was coming forward now, his ship's crew closed up behind him in a disciplined formation.

At the same moment some inner warning told Shef another face was staring at him fixedly. He turned, met a pair of black, implacable eyes. Recognized them instantly. Erkenbert the black deacon, whom he had seen first at the death of Ragnar in the snake-pit, and seen last being loaded aboard the transport-ships after the defeat of the Christian Crusade at Hastings. He was standing next to the rescued black-robe priest, talking rapidly to the blond German, and pointing.

"Skjef Sigvarthsson Ivarsbane," said Skuli, grinning, now only a few feet away. "I'm ready to pay more than market price for you. I reckon Ivar's brothers will pay me a man's weight in silver in return."

"If you can collect," snarled Shef, backing away and looking swiftly over his shoulder for a wall to set his back against. Karli was with him, he realized. He had drawn his sword, was shouting defiance in a growing hubbub. Shef saw instantly that he had forgotten everything he had been told, was holding the weapon like a thatcher cutting reeds. If the tension snapped, Karli would be dead within five heartbeats.

The blond German was within Shef's line of vision now as well, sword also drawn, his men trying to make a line between Shef and Skuli. He too was shouting something about a price. In the background traders and slaves were scattering, some trying to get well away, others drawing, seeming to align themselves with one faction or another. The guards of King Hrorik, taken off guard by this sudden outbreak among the customers, were trying to form a wedge to drive into the midst of the likely battle.

Shef drew a deep breath, hefted his spear. He would go straight for Skuli and take his chance with Erkenbert and the Christians. One act of charity first. He turned, meaning to club the unsuspecting Karli with the spear-shaft. If the little man was on the ground, maybe no-one would kill him, as they would if he tried to fight.

Something clung to the spear-point, weighing it down, hampering him. Something else over his face, blinding him. As he tore frantically at the blanket, trying to wrestle free, a soft concussion caught him on the side of the skull, and he found himself on one knee, struggling to rise, struggling to see. If he lost consciousness the next thing he might know was a Ragnarsson face intent on cutting the blood-eagle through his ribs.

Someone kicked Shef's feet from under him, and his head met the ground.

CHAPTER EIGHT

orry about that," said the fat face from the other side of the table. "If I'd heard about you just a little bit earlier I'd have bought you off your Ditmarsh friends myself, and no-one would have been any the wiser. But as a king yourself, you must know how it is. No king is cleverer than the information he gets."

Shef stared, trying to bring the face into focus, shook his head to clear it, and winced.

"There," said the face. "I don't think you've heard a word I've been saying. Where does it hurt?"

Shef rubbed his left temple, realized at the same time that the lump on his skull was on the right. A hand passed in front of his eyes, and he realized he was being tested for concussion.

"Lump on one side, pain on the other. Makes you think the brain is loose inside the skull, doesn't it?" the face went on conversationally. "That's why so many veteran warriors are—well—a little strange. We call it vithrhögg, the counter-blow. But I can see you're recovering now. Let me just run over some of what I said again.

"I'm King Hrorik of Hedeby and South Jutland. And you are?"

Shef grinned suddenly, realizing the gist of what was said to him. "I am your fellow-king, King Shef of the East and Middle Angles."

"Good. I'm glad it's all coming back. We have these riots in the market-place pretty often, you know, and the lads have a drill for it. Throw sailcloth over all the weapons, and then clip everyone who looks dangerous while they're trying to get their blades free. We don't like losing customers permanently." A large hand poured wine into what Shef realized was a golden cup. "Take some water with that and you'll soon feel better."

"You lost a customer today," said Shef, remembering the knife standing from the Swedish buyer's heart.

"Yes, bad business that. But my jarl reports that the dead man gave provocation. Besides . . ."

A plump finger jerked Shef's pendant from under the tunic which, he realized, someone had found and put back on for him.

"You're a man of the Way, right? So you don't have much time for Christians. None at all, from what I hear of your victory over the Franks, and I dare say they have even less for you. But down here I have to keep a very close eye on them. There's only the Dane-dyke between me and Othin knows how many German lancers. It's true they fight among themselves all the time, and it's truer that they're even more frightened of us than I am of them. But I really don't like to go stirring up trouble, especially in matters of religion.

"So I've always let the Christians send their priests up here and appeal for converts, and never said a word when they started baptizing the slaves and the women. Of course, if the poor souls wander off into the countryside and end up sold, or thrown into the bog for good luck, I can't do anything about that. I keep order in Hedeby and along the trade-road, and I judge disputes at the Thing. Telling my subjects what to believe or who to leave alone . . ." The fat man laughed. "*You* know how risky that would be.

"But this is something new. This spring, when the priests came north from Hamburg, three or four of them, each one had an escort with him. Not big enough to call an army, not even big enough to be a serious menace, and plenty of cash to pay their way. So I let them in. But I tell you something," the face leaned forward, "as one king to another. Very dangerous men. Very valuable men. I wish I could hire half-a-dozen of them. That one you saw, the blond one with the hair like stiff wire, my guard captain says he's the fastest man he's ever seen. Very tricky too."

"Faster than Ivar Ragnarsson?" asked Shef.

"The Boneless One? I was forgetting that you had bested him." Shef's vision seemed to clear as the wine did its work, and he looked more sharply at the big man leaning back in his wooden chair till the stout back of it creaked. Gold circlet on his head, heavy gold chain round his neck and thick bracelets on his arms. An air of simple good-nature, like the host of a peaceful town tavern. But sharp eyes under heavy brows, and a network of scars along the muscled right forearm, the places where a dueller picked up cuts. A successful dueller, for failed ones did not live long enough for the scars to heal.

"Well. I certainly owe you one for that. He used to worry me badly, and his brothers still do." A heavy sigh. "It's a hard life for a king down here, with the Empire and the Christians growling the other side of the Dane-dyke, and fifty sea-kings to the north forever disputing which shall be king over all. The Christians say they need an emperor now. Sometimes I think we do too. But there. If we thought that we'd have to decide who it was. Maybe me. Maybe you. Maybe Sigurth Ragnarsson. If it was him neither you nor I would live to see the day, nor want to.

"But I'm forgetting myself. You've had a hard time, I can see that, and you look as if you could use a good dinner too. Why don't you sit in the sun somewhere this afternoon, till it's time for the night-meal? I'll see it's all safe."

"I owe some money," said Shef. "That man I hit in the slave-ring—he did bring me here, and feed me for a week. I ought to pay him. And then I need money to buy passage home. If there are English traders in the port, I can borrow from them, on my own credit and that of my co-king Alfred."

Hrorik held up a ringed hand. "All dealt with, all paid for. I sent the Ditmarshers off very happy, I always try to keep in with them too, they can be a nuisance when they're angry. The one young one insisted on staying behind, though. Don't thank me, you can always pay me back.

"But as for the passage home. Well, not just yet."

Shef looked at the shrewd, jolly face. In the corner behind it he could see 'Gungnir' propped against the wall. He had no illusions about being able to reach it.

"Stay here with you?"

"I've sold you on, as a matter of fact," said Hrorik, winking.

"Sold? Who to?"

"Don't worry, not Skuli. He offered me five pounds of silver. The Christians went to ten, and a pardon for all sins from the Pope written in purple ink."

"Who then?"

Hrorik winked again. "Your friends from Kaupang. The priest-college of the Way. Made me an offer much too good to refuse. Said something about a trial. Better than being tried by Sigurth Snake-eye, though? Wouldn't you say?"

*   *   *

With a length of stout blood-sausage in his belt, a long black loaf under his arm, and a twist of salt in one hand, Shef strolled out into the strong afternoon sunshine, bidden by King Hrorik to go out and rest till dinner. Half-a-dozen guards surrounded him, there to ensure at once that no-one molested him and that he did not escape from the town. Karli, for once rather subdued, accompanied them, sword still slung from his belt, and carrying Shef's spear over one shoulder.

For a few minutes the little group walked through the crowded streets of Hedeby, full of booths selling amber, honey, wine from the south, fine weapons, bone combs, shoes, pig-iron and everything else that might be traded into or out of the Scandinavian lands. Then, as Shef grew tired of the constant edging and jostling, he caught sight of a low green mound, within the town-stockade but without buildings or people on it. He pointed to it wordlessly and headed over. The pain in his head had gone, but he still walked slowly and carefully, afraid to set if off again by some movement. He felt also as if information from the outside was filtering through to him slowly, as if he were under a foot of clear water. He had a great deal to take in and think about.

He reached the mound and sat down on the top of it, looking out over the bay of the Schlei and the green fields to the north of it. Karli hesitated, then drove the butt-spike of the spear into the soft turf and sat down also. The guards exchanged glances. "You have no fear of the howe-bride?" asked one of them.

"I have been in a howe before," said Shef. His belt-knife had gone, he noticed: Hrorik was taking no chances at all. He passed the sausage to Karli to cut up, and began to break up the bread. The guards gingerly sat or squatted in a ring around them.

After a while, belly full, back pleasantly warmed by the sun, Shef pointed out to the fertile landscape facing them outside the town's perimeter. The river Schlei ran to the north of the town, and on the opposite shore he could see hedged fields, plowmen driving their ox-teams, brown furrows growing along the green, and rising out of the trees here and there, the curls of smoke from chimneys. To an Englishman, the Viking lands appeared as the home of fire and slaughter, its inhabitants seamen and raiders, not plowmen and charcoal-burners. Yet here, at the center of the Viking storm, the land looked more peaceful than Suffolk on a summer day.

"I have heard that this is where the English came from once upon a time," Shef said to the nearest guard. "Are there any Englishmen still living over there?"

"No," said the guard. "Just Danes. Some of them call themselves Jutes, if they don't want to admit connection with the sea-kings from the islands. But they all speak the Danish tongue, just like yourself. That bit of land is still called Angel, though. It's the angle between the Schlei here and Flensborg Fjord on the other side of it. I dare say the English came from there right enough."

Shef reflected further. So much for his hope, once upon a time, of rescuing oppressed Englishmen from Danish rule here in Denmark. Still, it was strange that the Ditmarshers did not speak Danish, living next to them as they did. Strange too what they did speak: not English, nor Danish, nor yet exactly that strange language the priest had spoken this morning, a kind of German. Something with bits of all of them, and yet perhaps most similar to the Frisian Shef had got used to hearing from the men of the islands off the Dutch coast. Once upon a time this borderland had been a melting-pot of tribes. Now lines were being drawn more carefully: Christians this side, heathens that, German spoken here, Norse there. Yet the process was a long way from finished. The guard called his language Danish, *dönsk tunga*, others called the same language Norse, *norsk mal*. The same people called themselves Danes one day and Jutes the next. Shef was king of the East Angles and Alfred of the West Saxons, but both sides would agree that they were at bottom Englishmen. The German tribes were ruled by the same Pope and the same royal family as the Frankish tribes, but did not think of themselves as connected. Swedes and Gauts, Norwegians and Gaddgedlar. One day all of this would have to be sorted out and made clear. There was an urge to do it already. But who would succeed in drawing the lines, in imposing law on some level higher than Hrorik's "good for business" ethic?

Without much surprise Shef observed the blond German walking towards them out of the town, the man who had killed the Swede and rescued the priest-slave that same morning. Hrorik's guards saw him too, reacted without even a pretense of warriorly calm. Two instantly barred his path with swords drawn and shields raised, the other four poising javelins at ten feet range. The blond man smiled, unbuckled his sword belt with exaggerated care, let it drop to the ground. As the guard commander snapped orders at him, he stripped off also his leather jacket, set it down, peeled a heavy throwing-knife from under his sleeve, a short needlepoint from inside his boot. One man closed, searched him roughly and thoroughly. Finally, grudgingly, they stood back and let him pass, the javelins still poised. As he stepped the last few feet towards Shef Karli, too, drew his sword and stood in a posture of suspicious truculence.

The blond man looked at the way Karli held the sword, sighed, and sat down cross-legged facing Shef. His smile this time indicated a secret complicity.

"My name is Bruno," he remarked. "I am here with the mission of the Archbishop of Hamburg-Bremen to the Danes. Ransoming some of our people back, you know. And they tell me you are the famous Shef Sigvarthsson, the bane of the even more famous Ivar." He spoke Norse with a marked accent that made the name "Sigvarth" almost into "Siegfried."

"Who told you that?"

The smile of complicity and understanding again. "Well. As you guessed, it was your little countryman, the deacon Erkenbert. He is a passionate little fellow, and will hear no good of you at all. Yet he cannot deny that you beat the Ragnarsson sword to sword."

"Sword to halberd," corrected Shef. He added no further details.

"So. That is not often a winning game. But you use odd weapons. May I glance at your spear?" Bruno rose and studied the spear planted in the grass at Shef's side, carefully not touching it, hands behind his back.

"An excellent weapon. Newly-forged, I see. I take an interest in spears. And in other things too. May I see what you have round your neck?"

Ignoring the growl of doubt from Karli, Shef pulled out his silver pendant with the Rig-sign on it, and let Bruno, seated once more, stare intently at it.

"And what would you call that, now?"

"It is a *kraki*," said Shef. "A pole-ladder. A center pole, with rungs either side. It is the emblem of my god."

"Yet I believe you were baptized a Christian? Such a shame, that one who belonged to the true God should go over to a pagan idol. Do you feel no urge to change back? Might you not, if certain—difficulties—were cleared from your path?"

Shef smiled for the first time in their exchange, remembering the horrors inflicted on him and on others by the black monks, by Wulfgar and Bishop Daniel. He shook his head.

"I would not expect you to change your mind the first time anyone suggested it. But let me give you two things to think about," the blond man went on.

"One is this. I have no doubt all this fighting and struggling looks as if it is about land and money. And it is! Hrorik would not let me have you because he thought he had a better deal elsewhere, and he does not want to strengthen us in any way. I know you won over the

English kingdoms to your heresy of freedom for all gods by abolishing the tithes men have to pay to the Church. But beneath that struggle, I am sure you know well that there is something deeper. A struggle not just of men, but of other powers."

Remembering the strange sights he had seen, the compelling voices of his protectors and the other gods in the strange Asgarth-world of his dreams, Shef slowly nodded.

"There are powers which it does no man good to be associated with. Our Church calls them devils and demons, and you may think that is just the Church's prejudice, protecting its—what is the word?—its single-trade in salvation for the soul. Well, I know priests too, and I too despise their concern for money, for buying and selling the things of God.

"But I tell you, Shef Siegfriedsson, as one warrior to another: a great change is coming, and there is One coming who shall bring it. On that day the kingdoms will be overthrown and cast into a new mold, and the priests—yes, and the archbishops and the Popes who think to control it, they will be controlled. On that day you do not want to be on the wrong side."

"And how will anyone know which is the right side?" said Shef, observing the gleam of passion on the hard, stony face. Hearing the ring in Bruno's voice the guards edged closer, as if expecting some outbreak of sudden violence.

Bruno's face split in another of his unexpected and strangely winning smiles. "Oh, there will be a sign. Something pretty unmistakable, I expect. A miracle, a relic, something sent from God to work in the world, a chosen leader to use it." He rose to his feet, prepared to go.

"You said you had two things to tell me," prompted Shef. "Be on the right side when the kingdoms are shaken, that was one. The other?"

"Oh yes. Of course. I have to tell you you are in part mistaken about your own sign. I hope you recognize others better. What you have round your neck, you may call it a *kraki* in Norse, or a 'ladder' in your language and mine. In Latin, though—you have heard Latin from the priests? Well, they would call it a *graduale*. From *gradus*, a step, you know."

Shef waited, not sure of the point.

"There are those who believe in the Holy Graduale. The Franks call it the Holy Graal. Dreadful the way the Franks talk Latin—can you imagine a language in which *aqua* turns into *eau*? Yes, the Holy

Graduale, or Grail, that is what you have round your neck. It's supposed to go with the Holy Lance, some say."

Bruno stepped over to his pile of clothes and weapons, and slowly resumed them, covered all the time by javelins. Finally he looked at Shef, nodded a farewell, and strolled peacefully back towards the town and the markets.

"What was all that about?" Karli asked suspiciously. Shef did not answer. The feeling of being underwater was growing on him, as if he were now fathoms deep, but in clear water which hid nothing from his view. Still looking out over the peaceful fields of the Angle, he felt the pinch on his neck that told him his sight was being directed. On top of the green fields and the furrows and the curling smoke-plumes of cottages, other pictures began to impose themselves.

He was still looking at exactly the same place, but the buildings of Hedeby were no longer there, there were more trees, less plowland. This is the Angle as it was when the English left it, something told him. Ten long warboats were cruising into the Schlei, much the same as those of Sigurth Ragnarsson, but different, more primitive in design: no mast or sail, only oars, and a stiffer, crankier air, without the living suppleness of the full-fledged Viking ship. War canoes with rowlocks. Shef's sight followed them as they pulled up river, found an inlet, paddled along it into a small, shallow lake. The crews streamed out, never more than thigh-deep in the water, dispersed into the countryside, began to come back late in the day, laden with metal, with sacks and barrels, cattle and women. They settled down by their ships, lit fires as night came on, began to slaughter the beeves and rape the women. Shef watched unmoved: he had seen worse in reality, without the distancing of his vision.

The men of the land had not gone, had fled only to find their weapons and gather their strength. Now they had a leader. Where the canoes had paddled into the lake he felled trees, threw them in to block the exit. Then the land-folk began to close in on the scene of rape and riot. Arrows flew from the trees. The raiding party abandoned their entertainments, ran to their weapons, gathered to beat off the attack. Some women slipped away, crawled into the darkness or into the black water of the lake. Others were struck by flying arrows, cut down by angry raiders.

The people of the land made a line and pressed forward, shields raised. The raiders met them, the two sides hacked at each other over yellow linden shields for a few minutes, then the land-folk fell back. Once more arrows flew from the trees. A voice called out from the dark forest, promising to give all the raiders to the war-god, hang them on trees for the birds. The raiders gathered their ships, tried at dawn to break out the way they had come, met the tangled tree-trunks of the barricade. During a long morning's fighting, Shef saw—speeded up as if all was done by two armies of ants—the raiders defeated, split up, blankets thrown over their weapons so that the survivors were borne down or pinned between shields. In the end ten war-boats, their gunwales hacked and splintered, lay on the edge of black mud, a hundred and twenty grim-faced prisoners standing or lying by them.

The victors cleared the site of bodies and weapons, brought them all to the captured ships, urged on by the orders of their leader. Shef expected to see the prisoners stripped of armor and valuables, the loot divided. Instead the men began to smash holes in the boats' planks. They drove the captured spears into tree-trunks and bent them so that the iron shafts were useless. They snapped the bows and arrows, punched holes in the bronze helmets, took the swords, heated the blades in fire to destroy their temper, and then rolled the blades up with tongs into twisted spirals. Finally they turned to their prisoners, marched each one to a cauldron, bent him over it, cut his throat and bled him into it like a Michaelmas pig. The bodies were stacked in the boats, pushed out into the lake to sink, the broken weapons left on the boggy shore.

Everyone went away. For years everything lay as it had been left, the place avoided by all except the occasional awed or daring child. The boats and bodies and weapons sank slowly, maggot-ridden, into the black mud. Even more slowly, the lake dried out. Now cows pastured on it, all memory of what had happened there long gone, both among the victor-Angles whose descendants now lived far across the sea, and among the men of the islands to whom no word of their defeated expedition had ever come back.

And why do they do that? Shef found himself asking. The scale of what he was watching changed, he was no longer looking at real earth, at real history, instead he seemed to be viewing a drawing, a drawing that moved. Across a bare plain, the sun rose. Only it was not the sun, it was a ball of fire in a chariot, drawn by horses. The horses ran in terror, foam-flecked. Across the sky behind them ran giant wolves, tongues lolling, determined to pull down the horses and eat the sun. When the sun is hidden, or the moon, something told him, it is a wolf's shadow falling across it. One day the wolves will catch up and blood rain from the sky before sun and moon go out.

From the plain a great tree rose, giving air and shade and life to all the worlds beneath its branches. Looking closely, Shef saw that it twisted continually in pain. Beneath the earth, at its heart-root, he could see a giant serpent gnawing on it, venom dripping from its jaws. In the sea swam an even more monstrous serpent, rising from time to time to draw down a ship under full sail with one snap of its jaws. Deep beneath both the tree-serpent and the ocean-serpent Shef's new sight could see the dim outlines of some even more monstrous shape, chained to the foundations of the world, but writhing in pain so that the earth shook. It too was tormented, continually it struck back, one day it would break free to urge on the wolves of the sky and the serpent of the sea.

That is the world the pagans know of, Shef thought. No wonder they hate and fear their gods and seek only to propitiate them with cruelty. Their gods are afraid too, even Othin Allfather fears Ragnarök but does not know how to avert it. If there were a better way for the pagans to follow, they would take it. He thought of Thorvin's preachings of the Asgarth Way. Thought too of the White Christ, the suffering face under a crown of thorns which he had once seen on a wooden statue at Ely Cathedral, of the martyred King Edmund who had died under Ivar's chisel.

But that is not the whole story, something told him. Only a part. One day you may see the world as the Christians see it. Till then, remember this. Remember the wolves in the sky and the serpent in the sea.

The pleasant warmth on Shef's back had faded. As his normal sight slowly returned to him he realized that he was still looking out across the Schlei, his eyes wide open and unblinking. The green fields were still there, but the afternoon sun had faded, clouded over. His guards had drawn back, were muttering anxiously to each other as they stared at him.

Closer, a man knelt on one knee, looking deeply into his face. Shef recognized the white clothes and rowan-berry necklace of a priest of the Way, noted the silver boat which said that this was a priest of Njörth, the sea-god.

"I am Hagbarth," said the priest. "I am here to take you to Kaupang. My colleagues have been very anxious to meet you, to test you on their own ground. Fortunate for us that you came here from England."

He hesitated. "Will you tell me what you have just seen."

"Nothing but the world as it is," said Shef.

"To see things the way they are, that is a rare skill," answered Hagbarth. "And even rarer in broad daylight. Maybe you are the true prophet that Thorvin says, and not the false emissary of Loki that others declare. I will bear witness for you. We must go now."

"To Hrorik's hall?"

"And on to Kaupang."

Shef rose from the ground, stiffer and more cramped than he should have been. As he plodded down from the knoll towards Hedeby, he reflected on what he had seen. Was it his own mind telling him to accept the Christian Bruno's offer? Was it a warning, telling him of the true nature of the world he was entering, the world of the sea-kings, shaped by blood and horror over a hundred generations?

As they came to the edge of the town, they saw a coffle of slaves marched by. Shef looked at them, surprised to see such wretched folk find a market: old men, old women hobbling along, all with faces marked by a lifetime of toil, mere bags of bones like old oxen fit only for slaughter and the broth-pot.

"Are they worth bringing to market?" he asked.

"The Swedes buy them for the sacrifice at Uppsala," said one of the guards. "Summer and winter, a hundred oxen, a hundred horses, a hundred men and women they sacrifice and hang in the great oak groves at Uppsala. They say that without it the kingdom of the Swedes would fall, and the sky come down on their heads. If you can get no more work out of your thrall, you can always get one last payment that way."

One of the other guards laughed. "Keeps all the thralls working as hard as ever they know how, too. Maybe it's us should pay the Swedes."

CHAPTER NINE

Against the startling blue sky the great mountain line stood out in brilliant white. In fold after fold the range tumbled down to the black water at its foot—black only where the outflowing river kept a channel clear. Elsewhere thick ice still covered the shallow water of the bay, joining the mainland to the islands scattered along the shore. A thin powder of fresh snow covered the trees on the islands, and the ice between them. Where wind had swept the snow away, the ice lay old and transparent, still feet in thickness, but taking its color from the black depths beneath.

In the prow of the longboat, Shef and Karli watched, awestruck. In the land they had left, spring was far advanced, the buds out and the birds singing and nesting. Here there was no fresh green, only the dark gloom of the conifers, and the bright sun seemed only to be thrown back by the hard snow. The longboat was moving slowly now, under oars alone and they at no more than the paddling stroke. Hagbarth had furled sail in the night, as soon as he felt the loom of the land on either side, as soon as he knew they were within the deep bay that ran up in the end to the town of Oslo. Now, from time to time, the crew heard the sharp rap-rap of ice chunks striking the boat's fragile planks. Standing above them on the very gunwale itself, holding on with one hand as he leaned outboard, a crewman called sharp directions to the helmsman at the steering-oar, directing him away from the greater ice-lumps, the small islands that came drifting down the current from the land.

"Not much risk from ice this late in the spring," Hagbarth had
said, the first time his southern passengers had jumped to their feet in
alarm at the knocking beneath their feet. "But we won't risk it just the
same."

Shef had been profoundly glad, and Karli even gladder, of the
reduction in speed, and not just out of fear of what awaited them at
journey's end. Neither man, not even Shef, had made a fast passage in
a Viking longboat before. It was an experience very different—Shef
now realized—from the stately waddle of the *Norfolk* up the Dutch
coast, the sickening roll and lurch of sailing in a Yorkshire fishing-
coble. The Viking boat, Hagbarth's own *Aurvendill*, had seemed to
slide over the water like a great, supple snake. Each wave as it came
towards them rose far above the gunwales, looked down on the
undecked hull, seemed certain to crash down on it in a swamping
torrent. Then the prow rose, swarmed up, seemed like an intelligent
creature to look over the other side and begin its downward curve
while the stern-post was still rising. After a while Shef, his nerve
starting to return, found Karli sitting staring in horror at the lower
planks below the waterline. They shifted continually, moving away
from the boat's ribs and then moving back again, held only by lashings
of twisted root or sinew. Often the gaps were large enough for a man to
put foot, hand, or even head through. At such moments there seemed

to be nothing except habit holding the side-planks together at all. For a while after that both Karli and Shef sat together, convinced deep in their bellies that if they slackened the tension of their watch, the charm would break and the sea come rushing through.

As for anything striking the egg-shell's sides, the thought was unbearable. Shef had once asked Hagbarth if Norsemen ever carried horses or oxen from place to place, and if so, how they prevented the beasts from rushing to and fro in panic. Hagbarth had laughed. "If you put a horse in my *Aurvendill*," he said, "I have always found that any of them, even the fiercest stallion, takes one good look round him and then stands very, very still." Shef could see why.

And yet they had had to hurry, ice or no ice, running under full sail all the time during daylight, moving at a speed only a little under a horse's full gallop or a man's all-out sprint, as fast as a young man would go if he had nothing to carry and no more than a quarter of a mile to cover. For hour after hour. In the twelve hours of daylight on their first day Shef thought they might have traveled more than a hundred and fifty miles, though it was true they had tacked continually, making it less than that in a straight line. In the two nights and two days of their voyage, maybe four hundred all told—four hundred miles to bring them from the spring of flatland Denmark to the settled chill of Norway and the mountains.

All the way Hagbarth, explaining their haste, had commented on the immediate dangers on one or either side. Ships of King Hrorik had convoyed them up the South Jutland coast by night and through the Great Belt, the gap of water between the Danish mainland and Othin's own island of Fyn. Not too much risk there, Hagbarth had said. Hrorik has an arrangement with King Gamli of Fyn. But then they had swerved sharply out to sea with dawn and the turn-back of Hrorik's escorts. King Arnodd of Aalborg, Hagbarth had explained. Not hostile, does business like anyone else. But part of his business is robbing ships. Anyone without his leave, not related to him or his jarls, or just too weak to resist. Anyway, he feels threatened now: has to keep up a reputation.

Who's threatening him, Shef had asked, wondering already if the sea-legs he had acquired weeks before would keep off sea-sickness in the strange swoopings of the *Aurvendill*. Hagbarth had spat carefully past Karli's vomiting form and jerked a thumb to starboard, to the dim shapes of Fyn and Sjaelland beyond.

"The real bastards," he had said briefly. "Your friends. The Ragnarssons. Their base is over there, the Braethraborg, and the Emperor of the Greeks himself wouldn't want to meet them at sea.

Don't worry," he had added. "As far as we know the Snake-eye took the whole lot south to meet you, and they haven't come back yet. If they have, they'll be coming round the point over there on the backboard right about now. Unless they've strung out to make a nice long line from coast to coast just ahead."

Even after they had cleared the menace of the Skaggerak and were sailing, wind abeam, ten miles off the long coast of the South Swedes, Hagbarth's conversation was a long list of human hazards: King Teit of the East Gauts, King Vifil of the West Gauts, reports of independent pirates off the Weder islands, rumors of a fleet of broken men out of the Small Lands trying their luck up towards Norway, King Hjalti of the Farmsteads, and always—or so Hagbarth had said, though by this time Shef was suspecting him of deliberate terrorization—the possibility of the fearsome kings of the West-fjords taking a change from their usual raiding-grounds in the Atlantic islands and against the Irish, and coming over to vex the Swedes, whom they hated.

"In your country," Karli had asked once, pale with sickness and terror, "can anyone call himself a king?"

"Not *anyone*," Hagbarth had said with all seriousness. "It helps if you can call yourself one of the god-born, and there are plenty of people to check that. Us for a start, we priests of the Way. And there are some who are too proud to lie about their ancestry, like the Hlathir jarls—if they are descended from anyone it must be the trolls.

"But as a rule, if you can raise a fleet, say sixty ships or so, and you can find yourself a base on land, even if it is only a few square miles like the Braethraborg—the Ragnarssons took that from old King Kolfinn of Sjaelland, and defied him to take it back—then you can call yourself a king. Sea-king is what they usually say."

"And how do you get to be a king of somewhere? Like the Farmsteads or the Small Lands or the Midden-heaps or the Further Cow-byre," asked Shef, temper strained by fear.

"Get a Thing to accept you," said Hagbarth briefly. "Easiest way to do that is to stand in the clearing and say you're king and you're going to tax everybody. If you get out of the clearing, you're probably a king. God-born or no."

The tension had only slackened at dawn that day when Hagbarth, looking carefully round him at the first blink of dawn, had pronounced them within the waters of the Norwegian kings, Olaf and Halvdan.

"Kings of Norway?" Shef had asked.

"Kings of the Westfold and the Eastfold," Hagbarth replied. "One each, but co-kings of both. And don't look like that, what about you and Alfred? You're not even brothers. Half-brothers, that is."

Further argument had been cut out by the appearance from either side of heavily-manned warships, each half the size again of the *Aurvendill*, long pennants flying. Shef knew enough of the sea to recognize them as coast-defense craft only, unfit for a deep-sea passage or a hard gale because of their riveted keels, but capable of jamming in a hundred warriors each for a short while, untroubled by the need to carry rations and water. As the ice narrowed in from either side they closed up, eventually falling into line astern, each ship paddling gently into the whirlpools made by the one ahead, as the oars dipped and pulled in the dark water.

Ahead Shef could see what looked like a substantial township, many log houses with plumes of smoke rising from all of them. At its center rose a large hall, horns jutting from ridge and gables. Further away, outside the town but below the mountains, he could see with his one sharp eye a collection of larger buildings, some of them strangely shaped, but all half-hidden by the firs. Where the town ran down to the shore, dozens of boats of all sizes lay at jetties. And, at the largest and longest of the jetties, he could pick out what seemed to be a welcoming committee. Or a group of jailers. Shef looked longingly at the islands scattered thickly to the left. The ice was barely fifty yards away now. Then a few hundred yards more to the land, and on every island plumes of smoke to show shelter and habitation.

All ruled by the co-kings, of whichever Fold it was. If your heart did not stop beating as soon as you touched the freezing water. If you did not freeze solid as soon as you climbed out of it.

Shef belatedly realized that he cut hardly a kingly figure himself. He had started the trip in exactly the same tunic, breeches and leather shoes that he had worn continually since he had struggled ashore on the Ditmarsh two weeks before: bemired, salt-stained, blood-stained from his own blood and the Viking he had killed on the sandbanks, with a fortnight's accumulation of tar-patches, spilt broth, and sweat on top. It was no worse than what he had worn most of his boyhood in the Norfolk marsh, but Vikings, he had noticed, were cleanlier than Englishmen, or at least than English churls. Only Karli sat next to him when they came to eat. As they sailed further north and the sea-wind came keener, Hagbarth had tossed each of them a thick blanket, which they now hugged round them.

By contrast to their squalor, Shef could pick out on the jetty scarlet capes, gleaming armor, polished shields reflecting the sun, and in a solid body at the water's edge, the shining white clothes of the priests of the Way, competing with the snow behind. Shef ran a hand ineffectually through his hair, dislodging a louse, and turned for advice to Hagbarth. Then turned back again, with sudden incredulous joy.

One figure over there by the shore stood out even among the tall shapes around him. Surely—yes, that must be Brand. Scanning quickly along the jetty, Shef realized that there were other men there in a little knot, smaller than the rest as Brand was bigger. And one of them showed up in a bright flash of scarlet—it was the silk tunic the ex-slave Cwicca wore for great occasions. Now that he knew what he was looking for, Shef could pick them out readily. Brand there well to the fore, Guthmund the Greedy standing beside him, and in a self-effacing clump to the rear Cwicca and Osmod and a gang of their mates. Shef looked again at the white tunics and cloaks of the priests of the Way, standing at the very edge of the jetty. Yes, Thorvin was there among them, and Skaldfinn too, and Hund: outnumbered, though, by a cluster of other priests, one formidable figure near the front almost rivaling Brand even in size. And there was another group there as well, standing separate both from the priests and from Brand and his friends. A puff of wind from the mountains caught the pennants held by standard-bearers, and for a moment Shef saw the Hammer of the Way, white on black, and from the group he could not identify a blue streamer with a strange design he did not recognize. He looked a mute question at Hagbarth.

"It is the Gripping Beast," said Hagbarth, dropping his voice, the jetty now only fifty yards away.

"Of King Halvdan? Or King Olaf?"

"Neither," said Hagbarth with a touch of grimness. "Of Queen Ragnhild."

The crewmen tossed oars, dropped them clattering into the bottom of the boat. Ropes flew out from prow and stern, were caught and snubbed to tree-trunk bollards. The *Aurvendill* settled gently alongside the jetty. The gangplank was thrown across.

Shef hesitated, conscious of his own appearance. Facing him, the big unknown priest looked down, what seemed to be scorn and mistrust on his face. Shef remembered the last time he had stood face to face with an enemy on a gangplank: when he had killed Ivar, Champion of the North. No-one else could ever say that. Shedding his blanket, and snatching the 'Gungnir' spear from Karli's ready hand, he stepped on to the gangplank, strode across it, meaning to force the priest to stand back.

As he reached the other end an arm like the base of a mast quietly thrust the priest aside, and Brand shoved forward, holding out an immense fur cape, made from the skin of a white bear, its brooch and chain of gold. In an instant he had wrapped it round Shef's shoulders, fastened the links. Then he fell to one knee, his face still only just below Shef's own level.

"Hail, King of the East and Middle Angles," he called. On the signal, Cwicca and his mates, and the crews of the *Walrus* and the *Seamew* further behind, cheered and clashed their weapons.

Brand, who had never knelt in his life before, winked one staring eye, and jerked his head infinitesimally at the others on the jetty. Shef caught the hint, turned to Hagbarth, who had followed him up the gangplank.

"You may present your colleagues," he said imperiously.

"Why, this is—ah—King Shef, may I present to you Valgrim the Wise, Head of the College of the Way and priest of Othin? Valgrim, this is . . ."

Valgrim was paying no attention. With a scowl for Brand, he reached out one hand, seized the spear in Shef's grip, and turned it so that he could read the runes on it. After a moment he released the spear, turned and walked wordlessly off.

"He didn't like that," muttered Brand. "What do the runes say?"

"Gungnir. It's not my spear anyway, I took it from Sigurth Ragnarsson."

Most of the other priests of the Way had moved off after their leader, leaving Thorvin and Hund behind. As they departed, Shef saw the other group coming towards them under the blue and silver banner. He gaped up at it: a strange design, of a beast with snarling face, seemingly throttling itself with one paw while clutching its own ankle with another. He dropped his eyes, found himself face to face with the most striking woman he had ever seen.

He would not have thought her beautiful if some one had described her. Since his childhood Shef had framed his ideas of beauty on Godive: tall but slight of figure, with brown hair, gray eyes, and the perfect complexion she had inherited from her Irish slave-concubine mother. This woman was tiger to Godive's sleek leopard: as tall as Shef, with broad cheekbones and great green eyes set wide apart. Her breasts swelled out the dark green gown she was wearing, and heavy hip-bones showed through as she walked. Two long plaits hung round her face and over her shoulders, held in place by a heavy gold band low over her forehead. She was not a young woman either, Shef realized belatedly, but double his age or Godive's. At her side walked a young boy, maybe ten years old.

Confused, and unwilling to face the woman's stare, Shef dropped on one knee to the boy's level.

"And who are you?"

"I am Harald, son to King Halvdan and Queen Ragnhild. What happened to your eye?"

"Someone put it out with a hot needle."

"Did it hurt?"

"I fainted before it was finished."

The boy looked scornful. "That was not *drengiligr*. Warriors do not faint. Did you kill the man who did it?"

"I killed the man who caused it. The one who did it is standing over there, and the one who held me. They are friends."

The boy looked nonplused. "How can they be friends if they blinded you?"

"Sometimes you will take from your friends what you will not from your enemies."

Belatedly Shef realized the boy's mother's thigh was only inches from his blind side. He rose to his feet, conscious as he did so of the strong female warmth. There, on the jetty, with dozens of men all around, he could feel his manhood stirring as it had not for all the Ditmarsh girl's efforts. In another moment he would feel the urge to throw her down on the wooden deck—if he were strong enough, which he doubted.

The queen looked scrutinizingly at him, seemingly aware of what he felt. "You will come when I call you, then," she said, and turned away.

"Most men do," muttered Brand again in Shef's ear.

Over his voice, as he watched the green gown retreating magnificently towards the snow, Shef heard a sound he would once have picked out through any distractions: the clink-clink, beat-beat of light and heavy hammers working at a forge. And other sounds too which he could not place.

"We've a lot to show you," said Thorvin, finally making his way up to his former apprentice.

"Right," said Brand. "But first, the bath-house. I can see the lice in his hair, and it puts me off even if Queen Ragnhild likes it."

"He came stalking ashore with one eye and a spear in his hand with the 'Gungnir' runes on it," growled Valgrim. "What else has he to do to declare himself Othin? Ride an eight-legged horse? He is a blasphemer!"

"Many men have one eye," replied Thorvin. "And as for the 'Gungnir' runes, he did not have them cut. The only reason he has the spear is that Sigurth Snake-eye threw it at him. If there is a blasphemer, it is Sigurth."

"You have told us that when he first appeared to you out of nowhere two winters ago he said he came from the North."

"Yes, but all that he meant was that he came from the north of his kingdom."

"And yet you have presented this to us as if this accident were proof that he is the One we await. That he is the One who will come from the North to overthrow the Christians and put the world on its better path. If this aping of Othin is an accident, then what he said to you was an accident. But if what he said to you was a sign from the gods, then this too is a sign. He is setting himself up as Othin. And I, the priest of Othin in this college, I say that such as he cannot have Othin's favor. Did he not refuse the Othin-sacrifice when he had the Christian army at his mercy?"

Thorvin fell silent, unable to see a way round Valgrim's logic.

"I can tell you that he is one who sees visions," put in Hagbarth. "And not only in his sleep."

The listening priests, a score of them together, looked at him with interest. They had not formed their holy circle nor set up the holy cordon of rowan-berries round the spear and the bale-fire: what they said was still unprivileged, not done under the guidance of the gods. Still, they were not forbidden to speak of holy things.

"How do you know?" grunted Valgrim.

"I saw him in Hedeby. He sat on a mound outside the town, a grave-mound, an old king's howe. They told me he made his way there unprompted."

"Means nothing," said Valgrim. He quoted derisively lines from one of the traditional poems of the past:

"Then the bastard sat on the barrow,

When the princes parted the spoil."

"Bastard or not," Hagbarth went on. "I saw him with his eyes wide open, seeing nothing and replying to no-one. When the fit passed I asked him what he had seen and he replied, he saw things as they were."

"What did he look like when the fit was on him?" asked a priest with the sign of Ull the hunter-god round his neck.

"Like him." Hagbarth jerked a thumb at the most respected of the priests in the conclave, Vigleik of the visions, seated unspeaking at the end of the table.

Slowly Vigleik stirred. "One other thing we must remember," he offered. "The evidence of Farman priest of Frey, our brother still in England. He says that two winters ago he was in the camp of the Ragnarssons, searching for new knowledge, trying to see whether even among the Loki-brood there might be the One we await. He had seen Thorvin's apprentice whom they now call King Shef, but he knew nothing of him, thought him only an English runaway. Yet the day after the great battle with King Jatmund he too saw a vision, in daylight. A vision of the smithy of the gods. In it he saw Thorvin's apprentice in the shape and place of Völund, the lame smith. And he saw Othin speak to him. Farman told me, though, that Othin did not take him under his protection. So maybe Valgrim, as priest of Othin, is right to fear him. There may be other plans than Othin's."

Valgrim's chest swelled with rage, both at the challenge to Othin's plans and at the thought that he might be a prey to fear. He did not venture to defy Vigleik. Among the priests who had gathered to the College from the whole of Norway, and the other Scandinavian lands, there were more who knew of Vigleik the Seer than of Valgrim the Wise—wise in the ways of kings and the arts of government. One of the arts of government was to keep silent till the moment came.

"Guidance may come to us," he said pacifically.

"Who from?" asked a priest from Ranrike to the north.

"From our holy circle, when the time comes to form it."

"Also," said Vigleik, "if we are fortunate, from King Olaf. He is the wisest of kings on the earth, though not the most lucky. I suggest we invite him to attend our conclave, to sit outside the circle. He is not the One, though once we thought he might be. Yet if anyone may recognize a true king, it is he."

"I thought Olaf Elf-of-Geirstath was dead," muttered the Ranrike priest to one of his back-country fellows.

Washed from head to foot in a great tub of heated water, his hair cut short and scrubbed again and again with lye, Shef stepped cautiously across the old, hard-packed snow of the College's precinct. His clothes had been taken away and replaced with a hemp shirt and tight-fitting woolen drawers, a thick wool tunic and trousers over them. Brand had repossessed the bearskin cape, muttering that if he found lice in that he would send Shef out to hunt down another one, but he had replaced it with a mantle of homespun. His gold bracelets again shone on Shef's biceps, though he had refused to replace the gold circlet of kingship on his cropped head. He walked clumsily in a pair of thick winter boots borrowed from Guthmund, padded out with wound rags. In spite of the cold and the snow, he felt warm for the first time in days.

Udd the undersized steelmaster kept pace with him. After the rough administrations of Brand, Shef had greeted Cwicca and the rest of his faithful gang, handed Karli over to them, scowling distrustfully, and told them to consider him a new and valued recruit, and then become aware that Udd was standing to one side, tongue-tied as ever. One only became aware of Udd when he had something to say or to show. It was certainly something to do with metal. Remembering the forge-noises he had heard from the jetty, Shef clapped Udd on the shoulder, added a final warning about good behavior to Karli, and followed Udd out into the open. Cwicca and the other English ex-slaves who had come to this unknown land in the north had promptly slammed the door, wedged every chink they could find, and returned to their normal habit of clustering round the fire in as much animal warmth as they could manage.

Udd was not heading towards the place from which familiar forge-noises came, but to a small building separate from the main frequented halls and dormitories. As they walked a figure shot suddenly past them at a speed no man could match. Shef jumped to one side, fumbling for the sword at his belt, saw the figure sweep away down the slope to the township well below.

"What was that?" he gasped. "Skates? On snow? Downhill?"

"They call 'em skis," said Udd. "Or ski-runners or something. Wooden boards you tie to your feet. They all use 'em up here. Strange folk. But now look at this." He pushed the door open and led Shef into an empty shed.

For a few moments Shef could see nothing in its dark interior. Then, as Udd fumbled open a shutter he saw a great stone wheel lying in the middle of the shed. As his eyes grew used to the dimness, Shef realized that there were actually two wheels, one over the other. A machine of some kind.

"What do they do?" he asked.

Udd lifted a trapdoor, pointed under the shed to a channel below. "When the snow melts there's a stream under here. See the wheel down there? With the paddles on it? Water flows, turns the paddles. Axle on that wheel turns these two above. The surfaces touching each other have channels cut in 'em. Pour grain in. Grinds the grain."

Shef nodded, remembering the monotonous noise of the old woman grinding corn in the Ditmarsh hut, the job that never ceased, the job that warriors hated.

"Does it much faster than women with the old pestle and mortar," Udd added. "Mind you, it's been frozen solid since we got here. They say when it's working it grinds as much corn as forty women working all day. The folk come up from the town and pay the priests to use it."

Shef nodded again, reflecting on how the monks of Saint John or Saint Peter would have appreciated such an addition to their income. He saw the potential of the device. But he could not understand Udd's interest: it was notorious that the little man cared for nothing but metal. Best not to rush him.

Silently Udd led his king out and down the slope to a second shed. "This is like rung two," he said, with a glance at Shef's ladder-emblem. "And this is down to us. See, ever since last year the priests here have been fascinated by what they heard of our catapults. Cwicca and his mates have already built a couple, to show 'em how we do it. But they'd already got the idea of the little wheels: the cog-wheels, you know. And the priest who was working with the mill, he got the idea of using real big cog-wheels not to wind a catapult but to make a different mill."

The pair approached the second building. On one wall of it, another big wooden wheel with paddles, exactly like the first one: but set vertically in the snow-choked ravine, not horizontally. Clearly the water would turn this even better, with a better purchase. But what use would an axle be turning two vertical millstones? The corn would run straight through them and never be ground at all. It was the weight of the stone that did the grinding.

Still silently Udd led Shef in and pointed to the gearing. At the end of the millwheel-axle an immense iron cog-wheel stood vertical. Its teeth meshed into a matching horizontal cog, fitted over a stout oak axle. Below it, on the same axle, the two familiar stone wheels. Above them, a hopper showed where men could stand to pour in sacks of kernels.

"Yes, lord, it's well-done. But what I wanted to say was there's something to do with this that these folk haven't thought of yet. See, lord," Udd dropped his voice, though there was no-one near, no-one within a furlong of them. "What's our problem with iron? With making it, like?"

"Beating it out," said Shef.

"How many days does it take a man to get fifty pound of iron out of, say, five times that amount of ore?"

Shef whistled, remembering the hours he had spent pounding out the slag for his first home-made sword. "Ten," he guessed. "Depends how strong the smith is."

"That's why smiths have to be strong," agreed Udd, looking down at his own puny frame. "I couldn't ever be one. But then I thought, if this mill does the work of forty grinding-slaves, women that is, could it not do the work of, say, twenty smiths?"

Shef began to feel a familiar warning itch in his brain. Many minds were working here, as they had worked to make the catapults, the pulley-wound crossbow. Some priest of the Way had thought of the water-mill. Some long-dead Roman had left behind the cog-wheels. Shef and his crewmen had rebuilt the catapults. And from hearing about that alone, some other priest had worked out how to transfer the force in the flow of a river to the task he needed in a different dimension. Now Udd had returned that thought to his own obsession. It was as if people too were cog-wheels, the one fitting into the other, one brain turning the next.

"How could stone wheels grind iron?" he asked cautiously.

"Well, lord, what came to me was this." Udd dropped his voice even further. "What everyone's always thought in this line is, a wheel drives a wheel. But I thought, what if it doesn't? What if it drives something a different shape? And much, much bigger? See, axle turns here. Turns a shape like this. The shape turns, and all the time it's turning, it's lifting a heavy weight, as heavy as a millwheel. Only not a millwheel, a hammer. But when it gets to this point here—it stops lifting. The hammer drops instead. A really heavy hammer, a hammer six smiths couldn't lift, not even if they were as strong as Brand! And hammering as fast as the axle on this millwheel turns. How long would it take to beat out fifty pounds of iron then? Five hundred pounds?"

The little man's pale face shone with excitement, the thrill of the inventor. Shef caught the feeling, felt his palms itch to start the work.

"Listen, Udd," he said, trying to keep a cool head. "I don't see what you mean about the shape to lift and to drop."

Udd nodded energetically. "That's what I've been thinking about every night in my bunk. What we need, I reckon, is something like this . . ."

On the floor of the hut, planks overlaid with a thin layer of drifted snow from under the warped door, Udd began to draw a cross-section of a reciprocating cam. After a few moments Shef seized his own straw and began to draw as well. "If it turns like this," he said, "you'd have to have a groove on the handle of the hammer, to stop it flying off. But does it have to have a hammer-shape?"

An hour later Thorvin the smith-priest, coming from his doubtful meeting, saw the tall king and the puny freedman walking down the snowy path, their arms waving wildly as they designed imaginary machines. For an instant he understood Valgrim's doubts. Farman and Vigleik might see the One King in their visions. No vision or prophecy had ever included a word, he was sure, about scrawny foreign thrall-born assistants.

CHAPTER TEN

In the Scandinavian lands, in the year of Our Lord 867, the peoples were much the same, but the lands themselves greatly different. In spite of centuries of bickering, jealousy and war, the Danes, Swedes and Norwegians were all much more like each other than anyone else. There is every difference, though, between the fertile pastures of the Danish islands and the Jutland peninsula, or the long coastline of Sweden in the sheltered tideless Baltic, and the fjord-splintered Atlantic-facing stretch of Norway, with its immense and almost pathless spine of mountains, the Keel. The Norwegians said even then of the Danes that only Danes could have an eighteen-hundred foot hillock as the highest spot in all their kingdoms, and call it Himinbjerg, Sky Mountain. The Danes said of the Norwegians that if you put ten Norwegians together, eleven would call themselves kings and lead fifteen armies to war against each other. The jokes had a basis in fact, in geography and history. Travel for the Norwegians was not impossibly difficult, for there were passages all the way up the coast with its thousands of islands, and in the long winter ski-runners could travel over the snow faster than any horse could gallop. Yet it might take two days to go round by sea rather than cross a ten-thousand-foot sheer-rising mountain mass. It was easier in Norway to divide than to unite. Easy too, in a land where there was a boatyard on every one of a thousand fjords, to raise a fleet and crew it with the younger sons who counted their fathers' farmlands in fractions of an acre.

In this land of little kingdoms and brief alliances, forty years before,

there had been a king called Guthroth. He was king of the Westfold,
the land to the west of the great fjord that runs up to Oslo and divides
the main Norwegian mass from the borders with Sweden. He was a
king not much better, or much worse, than his neighbors and rivals
the kings of the Eastfold, of Ranrike, Raumrike, Hedemark, Hedeland,
Toten, Akershus and all the others. His subjects, a few score thousand,
maybe enough to make the population of a decent English shire, called
him the Huntsman because of his hobby, which was hunting
women—a dangerous and difficult hobby, even for a king, in a land
where every cot-carl had spear, axe and half-a-dozen Viking expedi-
tions behind him.

But Guthroth persevered. In the end his first wife Thurith, daughter
of the king of Rogaland, died, worn out with vexation at her husband's
infidelities and the trouble and expense they caused, and Guthroth
thought at once of replacing her. His eye fell on the daughter of the
king of the tiny kingdom of Agdir, no more than a town and a handful
of villages: Asa, daughter of Hunthjof the Strong, a virgin of un-
matched beauty. To Guthroth it seemed that her charms might stir
again in him the youth that seemed to be passing. But Hunthjof the
Strong refused Guthroth's offers, saying that his daughter would not
need to go sniffing other women's beds to see who had been in them.
Stung by the insult and the rejection, Guthroth did his only great deed
beyond the normal expected from kings of a warlike people: he
gathered his men and came down on Agdir on skis on a dark winter's
night, just after Yule, when men were still sleeping off the Yule-ale. He
killed Hunthjof the Strong in fair fight at the door of his bedchamber,
though it is true that Guthroth was fully awake and fully armored,
while Hunthjof was half-drunk and wholly naked; then seized Asa,
bundled her into a sleigh and dragged her back to the Westfold roped
to the sleigh-posts. There Guthroth's own priests declared the
wedding, and Asa was dragged off willy-nilly to the bedchamber.

Her beauty fulfilled Guthroth's expectations, and nine months later
she gave birth to her son Halvdan, later called the Black from his hair
and his rages. Guthroth slowly let out the breath he had been holding,
and forbore to tie Asa's wrists to the bedposts every night when he
slept, knowing that women with a child to defend would become more
sensible and less grudge-bearing than before. He still made sure even
the knife she used to pare an apple with was pointless and no sharper
than would serve to cut soft cheese.

Yet he had forgotten that a woman can work through other men as
easily as in her own right. One dark evening, just after Yule the year
after Asa's father's death, Guthroth emptied the great aurochs-horn of

beer which he kept on his table without a stand, so that it had to be drained in one draught, and shortly staggered out to piss on the snow. As he did so, while his hands were occupied with his breeches, and before he had begun to empty his bladder, a young lad stepped round the corner of the royal hall and thrust a broad-bladed spear through his belly, fleeing instantly on skis. Guthroth lived long enough to say that the killer had said only, "Those who kill drunken men should always stay sober," and then died, trying still to complete his piss.

Guthroth had an acknowledged and legitimate son by his first wife Thurith, a strong lad of eighteen winters called Olaf. Men expected that he would appease his father's ghost by sending Queen Asa into the howe with him, and make a clean sweep by leaving the child Halvdan, his half-brother, out in the forest for the wolves. He did not do so. And when asked why not—it was a sign that men did not fear him as much as a king should be feared that they were able to ask—he said that he had dreamed a dream. In it he saw a great tree spring from his step-mother's womb, a tree with blood-red roots, a white trunk, and green leaves that spread all over Norway and even further across the world. So he knew that a great destiny waited for Asa's children, and would not thwart the gods and bring down bad luck by trying to avert it.

Olaf, then, spared his stepmother and protected his half-brother, but from that time he himself had little good fortune, and men said that he had thrown away his own luck. In the years to come he was overshadowed in battle by his half-brother, Asa's son, who won himself a kingdom across the fjord in the Eastfold. And Olaf's own only son, Rognvald, whom men called the Magnificent for his courage and his gifts to poets, died when a trifling scratch in a mere skirmish swelled and went bad and defied the leeches even of the Way.

By contrast Halvdan won himself not only the new kingdom of the Eastfold, which he loyally shared with his one-time protector, and his grandfather's kingdom of Agdir, but also a wife whom even the imperious Queen Asa could not despise, as she did all other women. This was Ragnhild, daughter of King Sigurth the Hart of Ringerike. Like Asa, she too had been carried off from her father, but not by Halvdan. While her father was traveling through the mountains, he was ambushed by a mountain-chieftain, a wild man and a berserk called Haki. For all his berserkergang, Sigurth wounded Haki three times before he was killed, and cut off his left arm, so that Haki lay abed for a long winter, unable to enjoy his virgin bride. Just about the time he might be calculated to have recovered enough to do the deed, Halvdan struck first like his father. He took fifty picked men into the mountains and fired Haki's hall in the night. As Ragnhild ran out to greet her rescuers, they snatched her up and drove away across a frozen lake. When the pursuers got to the lake and saw the reindeer-sleighs disappearing, Haki knew that he would never catch them up nor live down the shame of losing both his arm and his bride. He threw himself on his own sword's point to rise again unmaimed in Valhalla. And so Halvdan won the most beautiful bride in the North and the only woman fit to match the mother-in-law for temper, and did so in time to enjoy her virginity despite the appearances: or so he always believed. Before long she too gave birth to a son, Harald, whom men called the Fairhaired in contrast to his father.

These, then, were the rulers of the Westfold in the time that the priests of the Way settled there and made the trading town of Kaupang their center and headquarters: first King Guthroth, then King Olaf, then King Olaf and King Halvdan together, with Harald Fairhair the only son of either of them able to succeed. And as important at least as any of the men, Queen Asa mother of Halvdan, and Queen Ragnhild mother of Harald.

Seated on a bench before an open window in Hedeby, Erkenbert the deacon considered the names both of King Halvdan (the Black), and King Olaf (Elf-of-Geirstath, whatever that might mean), and attached carefully the name of their kingdom or kingdoms: the Eastfold and the Westfold, both parts of that larger grouping that men called *Northr Vegr*, the Northway. He did not think that either of them was the man he had been told to look for. Olaf the Elf, certainly not. Erkenbert's notes said this man was over fifty, and notorious for his bad luck, though he did seem nevertheless to have retained his kingdom. But he also did not occur on any of the lists Erkenbert had made—doubtful and based on shaky memories though they were—of who had and had not been present at the great raid on Hamburg after which the Holy Lance of Longinus had disappeared.

The other one might be a bit better as a possibility. He was widely feared and respected, something of a conqueror on the tiny depressing scale of the Northern lands, said to be the main obstacle in Norway to the Ragnarssons' goal of spreading their power. His ships challenged quickly and kept all interlopers at a distance. Yet Erkenbert did not think this Halvdan fitted the bill either. When Bruno had given him the task of collecting all available information on the kings and chieftains and jarls of Scandinavia, to try to determine who might hold the Holy Lance, he had told him to look for three things. One, success. Two, connection with the raid on Hamburg. Three, sudden change: a failure who suddenly became a success would betray the mighty influence of the great relic more surely than anything else. There was no sign of that with Halvdan. He seemed to have ground his way to power in an unremitting way from birth, or at least from his youth.

Against his will—for he had not wanted to come on this mission to the north, and would rather have stayed in Cologne or Trier or even Hamburg or Bremen, finding out more of the mysteries of power— Erkenbert was beginning to feel the intellectual challenge of the problem Bruno the count's son had set him. "Someone must know the answer," Bruno had said. "They just don't know they know. Ask everyone we meet about everything. Write all the answers down. Look to see what kind of pattern emerges." And this Erkenbert had done, interrogating first the few Christian converts they had made in Hedeby—low-value informants these, mostly women and thralls who knew nothing of the reputations and records of the great ones—then the Christian priests they had rescued, then those guards of King Hrorik who would speak to them out of politeness, and finally, paying heavily in wine from the South, the skippers and helmsmen of the boats that put in, often famous warriors themselves and sensitive as harlots to shifts in reputation.

A shadow darkened the door and the senior knight of the Order of the Lance, Bruno himself, edged his freakishly broad shoulders through the opening.

He smiled, as he did so readily. "What is the betting today?" he asked. "Any new runners in our little horse-race?"

Erkenbert shook his head. "If we have heard the answer already, as you say, I cannot recognize it," he said. "The one most like the picture you want is still the young man who killed Ivar and bested Charles. He has come from nowhere. Everyone talks of his deeds and his luck. He is a close associate of Viga-Brand, Brand the Killer, who was certainly present at the sack of Hamburg."

Bruno shook his head regretfully. "I thought so too," he said. "Right up till the time I spoke to him. He is a strange one, and I think maybe he has something to do with all this. Yet he had only one weapon, and though it was a spear it was most certainly not *the* spear. Too new, wrong shape, marked with heathen runes, though I could not read them. I think you have got him on your brain, and will not drop him. Maybe that is preventing you from recognizing the true holder. Tell me some more about some of these heathen kings."

Erkenbert shrugged, picked up once more his mounting pile of vellum. "I have told over to you the kings of Denmark and Norway," he said. "Now in Sweden and Gautland between them there may be as many as twenty more. From the north, King Vikar of Roslagen, aged fifty, elected at the Ros-Thing twenty years ago, said to be rich but peaceful, takes tribute from the Finns and never comes south."

Bruno shook his head.

"How about King Orm of Uppland, controls the great Kingdom Oak and the temple-sacrifices at Uppsala, said to be powerful but disinclined to personal combat, took the kingdom by force twenty years ago?"

"He sounds a bit more likely, but not much. We'll keep an eye on him. You know," Bruno reflected, "for all their recent defeats, I wonder if Sigurth Ragnarsson or one of his brothers couldn't be our man. After all, even Charles the Great had some setbacks, against the Saxons."

Erkenbert was unable to repress an involuntary shudder.

"I think we may have to get a little closer to the action to find out for sure . . ." Bruno went on.

In the hut to which they had been assigned in the college precinct at Kaupang, the English ex-slaves and Karli the Ditmarsher were exchanging stories of the Hidden Folk. There was a companionable mood in the warm tight-closed room. Hama, one of the catapulteers, had a split lip. Cwicca had an eye swollen shut. Karli was nursing a bitten ear, and had a lump on the side of his head where Osmod, seeing man after man knocked down by Karli's fists, had hit him over the head with a billet of firewood. The group had ceased to mock each other's accents, and were trying to find common ground in explaining the strange world around them.

"We believe in things called thurses," said Karli.

"Us too," agreed Cwicca the fen-man. "They live in holes in the marsh. If you're out in a punt after wild duck, you don't want to go putting your pole into any old thurs-nest. Fowler who does that, he don't come back."

"Where do these creatures come from?" asked one of the men.

"They don't come from anywhere, they've always been here."

"What I heard," said Cwicca, "is this. You know we're supposed to be descended from Adam and Eve. Well, one day the Lord God came down and asked Eve to show him her children. Well, she showed him some of them, but some of them weren't washed, 'cause she was an idle slut, so she told them to hide. And at the end the Lord God said 'Those children you hid from me, let them remain hidden.' And since then those of us who come from Eve's children who were seen, we're human, but those who come from the others, they're the Hidden Folk, who live in the marshes and on the moors."

The story was considered, but not much liked. Every man there but Karli had been a slave of the Church, first recruited and then freed by Shef and the army of the Way. Christian doctrine was familiar to them, but they associated it with slavery.

"I can't see that has anything to do with what they've got up here," said another voice. "No thurses up here, 'cause there's no marshes. What they've got up here is nixes. In the water. Only there's no water 'cause it's all frozen."

"And trolls," put in another.

"I never heard that word," said Osmod, "what's a troll?"

"Great gray things what live in the rocks. And they call 'em trolls because they trundle down the hill at you."

"One of the locals told me this," said the split-lipped Hama. "There was a man lived up in the mountains, called Lafi. And one day when he was hunting, two troll-wives caught him and dragged him off to their lair in the mountains, and used him as a stud. They wore nothing but raw horse-hides, and they lived on nothing but meat and fish. Sometimes the meat was horse or sheep, but sometimes they wouldn't show him where it had come from, but he had to eat it just the same. After a while he pretended to fall ill, and while the young troll-wife was out hunting, the other one asked him what would cure him. And he said, nothing but rotten meat that had been buried for five years. So she said she knew where there was some of that, and off she went. But because she thought he was too sick to get out of bed, she didn't roll the stone quite shut in front of the cave. And he got out and ran for it. They picked up his scent and came after him, but he smelt wood-smoke and ran till he got to a camp of charcoal-burners, and they got their weapons and faced out and kept the troll-wives off. And then they all went down the mountain and got to safety.

"But nine months later, when he came out of his house, there was a baby on the doorstep all covered in gray hair. After that he was afraid ever to go out at night. I don't know what happened to the baby."

"So they aren't animals, then. They can breed with us, like," reflected Osmod. "Maybe there's some truth in Cwicca's story."

"Maybe we better leave Karli out for the troll-women," came a suggestion.

"Yes, and then if there's any trouble from any old troll-daddy, he can just knock him down."

* * *

Outside, ignoring the laughter coming from the dark hut, Brand was trying to talk seriously to Shef.

"I tell you," he said, "she's dangerous. Deadly dangerous. The most dangerous thing you've met since you stepped on the gangplank to face Ivar. Worse than him, even, because when you faced him he already knew he was bound to lose in the end. She doesn't think that. She has more to play for."

"I don't know why you're worried," said Shef. "I've never so much as spoken to her."

"I saw the way you looked at her. And her at you. What you need to realize is that she's only interested in one thing, and that's her son Harald. There are prophecies about him. First people thought the prophecies meant his father. Then they switched to thinking it meant him. Ragnhild certainly thinks it means him.

"But now you come along and people start saying maybe you're the one, the big king that everyone's been waiting for, the one who'll rule all Norway."

"I wouldn't even have *got* to Norway if they hadn't bought me off Hrorik and brought me here."

"Well, you're here now. And people like Thorvin—he means no harm, but he's responsible just the same—people like Thorvin telling everyone you're the son of the gods and the one who comes from the north and I don't know what else. You have visions, you're *in* visions, Hagbarth says one thing and Vigleik says another. You have to expect people to listen. Because behind it there are things no-one can just laugh off as old wives' tales: you're a thrall who got to be a king, I saw it myself. You put Alfred to one side, and he was one of the god-born, descended from Othin, even the English admit that. You took the surrender of the king of the Franks. What are a few hedge-wife prophecies to that? Of course Ragnhild thinks you're dangerous. That's why she is."

"What happens tomorrow?" asked Shef.

"The priests of the Way meet in holy circle. They have to decide about you. You won't be there. Nor I."

"What if they decide Thorvin is wrong? Surely then they can just agree I'm nothing to do with them and let me go. After all I have supported the Way, I wear its pendant, I have helped them establish themselves on Christian soil. Any of its priests are welcome to come to my kingdom any time and pursue new knowledge. More than welcome," Shef added, thinking of what he and Udd had discussed.

"And if they decide the other way, that you are the one they seek?"

Shef shrugged. "If there's going to be any change in the world, I'm more likely to start it in England than stuck up here where no-one ever comes.''

Brand frowned, displeased to hear Norway disregarded. ''And what if they decide you are not the one they seek, but you have been masquerading as him? Or even more likely, that you are not the one they seek, but a rival and an enemy. That is what Valgrim the Wise thinks, and he has a point. He is sure that the great change in the world which shall destroy the Christians' power must come from Othin. And everyone agrees you are not from Othin.''

He tapped Shef on the chest with a mighty forefinger. ''Though you go round looking as if you ought to be, with your one eye and that damned spear. Valgrim thinks you are a threat to Othin's plan. He will try to have you condemned for that.''

''So Valgrim thinks I'm a threat to Othin's plan. And Ragnhild thinks I'm a threat to her son's future. And all because I learnt to build the catapults and the crossbows, to twist rope and forge wheels and bend steel. They ought to realize the real danger is Udd.''

''Udd's only five feet tall,'' snarled Brand. ''People don't think he's a danger because they don't even know he's there.''

''That's a real danger for you, then,'' answered Shef. Musingly he added words he had learnt from Thorvin:

''All gates, ere you go through,
Look round you, peer round you.
Not evident to any, where un-friends sit
    In every hall.''

Far up the mountain-side, a man sat amid the dark, who had forfeited the family luck, had felt it go out of his possession. Some men said they could see the luck, the *hamingja*, of a family or a land or a kingdom: usually a giant woman, fully-armed. Olaf had not seen that. But he had felt the luck flow out of him all the same. It was the loss of luck that had been the death of his son, Rognvald the Magnificent. His father had killed him.

Now the same father had to decide whether the sacrifice he had made had been pointless. It was the new one, the one-eye. Olaf had watched him come ashore, to be greeted by the Way and his dangerous bitch of a sister-in-law. Even from a distance, Olaf had felt the luck flowing from him. So great it was that it had overpowered the luck of the Othin-born kings of Wessex. It could easily now overpower even the destiny that Olaf had foreseen for his half-brother's family. For the future, as Olaf well knew, was not fixed. It was a matter of potentials. Sometimes the potentials could be changed.

Should he intervene? Olaf had brought the Way to Westfold many years before, respecting both its material power through new knowledge and the spiritual power of its visionaries and dreamers. With material power he had had little to do. With the mystical power, much. If he had not been a king, he could have rivaled Vigleik in visions. Except that Vigleik saw what had happened, what was happening. Olaf saw what would happen. If he could blot out the desire to do so.

Olaf reflected wordlessly on what part he would play in the morning, when the Way formed its circle, and called on him, as it would, to sit outside it, to listen and advise. If he chose to put down the one-eye, he knew, he would gain a majority and reestablish the plan to which he had sacrificed his own life and his son's. But if he did that, he would be sacrificing another future. From very far away, Olaf felt the faint tingle of a thought searching for his own, searching for what he knew and trying to pick a path out of the same tangled indications as his own. There were Christian priests as sensitive in their inquiries as himself. Yet they were too late: he already knew what they were looking for, he was closer to the balance point.

As the sun left the sky entirely, the man in the grove found his skis, walked to where the snow began out of the protecting trees, and began to snake his way down the hill. Behind him, wolf-howls rose. As his skis hissed past the outlying farms, the bonders caught sight of him and muttered to their wives. "There is the elf-king. He has been again to the stone ring, to Geir-stath, to take counsel from the gods."

CHAPTER ELEVEN

Inside the great boat-shaped hall, the priests of the Way had formed their holy circle. White cords marked it off from the outside world, with the sacred rowan-berries hanging from them—berries faded now, with the spring coming on, from their autumn scarlet. Inside the circle, more than forty priests sat together, the largest conclave any of them had ever known, drawn for the most part from Norway, where the Way was strong, but also from Denmark, from Sweden, with a few scattered converts or missionaries even from the isles of the Atlantic, from Ireland, or from Frisia where the Way had been born almost two centuries before. One even, Hund the leech, from England, accepted formally at the sponsorship of his master Ingulf the week before.

At one end of the circle stood the silver spear of Othin, at the other the burning bale-fire of Loki. By tradition, this fire, once the conclave had begun, could not be refueled: nor could conclave continue once the fire was so far dimmed that no spark could be seen in the ash.

Valgrim the Wise stood by the spear of Othin, not touching it, for no man had the right to claim it for himself, but reminding them that he was the only priest among them who dared take to himself the dangerous service of Othin. He served the God of the Hanged, Betrayer of Warriors, rather than the homelier or friendlier gods like Thor, the farmers' help, or Frey, bringer of fertility to men and animals. Ten paces behind him, almost hidden in the shadows of the shuttered hall, there stood a great chair of carved wood, with built-up sides and a canopy covered in a design of interlacing dragons. A pale face looked out from the deep shadow, the gold circle on its brow catching ruddy gleams from the Loki-fire: King Olaf, host and protector of the Way, there by invitation to observe and if need be advise, but not to vote, or speak without express request.

The shuffling of stools and muttered conversation slowly died. Valgrim let it die away, waiting for his moment: he had opposition, he knew, and needed every advantage to overbear it. The only man standing, he looked round, waited till all eyes were on him.

"The Way has come to a turning-point," he said suddenly. He waited again. "We have our first false prophet."

That is what we are here to determine, thought Thorvin. But he let Valgrim continue. Better to have the issue out in the open.

"For a hundred and fifty years the Way has spread. At first slowly, and only here in the North where the words of Duke Radbod took root. Now we begin to have followers in many places. Even followers of alien blood and language. Even followers baptized in infancy to the Christ-god. And who can doubt that this is good?

"For we must remember our aim and our purpose. Aye, and our vision. Duke Radbod saw that we who worship the true gods would be brushed aside by the Christ-god, if we did not do as his followers do: preach a word, say a message, bring news of where our spirits go to, and where they come from. And do one thing they do not do: allow all words and all messages to be spoken, not say like the Christ-priests that those who do not obey them in every respect must be tormented for ever for no sin other than disobedience.

"That was our first aim. To preserve ourselves and our peoples and our teaching against men who would destroy them all utterly. But after the aim there came the vision. I have not seen it, but there are others in this hall who have. Different men"—Valgrim looked round the circle, nodding at this face and that, showing the others that he knew exactly who he meant and that they were present to deny him if they did not agree—"different men who yet saw the same vision.

"And that vision is of another world than this one. A world where every land we know, ours among them, obeys the Christian god. But where men live like beasts on a slave's holding, so crowded that they cannot breathe, ruled by rulers they never see, sent to war like pigs to the slaughter-place. And worse things than that. Our wise men and seers call this the Skuld-world: the world that shall be—unless we stop it.

"Yet stop it we can! There is another world wise ones have seen. Aye, and this one I have seen myself"—Valgrim's gray bush of a beard nodded as he stared round. "A world so strange we see it only in fragments, and cannot understand all of those. I have seen men floating in the black of an airless sea, somewhere between the worlds, and thought at first they were the most wretched of all sinners, cast out from all the worlds because even Nithhögg could not bear to gnaw their bones. But then I saw their faces and saw that they were like men on some great adventure: and some of them men of our own blood and language, world-farers so great that any skipper alive today would be no more than a child to them. I do not know how this came about, or will come about, but I know that is the true path for true men: not the path of the Christ-fearers. So all my days I have sought new knowledge.

"One more thing I know, and that is why we must take this path besides the desire for knowledge and power and glory. That is because we are not alone."

Valgrim looked round again, trying to impress these last words, his own conviction, on men who might have agreed with everything he said so far.

"All men know that around us there are the Hidden Folk. Not dangerous to us here down in the settlements, dangerous only, it may be, to the hunters in the mountains and the children playing by the water-side. But they are not the only Hidden Folk. Somewhere out there, we know, are creatures with power to match the gods, not trolls or nixes, but the *iötnar* themselves, foes of god and man. And the Loki-brood as well, those who are not of one skin, those who walk in different shapes, half-human, half-dragon, or half-whale.

"In the end, we believe, the great day will come when gods and men on one side will battle the giants and the Hidden Folk on the other—and on that other side too there will be many men, the Christ-worshipers, the deserters. Those who have been misled. That is why Othin takes the warriors to him, to form the host that will march out from Valhalla on that day of Ragnarök. Other hosts there will be too, from Thruthvangar for Thor and Himinbiorg for Heimdall, and from all the others, sailors and ski-runners and leeches and bowmen. But Othin's host will be the greatest and the hardiest, and most hope of victory lies in it.

"We dare not divide our hosts. The battle is not yet certain. If the Way takes the wrong path now, we will be divided and lost. I say that the one-eyed Englishman who carries the Othin-spear and yet does no homage to Othin, I say that he is the false prophet leading us on the false path. We must reject him now to fulfill our true destiny: which is to hail the One King, the One King whom our prophecies say will come to us from the North. The One King who will change the world and bring victory instead of defeat on the day of Ragnarök.''

Valgrim ceased, and settled the spear-pendant firmly on his broad chest. He waited for the denial he knew would come.

It came from a quarter he had hoped would support him. Vigleik of the many visions stirred on his stool, looked down at the unusual emblem he bore, the bowl of Suttung the mead-guardian, bringer of inspiration, and spoke.

"What you say of visions may be true, Valgrim, but while what we see is one thing, what we understand of it is another. Now I have said this to you before, and if you cannot deny it you must tell me what it means. We know our brother Farman saw the one-eyed English-man—saw him when he had two eyes. Saw him in vision in Asgarth, home of the gods, and set in the place of Völund, lame smith of the gods. And Farman saw All-Father speak to him. None of us has seen this of any other mortal man. So why should I not think that this man has a divine destiny?''

Valgrim nodded. "I know your visions are true, Vigleik, and Farman's also. You saw the death of the tyrants last month, and news has come through on the trade-ships since, that you saw the truth. So the one-eye may have been seen as Völund. But just as you say, seeing is one thing and understanding is another. Now what does the story of Völund tell us?''

He looked round again, sure his audience was with him, all keenly interested in the story of their sacred myths. "We all know that Völund's wife was a swan-maiden, but that after she left him he was taken by Nithhad, king of the Njar-folk. Nithhad desired his craft as a smith, but feared his escape, so he cut his hamstrings with a knife and set him to work in the smithy at Saevarstath. And there what did Völund do?''

Valgrim's voice fell into the deep chant of the Way-priests:
"He sat, he did not sleep, he struck with the hammer.
Always he crafted the cunning thing for Nithhad.

"He made him fine bracelets and necklaces of gold and gems. He made him bowls for his ale and cunning runners for his sledges. He made him swords that would cut linen by sharpness and anvils by strength. But when Nithhad's two young boys came to see the marvels, what did he do? He lured them into his smithy, promised to show them fine things, showed them a chest.''

Again Valgrim's voice turned to the chant:
"They came to the chest, they craved the key.

It was malice they opened when they peeped in.

"He killed them, he buried their bodies under the forge, of their teeth he made necklaces, goblets of their skulls, brooches of their shining eyeballs. Gave them all to Nithhad. And when Nithhad's daughter came to him to mend a ring, what did he do? Stupefied her with beer, raped her, thrust her out.

"She told her father, weeping. He came to Völund to take his head. And Völund, his hamstrings severed—he put on the wings he had made in the smithy, and flew away. What was the cunning thing he had made for Nithhad? It was his revenge. For that is his name, Völund. From the cunning thing, *vel*."

The conclave sat silent, pondering the story they all knew. "Now I ask you," said Valgrim, "who is the hero of this story? Völund for his cunning, as we are told? Or Nithhad for his attempt to restrain it? I tell you, Vigleik, where this Englishman is concerned, he is Völund, right enough. And we are Nithhad! He will kill our sons and rape our daughters. That is to say, he will deny us our own issue and turn us into creatures to breed his getting for him. Nithhad made only one mistake, which was to try to use Völund's skill and think he was safe when he was only lamed. He should have killed him and made sure work! For men like Völund or the Englishman are not safe when they are crippled. For they are like Völund's wife, the swan-maiden: they are not men of one skin. But it is not a swan that the Englishman turns into, on the other side. Rather, a dragon, or a mound-dweller, a mold-man. Hagbarth, I ask you: did you not report that he said *he had been in a mound before*?"

The hall stirred with excitement and appreciation at Valgrim's unexpected explanation. They saw Hagbarth nod slowly, reluctantly confirming what Valgrim had said.

Thorvin broke out in reply, as Valgrim had known he would. "This is all well enough, Valgrim, but you are only twisting words. Of course the lad had been in a mound before—he took the old king's treasure from it. He dug his way in with a mattock and fought his way out, like a hero. He did not *live* in one. If Viga-Brand were here he would mock you for saying he should have left the money in the ground. I ask all here, look beyond words. Look at actions. Shef Sigvarthsson, give him his proper name, he turned a whole country to the Way. He drove out the Christ-church. If he let Christ-priests stay, it was only as if they were any of us, made to pay their own way and work for their own believers. He killed Ivar Ragnarsson. And is there any doubt that he is a seeker for knowledge, who will give up anything for that knowledge?"

Thorvin raised his hand for silence. "If you do not believe me, listen."

Outside, not far away, the priests could hear a familiar sound, but not one they had expected to hear with all of them in conclave. Across the precincts of the college, across the old, much-trodden snow, there came the clink-clink of the heavy hammer, dimly over it the roaring of forced draught from a bellows. Men working at the forge.

At the forge, Shef had just completed the careful reforging and re-tempering of the sword he had given Karli. Now it was set aside to cool, before reassembly of blade, guard, hilt and pommel. Now Udd had taken over. The little man was conducting a demonstration. He stood to one side of the fire, directing, while Shef, stripped to his breeches and a protective leather overall, handled the pieces of iron and steel with tongs. Cwicca crouched on one knee, pumping the leather bellows that fed the draught to the charcoal-glowing forge. The rest of the English catapulteers, seven of them, Hama, Osmod and the others, with Karli making an eighth, squatted on their heels along the wall, enjoying the warmth and adding their comments.

"Right," said Udd. "They're all red-hot. Take the first spike and lay it down to one side."

Shef took a red-hot iron spike, the raw material for a dagger or spear-head, and laid it carefully across the mouth of a pottery bowl, not letting it touch the still-frozen earth of the floor.

"Take the next one and put it straight away into the snow-water."

Shef lifted it with the tongs and plunged the red-hot metal into a leather bucket full of barely-melted snow, gathered a few minutes before from outside. A cloud of steam rose with violent hissings.

"When the metal's cold, take it out and bend it between your hands."

Shef waited a minute or two, plucked the spike out, felt it gingerly to make sure there was no residual heat. Bent it between his hands. He had a good idea of what would happen, but was content to let Udd make his demonstration his own way. As the muscles stood out on Shef's forearm, the metal spike suddenly snapped in two.

"Now try the other one."

Shef handled this one, still warm even in the chilly air, with rags. This time he needed no force. The metal bent in his hands like wire, remained bent without any sign of springing even after he let it go.

"Same metal," lectured Udd. "If you quench it, it gets hard and brittle—takes a good edge, but no strength. But if you just cool it, it bends. Neither hard nor strong."

"As much use as an old man's dick," said a catapulteer companionably.

"More use than yours," retorted Karli.

"Shut up," said Udd, bold only in the making of steel. "Now, Shef, my lord that is to say. Take the bent one. Bend it straight again. Put it back in the fire and heat it red-hot once more.

"Now, quench it." Again the hissing and the cloud of steam. "Return it to the fire. But this time, don't let it get red-hot. Heat it gently—slow down on the bellows there, Cwicca. Let it get to the color of straw."

Udd peered over with near-sighted anxiety. "Now, that's enough. Take that out and let it cool slowly."

Shef followed instructions, this time more unsure of what would happen. As a working smith, he knew well the virtues of quenching and the dangers of annealing. His way of combining the qualities of strength, hardness and suppleness, however, had always been to work different grades of metal together in strips. The thought of going back to a strip once annealed had never occurred to him. Nor did he see the significance of the third gentle heating. As the metal cooled he looked with satisfaction at the returning blisters on his hands. They had got too soft while he had played at being a king.

"All right," said Udd. "Now try it."

Shef picked up the iron spike and bent it in his hands. It flexed powerfully, giving but then striving to regain its shape.

"This is how you made the crossbow strips," he remarked.

"In a way, lord, yes. But this is different." Udd's voice dropped with a kind of reverence. "This iron is the best I have ever seen. The ore it comes from takes half—a quarter—of the working we are used to. How long does it take a forge to make ten pounds of iron in England?"

"Two days," suggested Shef.

"Here you would get forty in the same time for the same labor. That is one reason the Vikings are so well-armed, I think. Their iron is better. It costs far less time and charcoal to make. So every man can have iron tools and weapons, not just the rich. The iron comes from Jarnberaland, far to the east across the mountains. The Way-folk say they have a mine there and men to run it.

"But there is still more we have discovered, lord."

In the heart of the forge there lay a pile of what appeared to be ash. Using long tongs, Udd hauled it out, dragged it onto the earthen floor, briskly swept away the covering cinders to reveal a metal plate.

"This has been in the fire for hours, since last night. I have kept the fire going all that time, while the rest of you were snoring."

"Karli wasn't snoring, he was out after women."

"Shut up, Fritha. It is a plate made like the spike, by cooling, and then quenching, and reheating, so it was strong and springy. Then I heated it again and kept it in the fire. And all the time it was in the fire, I kept piling the charcoal round it. Now lord, when it has cooled, I want you to thrust it with your spear, with the great spear you took from the Snake-eye."

Shef raised an eyebrow. The 'Gungnir' spear's massive head was made of the best steel he had ever seen. The plate Udd had been working on was perhaps an eighth of an inch thick, the thickness of the metal guard that protected a warrior's hand in the center of a shield. Much thicker and the shield would be too heavy to move easily. But Shef had no doubt the steel spear-head would punch straight through.

As the plate cooled, Udd set it up directly against the wooden logs of the forge wall. "Strike now, master."

Shef stepped back, balanced the shaft, imagined he had in front of him a deadly enemy. He stepped forward onto the left foot, swung body, arm and shoulder, trying to strike through plate and wall to a space a foot behind both, as Brand had often taught him.

The shaft jarred in his hands, sprang back. Incredulously, Shef looked at the thin plate. Unmarked. Undented. He looked again at the needle-point of 'Gungnir'. For half an inch the triangular point had been punched flat.

"That's hardened steel," said Udd flatly. "I thought it would be good stuff for mail. But I found you can't work it. It's unbendable. But if you made the mail, and then hardened it . . ."

"Or if you made thin plates like this and then just sewed them on . . ."

In the considering silence one of the catapulteers remarked, "What I don't see is how it all comes from the same stuff. Some's hard and brittle, some's soft and bendy, some's springy, some's so hard you can't scratch it. What makes the difference? Is it something in the water?"

"Some of the Vikings think that," said Udd. "They believe it's best to use a slave's blood for the final temper."

The ex-slaves looked at each other, reflecting on fates they had missed.

"Or some try oil. There may be some sense in that. All this steam. You've seen sweat jump off a hot blade? Well, water tries to get away from hot metal, and when you're quenching you don't want it to get away. So oil might be better.

"But I don't think it's that. It's the heating and cooling that do it. And I think it's something to do with the charcoal as well. If you can keep the metal touching the coal, something passes between them. That's my belief."

Shef walked to the door, stared out across the snow to the fjord and the islands lying in it, still trapped in thick ice. Out there on one of the furthest islands, he knew, was the queen he had seen on his first arrival, Queen Ragnhild, with her son, her husband away seeing to his taxes in the Eastfold. Out there on the island they called Drottningsholm, Queen Island. He watched his breath condensing in the frosty air, and wondered about sweat on iron, iron sizzling in the water-bucket, men blowing on their hands to warm them, steam rising from hot bodies in cold air. What was steam, he wondered?

Two men were carrying a bucket towards him across the snow, slung between them on a pole. There was something strange about that. You would expect slaves to be given a task of that kind, but those men were not slaves: too tall, too well-dressed, swords at their belts. Behind him Shef could hear Cwicca ordering Karli to the bellows and taking a turn at following Udd's instructions. Through the inexpert beating of the hammer he could hear the faint squeak of leather shoes on snow.

The men reached the forge door, set their bucket down carefully. Shef found himself, as so often with these Norwegians, looking up to meet their eyes.

"I am Stein, of the guard of Queen Ragnhild," said one of them.

"I did not know guards carried buckets," observed Shef.

Stein scowled. The noise at the forge had ceased as the men inside heard conversation, and Shef knew they were crowding into the doorway, ready to support their leader if needed.

"This is a special bucket," said Stein, mastering his temper. "A gift from the queen to you, the Ivarsbane. It is winter-ale. Do you know what that is, southerner? We brew our strongest ale, and then in the hardest of the frost we set our vats outside. The water in the ale freezes, we break the ice off the top and throw it away. The longer you do it, the more water the ale loses, and the stronger is what remains. It is a drink for heroes—like you, if you are the slayer of Ivar."

Stein's expression showed doubt, increasing as Cwicca and the others jostled their way out to peer into the tawny liquid. Not one of the Englishmen was less than head and shoulders shorter than the two Norsemen, and even the stocky Karli was dwarfed.

Stein fumbled at his belt. "The queen told me also to say this. The drink is for you and your men, as you choose. But the queen said you came ashore with nothing, so she sent you a cup. The cup is for you alone. For you alone."

He freed what he had been carrying and passed it over. Shef turned it over in his hands, surprised. From the way Stein talked he had expected a goblet of gold or silver, something precious. Instead it was a plain mug of hollowed beechwood, such as any churl might drink from. As he turned it over he saw marks on the bottom. Runes. A message.

His errand done, Stein turned away with his companion, not waiting for thanks. Shef recovered himself, called to his own companions. "All right, let's get that inside where it's warm. Fritha, run down to the hut and get your mugs and a ladle if you can find one. Let's at least have a drink. And Udd, heat up a couple of spikes, we can mull this ale and see what it's like hot. Just the thing for this country. Hama, get on the bellows for him, Osmod, get some more fuel for the fire."

As the ex-slaves bustled round, Shef stepped into the cool bright sunlight to read the scratched runes. They were in the Norse style he had learned from Thorvin, but unfamiliar in some ways. Slowly he puzzled out their sense.

"*Bru er varthat, en iss er thykkr,*" they read. "The bridge is guarded, but the ice is thick."

What bridge? Shef looked out again over the fjord. Out there the islands lay in the dense ice. Now he looked for them, he could see thin strips running from one island to the next: long lines of logs, set in the water each autumn and allowed to freeze there. The furthest island out was Drottningsholm. She had said he would come to her when she called him. And now she had. Shef realized Karli was watching him with a raised eyebrow. For him alone, she had said. But if he were to go prowling like a tomcat, it might be best to take an experienced companion.

In the hall of conclave, tempers were running high. The higher because everyone there knew they would soon have to make a final decision. The bale-fire had long since fallen from a blaze to a glow, and now in the darkening hall only a few embers shone out. The fire might not be refueled, nor the conclave continue once no spark could be seen.

"So what is it you propose?" said Valgrim to Thorvin. As the debate had gone on, the two men had emerged as leaders of factions, increasingly speaking against each other. With Thorvin were the majority of the priests of Thor, of Njörth and of Ithun, practical men with clear skills to which they were devoted, smithcraft, seamanship and shipbuilding, medicine and surgery. These men appreciated the advances and the experiments that Shef's Way-kingdom had made, and were eager to continue on that path. Thorvin's followers also included the alien priests, the Frisians, those whose native language was not Norse. Against him were Valgrim, the one priest of Othin, and the majority of the priests of Frey, along with those of Ull, Heimdall, Tyr and the lesser gods. Devotion to them was strongest in Norway itself, and among the least-traveled or most-isolated of the followers of the Way.

"Let the lad return to England," said Thorvin promptly. "Take as many of us as we can with him. Make his kingdom there the strongest in the North, a place where we can recruit wealth and followers. From it, set up our challenge to the Christ-god. Never before have we taken followers from him, always his priests have crept into our lands to steal followers from us. Let us support this, the first true success we have had.

"And what is your proposal, Valgrim?"

The big man replied as promptly. "Hang him on a tree as a sacrifice to Othin. Fit out the greatest fleet we can, with the assistance of King Halvdan and King Olaf, and go down to take over his kingdom before the English know what has become of him. Then do as you say, Thorvin. Only with the priests of the Way in charge, not some unknown foundling."

"If you hang him on a tree you reject the messenger of the gods!"

"He cannot be the messenger of the gods. He is not a Norseman, not even a Dane. Most of all, Thorvin, even you have admitted it. He may wear a pendant, he may see visions, but he has no belief. He is not a true believer!"

"You talk like a Christian!"

Valgrim's face purpled, and he started to stride towards Thorvin, who slipped his hand down the haft of his ceremonial hammer. As the other priests started to rise from their stools, to come between the two men, another voice cut through the chill air, one that had not spoken during the angry debate: that of Vigleik of the visions.

"You spoke of fitting out a fleet, Valgrim, and you of setting up a kingdom, Thorvin. Maybe it is time, before the bale-fire goes out, to call on the advice of a king and a commander. You have heard our words, King Olaf Elf-of-Geirstath. What wisdom do you have for us?"

The figure in the carved chair rose to his feet and walked forward to the very perimeter of the corded circle. His face was grave, lined with care. In it there was something of the air of majesty: none, though, of the air of instant decision seen in every Viking jarl or skipper, let alone king. His eyes seemed to look through what was in front of them, to some event or chance beyond.

"Have I leave to speak?" asked Olaf. He waited for the growled assent of the conclave. "Then I have this to say, having heard all that has been said here on both sides.

"All of you know, I think, though you may not wish to say it to my face, that I am a man who has lost his luck. The luck of his family. I can tell you that I did not lose it, nor give it away. I only knew that it would go, and then that it had gone. I am different from other men only that I knew it, instead of finding out much later, or never. I know a great deal about luck.

"Some men will tell you that the luck of a family, the *hamingja* as we say, is like a giant-woman fully-armed, that the lucky can see as they see the spirits of the land. There are stories of men who saw their guardian-spirit leave them and go to another. They may be true. But that is not what I saw. Truly I saw nothing—except the dream of the great tree of which you have doubtless heard.

"What I felt was like the feeling in the air before the lightning-flash. I knew the flash would come, I knew it would go from me to another. I knew that that other was of the line of my brother. When I was young I thought it was my brother Halvdan. Now I know it was not. Till a few days ago I thought it was my brother's son Harald, whom they call Fairhair.

"Now I am not sure again. For again I have the feeling, the feeling before the flash. It comes to me that luck is going to shift again, to pass out of my line altogether—and maybe to the young man Shef."

The listeners stirred, and Valgrim's faction eyed each other doubtfully.

"Yet I was wrong before, over Halvdan. Maybe I am wrong again. But not, I think, wholly. As I grow old it seems to me more and more that luck is not a thing that one has or has not, like youth or strength. It is more like light, where a lesser light remains what it was, but cannot be seen any longer when a greater light outshines it. Like a candle still burning in a sunlit room. Except that maybe the greater light steals light from the lesser even, even puts it out.

"I have heard the history of the young man Shef. He brought bad luck to his own king Jatmund. He did not quail before the luck of Ivar. He was rescued, they tell me, by one of the god-born, the king Alfred, descended from Othin. Soon after the rescue that king was a beggar, to be rescued in his turn. I think this young man draws the luck from others. Where he comes, luck goes. He may take it even from my own blood, where I thought the luck of Norway rested—where it did rest, till you brought him here to challenge it."

"All this is mere talk," rumbled Valgrim. "We must have proof."

"Proof comes from a test. Let us test his luck against the luck of Harald and Halvdan, against the queens Asa and Ragnhild."

"How do we do that?"

"Agree to the test and I will tell you. But agree quickly, before the bale-fire goes out."

The forty priests looked at the tiny glowing spark that was all that was left, muttered together. Then, slowly, both Thorvin and Valgrim nodded their agreement. As a Tyr-priest knelt down and blew gently on the last remaining ember, King Olaf began to speak. Before he had finished, Valgrim was already shaking his head in dissatisfaction.

"Too unsure," he growled. "I need a clearer sign."

"You may get a clearer sign than you wish, Valgrim. I spoke of light and luck. There is another way to see it. Some of you believe that all our lives are spun by the three spinners, Urth, Verthandi and Skuld. But they spin not single threads, rather a great web, the threads crossing over each other. Where the threads cross each other, they fray! Beware the man with a strong life-thread, Valgrim. Especially if that thread crosses yours."

Vigleik stirred himself to speak. "I have seen the Spinners," he said. "Their loom-weights are skulls, their shuttles are swords and spears, their web is human gut."

"That is in the Skuld-world," said Thorvin flatly. "That is what we mean to change."

CHAPTER TWELVE

The two men crept cautiously through the dark woods to the edge of the ice. The snow had hampered them badly, lying in uneven drifts in the hollows and forcing them to push through the tangled fir-branches. Yet they had not dared to use the paths through the woods—anyone who saw them might have challenged them, and while they were not forbidden to move around at night, they had no wish to cause stir or comment. Karli had grumbled steadily at first as snow fell from the trees and crawled down his neck, repeating that he knew plenty of places where they could find friendly women without all this trouble. But as Shef pushed on Karli had fallen silent, accepting the expedition as one of the strange preferences for a particular woman that even the sanest of men might have. It would be an exploit, after all, he told himself, to seduce a queen. Maybe there would even be a princess for himself.

Where the wood ran down to the ice, the snow stopped, brushed away by the wind, or melted by the sunlight that got through the fringes of the fir-trees during the lengthening days. Shef and Karli walked forward more easily and stood for a few moments looking out at the scene, considering their course.

They had made a circle away from the college and the town behind it, and were now on the end of a long point jutting out on the western side of the bay. On the far side of the bay, maybe a quarter-mile off, were the chain of islands that led to Drottningsholm. There was no moon, and the sky was covered by thick cloud driven on by a strong wind from the south-west, but even so they could see the tree-covered island nearest the shore standing out black against the mirk of the sea and sky. Just visible as a black streak was the long line of logs which led from mainland to island. They could not see the guard-posts at either end, but there was no doubt they were there. The question was, could the guards see two men silhouetted against the ice?

"The wind has swept the snow off," Shef whispered to Karli. "We won't stand out against the white."

"But why isn't the ice white too?" Karli replied.

Both men knelt and looked closely at the ice-cover in front of them. It seemed black and forbidding, yet still thick as cathedral walls. There was no give in it, clearly frozen still all the way down to the mud at the bottom. Shef stepped out cautiously, jumped up and down in his leather-soled boots. Both men had tied rawhide round their footwear for better grip and less noise.

"It's solid. We can do it. And if the ice is black, better for us."

Cautiously, both stepped out and began to walk gingerly across the ice to the center of the island before them. Both crouched, as if that would make them harder to see. At each step they planted their feet carefully and delicately, as if the ice might shatter beneath them at a sudden shock. Every now and then one or the other would tense, thinking he felt the first shiver that would mean thin ice. Then they plodded on again. Shef had his spear in one hand, the point carefully beaten and filed out once again to needle-sharpness. Karli had taken the wooden sword-scabbard from his belt, frightened to trip over it, and now held sword and scabbard together in both hands, as if it were a balance-pole.

As the island drew nearer both men began to breathe more freely. At the same time the sense of exposure grew on them. The trees ahead were a dark menace, they themselves out on the flat without a vestige of cover. Sense told them that the black night and low clouds covered them, that there was no light in the sky to pick them out. Nevertheless, if they could see the island, surely the island could see them. As they came up to the shore, they both accelerated their pace, darted instantly into the shadow of the trees.

They sat for a while, hearts thumping, waiting for noise of movement or challenge. Nothing came. Only the steady hiss of the wind in the trees.

Shef turned to Karli, muttered, "We'll go round the edge of this island, keeping to the ice by the shore. When we see the next bridge ahead of us we'll decide what to do about it."

For some minutes they shuffled warily round the edge of the island. Once they caught a whiff of wood-smoke and stood stock-still. But the trees remained unbroken, not even a cottager's landing-stage jutting out into the water. They shuffled on.

The bridge to the next island almost caught them by surprise. They shuffled round a small spit of land, and saw it in front of them, not twenty yards off, and plain to see, two tall men leaning on their javelins. Could even hear their muttered conversation. Quickly the two intruders pulled back into shelter.

"What we ought to do," whispered Shef, "is make a detour out to sea, to keep well away from them."

"Don't fancy that," muttered Karli. "I want to keep where the ice is thick."

"If the ice wasn't thick enough, she wouldn't have told us to take it."

"Women are funny. And she could be wrong. Anyway she's not out here with fifty feet of cold water under her."

Shef reflected for a moment. "Let's try this, then. We'll start from here, and go parallel with the bridge, where the water's shallowest and the ice thickest. But we won't walk, we'll crawl. Keep right down, there's not so much for them to see. Anyway, they're watching the path, not the ice."

As they set out, crawling awkwardly in their heavy clothing, beards skimming the ice, Karli began to wonder. If the ice is so thick, why are these Norwegians only guarding the bridges? Why are they guarded at all? Are these people just stupid? Or does the queen . . . ?

His friend was yards in front of him and moving like an angry adder. No time for debate. And the ice seemed thick as ever. Karli crawled quickly behind, trying not to eye the seeming safety of the log-bridge twenty yards off.

As soon as they reached the second island both men crawled to the side away from the bridge, slithered round behind another of the many tiny spurs jutting out from the shore, stood up and bolted once more into the cover of the trees, breathing hard. The cold of the ice had bitten through their layers of wool and leather. They put their weapons down carefully, pulled off the sheepskin mittens Brand had given them, blew on frozen hands. Carefully Shef eased a leather bottle from its belt-sling, pulled out its stopper.

"Winter ale," he muttered. "The last of it."

Each took a long pull. "Tastes like ale," muttered Karli, "but it doesn't feel like it. You can feel your gullet glowing as it goes down, no matter how cold it is. Shame we can't make this stuff where we come from."

Shef nodded, thinking again for a moment of water freezing on ale, of steam leaping from a hot blade. No time to pursue that thought.

"Drottningholm's the next island," he said. "We know the king isn't there, and that no men are allowed to sleep overnight on it. One more crossing . . ."

"And we're like two cocks in the hen-roost," completed Karli.

"At least we can see what the queen wants from us."

I know what she wants from *you*, thought Karli, but kept silent. Slowly, they worked their way round the shore of the second island.

The bridge this time was easy to spot, but well away from the point where they caught their first sight of Drottningsholm. They stood in the trees, looking across and calculating the odds. They were on the western point of another small bay, Drottningsholm perhaps a furlong off. The eastern point was another furlong away, and the bridge ran from its tip to the further island.

"Just as easy to start from here as go over near the bridge," said Shef. "And we won't need to crawl. We're far enough away so no-one will see us from the guard-post, and we'll be getting further away all the time."

"All right," said Karli. "I guess if the ice was going to break, it would have broken by now. We've seen no holes in it. It hasn't creaked or anything."

Shef gripped his shoulder, took his spear in both hands, and set out across the flat, black, windswept expanse.

"All right, where is he?" Brand stood in the doorway of the fetid communal hut, glowering down at the eight Englishmen facing him. He had been drinking worriedly in a tavern in the port of Kaupang with Guthmund and their crews, when he had been called away by news that the Way-priests' conclave had ended. After a brief interview with Thorvin he had headed straight for the quarters Shef shared with Karli, now treated as his bodyservant. Found both missing, and headed on to the catapulteers' hut.

Faced with an angry man nearer seven feet high than six, the ex-slaves reverted to servile custom. With imperceptible shuffles they moved into a tight group with at its front Osmod and Cwicca, the burliest and most self-confident of them. Their faces took on a look of stony ignorance.

"Where's who?" said Osmod, playing for time.

Brand's enormous fists opened and closed. "Where—is—your— master—Shef?"

"Don't know," said Cwicca. "Ain't he in his quarters?"

Brand took a step forward, murder in his eye, paused as he saw Osmod, once captain of the halberdiers, cast a quick glance towards a rack of weapons. He turned, marched out, slamming the door.

Outside Hund, Shef's childhood friend, now a faithful priest of Ithun, stood patiently in the crusty snow. "They won't talk to me," Brand snarled. "You're English. They know you're his friend. See if you can find out what's up."

Hund stepped into the hut. A murmur of voices, all talking English in the thick Norfolk dialect common to them all. Finally Hund appeared, beckoned Brand once more into the hut.

"They say they don't know for sure," he translated. "But putting one thing and another together, they're fairly sure he got a message of some sort. They suspect that he has gone to visit the queen Ragnhild at Drottningsholm. He has taken Karli with him."

Brand goggled. "Gone to Drottningsholm? But no man's allowed on the island overnight. And the bridges are all guarded."

Cwicca grinned, his gap teeth showing. "That's all right, skipper," he said in the Anglo-Norse pidgin of the Wayman army in England. "We're not so dumb. We know that. If he's gone, he'll have slipped across on the ice, see? We went down and had a little look this afternoon. It's still plenty thick enough, no sign of cracking."

Brand stared at Cwicca and the others, horror evident on his face. He tried to speak, failed, tried again.

"Don't you English fools know anything?" he said in a hoarse whisper. "In the fjords this time of year, the ice doesn't crack. It rots from the bottom up. Fills with water. Then one morning it isn't there any more. It doesn't crack. It just sinks!"

The wind struck them with redoubled force as soon as Shef and Karli were well out on their last stretch of ice, as if they had come out from under the lee of some unseen headland. With it came a whirl of horizontal, driving rain. Shef flinched as the first drops struck his face, expecting stinging hail or ice-storm. Then he put his hand up to the drops that trickled down his face, and wondered. Rain. So the frost had broken. Would they be able to get back, once across? No time to worry about that now. And in the rain they had no need to fear being seen by the bridge-guards.

"Listen," he said to Karli. "I don't like this rain. The ice may crack. We can both swim. The thing to do, if it cracks under us, is keep your head up. Don't get caught under the ice and not know which way to turn. If we're in a hole in the ice, swim to the edge of it and put your weight on the ice. If it cracks, go forward and try again. When we get to somewhere thick enough to bear us, crawl out and keep crawling. And Karli, tuck your sword in your belt again. You may need two hands."

As Karli fumbled to obey, moved by some impulse, Shef looked up at the dark shore still a hundred yards in front, hefted the 'Gungnir' spear in his hand, trotted two paces forward, turned and hurled the spear ahead of him. He saw it streak forward, land, and skid on along the ice, its clatter drowned by the hiss of the rain.

As his foot came down he felt the ice give. Both men stood motionless for a moment, listening for the crack. Nothing. Still ice under their feet.

"Maybe it just came loose from the shore," muttered Karli.

They stepped on, cautiously, planting their feet with utter delicacy. One step. Two.

Cold bit into Shef's boot as he put it down. Water. A puddle on the ice? Water in the other boot. Suddenly the cold was at his knees, his thighs, he felt his vitals retract convulsively. Shef stared round for the break in the ice, but there was nothing there, his feet were still planted solidly but the ice was dropping beneath . . .

The black water closed over Shef's head and he found himself struggling desperately to stay afloat. There were hands round his neck, clutching from behind, hands like Ivar's, as if Ivar were back from the dead.

Shef turned furiously inside Karli's panic clutch till they were face to face, brought his hands up together inside Karli's embrace, joined them and swung them down edge first on the bridge of Karli's nose. Reared up out of the water and swung again, felt gristle give beneath the blow. Reared up to swing again, felt the strangling clutch release.

"Sorry, all right, I'm all right." Karli let go and began to tread water. Shef realized at once the furious bite of the water. He had swum in cold water often enough, in the fens, for sport or to cross where there was no bridge. This was different. The cold had bitten through every garment he wore, filled them all, was draining the strength from his body with every instant that passed, the cold and the waterlogged wool and leather both combining to drag him down into the mud.

And he had lost any sense of direction. Shef thrust his body out of the water as high as he could manage, twisting his one eye round to see if he could see the island, or the other shore, or ice still solid to swim towards. Nothing. Nothing.

Or there? Was that a deeper black in the night? He caught the shape of Drottningsholm against the sky, seized Karli's shoulder, dragged him in the right direction. Both men began to strike out with the strength of panic, first with a clumsy overarm stroke, then as their sodden clothes pulled them down with a gasping short-armed breast-stroke. Their legs trailed under them. Kick your boots off, thought Shef. They always say, kick your boots off. But mine are laced with rawhide, and anyway. Anyway it's too cold. I have to get out or die.

The first touch of mud under his feet made him try to stand immediately, and his head sank instantly beneath the surface. He pulled himself up, flailed again overarm till he felt mud beneath his belly. Staggered up, felt his feet slide from under him, seized a tree-root on the shore and dragged himself forward and out. From behind came a gasp, feeble splashing. Shef marked the helpful root, turned, plunged back into the water, seized Karli and dragged him by main force the last few yards to shore. With one hand he grabbed the root again, twined the other in Karli's curly hair and shot him forward onto the freezing beach. Both men rose gasping and choking to their knees.

As they did so Shef knew for certain that if they did nothing they would die there of cold, in less time than it would take a careless priest to say a Mass. The water had burned like fire. Now they were out in the air the cold was even worse. Already he had little sensation across his body, the feeling of bitter pain was going, he felt a pleasant relaxation pulling him down.

"Strip," he snarled to Karli. "Get your clothes off. Wring them out."

His own hands fumbled at the toggles of his coat, seemed unable to find them. Karli had somehow got his sword out of his belt and out of his scabbard, was sawing at his own fastenings. He passed it to Shef, who dropped it from numb hands. For moments, a desperate silent struggle in the dark as they peeled off layer after layer. Naked at last, they were flayed by the wind, doubled over. But the rain flurry had gone, the harsh wind dried them in seconds. Shef groped for his tunic, wrung it out, doubled it and wrung it out again, driving out the half-frozen salt slush. As he struggled into it again, for an instant he felt an illusion of comparative warmth.

Pure illusion. They would still die here on the shore before daybreak. But at least a moment to think.

As Shef groped for his breeches, he saw movement in the trees. Not men. Too low down for the queen's guards. Wolf-shapes creeping closer, belly-down, lips already drawn back over snarling teeth. But not wolves. The queen's wolfhounds, bought at fabulous prices from the market in Dublin, and turned loose each night for her safety.

Only the water's edge saved the two men in their first rush, for the men backed into it by some primeval instinct, and the dogs could not come at them from all sides. As the big leader ran silently in, Karli, sword snatched up, swung a violent blow at its head. The edge turned as it connected, still gripped in inexpert hands, and the dog seized Karli's wrist in its jaws.

It had seized a fighter of instant reflex, poor swordsman though he was. In a moment Karli had thrust his left thumb deep into its eye, shaken it off, mad with pain, and thrust the sword into Shef's hands, snarling incoherently. Shef met his first attacker with a barefooted kick in the throat. As it came back for a leap at his groin he snatched the sword, dropped the point, and spitted its heart as it sprang.

The pain-crazed leader had seized another dog in its jaws and the two were rolling over and over in a snarling tangle. Padding round them a fourth animal the size of a calf gathered itself and made a leap for Karli's throat. He met it as he would a rough-and-tumble fighter in the brawls of the Ditmarsh, dropping his head instantly to butt it in the teeth, hooking with both hands at its body, trying to break ribs, rupture liver. The dog fell back, off balance, caught itself and poised for a second spring.

As it did so Shef leaned across and swept off one foreleg at the knee-joint, flashed the point in the muzzle of the dog that was threatening him, cut forehand at the dogfight still going on a yard away and instantly backhand at the last dog springing forward. Don't go for the kill, he thought. Take the easy maim instead. Dogs are safer than men for you only have their jaws to worry about.

One wolfhound was down dead, another hobbling off on three legs. The half-blind leader, further disabled by a slash on the side, had had its throat torn out by the dog it had attacked. That animal was backing off, disconcerted, a low rumble in its throat as warning, but not ready to continue the fight. Only one hound still faced them, teeth showing, lunging a few inches forward and then backing off again as it eyed the menace of the sword-point. Karli, bleeding now from both head and wrist, scrabbled in the water for a rock, dragged one out and hurled it furiously at three feet range. Struck on the shoulder, the dog whuffed indignantly, turned and streaked into the shadows.

The two half-naked men staggered again towards their clothes, groped in the freezing pile of wool and leather, struggled again to wring them out and get them on. As the adrenalin of the fight faded,

Shef realized that he had no movement left in his fingers at all. He could use them as hooks, but tying a lace or fastening a belt was beyond him.

Slowly he wrapped his fingers round the sword-hilt again, knelt by the body of the dog he had spitted. Drove the point deep into its belly and sawed feebly downwards. A rank smell of punctured gut and coils of pale intestine pushing their way out. Shef dropped the sword, pushed his frozen hands into the body cavity and groped for the creature's heart.

A dog's body temperature is higher than a human's. The still-hot blood poured over Shef's fingers like liquid fire, seemed to run up his body. He thrust his arms deeper into the body cavity, up to the elbows, wishing he could crawl entirely inside. Karli, seeing what he had done and why, hobbled painfully over and fumblingly followed his example.

As sensation came back, Shef withdrew, pulled on his wet but no longer dripping breeches, fastened the belt, clambered into his water-sodden leather coat. His woolen hat was somewhere in the waters of the fjord, the sheepskin mittens lost in the darkness. Against his warmed hands, his feet felt like blocks of ice. Slice open another dog? Short of absolute necessity, he could not make himself do it. Clumsily he tipped water from his boots, thrust his feet inside, feeling as if the toes might break off at any moment. He made no effort to refasten the cut thongs on boots or coat.

"What do we do now?" asked Karli. He passed Shef the sword, holding on to the wooden scabbard as a makeshift club.

"We came to see the queen," said Shef.

Karli opened his mouth to reply, then closed it. The woman had trapped them, that was obvious. Unless maybe it was her husband all along. He had known deceits like that before. But the queen's hall and its outbuildings were the only shelter on this island. If they did not have shelter and fire they would be dead before dawn. Karli plodded after Shef through the fir-thickets, hoping to stumble on a path. He had hoped for a princess. He would settle now for a friendly drab, any draggletail housemaid with a fire and a blanket in a corner.

In the endmost room of the queen's hall at Drottningsholm, two women sat facing each other from either side of a glowing fire. Each sat straight-backed in a hard wooden chair, each glittered with ornaments, each had the air of a woman rarely refused, and never safely. Other than that they were dissimilar. They had hated each other from the moment of first meeting.

Queen Asa, widow and murderess of King Guthroth, mother of King Halvdan, had centered all her hopes on her boy. But as soon as he grew beyond infancy he had feared and distrusted her. Had she not killed his father? In youth he had pursued women as had his father and in contempt of his mother, in manhood he had turned Viking and spent every summer on campaign, every winter planning the next or consolidating the last. Disappointment had withered Asa, turned her brown, shriveled and cruel.

Queen Ragnhild, wife of King Halvdan, had no liking for her mother-in-law or the son whose bed she occasionally shared. Often she wondered whom she would have chosen for herself, if her father had been spared to arrange marriage for her. Sometimes she wondered if even Haki the one-armed berserk might not have made a better match, mountain-troll though he was. As she came to her full strength and influence she consoled herself when necessary with one or other of the stalwarts of her guard. Her husband insisted that no man might stay overnight on her island, for the sake of his own good name and the legitimacy of their one child. But much could be done in the daytime. Ragnhild was like Asa in only one further respect: she too centered her life on her only son, the boy Harald. If Ragnhild had allowed it, the boy's grandmother might have turned a fraction of her disappointed love from son to grandson. It was one theme where their interests ran together.

"Midnight already," said Ragnhild in the warm silence. "He will not come."

"Maybe he never bothered to try."

"Men do not turn their back on invitations from me. I felt his mind as he stood on the dock. He could no more refuse me than my hounds a bitch in heat."

"You describe yourself well. But you could have done as much without the play-acting. Bitch that you are, you could have sent your hound Stein to cut him down."

"His friends of the Way would have protected him. That would have drawn in Olaf."

"Olaf!" The old queen spat out the word. She owed her life to her stepson's forbearance, and the life of her child. She hated him the more, and the more still because her child did not feel as she did, consistently respected and deferred to his elder half-brother, for all Olaf's name for bad luck and Halvdan's history of conquest.

"And your son, my husband, would have supported his brother," added Ragnhild, twisting the knife she knew was there. "It was better done as I did it. His body will be found in a week's time, when it swells, and men will say what fools the *Enzkir* are, to walk out on rotten ice.''

"You could have left him," suggested Asa, determined to give her daughter-in-law nothing. "He was no risk. A one-eyed stripling from a country far away, from the slavelands. Who would think such a man a risk to a true king like Halvdan? Or even to your puny Harald? You would do better to fear that half-troll Viga-Brand."

"It is not size that makes the king," said Ragnhild. "Or the man."

"You would know," hissed Asa.

Ragnhild smiled contemptuously. "The one-eye had luck," she said. "That was what made him dangerous. But luck lasts only till it meets a stronger luck. The luck that is in my blood, the luck of the Hartings. It is we who will make the One King in the North."

The door behind them creaked open, letting in a blast of freezing air. Both women sprang to their feet, Ragnhild seizing the iron stake she used to summon her thralls. Through the door stumbled two men, one tall, one short. The short one pushed the door closed, dropped its latch, this time pushed home the peg that prevented it being opened from the other side.

Shef pulled himself straight, walked wearily across the room, sword still in hand, forced himself not to drop groveling in front of the blessed glowing embers. His features were barely recognizable, caked with mud and the filth of shore and forest. Blood and slime covered his hands and matted the hair on his forearms. Where his skin showed it was blue with cold, a touch of deadly white on his nose and forehead.

"You sent me a message, lady," he said. "You warned me of the bridge-guards, but you lied about the ice. I met your dogs, too, here and there on the shore. Look, this is their hearts' blood."

Ragnhild raised the iron spike she had snatched up, beat with it on an iron triangle hanging above the fire. As Shef moved forward, sword raised, she stood motionless.

The slave-girls had been asleep, though not yet dismissed, on pallets out of sight. Four of them tumbled through the door that led to the main hall and the other apartments, rubbing their eyes and pulling dresses straight. It was not wise at any time of night to be slow in answering the summons of either queen. As Asa often said, she would be entering her grave-mound soon now, and she still had not chosen who should keep her company in death. The women, young or middle-aged but all with weary careworn faces, lined up hastily, daring only to cast side-glances at the two strange men. Men? Or marbendills from the deep? Queen Ragnhild might press even a marbendill into her service.

"Hot stones into the steam-room," snapped Ragnhild. "More fuel for this fire. Heat water in basins and bring towels. Bring two blankets—no, one blanket for that one and my fine robe of ermine for the English king. And girls—" The women halted in their first obedient scurry. "If I hear that anyone hears of this, I will not ask which one of you told them. There is always a Swedish ship in port, and space on the temple trees at Uppsala."

The women ran out. Ragnhild looked from her full height down at Shef, still standing irresolute in front of her, and then across at Asa.

"There is no arguing with the stronger luck," she said. "Best to join with it."

CHAPTER THIRTEEN

hef sat on a broad wooden bench which almost filled the tiny dark room, lit only by a single wick burning in a dish of whale-oil. Beneath it a covered trough of hot stones radiated heat, scorching heat that shriveled the mouth-lining and stung the nose with the stink of pine-resin from the wooden walls. He luxuriated in it, feeling the deep chill thaw from his bones. Feeling also the need for instant decisions recede. He was in others' hands now. Even Karli was no longer his responsibility. He did not know where they had taken him.

At the queen's instructions, the slave-women had pulled him away, taken off his filthy, clammy clothes. One of them had rubbed his face furiously with handfuls of snow taken from the fast-shrinking drifts outside, to prevent the frostbite that had already attacked it. Others had poured warm water over him, rubbed him with lye, scrubbed off the dirt and blood and animal fat from his hands. Dimly he had realized that they had also taken his sword, that something or other of the same kind was happening to Karli, but the sudden entry into warmth had half-stupefied him. Then they had led him into the steam-room and left him.

For a while he sat, not even sweating in the fierce heat, just letting the warmth soak through to his half-frozen marrow. Then as weariness came over him he lay back, propping his head against a wooden billet, and fell into a light, uneasy sleep.

* * *

Somewhere in the dark above him, his fate was being discussed. He heard the now-familiar rumble of mighty voices. One spoke for him, he realized, one against.

"He should have died on the ice," said the hostile voice: cold, authoritative, unused to contradiction, the voice not only of the Father but the Ruler of gods and men.

"No-one should blame a man for saving himself," argued the second voice: Shef knew he had heard it many times, recognized it as the voice of his patron, perhaps his father, Rig the cunning.

"He threw away the spear, the spear with my own runes on it. He denied me sacrifice. He does not follow the heroes' road."

"The less reason, then, for taking him to you. He would not find a place in Valhalla, would not be an obedient recruit for your Einheriar."

The first voice seemed to hesitate. "And yet . . . There is a cunning there. Too few of my champions have that. Maybe it is a quality I will need on the day of Ragnarök."

"You do not need it yet. Leave him where he is, let us see where his luck takes him. He may do you service in his own fashion." The second voice was lying, Shef knew, he could tell it by the sweet reason that dripped from its tongue. It was buying him time.

"Luck!" said the first voice, suddenly amused. "Let us see that, then. If he has a luck, it will be his own, for mine he has thrown away. And he will need powerful luck to survive the dangers of Drottningsholm. We will watch."

The two voices drifted away in a rumble of agreement.

Shef came to himself with a start. How long had he slept? Not long, he thought. It was too hot for anyone to lie comfortably. He was sweating now, and the bench under him was damp. Time to get up and look about him. He remembered the lines of poetry he had heard from Thorvin:

Not evident to any, where un-friends sit
    In every hall.

As he rose to his feet, the door of the tiny room creaked open. There was a fire lit in the room outside, and from the glow behind her, he realized that the figure standing in the doorway was the queen, Ragnhild. He could not see what she was wearing. As she came forward, closing the door, she pressed close to him.

"You have shed your jewelry, queen," he said with a roughness in his throat. He could feel himself stirring at the woman-smell that came from her, stronger even than the pines.

"No-one can wear gold in the room of hot stones," she replied. "It would burn. So I have shed my rings and armlets. See, even my brooch has gone."

She caught his hands, held them to her gown, ran them down its lapels. The gown fell open. Shef's hands cupped the heavy swell of her breasts, realized she wore nothing but the one open garment. His arms went round her, his hands stroked down the long muscular slope of her back, gripped her buttocks fiercely. She pressed forward, thrusting her pelvis into him, pushing him back. The bench caught him behind the knees and he sat back with a thud.

As the sweat poured suddenly from his body, the queen straddled over him, thrust herself down on his rigid erection. For the first time since he had entered Godive two years before in the Suffolk wood, Shef felt the inner warmth of a woman's body. It was as if a spell had been released. Half-amazed at his own ability, he tore the gown aside, seized the queen by her hips, began to thrust upwards violently, still sitting.

Ragnhild laughed, steadying herself on his shoulders. "I have never known a man so active in this room," she said. "Usually the heat makes them as slow as a gelded steer. I see that this time I shall not need the birch-twigs."

Unknown time later, Shef walked to the outer door of the hall, opened it, peeped cautiously out. In front of him, to the east, he could see a thin line of light over the Eastfold hills far on the other side of the fjord. Ragnhild looked over his shoulder.

"Dawn," she said. "Soon Stein and the guards will be here. You will have to hide away."

Shef pushed the door open, let the air in on his naked body. In the last few hours he had been first frozen, then all but roasted. Now the air felt only pleasantly cool and fresh. He took deep breaths of the clear air, thought he could scent in it the green smell of grass thrusting up through the vanishing snow. Spring came late to Norway, but then plants and animals and people all made up for lost time. He felt more alive and alert than he had since his boyhood. The danger threatened in his dream was forgotten.

He turned, seized Ragnhild once again, began to push her to the floor. She resisted, laughing. "The men will be here. You are very vigorous. Have you never had your fill before? Well, I promise you—you will have it again tonight. But now we must hide you away. The girls will not talk, and the men will not look. They know better. But we must not give Halvdan any excuse for trouble later."

She pulled Shef, still naked, away from the door.

Karli wondered where they had hidden his friend—he supposed he now had to call him, his master. He himself was lying on a straw mattress in a garret reached by a ladder through the slave-women's quarters. A small unshuttered window gave light, but he had been warned not to look out. His gashed wrist and head had been bandaged, and he was wrapped in a warm blanket.

The ladder creaked, and he reached for the sword which he had picked up when they separated him from Shef. But it was only two of the slave-women coming up together. He did not know their names: plain, brown-haired women, one his own age, one ten years older with a deep-lined face. They carried his clothes, washed clean and dried by a fire, a loaf of hard bread, a crock of ale and another of curds.

Karli sat up, grinned, reached appreciatively for the ale. "I would stand up and thank you properly, ladies," he said. "But all I have on is this blanket, and what I have behind it might shock you."

The young one smiled faintly, the older one shook her head. "There is not much that shocks those who live on this island," she said.

"How is that?"

"We have other things to worry about. The queens play their games, with men and the king and the boy Harald. In the end one of them will lose, and pay the forfeit, and be carried to the grave-mound. Queen Asa has already started to put aside the things that will go in it with her, the sledge and the cart and the jewels and the fine clothes. But neither she nor Ragnhild will go alone, when they go. They will take attendants—maybe one, maybe two. I am the least valuable of those here. Maybe Asa will take me, or Ragnhild send me. Edith here is the youngest. Maybe Ragnhild will be jealous and send her."

"Edith," said Karli, "that is no Norse name."

"I am English," said the younger girl. "Martha here is a Frisian. They took her from her island in a mist. I was caught by the slavers and sold in the market at Hedeby."

Karli stared at them. Up till then all three had spoken in Norse, the women quite fluently, Karli still uncertain. Now he changed his speech to the Ditmarsh language, related to Frisian and English, which he knew Shef could easily understand.

"Did you know that my friend and I are not Norsemen either? He is a king in England. But they say he was once a thrall, like you. And they tried to sell him in Hedeby only weeks ago."

"Tried?"

"He knocked the man who said he was his master down, and threatened to sell him instead. A good joke, and not a bad punch. But listen—I know my friend, and I know he has no love for slavers. When we get back to our friends, shall I ask him to buy you from the queens here? He would do it if he knew you were English, Edith, and he would take Martha too."

"You aren't going to get back to your friends," said Martha flatly. "We hear a lot. Queen Ragnhild fears your friend. She thinks he may take the place she means for her son. She meant to kill you both last night. Now she means to drain your friend's manhood, get a child from him, in case his blood is the one destined for rule. Once she has that child in her belly, your friend will find the henbane in his porridge. And you too."

Karli looked uncertainly at the loaf he had been gnawing.

"No," the woman went on, "you are safe yet. As safe as we are. Till she has got what she wants."

"And how long will that take?"

Martha laughed for the first time, a short and mirthless bark. "Putting a child in a woman's belly? You are a man, you should know. As long as it takes to walk a mile? Less, with most of you."

"More with me," muttered Karli. His hand had strayed automatically and unresisted to Edith's knee.

Valgrim the Wise looked carefully at the dripping spear, its steel head already showing rust. He spelled out the runes on its iron shaft.

"Where did you find this?" he asked.

"On the shore of Drottningsholm," said Stein, the guardsman. "When we went back on to the island this morning, as usual, I sent men to round up the dogs as we always do. They couldn't find them, and the queen Ragnhild told me she had been disturbed by their howling and sent her maids out to bring them in. When I asked more, she flew into a rage and told me to get out before she had my ears cut off. I guessed something was wrong and sent out a guard-boat to row along the shore, now the ice has gone. They found this."

"Floating?"

"No, the head's too heavy. They said it was close to the shore, in about three feet of water. The head was lodged on the bottom, but the shaft was still bobbing about."

"What do you think it means?"

"They could have drowned on the rotten ice," suggested Stein. "It all went quite suddenly early last night, when the rain came on."

"But you don't think so?"

"It's the dogs," said Stein. "There's something fishy there, and Ragnhild is hiding something."

"Maybe a man?"

"Probably a man."

Both heads turned to the third man in the room, the remote unbending figure of King Olaf.

"This seems to affect the good name of your family," said Valgrim, a trifle uncertainly.

The king smiled. "What you are thinking is that it is also a good test of luck. If King Shef was on the rotten ice last night, and survived, that was one test passed. If he got past the wolfhounds, that was another. You want me to set him a third?"

"Third time pays for all," said Stein.

"I agree. A third test it is, and then no more, from me or from you. Agreed."

Valgrim nodded, reluctantly, eyes full of calculation.

"Then I will send word to my brother that there is reason to think things amiss on Drottningsholm. I have never done that before, and he knows I would not do it lightly. So he will believe me and give permission for a thorough search of the island and every building in it, from end to end. You must think how you would make it, Stein. And if intruders are found there, hiding, then they must go to the king's justice. It will be heavy, when he thinks the good name of his son Harald is concerned.

"Till then, Stein, you had better double the guards on the bridges, both from Drottningsholm to the second island, and from that to the third and to the mainland. A bold man could swim between the islands too, so have your guard-boats out between them. I need not tell you to make sure there is no boat a man could steal.

"If this is to be a test, it is in your hands to make sure it is a strict one. Do not come to me afterwards and say, this was no fair test, any man might have escaped. You must make sure that the only escape is by Völund's path, through the air! Then if King Shef escapes, we will know that Völund he is, in whatever shape."

Stein and Valgrim nodded again.

"And no word to his friends," added Valgrim. Out of the window of the high room where they sat, he could see Thorvin walking across the college precinct, Brand at his side. Both men looked deeply anxious.

"No word to his friends," Olaf agreed. "I will play fair on this one, Valgrim. See you do too. Otherwise it is no test of king's luck."

As he turned and went out, Valgrim and Stein looked at each other.

"He said make it a strict test," said Stein. "I could make it a little stricter than he plans."

"Do that," said Valgrim, looking again at the 'Gungnir' runes on the spear he still held. "No strictness is too harsh for the man who pretends to come from All-father."

"And if his luck does prove stronger?"

Valgrim hefted the spear, shook it like a man about to strike. "I think it has left him already. I hated him for aping my master Othin. I hate him more now he has thrown away my master's token."

From the shadows of the great hall, Karli watched his friend-and-master musingly. All the signs, he thought. I should have realized earlier.

Almost from the moment of their first meeting—certainly from the first time they had talked together—Karli had unconsciously assumed that Shef was the elder of the two, the wiser, the more widely-traveled, the more weapon-skilled. It had given Karli no sense of inferiority. His own animal spirits were too strong for that, and he remained unshakably confident in his own ability to knock any man down with his fists, and bed, if not any woman, at least any woman reasonably good-humored. He did not feel inferior to Shef. But he had assumed that Shef knew as much as he did.

A mistake. He should have realized that where women were concerned, this tall warrior with the scars and the mighty friends was no more than a boy. He was behaving like a boy now. A boy who has met his first woman. What he had been doing with Queen Ragnhild all day, Karli did not know, but now night had fallen and the guards had been withdrawn he still could not take eye or hand off her. As he spooned the strong salt stew into his mouth, his left hand lay on the queen's bare arm, lightly stroking it. Every time she spoke he leaned close to her mouth, laughed, took every chance to touch her again. Karli had heard stories of witches who sucked away a man's manhood. In his experience there was no need of witchcraft. Sexual skill, consciously exercised, worked on any man—the first time anyway. Once you realized there were more fish in the sea than ever came out of it, you might be protected. But Shef did not know that yet. And there was no way of telling him. When Karli had approached him after being freed from the garret, Shef had been pleased to see him, but vague, reluctant to talk or plan or even think about what had happened. He was slit-struck.

It was up to him, then. Karli had no doubt that for all the warmth and the food and the careful attention, he and Shef were in greater danger than they had been on the ice. What Edith and Martha and their two friends had told him had chilled him deeply. Shef was against slavery because he had been threatened with being a slave. Karli was against it because he had no experience of it. In the uncivilized and poverty-stricken Ditmarsh there was neither room nor work for slaves. They might sell shipwrecked strangers to other strangers, but they kept no thralls themselves. The constant fear under which a thrall like Edith or Martha lived was a new thought to him.

And fear made people good listeners. Their lives depended on knowing what might happen and taking the few pitiful precautions open to them. So Martha not only bore with the contempt and bullying she received from the Norwegian female housekeeper who came in with the guards each morning and left with them each night. She encouraged it, making mistakes to provoke a beating and a flood of words. What the massive Vigdis had said after Martha dropped the pan was that a time was coming for idle sluts. Aye, and maybe not them alone. Why else the doubled guards? And don't think to swim off like the spineless eel your father. The men have brought up boats to the channel between each island. When the king comes we'll see who's useful enough to let live and who is fit only for howe-bridal.

Vigdis obviously did not know what the guards were for, and thought it some royal intrigue: maybe King Halvdan tired of his mother waiting to die, or of his wife and her independence. But the slave-women knew better. The dogs, they said. Men coming round to look in their pens, ask where the others were, why they had not all come home, why they could not be heard baying if they were still loose somewhere on the island. We cleared up the bodies before first light, Edith had said, and the rain washed away the blood, but in the soft ground it would not take a tracker to see that people had been doing something.

A night or two's grace, thought Karli, still watching Ragnhild and Shef, the sour queen Asa sitting glaring at both across the table. I know. The slave-women know. Shef will not listen. And Vigdis has not told the queens. Well, one thing is for sure. They will not notice if I am not there. Quietly he went through the door to the little cramped room where the slave-attendants waited.

"Have you thought what to do?" whispered Edith.

Karli squeezed her hip. "I am a Ditmarsher," he said. "I know something about water. I need to build a"—he hesitated for the right word—"a boat?"

"There are no boats on the island. No planks, no tools. It would take weeks to fell trees. And anyway, they would hear you!"

"I don't mean a boat like that," said Karli. "I mean"—he turned to the Frisian woman Martha—"we call it a *punt*."

"For the duck-hunters," said Martha, nodding. "But what do you need to make that?"

Hours later Karli bent sweating over the contraption he had put together on the island's seaward shore, furthest removed from the guard-posts. Its flat bottom was simply a door. There had only been one whose absence would not be immediately noticed the next day—the one that led to the slave-women's stinking latrine. Probably neither the guards nor the queens knew such a place existed, let alone whether it had a door or not. Karli had lifted it bodily off its hinges and carried it out. He could have stood on that alone and poled himself along if he had been able to keep to shallow water. But he knew he would have to do better than that, make a seaward circle before he ran in to the shore. He needed a place to stand if he was not to be tipped off by every wave. And something like a bow to cut the water. Done with no tools and no noise.

Slowly and clumsily he had cut away one edge of the door with his sword, sharp but not serrated. Iron skewers from the kitchen had nailed down billets of firewood toward the stern, hammered in with a flat stone muffled by layers of cloth. On top of that he had fixed a flat wooden tray with four nails worked loose with his fingers and pulled stealthily out of the ornate wooden planking at the rear of the hall. Finally, growing impatient and trusting to luck that the damage would not be seen next morning, he had pulled away one strake of planking low down to the ground, snapped it over his knee. He was trying now to drive three more nails through the planking into the cut-away edge of the door, to make a bluff, square bow. Once it was done he would have a makeshift imitation of the craft the Ditmarsh fowlers steered through their everlasting bogs. He would neither row nor pole it, but scull it over the stern with a single oar—snapped planking again, wedged into a split fir-branch. It would do, if the water stayed calm. If no-one picked him out from a guard-boat close in, or one of the king's giant coastal patrol warships further out. If he met no creature of the deep.

At the last thought Karli's hair bristled. Deep within himself, he knew he was afraid. Not of water, not of men. He and the English catapult-men had idled away too many hours telling each other monster-stories, and passing on those they had heard from the Vikings. In his own land Karli feared the fen-thurses. The English feared boggarts, hags, and groundles. The Vikings told stories of all of them, and stranger creatures still, skoffins and nixes and marbendills and skerry-trolls. Who knew what might not be met, out at sea, in the dark? All it would take would be a gray-haired hand reaching up and seizing an ankle as he sculled six inches above the water. Then the things would feast at the sea-bottom.

Karli shook himself, drove home the last nail with a flat stone, straightened up.

The voice in his ear murmured, "Going fishing?"

Frightened already, Karli leapt straight over his punt, turned in the air, came down braced for flight, gaping to see what threat had crept up on him. Almost, he relaxed when he saw the amused, contemptuous face of Stein the guard-captain, standing there fully-armed but thumbs still hooked in his belt.

"Surprised to see me?" suggested Stein. "Thought I wouldn't be back till morning? Well, I thought a little extra care wouldn't hurt. After all, if men aren't allowed on Drottningsholm after dark, nor are you. Eh?

"Now tell me, short-legs, where's your taller friend? Stallioning away up at the hall? He'll lose more than an eye when we hand him over to King Halvdan. Do you want to go along with him?"

The sword Shef had retempered for Karli still lay on the ground where he had been using it. Karli lunged forward, seized its hilt, straightened up. The shock had worn off. No hag from the deep. Just a man. On his own, seemingly. With helmet and mail, but no shield.

Stein dropped a hand to his own sword-hilt, drew and stepped round the boat. Karli was no dwarf, but Stein out-topped him by head and shoulders, outweighed him by fifty pounds. How fast was he? Plenty of farmers' sons in Viking armies, Shef had said.

Karli cocked his elbow and threw his weight into a forehand slash, not at the head, too easy to duck, but at the point where neck met shoulder, as Shef had taught him.

Stein saw the beginnings of the movement, knew before the sword was drawn back where the blow was aimed, where it would fall. He had time to tap his foot once before his riposte. In one movement he turned his own sword in his hand, drove the base of his blade in a short chord to intersect the longer arc of Karli's blow. The blades clanged once. Karli's shot into the air, knocked from his grasp. A twist of the wrist, Stein's point rested in the hollow of Karli's throat.

Not one of the farmers' sons, then, Karli thought sickly. Stein's face creased with disgust. He dropped the point to the ground.

"It's not the skin that makes the bear," he remarked. "Nor the sword the warrior. All right, you little freckle-faced bastard, talk or I'll cut you up for bait."

He bent forward, thrusting his chin out and up. Karli's feet shuffled from the fencing position he had taken to the one that came naturally to him. He shrugged a left hand feint out of habit and swung instantly with the right hook to the side of the jaw.

This time Stein's decades-drilled reflexes failed him completely. The blow caught him standing flat and still. As he straightened his sword for the killing counter-stroke, another blow snapped his head back and a third from six inches' range crashed into his temple. As he slumped forward Karli side-stepped and swung a hand-edge chop at the back of his neck: illegal in the Ditmarsh ring, but not against husbands or rivals met at night. The veteran sprawled his six foot four full-length at Karli's feet.

Out of the shadows came Martha, the middle-aged slave-woman. Terror stood in her eyes as she saw the lying man.

"I came to see if you were gone. That is Stein the captain. It is the first time he has ever come spying at night. They must know you are here! Is he dead?"

Karli shook his head. "Help me to tie him before he comes round."

"Tie him? Are you mad? We cannot guard him for ever, or keep him silent."

"Well . . . What are we going to do with him?"

"Cut his throat, of course. Do it now, quickly. Put his body on your boat and roll it off in the water. It will be days before he is found."

Karli retrieved his sword, stared at the unconscious man. "But I've never killed anyone. He's . . . He's done me no harm."

Martha's face set, she stepped forward, bent over the man now starting to push himself up from the ground. She snatched the short knife from the sheath he carried on his belt, felt its edge for a moment, hurled the helmet aside and pulled his head back by the hair. Reached forward and round, drove the point in deep under the left ear. Dragged it round in a deep, slicing semi-circle. Blood spouted from the severed arteries, Stein cried out, his voice coming as an expiring whistle from the great hole in his windpipe.

Martha released his head, let the body fall forward, wiped the knife automatically on her filthy apron. "You men," she said. "It's just like killing a pig. Only pigs don't steal other pigs from their homes. Don't bury them alive. He'd done you no harm! How much have he and his like done me? Me and my kind?

"Don't just stand there, man! Be off with you. And take this carcass with you. If you are not back within two days we'll all go to join him. Wherever he's gone."

She turned and fled into the darkness once more. Karli, his throat dry, queasily began to drag his clumsy craft into the shallow water and then to load the dead weight on it.

CHAPTER FOURTEEN

An hour later, Karli tucked his single oar cautiously between his thighs, straightened up on his precariously rocking craft, and stretched his overworked shoulder muscles. As soon as he started he had realized how different the sea was, even the sea of a landlocked fjord, from the shallow muddy waterways of the marsh. The gentlest of waves made the door pitch and toss. To keep his balance at all he had to straddle as near as he could to the center, which meant that his sculling-platform was behind him, not where he needed it. By trial and error he had found a way to stand, one foot far forward, one braced against the edge of the wooden tray. Fortunately he had made the oar long enough to reach the water even so.

There were two ways for a Ditmarsh fowler to scull, an easy way and a hard way. The balance problem ruled out the easy way— standing upright on one leg with the oar in the crook of the other knee, swinging it with both hands. He had had to switch immediately to the hard way, oar under one arm, other arm swinging the oar up and down, left to right in a continuous figure-of-eight. Karli had unusual balance, unusual strength in the arms and shoulders for a man of his weight. He could manage. Only just, and only slowly.

Still, no-one had picked him out. At the beginning he had poled his way out into water deeper than the length of his oar, then with relief pushed the dead body off the front edge and felt his wooden plank rise. The mail took the body down. It would rise again soon, but by then Shef would be rescued or Karli gone to join Stein in the next world.

Then he had sculled away from the island in a straight line towards the black shape of the Eastfold hills across the fjord. Five hundred weary strokes, fighting to keep his balance all the way. Then he had turned, looked cautiously behind him to Drottningsholm and the islands. He could make them out, but with no detail. He did not think that in the clouded, moonless night anyone from the guard-posts could see a crouching man on an invisible raft against the black sea.

He had turned and started to make his way towards Kaupang harbor to the north. Wind and tide were behind him. He kept changing arms as the weariness grew. It was discouraging to be able to see nothing, no lights, no sign of progress. He could have been on a shoreless sea, paddling from nowhere to nowhere.

As long as there was nothing out here with him. Over the hiss of the wind and the surge of the sea, Karli realized he could pick out something else. A steady creaking, something rhythmic, something chopping the water. He looked behind him, full instantly of terror at some strange water-hag swimming behind him for its prey.

Worse than that. Against the black sea and the sky Karli made out a shape, a fierce head lifted high, like a monster questing for swimmers. The dragon prow of one of King Halvdan's giant warships, out rowing his endless summer blockade. Karli could see the white splash of the oar-thresh, hear the rhythmic creak of the rowlocks, the grunting of the rowers as they put their weight on the oars. They were rowing very slowly, not going anywhere special, conserving their strength. Look-outs stood at prow and stern, alert for skippers trying to evade King Halvdan's taxes, for pirates sneaking by to raid Eastfold or Westfold. Karli lay down immediately on the plank, careless of the water soaking him. He dropped his face, pulled his hands back into their sleeves, trapped the oar beneath his body. On a dark night, he knew from much avoidance of husbands and fathers, nothing showed up more than white skin. He tried to look like a piece of floating wreckage, skin crawling as he imagined the bowmen taking aim.

The oars thundered in his ear, the door pitched and heaved as the bow-wave of the great warship went by. No challenge, no shot. As the stern-tail crawled past the corner of his eye he heard the lookout call something, an indistinct reply. Still no challenge. Nothing to do with him.

Carefully and shakily he climbed back on to his feet, retrieved the oar, began to scull slowly after the warship's receding stern. As he began to count off his strokes once more he felt the door begin to rise again beneath his feet. Another bow-wave? No, something greater, something closer, the whole clumsy contraption tipping over almost on to its side. Karli dropped on to his knees, clutched the edge, as he did so heard a great snort in the water not six feet away.

A fin his own size cruised gently past, standing straight up almost at right angles to the water. Beneath it a huge body rolled black and gleaming. Ahead of him the fin turned, cruised back to intercept. A head came out of the water, broad enough to engulf the door in one snap. Karli caught the flash of brilliant white barring beneath the black upper body, saw an intelligent eye observing him.

The killer whale, a bull orca out foraging for seals ahead of the rest of its school, considered tipping the man-thing off its floe and snapping it to pieces in the water, but decided against. Men-things were hardly fair prey, a gentle, irresistible voice told it. There was no excitement in chasing them. Sometimes porpoises followed their ships, and porpoises were a good catch. Not tonight. It ceased to follow the warship, ignored the thing on the floe, swam inexorably off to find its companions.

Karli straightened again, realized the warmth inside his breeches was his own piss. Shakily he took up the scull, began to count off his strokes. This country was not safe. Both the men and the animals were just too big.

In their hut, the English catapulteers were preparing their breakfast and at the same time checking their weapons. Light was just showing in the sky, but ex-slaves rose early, out of habit. Besides, in spite of the pendants they all wore, in spite of being at the heart of their adopted religion, they felt uneasy, isolated, unsafe. Their leader had vanished, no-one knew where. They were surrounded by men of alien speech and unpredictable temper. In their hearts they knew that most of the Norsemen they met thought all foreigners were just slave-material waiting to be seized. They had come to Kaupang as men of a conquering army. Slowly their status seemed to be slipping away. If they were disarmed they would be back to tilling fields and herding goats, working under the lash once more. Without saying it, every one of them had determined that that was not to happen. If need be, they would have to break out. But how?

In the army of the Way in England there had been three main divisions: crossbowmen, halberdiers, catapulteers. No-one had made any effort to train them as swordsmen, though each carried a broad, single-edged sax-knife in his belt, as useful for firewood as for enemies. But Udd had made sure that each man there, whatever his original trade, carried and knew how to use one of the latest model crossbows, no longer wound by belt-pulleys, the spring-steel bow cocked instead by a long, pronged lever. It fitted under the bowstring and latched onto inset bolts. With a single, heaving effort the bow was cocked as the pull was exerted against a foot stirrup on the front of the bow's wooden frame. Osmod and three of the others also carried their unwieldy halberds, the combination axe and spear that Shef had invented for himself to make up for his lack of weight and training.

But the group's main weapon stood outside the hut: the mule, the stone-hurling catapult they had unshipped from the *Norfolk* and loaded into Brand's *Walrus*. The Thor-priests had been busy ever since they arrived, observing it, watching them shoot it, getting them to build further models of the two other styles of catapult they knew, the twisted-rope dart-shooter and the simpler stone-lobbing pull-thrower that the Way had already deployed on three battlefields. It was said that King Halvdan had ordered experiments on fitting mules to bow and stern platforms on his coastal patrol craft, large enough to take them if maybe too weak in the keel to stand the repeated shock of recoil. But till then the mule outside was the only one in the North.

There was one further innovation that no-one as yet had tried. Udd's invention of case-hardened steel as yet seemed all but useless. The material, once hardened, was too hard to work with any tools they had. Udd had suggested hardened crossbow-bolts, but as the others pointed out, the ones they had would go through any known armor anyway, so why bother? In the end Udd had made one thin round plate of the new steel, two feet in diameter, and pegged it on to a standard round shield of linden wood. Few warriors if any carried iron shields. The weight was so great that the shield could not be wielded for more than a few moments. Soft linden wood was used instead, to catch and trap the enemy's point or edge, usually with an iron boss as hand-guard. The plate Udd had made was so thin that if it had been normal iron it would have added no protection. But the case-hardened steel would turn any ordinary sword, spear or arrow, and weighed no more than a second layer of wood. Udd and the others had not yet worked out what the utility of the new shield was—none at all to men who fought as they did. It was a case where a new technique had not yet found a use.

At first, in the early-morning hubbub, no-one heard the scratching at the door. Then, as it was repeated, Cwicca paused. The rest fell silent. Fritha and Hama snatched up crossbows, cocked them. Osmod stepped to one side of the door, poised his halberd. Cwicca jerked out a peg, lifted the latch, swung the door open.

Karli fell in on hands and knees, barely able to support himself. The seven men inside gaped at him, then slammed the door shut and sprang to help.

"Get him on the stool," snapped Osmod. "He's soaked. Hah, not all water either! Get his clothes off, one of you bring him a blanket. Rub his hands, Cwicca, he's half-frozen."

Karli, supported on the stool, was pointing towards a mug. Osmod passed him the strong warmed beer, watched it go down in a dozen gulps. Karli finished, breathed out, sat up straighter.

"All right. I'll be all right in no time. Just cold and wet and dead-tired. But I've got news.

"First, Shef is alive, on Drottningsholm. The message he got was a trap but we got there just the same. So he's on the island, he's alive but he won't be much longer if he stays there. Trouble is, that queen of theirs is screwing him senseless and he won't leave. We're going to have to go and get him. But he won't come of his own free will and they've reinforced the guards over the bridges. And he's not the only one there who needs rescuing . . ."

Karli poured out his story to a ring of faces that grew grimmer as he went on. At the end Osmod silently passed him a refilled mug, looked at Cwicca, who as catapult-captain shared the leadership with him in Shef's absence.

"We've got to get him off. We could do it ourselves, but we'd never get away afterwards. That's what we've got to think about. Now, who in this place can we trust?"

"How about Hund the leech?" asked Cwicca.

Osmod considered a moment. "Yes, I'd like to have him with us. He's English, and he's the lord's oldest friend, and he's a Way-priest besides."

"Thorvin the priest, then?" suggested one of the hammer-wearers. Faces round him twisted dubiously. Cwicca shook his head.

"He's more loyal to the Way than he is to King Shef. This is Way business, somehow. You can't tell which road he'd turn."

"Can we trust any of these Norskers?" asked one of the others.

"Maybe Brand."

A pause while they thought it over. Finally, Osmod nodded. "Maybe Brand."

"Well, if we got him on our side, it's easy. He's nigh seven foot tall and built like a stone wall. He's the Champion of wherever-it-is, isn't he? He's just going to walk through them guards like piss through snow."

"I'm not so sure about that," muttered Osmod. "He got a sword right through his belly last year. They've patched him up, right. But they didn't patch his head up, did they? I don't know that he'd be champion of anywhere any more."

"Are you saying he's gone yellow?" asked Fritha, incredulous.

"No. But I'm saying he's got a bit careful, like he never was before. In this country full of berserks, or whatever they call 'em, that's almost the same thing."

"But you still think he'll help?"

"As long as we don't ask too much." Osmod looked round, frowning. "Seven of us here, and Karli. Where's Udd?"

"Where do you think? Now the water's running he's up at the mills, seeing how they work. Took a hunk of bread up as soon as light showed."

"Well, go and get him back, someone. The rest of you, listen. Because here's what we'll do . . ."

". . . So that's our plan," concluded Osmod, looking grimly across the table at Brand. "And that's what we're going to do. The only question we've got for you is, are you in or are you out?"

Brand stared down consideringly. Though both men were sitting, Brand's face was still a foot above the Englishman's. It was a real surprise, he reflected, how these men of Shef's had changed. Everything in Brand's make-up, culture and experience had told him all his life that a slave was a slave and a warrior was a warrior, and there was no way of making the one into the other. A warrior could not be enslaved—or only with massive precautions, like those King Nithhad had taken for Völund, and look where that had got him. And slaves could not be made into warriors. Not only did they not have the skills, they didn't have the heart either. During the battles in England the year before Brand had revised his opinion, a little. Ex-slaves were useful, he concluded, for war-with-machines, because they could be made into machines themselves: doing what they were told, heaving on ropes and pulling toggles to order. That was all.

But now here was one not just making up a plan of his own, not just telling him, Brand, that he was going to do it, but defying Brand to stop him. The giant Halogalander felt a mixture of irritation, amusement, and something like—anxiety? Fear was not something he would ever readily admit to.

"Yes, I'm in," he said. "But I don't want my crew mixed up with it. And I don't want to lose my ship."

"We want to use your ship to get away in," said Osmod. "Sail back to England and get out of here."

Brand shook his head. "Not a chance," he said. "King Halvdan's got this coast sewed up as tight as a frog's ass. And the *Walrus* can't fight off one of his patrol ships, they're twice our size."

"Use the mule."

"You know how long that would take to ship, not just to carry, but to mount it so it can shoot. Anyway, any ship not specially designed will just fall to pieces if you shoot that thing off in it."

"So how do we get away after we've got King Shef back off this queen? Are you saying it can't be done?"

Brand chewed his lip. "We can do it. Maybe. Not by sea. I think the best thing is this. I'm going to invent an errand and get off now—say I'm going out in the hills for some sport, they'll believe that after a winter cramped up indoors. I'll buy horses for the lot of you. When you've done your bit, meet me at a place I'll tell you. Then we all have to ride like smoke till we're out of Halvdan and Olaf's territory—they won't know right off which way we've gone. Then we all cut across country to the Gula Fjord. My helmsman Steinulf will take over here for me. I dare say with the Way behind him, or anyway with Thorvin and Skaldfinn and their friends, he'll be able to get the *Walrus* free and take it round the coast to meet us. Even if there's trouble, Guthmund should be able to get away with the *Seamew*. All meet up at the Gula and head back to England, like you said."

"You don't want to be in on the attack?"

Brand shook his head silently. Osmod in his turn stared across the table. He too had always believed that a slave and a warrior were two different breeds, as different as sheep and wolves. Then he had found that given a reason and a fighting chance, he had wolf in him. Now he wondered about the giant figure facing him. This was a man famous even among the fierce, quarrelsome, everlastingly competitive heroes of the North. Why was he now standing out? Leaving the dangerous work to others? Was it right that a man who recovered from a wound that took him to the gates of death was never the same man again? He had stood by the door and felt the cold wind come through . . .

"You can leave that to us, then," said Osmod. "Us Englishmen," he added, rubbing the point in. "Do you think we can do it?"

"I think you can do it the way you said," replied Brand. "You Englishmen. What worries me is getting you all across the mountains to the Gula Fjord. You've only met the civilized Norwegians so far. The ones who live up in the back hills, where we're going—they're different."

"If we can handle King Halvdan's guards, we can handle them. And what about you? You're the champion of the men of Halogaland, aren't you?"

"I think taking you midgets across Norway will need a champion. I shall feel like a dog taking a troop of mice through Catland. They're going to think you people are just so many free dinners."

Osmod's lips compressed. "Show me where we are to meet you with the horses then, Lord Dog. I and the other mice will be there. Maybe with a few catskins."

The little convoy moving down to the bridge and the islands beyond it looked as ragged and unthreatening as it could be made. In the lead an old farm-horse pulling a battered cart, with one man walking by its side chirruping encouragingly to it. The cart's load was invisible, but a dirty tarpaulin held it all down, one end flapping loose. On the other side of the horse walked Udd, the smallest of the men, gaping near-sightedly at the horse-collar: a Norwegian invention which few Englishmen outside the catapult-teams had ever seen. It enabled a horse to pull twice the weight of the ox-style straight pole, and Udd, characteristically, had forgotten about the point of their journey in fascination at the new artifact.

Round and behind the cart straggled eight more men, the six remaining English catapulteers, Hund the leech, his white priest-clothes hidden under a gray mantle, and Karli. None carried a weapon in sight other than their belt-knives. Halberds were stowed inconspicuously on nails along the sides of the cart. The crossbows, already cocked, lurked under the loose tarpaulin.

As the cart dipped down to the shore, two guards by the side of the bridge straightened up, retrieved their javelins from the ground.

"Bridge is closed," one of them shouted. "Everyone's off the island. Can't you see the sun, nearly down?"

Osmod pushed forward, shouting indistinctly in poor Norse. There were six men on this post, he knew. He wanted them all outside. The man leading the horse joined in, continuing to walk forward.

One of the guards had had enough. He jumped back, javelin poised, shouted at the top of his voice. Other men came suddenly out of the hut to one side, handling axes, picking up shields. Four more of them, Osmod silently counted. That was right. He turned and raised a thumb to the others clustered round the cart.

In an instant the crossbows were out and leveled, six of them, with Udd slipping back to seize his and join in.

"Show 'em," said Osmod briefly.

Fritha, the marksman of the group, sighted and released. A sharp twang and an instantaneous thud. One of the men with shields gasped, his face suddenly white, stared down at the iron quarrel which had driven through his shield and deep into his upper arm. Fritha dropped the bow forward, thrust his foot into the stirrup, jerked over the goat's foot lever, dropped a second quarrel into place.

"You're all marked," called Osmod. "These bows will go through any shield or armor. You can't fight us. Only die. Drop what you're holding and go into the hut."

The guards looked at each other, brave men, but unnerved by the lack of face-to-face challenge, the threat of being shot down from a distance.

"You can keep your swords," offered Osmod. "Just drop those javelins. Go in the hut."

Slowly they dropped spears, shuffled backwards, watching their enemies, trooped into the guard-hut. Two Englishmen ran forward with bars, hammers, nails, quickly and roughly nailed bars across the door and the one shuttered window.

"We learnt something from King Shef," remarked Cwicca. "Always work out what you're going to do before you do it."

"They'll soon bust out," said Karli.

"Then they'll reckon they've got us trapped. That'll give us a bit more time."

The cart rolled on to the bridge, in winter logs embedded in ice, in summer with planks laid over the logs now floating. The men were carrying crossbows and halberds openly now, easy to see in the long Northern twilight. But there should be no-one to see or challenge till the other side of the first island and the next bridge.

Hearing the cart roll towards them, and knowing there should be no-one there, the pair of guards manning the second bridge had more warning and more time to decide what to do. Facing a line of crossbows, one of them immediately and sensibly turned and ran, hoping to get away and call for help. Aiming carefully, Fritha put a bolt through his thigh that brought him instantly down. The second man carefully grounded his weapon, eyes glaring vengefully.

Hund walked from his place at the rear to glance at the wound the crossbow-bolt had made, clicking his tongue at the spreading blood, the bolt buried firmly in bone.

Osmod joined him. "Nasty job getting that out," he remarked.

"Still, better alive than dead, and the best leeches in the world over at the college at Kaupang."

Hund nodded. "You, fellow, when you take him to master Ingulf to have his leg mended, give him the regards of Hund the priest and say the Englishmen spared this man's life, at my urging. Till then, pad the wound, check the blood-flow." He showed his silver apple-pendant, sign of Ithun goddess of healing, and turned away.

The cart rolled over the second bridge, over the second island, and on to the final span to Drottningsholm. Occasionally looking behind them for signs of pursuit, the freedmen closed up. This time, they knew, they would have to fight.

The third guard post was the main one, a dozen men. They had already spent the day in serious anxiety, following the disappearance of their captain Stein. They had searched every part of the island for him except the queens' quarters, found nothing. They waited now only for word from King Halvdan before they searched the queens' hall too, but even so they did not expect to find him. They knew enemies were nearby, whether human killers or monsters from the deep. Some had seen a school of orcas cruise by, their great fins showing, and wondered if Stein had been fool enough to enter the water. The faint shouts they had heard from the brief clashes to the north had alarmed them further. As the cart and its escort came into view they moved on to the bridge to block it, four men abreast, three deep.

From the rear rank an arrow flew, aimed at the horse's head. Whatever the cart and its cargo, they meant to block it. Wilfi, leading the horse still, now carried the new case-hardened shield. He lifted it, caught the shaft square on. It leapt back, point blunted.

Cwicca, Osmod, Hama and Lulla walked forward, halberds ready, dropped on one knee to make a hedge of points facing the Norsemen forty feet away. Four crossbowmen stood behind them.

"Drop your weapons," shouted Osmod. He had no hope that his order would be obeyed. A dozen veteran warriors surrender to less than their own number of strangers? Their mothers would disown them. Yet Osmod felt at least a flicker of compunction about shooting men down who were all but helpless, helpless against weapons they did not understand. He waited for the bows to be bent, the javelins to poise before he shouted again.

"Shoot!"

Four crossbows twanged together. At forty feet, against standing targets, no-one could miss. The Viking front line collapsed, one man lifted off his feet by the impact of the bolt, many foot-pounds of energy stored in sprung steel and delivered in a moment. A man in the second line gasped and flinched as a bolt passed through the man in front and plowed up his rib-cage.

Another man broke from the pile of fallen round his feet and hurled himself forward, sword circling back for one mighty slash. Foam splattered his moustache as he ran, desperate for glory and for one blow. He called hoarsely on Othin as he came. A crossbow bolt from the near-sighted Udd hissed past one ear, another from the inexpert Karli flew over his head.

As he came within three strides Osmod straightened from his kneeling position, gripped his long halberd close to the base, thrust forward in a long point from low down. The charging warrior ran straight on to it, splitting his own heart on the leaf-blade, running forward with the last strength in his body till the cross-fixed axe-blade and spike stopped him short. His last breath left him with a grunt, his eyes stared forward in shock.

The sword fell from his hand, the life left him. Osmod twisted the shaft once, cleared his blade, withdrew, dropped back to kneel. A series of clicks behind him as the crossbows cocked again.

The six men in front of him broke and ran, four sideways along the shore, two away along the bridge to Drottningsholm. Osmod gestured briefly. "Put those two down," he said. "Let the others go."

Bodies were dragged aside, and the cart rolled forward for the last time, the old horse now encouraged into a trot, some of the Englishmen behind it walking backwards, alert for pursuit. Osmod and Cwicca jogged in front of the others, eyes probing in the dim light for what they had been told to expect.

"There," said Cwicca, pointing. "Tell Udd and Hund to secure the boat, they're easily spared. They only have to push it off and row it round the point."

Osmod called directions, and the two men broke away. "The rest of you, put your shoulders to the cart and get it up this slope. The hall's on the other side, and we have to hurry now."

Heaved on by the horse and eight men, the cart rocked up a brief slope, came through a copse of firs, and broke out into a clearing. In the center of it stood the Hall of the Two Queens, steep-roofed, ornately gabled, stags' antlers nailed up above the doorways. No sign of life except a frightened face peeping from behind a low shutter, but smoke seeped into the air from its one chimney.

The men swung the cart round so that its rear pointed at the hall, whipped away the tarpaulin, dropped the tilt, clustered round the squat bulk of the mule in the wagon-bed.

"Not there," called Karli. "That's the slaves' room you're pointing at. They'll have him there, in the private chamber. Train round right, right another six feet."

The ton-and-a-quarter mule could not be lifted from its bed without immense effort. Instead the horse-holder slowly shuffled the horse round, inching the cart sideways on its solid axles.

"On!" grunted Cwicca hoarsely, raising his arm in the team's well-practiced drill. Fritha the loader lifted a twenty-pound water-smoothed rock from the bed of the cart, fitted it into the sling. The crew, all but Cwicca and Hama the launch-man, vaulted over the sides of the cart. They had not shot their weapon, with its monstrous kick, from inside a confined space before, and were not sure what effect it would have.

Cwicca checked his target again, dropped his arm in the signal to shoot.

Shef lay back in the great feather bed, in complete relaxation. In all his life he had never spent so much time lying down before, except when he was bedridden with the marsh-fever. A man who was awake should be working, or eating, or at rare intervals merry-making. That was what everyone he knew believed. The idea of rest did not enter their minds.

They were wrong. A day and a night now, he had hardly stirred from the great bed, except to eat his meals. Even those had been brought to him by the slave-women during the day. He had never felt better.

But then maybe that was the queen. She too had come to him at frequent intervals during the day, more frequent than he had ever imagined possible. In Shef's stern and gloomy home, dominated by the pious, angry Wulfgar his stepfather, all forms of sexuality were forbidden to all on Sundays, on the eve of Sunday, during Lent, in the Advent season, during the fasts of the Church. The servants had evaded his rules, of course, and even more the village folk, but sexuality had taken on an air of furtiveness, something to be snatched, got over in between bouts of work, or between sleep and wake. Someone like Queen Ragnhild had been the stuff of dreams, beyond the imagination or experience of any village-youth.

And what he had done had been beyond his imagination too. In amazement, considering what he had already performed, Shef felt his flesh beginning to rise again at the thought of what he had seen and felt. Yet the queen would not return for a while, gone out, she said, to walk along the shore. Better to save his strength. Better to sleep again, warm and well-fed. As he closed his eyes and lay back against the duck-down bolster, Shef thought vaguely of Karli. Better see what he was doing. One of the slave-women would know. He had never asked their names. Strange. Perhaps he was beginning to behave like a king at long last.

In his dream, Shef was standing by a forge, as he had before. It was not the great forge of the gods of Asgarth, which he had once visited, yet it was like that forge in that the whole working space was littered with boxes, logs, rough tables. There were hand-holds nailed here and there to the wall.

They were there, Shef remembered, because this smith was lame. In the body he now inhabited, he remembered the keen pain as they slit his sinews with the knife, the laughing face of his enemy Nithhad, the promise Nithhad had made him.

"You will not run far now, Völund, with your hamstrings cut, neither on feet nor on skis, hunter of the forest. And cut sinew never grows back. Yet your hands are unharmed, and you still have your eyes. So work, Völund, mighty smith! Work for me, Nithhad, make me precious things by day and by night. For there is no escape for you by land or by water. And I promise you, husband of the Valkyrie though you are: if you do not earn your bread every day, you will feel the lash like the lowest dog of a Finn among my thralls!"

And Nithhad had had him trussed up then and there and given him a taste of the leather for proof. Still Völund remembered the pain in his back, the shame of being beaten without reply, the glittering eyes of Nithhad's queen as she watched. His wife's ring had glinted on her finger as she did so, for they had robbed him as well as mutilated him.

Shef-who-was-now-Völund beat furiously on the red iron as he remembered, not trusting himself in this mood with copper or silver or the red gold that Nithhad demanded most.

As he limped and heaved himself from side to side he saw bright eyes watching him. Four of them. The two young sons of Nithhad, come to see the fire and the clangor and the sparkling jewels. Völund paused, looked at them. Nithhad let them come freely, sure that his slave could never escape, sure too that no matter how crazy he was for revenge, Völund would never take a revenge for which he could not escape retaliation. In the belief of the North, that would be exchanging one for two, neither sensible nor honorable. A revenge was no revenge unless it was complete.

High above, in the rafters to which his great smith's arms could swing him, lay the wings Völund had made: the magic wings to take him away. But first the revenge. The complete revenge.

"Come and see," called Völund to the watching faces. "See what I have in my chest here."

He reached inside it, pulled out a chain of gold links with a jewel between each one, red, blue and green in complex pattern. "Or see this." He showed for an instant a box of walrus ivory with carved scenes upon it, inlaid with silver. "See, in the chest, there is much besides. Come, look in the chest, just peep over the side if you dare."

Slowly the two boys came out into the light of the fire, holding each other's hands. One was six, the other four, the children of Nithhad and his second wife, the enchantress, far younger than their half-sister, the maiden Böthvild who also came to eye him sometimes from the shadows. They were fine boys, shy but friendly, not yet spoilt by their father's greed, their mother's cunning. One of them had given him an apple the day before, saved from his own meal.

Völund waved them over, opened the chest, held its massive lid open with one hand. He was careful to hold it by the handle. Many an hour had he spent, in time stolen from sleep, welding on the edge to it, the sharpest edge he had ever made in his life. They were good children, and he did not wish them to feel pain.

"Come, see!" he said again. They peered over, squeaking like mice with excitement. Their necks were over the iron lip of the chest. Völund, cruel man that he was, averted his eyes as he prepared to slam down the lid . . .

I do not want to be in this body, thought Shef, fighting against the god's fingers that held him firmly, forced him to watch. Whatever lesson I am being taught, I do not want to learn it.

As he began in some unknown way to squirm free he saw another sight, far below the forge, somewhere in the deep rocky bowels, not of Middle-earth, but of the walls that surround the Nine Worlds of men and gods and giants together. A great figure, with the savage unpredictable face of a god, chained with monstrous fetters to the foundations of the universe. A great serpent hissing and spitting venom in its face, the face contorted with pain and yet still aware, still thinking, still looking beyond the pain.

The figure was the chained god Loki, Shef realized, whom the Way-priests believed had been bound and tormented by his father Othin for the murder of his brother Balder. Yet who would break free and return to revenge himself on gods and men, with his monster-children on the Last Day itself. The enormous staple on one wrist-fetter had been pulled almost free from the wall, Shef saw. When it came loose Loki would have one hand free to throttle the tormenting serpent sent by his father Othin. Already he seemed free enough to beckon, to be signaling to his allies, the monster-broods in the forests and in the depths of the sea. For an instant his furious eyes seemed to look from his prison up towards Shef.

As he tore himself away again Shef felt one more trickle of the thoughts of Völund.

Do the deed, they ran. Do it now. And then, then to scoop out the skulls and carve them like walrus ivory, then to polish the teeth till they shine like pearls, then to take the glistening eyeballs from their orbits . . .

Back in his own body again, Shef felt a monstrous slam, saw for an instant a sharpened lid swinging down.

The slam was real. He could feel the tremors of it still shaking the bed. Shef kicked his feet free of the linen sheet and woolen blanket, leapt from the bed, lunged for tunic, breeches and shoes. Was this the queen's husband come for him?

The door swung open and the boy Harald rushed in. "Mother! Mother!" He stopped as he saw only Shef sitting on his mother's bed. Without a pause he pulled his little eating-knife from his belt and lunged at Shef's throat.

Shef parried the blow, caught the thin wrist, twisted away the knife, ignored the furious kicks and punches from the free hand. "Easy, easy," he said. "I was just waiting here. What is happening outside?"

"I don't know. Men with a—with something that throws rocks. The wall is all smashed in."

Shef let the boy go, darted through the door from the bedchamber to the queens' parlor. As he did so a concerted charge smashed down the door from the main hall, and a wave of men poured in, knives drawn and crossbows pointed. Shef recognized Cwicca at the same moment that they recognized him, began to step forward waving his arms frantically for them to stop.

Karli sprang out of the ruck and came forward, shouting something inaudible in the din of voices.

"There's no need for it!" Shef bellowed back. "I'm all right. Tell them all to stop."

Karli laid a hand on his arm, trying to drag him towards the door. Furiously, Shef threw it off, realized at once that Karli meant to knock him unconscious once more. He dodged the left lead, got a hand up in time to block the right swing, ducked his head into Karli's already-broken nose and grappled his arms, trying to prevent him getting in a clear blow. As they struggled, Shef felt other hands on him, arms and legs, men trying to pick him up bodily and carry him off like a sack. He heard a voice gasp in his ear, "Hit him with the sandbag, Cwicca, he won't stop fighting."

Shef dropped Karli, swung the men holding his arms into each other, trampled his way free of the man clutching his leg, filled his lungs for another and more commanding bellow.

Behind him, the old queen Asa had also entered the room. One of the English raiders stood goggling at the struggle in front of him, unable to bring himself to join in and lay hands on his master. Seizing the iron stake by which she summoned her slaves, the old queen struck him smartly over the head, snatched the seax-knife from his belt as he slumped. Took three quick hobbling paces towards Shef, the cuckolder of her son and danger to her grandson, still standing unawares with his back to her.

At the same moment the little boy Harald, also standing staring at the struggle, felt the prompting of generations of warrior-ancestors. With a shrill cry he too raised his knife again and ran forward to attack the invaders of his hall. As he ran past Shef at a line of grown men, Shef scooped him up and hugged him to his own body, wrapping both arms round him to prevent his struggles. He tried to shout again, "Everybody just stand still!"

The faces confronting him turned to alarm, men started to spring forward. Shef turned with the speed he had learned in the wrestling ring, Harald still clutched to his body.

Queen Asa thrust savagely upwards with the broad-bladed knife. Shef felt a thud, a prick of pain over his ribs. Looked down at the boy in his arms. Saw him turn up his face, start to ask some disbelieving question. Saw the knife driven clean through the boy's heart and body. The knife in the hands of his grandmother.

Somewhere, again, Shef heard a lid slam. Slam again and again.

The room had gone completely still and silent. Shef released his grip, slowly straightened the small body out, laid it on the ground.

As he looked down, his eyes seemed for a moment to blur. He seemed to be looking not at the slight shape of a ten-year old, but at a grown man, tall and burly, with a mane of hair and beard.

This was Harald Fairhair, said a cold, amused, familiar voice. *Harald Fairhair as he would have been. You are his inheritor now. You inherited his treasure from King Edmund, and paid with your youth. You inherited his luck from King Alfred, and paid with your love. Now you inherit destiny from King Harald. What will you pay with this time? And do not try to shirk my visions again.*

The moment passed. Shef was once more in the parlor, staring down at a bloodstained shape. Harald was dead now. Shef had felt the life go. Arms were at his shoulders again, hustling him away, and this time he did not resist. Behind him Queen Asa took slow step after slow step towards the body of her grandson, reaching out a tentative, shaking hand. Shef lost sight of her as they ran him through the door into the hall, out through the main door shattered by the catapult-stone, into the open.

Outside the hubbub broke out again, someone shouting, "But she's still got my knife," other voices snarling at him, Osmod counting, "Seven, eight, nine, all right, that's the lot, get moving." Cwicca appeared from somewhere with a firebrand and the barrel of dry kindling the slaves used, hurled first one and then the other into the cart, watched the flame spread as he slashed the horse free of its traces.

"They won't get our mule," he shouted.

"What are you doing with those women?" Osmod shouted as Karli came into the light, a woman in each hand and two more running anxiously behind him.

"They've got to come with us."

"It's only a six-oar boat, there's no room."

"They have to come. Especially now the boy's dead. Their throats will be cut at his burial."

Osmod, ex-slave himself, argued no more. "All right, move it."

In an untidy stream nine men and four women ran down the path leading to the little beach where Martha had killed Stein only the evening before, Cwicca and Osmod bringing up the rear, crossbows raised. Half way down it, Shef heard a great shriek split the air behind him. Ragnhild returned from her walk along the shore. Behind it, men's voices shouting. The guardsmen they had left behind, rallied and anxious to avenge their defeats.

The run turned into a headlong dash, each person making for the beach and the boat they could see waiting, Udd and Hund with oars poised ready to shove off. Men and women poured over the thwarts, seized oars or were pushed out of the way. The overloaded boat jammed on the shingle, Shef and Karli leaped out again and heaved it bodily out six feet, ten, till the beach shelved away and they were dragged in over the sides, only inches above the water. Six men found their places, braced their feet, took one pull, another, as Osmod hoarsely called the time.

Framed by the light from the now fiercely-burning cart, Shef saw the figure of Queen Ragnhild walking down the beach, her arms stretched out. Arrows from the men behind her skipped over the water, but Shef ignored them, waved down the crossbows poised to answer.

"Luckstealer!" she cried. "Bane of my son. May you be the bane of all those around you. May you never know woman again. May no son succeed you."

"It wasn't his fault," muttered Wilfi from the bow, rubbing his head where the iron stake had split it. "It was that daft old woman who took my knife."

"Shut up about your knife," growled Fritha, "you should have held on to it."

As the bickering continued, the boat pulled steadily away into the black dark, waiting for concealment before bending round away from Halvdan's cruisers to the mainland no more than a short mile off.

Shef stared over the stern till he could see no longer, at the woman still raving and weeping by the shore.

CHAPTER FIFTEEN

Alfred, King of the West-Saxons, co-ruler with the absent King Shef of all the English counties south of the Trent, watched his young bride with slight nervousness as she walked the last few steps to the top of the hill overlooking Winchester. There was some chance—the leeches could not yet be sure—that she might be carrying his child already, and he feared she might overtax her strength. He knew though that she hated protection, held his tongue.

She reached the top, turned and looked out over the valley. It was already a mass of white blossom, where the Hampshire churls had planted the apple trees for their beloved cider. On the broad fields the other side of the stockaded town teams could be seen plowing, men following the slow oxen up and down the furrows; very long furrows because it took the eight-beast teams so long to make a turn. Alfred followed her gaze, pointed to a spot in the middle distance.

"Look," he said, "there is a team plowing with four horses, not eight oxen. It is on your own estate. Wonred the reeve saw the horse-collars the men of the Way used for their catapult-teams, and said he would try it for plowing. He says horses eat more than oxen, but if they are hitched properly they are stronger and faster and do much more work. He says he is going to start breeding horses for size and strength as well. And there is an advantage no-one thought of. It takes a good part of a churl's day to get out to the further fields and back if he is leading a yoke of oxen. With the horses they ride out and back, so they have more time in the fields."

"Or more time to rest, I hope," said Godive. "One reason poor churls live so little time is that they have no rest but Sunday, and the Church takes that."

"Used to take that," corrected Alfred. "Now it is up to the churl."

He hesitated a moment, patted her shoulder gently. "It is working, you know," he said. "I don't think any of us ever realized how rich a country can be if it is left at peace, with no masters. Or only a master who cares for the country. But the good news comes in every day. What King Shef, your brother, told me is perfectly correct. There is always someone who knows an answer, but nearly always it is someone whom no-one has ever asked before. I had a group of miners visit me yesterday, men from the lead mines in the hills. They used to be owned by the monks at Winchcombe. Now the monks have gone, they work the mines themselves, for my reeve and the alderman of Gloucester. They told me that the old Rome-folk used to mine silver in the same hills, and that they think they could do the same.

"Silver," he mused. "If the black monks had known that, they would have whipped their slaves till they died in search of it. So the slaves did not tell them. They tell me because they know I will give them a share. And with new silver—it is not long ago that every time we minted the money was worse, and soon Canterbury money would have been as bad as York. Now, with the silver I put back from the Church hoards, a Wessex penny is as good as any in Frankland or the German lands beyond. And the traders come in from everywhere, from Dorestad and Compostella, and the Franklands too if they can evade their own king's ban. They all pay harbor-dues, and I use it to pay my miners. The traders are happy, and the miners are happy, and I am happy too.

"So, Godive, you see that things are not as bad as they were, even for the churls. It may not seem much, but a horse to ride and a full belly even in Lent is happiness to many."

A bell began to chime from the Old Minster in the town below, its strokes ringing out over the steep valley. Ringing for a bridal, probably: the priests who remained in Wessex had found that if they were to keep any worshipers for the White Christ they had to use their assets of music and ritual, more impressive still than the strange tales of the Way-missionaries from the North.

"It still rests on war, though," she replied.

Alfred nodded. "It always did. I saw this valley a desolation of burnt fields when I was a boy. The Vikings took the town and burnt every house in it except the stone Minster. They would have pulled that down if they had had time. We fought them then and we fight them still. The difference is that now we fight them at sea, so the land is spared. And the more it is spared the stronger we are, and the weaker they grow."

He hesitated again. "Are you missing your—your brother? I know well that all this goes back to him. If it had not been for him I would have been dead, or a penniless exile, or at best a puppet-king with Bishop Daniel holding my strings. Or some Viking jarl, maybe. I owe him everything." He patted her hand. "Even you."

Godive dropped her eyes. Her husband always referred to Shef, now, as her brother, though she knew that he knew that there was no blood relationship between them, that they were stepbrother and stepsister only. Sometimes she thought that Alfred had realized the truth of their relationship, maybe the truth too that her first husband had really been her half-brother. But if he suspected, he was careful to ask no further. He did not know that she had miscarried twice, deliberately, while she had been first married, taking the dangerous birthwort. If she had believed in any god, the Christian one or the strange pantheon of the Way, she would have prayed to him or them for a safe delivery for what might now be in her womb.

"I hope he is alive."

"At least no-one has seen him dead. All our traders know there is a reward for any news, and a greater one for the man who brings him back."

"Not many kings would pay to have a rival return," said Godive.

"He is no rival to me. My rivals are across the Channel there, or up in the North working mischief. It looks safe as we sit on this hill and look over the fields. I tell you, I would feel twenty times safer if Shef were back in England. He is our best hope. The churls call him *sigesaelig*, you know, the Victorious."

Godive squeezed her husband's arm. "They call you Alfred *esteadig*. The Gracious. That is a better name."

In the great tent of striped canvas many days' march and sail to the north, the conference was less happy. The tent had been pitched with its rear into the wind, and the front wall brailed up so the men inside it could also look out. They looked out over a drear landscape of moor and heather, marked here and there by columns of smoke rising, the marks of the harrying parties coming down on one clump of wretched bothies or another. The three Ragnarssons left alive sat on their camp stools, ale-horns in hand. Each had a weapon stuck into the ground beside him, spear or spiked axe, as well as their swords belted on. Twice already that spring, since the battle off the Elbe, one jarl or another had tried to challenge their authority. Sensitive as cats to the constant ebb and flow of reputation on which power rested, all three knew they had to offer their followers a scheme. A bribe. A proposition. Or there would be tents struck in the night, ships missing at the next rendezvous, men gone to try their fortune in the service of some sea-king better favored by luck.

"This is keeping the lads busy," said the grizzled Ubbi, nodding at the smoke-columns. "Good beef, good mutton, women to run down. No casualties to speak of."

"No money," completed Halvdan. "No glory either."

Sigurth the Snake-eye knew his brothers were just setting the problem up for him to deal with, not offering a criticism. The brothers never fought, hardly ever disagreed. Their relationship had survived even the psychotic Ivar. The other two waited for him to respond.

"If we go south again," he said, "we run into those rock-throwers again. We can sail rings round them, we know that. But they have the advantage now. They know we're up here in Scotland, because they kept us out of the Channel. All they have to do is harbor somewhere on the coast near their northern border, wherever they choose to draw it. If we sail down-coast, they hit us. If we go round them—and we don't know where they are—they get to hear about it, come down after us, and hit us in harbor, wherever we are. The risk is either meeting them at sea, or getting our ships battered to bits while we're on land. We might end up having to cut our way from coast to coast. And I don't think any of the lads, however big they talk, fancies meeting the rock-throwers at sea again. You can't fight standing on a bundle of planks."

"So we're beat," nudged Ubbi. All three men laughed.

"Maybe what we need is some rock-throwers of our own," suggested Halvdan. "That's what Ivar thought. He made that little black-robed bastard, what was his name? Erkinbjart? He made him make some. Pity the little bastard got away."

"That's for next year," said Sigurth. "Can't change horses in mid-stream, and for this year we have to go with what we have. This year we'll pass the word in the slave-markets that we pay high prices for men who can shoot these throwers. Someone will bring one in. And if they can shoot them they can build them. Put someone like that together with a real ship-builder, and we'll have something that can outsail those clumsy English tubs and outfight them too.

"But right now we need something to put heart into our lot and silver into their pouches. Or the hope of silver in their heads, anyway."

"Ireland," suggested Halvdan.

"We'd have to go north about round the tip of Scotland now, the place will be aswarm with Norwegians before we get there."

"Frisia?" offered Ubbi doubtfully.

"Poor as Scotland, only flatter."

"That's the islands. How about the mainland? Or we could try Hamburg again. Or Bremen."

"That hasn't been lucky water for us this year," said Sigurth. His brothers nodded, both of them showing their teeth in involuntary snarl. They remembered the humiliation on the sandbank, coming back from a fruitless hunt with no quarry and a man missing. The humiliation of being outmaneuvered, so that they had to stand back from a challenge from a single man.

"But I think that's the right idea," said Sigurth. "Or nearly the right idea. We'll keep the lads busy over here for a few weeks yet, give this whole country a complete shaking. Let them know they just have to enjoy themselves, there's something bigger coming. Then we'll go back across the North Sea, direct crossing, head for the granite isles."

His brothers nodded, knowing he meant the islands of the North Frisians, facing the Ditmarsh, Fohr and Amrum and Sylt, three islands of rock amid a waste of shifting sands.

"Then we go down the Eider and hit Hedeby."

Halvdan and Ubbi stared at each other, considered. "They're our own people," said Halvdan. "Sort of. Anyway, they're Danes."

"So what? Have they done us any favors? That fat trader-king Hrorik wouldn't even sell the man we want to Skuli. He let the Way-priests take him off to their bolt-hole."

"Maybe we ought to hit them instead."

"Right. What I'm thinking," said Sigurth, "is if England is ruled out for us right now, we'll find better returns in our own countries than foraging round these poor places. Riskier, I know. But if we take Hedeby and Hrorik's gold, then there'll be all the more to support us if we go for Halvdan and his idiot brother Olaf. Sure, there'll always be some who'll drop out, got a brother in Kaupang or a father in Hedeby. Plenty left. And the ones we beat in one place will join us for the next place."

"Roll up the North first," said Halvdan. "Set you in place as the One King of all the Northlands. Then come back to the South."

"With a thousand keels, and rock-throwers in the front of them," amplified Ubbi.

"To finish the Christians once and for all . . ."

"To fulfill our Bragi-boast long ago . . ."

"To get revenge for Ivar."

Halvdan got up, drained his horn, pulled his spiked beard-axe out of the ground. "I'll go round the tents," he said. "Drop a few hints. Say we've got a plan, and everyone will get a shock when they know it. Keep them quiet just a few weeks longer."

Erkenbert the deacon stood inside a great ring of ancient stones. It was the doom-ring of the Smaaland peoples, the Little Countries between Danish Skaane and the giant confederacy of the Swedes extending hundreds of miles to the north, a country with many kings striving always to establish one *Sveariki*, one empire of the Swedes. It was the Smaalanders' spring assembly, when men came out of their snowed-in cabins and began to prepare for the short but welcome summer.

Erkenbert had carefully dyed his worn black robe so that it shone even blacker, a violent contrast with the furs and homespuns that surrounded him. His attendant had also once more shaved every inch of his tonsure, so that the bald ring on his head stood out even more strongly. "We don't want to hide away," Bruno had said. "That's the old style. Trying to get by on sufferance. We want them to see us. Get Christianity in their faces." Erkenbert had meditated a sharp reply on the virtue of humility, but had withdrawn. For one thing few men any longer cared to answer back to the Master of the *Lanzenorden*, as men were already calling him. For another Erkenbert could see the sense in the policy.

The Smaalanders were selling off slaves, as usual. Mere bags of bones, most of them, ill-fed during the winter and now a doubtful speculation for the summer and the work-period. The emissaries of the Uppsala king Orm were buying the cheapest, as usual. Don't bother with most of them, Bruno had said. Funds are low. But this one he had to have.

A burly farmer pushed forward into the ring as his turn came, towing with him in one fist an emaciated figure. The slave was dressed in no more than tatters, and shook uncontrollably with cold. Through the rags his ribs showed. A cough racked his body every few seconds, and he stank of the midden where he had slept for warmth.

A chorus of jeers greeted the arrival, from the seller's neighbors. "What do you want for him, Arni? If he was a chicken you'd have to use him for soup. Even the Swedes won't take him. He won't live till the next sacrifice."

Arni glared round indignantly. His eye fell on Erkenbert advancing deliberately across the sale-ground. Erkenbert walked composedly up to the thin man, put his arms round him, held him closely.

"Don't worry, sirra, we have heard of you, we are here to rescue you."

The stink attacked Erkenbert's nostrils, but he bore it, remembering the Book of Job. The thin man began to weep, causing a fresh barrage of jeers and hooting from the crowd.

"How can you rescue me, they will take you too, they are animals, they care nothing for the rights of God . . ."

Gently Erkenbert disengaged himself, pointed behind him to the group from which he had come. Ten *Ritter* of the *Lanzenorden* stood in a double line, every man mailed, helmeted, with metal gauntlets shining. In each man's right hand was a short pike, butt on the ground, point forward at exactly the same angle. "These people are good warriors," Bruno had said. "But they have no discipline. We will show them some. It keeps them uncertain."

"What do you want for this man?" said Erkenbert, speaking loudly so the watchers could hear.

Arni, a devout disciple of Frey, spat on the ground. "To you, Christling, twenty ounces of silver."

Derision from the crowd. Eight ounces was a good price for a man in full vigor, twelve for a pretty girl.

"I will give you four," shouted Erkenbert, still playing to the crowd. "You have saved the other sixteen on food and clothes over the winter."

Arni did not see the joke. Face purpling, he strode forward towards the much smaller man.

"Shaveling! Four ounces! You have no rights here. By the law of the Smaalanders any man who catches a Christ-priest has the right to enslave him. What is to hinder me from taking you and your four ounces."

"You have the right to enslave a Christ-priest," replied Erkenbert unmoved. "Do you have the strength?"

At the psychological moment the uncanny shape of Bruno made its way out of the crowd, from the point opposite the watching ranks of the *Ritters*. He pushed gently through the watching men, edging them aside with his ape-like shoulders. He carried no pike, but wore the same armor as his men. His left hand rested on the pommel of his trailing, over-length sword.

Arni glared round him, observing the sudden silence, realizing that in an instant he had become the one under test. He tried to rally the crowd round him.

"Are we going to take this? Are we going to let these men come in here and steal our slaves away?"

"They're paying cash," observed a voice from the crowd.

"And what will they do with the men they take? Such as these—" Beside himself with fury, Arni turned and cuffed his slave violently across the side of the head, sending him sprawling and weeping to the ground. "Such as these should go to the groves of Uppsala, as a sacrifice to the true gods, not go back to preach more lies about sons of virgins and the dead risi—"

Arni's voice cut off in mid-syllable. Moving like the tufted lynx of the forests, Bruno had covered the four paces between them. His hand shot out faster than anyone could see. But they could all see now that his gauntleted fingers had closed on the throat-ball, the Adam's apple of the Smaalander, held it in steel pincers. He lifted slightly, and the farmer rose on struggling tiptoe.

"Filth," said Bruno. "You have laid hands on the servant of the living God. You have spoken blasphemy against our faith. I will not kill you in the doom-ring, where blood must not be shed, but do you care to meet me in the dueling-ground, with sword and buckler, or axe and spear, or any weapon you care to choose?"

Unable to move or speak, the farmer goggled helplessly.

"I thought not." Bruno released him, turned on his heel, barked a command. In one drilled movement the front rank of his *Ritters* stamped forward, paces one-two-three, stood at attention once more. "Continue with the sale."

"Four ounces," Erkenbert repeated. We mustn't rob them, Bruno had said, or they *will* fight. But we don't have to pay over the odds either. Still, we must rescue Sirra Eilif the priest. Only he knows anything of the kings in the back country behind Birka. We need him to help us with our search. I am anxious to hear more of this King Kjallak they speak of, from up on the borders of Iron-bearing Land.

Massaging his throat, the farmer wondered whether he dared hold out for more, met Erkenbert's black hostile eyes, decided he did not. He nodded.

Erkenbert threw a small purse at his feet, took Eilif the priest gently by one arm, withdrew with him to the ranks of the *Ritter*, now joined once more by Bruno. The priest and the deacon moved to the security of the central file, Bruno snapped commands, the armored men sloped their pikes and marched away, feet slamming down together like a single man.

The Swedes and Smaalanders watched them go, turned again to their business.

"What did you think of that?" said one tall Swede to another.

"Think of that? That's the bastard who killed King Orm's man at

Hedeby. He must make a habit of this. I don't know what he wants, but I'll tell you this. We're seeing some new kind of Christian."

The other nodded thoughtfully, looked round to see if any might overhear. "If there's a new kind of Christian around, maybe we all need a new kind of king to deal with them."

rand had protested briefly and furiously at the unexpected appearance of four women from the boat. Not enough horses. We'll have to leave them. When they told him what had happened on Drottningsholm his protests ceased. "We'd better get out of here," was all he said. "Now his son is dead Halvdan won't rest till everyone involved is dead as well. Or he is. I don't think he'll touch my crew, or not till he finds out that I left with you. But we have to be out of the Westfold faster than anyone has ever left before. You drop behind—you're left behind."

Shef said nothing to all this. Stumbled as he walked with his dark thoughts still on the island. And the dead boy. Some part of him was still trapped back there, sealed between the warm thighs, engulfed by large breasts.

They had set off along a path that led directly up into the mountains, twisting and winding through the everlasting dark pine- and fir-forest. Ten Englishmen, four women, Karli and Brand, with a dozen horses between them. And deadly pursuit sure to follow them in the morning.

Yet almost from the start it seemed that Brand's fears had less ground than he thought. One of the ex-slaves, Wilfi, had said immediately that in his life in England he had been a forerunner, the slave sent on ahead of his master when his master travelled, to see to his lodging and food at every halt. Running forty miles a day, Wilfi said, was as easy to him as walking twenty to another man. He needed no horse. The women rode double, or else one would ride while the men took turns trotting at their side with a hand on the saddle.

It was a long night's riding, dawn was slow in coming. At first light Brand called a halt to cook, water the horses at a stream, and give the mountain ponies a chance to forage in the new swift-growing grass. The slaves quickly built a fire, crushed grain and made their everlasting porridge. Then they were ready to start again while Brand was still groaning and massaging his stiff thigh-muscles. When he looked round in surprise at the column already forming up, Osmod told him with a certain relish: "You forget, master. A slave has to go on whether he wants to or not. It is free men who have to be persuaded, or think a blister, or hunger or thirst are good enough excuses to stop."

And Vikings, fast movers though they might be by the leisurely standards of the armies of the Christian West, were seamen or ski-runners rather than horsemen. For all his urgency it was Brand who held the party up. No horse the party had could carry his giant frame for long. During the long day that followed the long night, Osmod finally took charge, reorganized the mounts so that each man or woman in the party took a turn on foot as well as riding, and told Brand to take two horses, riding one and leading the other in turn, or else, on the flatter and broader stretches, running between the two with a great arm hooked over each saddle-pommel.

"Will we make it?" Cwicca asked finally when they stopped for a second time, to hobble the horses in a patch of thick new growth. The rest of the party listened anxiously for the answer. Brand looked round, tried to estimate where they were and how far they had come.

"I think so," he said. "We have come faster than I thought possible. And we must have had a start anyway, since Halvdan did not know which way we went."

"He'll find out, though?" queried Cwicca.

"There'll be riders out now to tell him who is moving through his territory. But they have to reach him, get his orders, come back and try to carry them out. All that time we're heading the other way. Three more stages like the two we've done and we're out of the Westfold. Won't stop Halvdan sending killers after us, but he can't order anyone to block the road."

"But we're not taking any risks," said Osmod. "As soon as the horses have eaten their fill, we move on."

"We have to sleep sometime," protested Brand.

"Not for days yet. When people start falling off their horses, then we can sleep. Or else tie them on."

The party pushed on again, wearily, with aching feet and grumbling bellies. But never a word of complaint. The women led the way, looked back sharply at the slightest sign of flagging.

Slowly, though, they began to realize that the real threat lay not behind them but in front. In mountainous and little-traveled Norway, all roads and paths went naturally through every farmstead on the route. A chance for the isolated farm-folk to hear news or to give it, a chance for the traveling pedlars to sell their clothes or wine or salt. To begin with, at every farmstead they came to, Brand had bargained for extra horses, buying one here and two there till the party were fully mounted with animals to spare. Yet though he paid immediately in good silver pennies, the farmers seemed loath to sell. "I'm being too quick," he explained. "They want me to hang around and bargain for half a day. Nothing much happens up here. They like to spin things out. Paying the price asked and moving on—it doesn't seem honest to them. Anyway, it's natural they're going to wonder who we are. Ten midgets who can't speak the language properly, four women in slave-gear, one man in a dream"—he pointed at the unspeaking Shef—"and me. They're bound to be uneasy. I told you, I'm taking a bunch of mice through Catland."

Trouble stirred first the day after Brand declared them free of the Westfold. They had crossed a watershed and were winding their way down through a steep valley, water rushing down on both sides of it, and animals newly-released from their indoor winter pens grazing gratefully wherever the new grass showed. The party came down, as they had a dozen times before, on a farmstead, a cluster of buildings arranged in a rough square. Work had stopped immediately as the men of the farm moved over to inspect the new arrivals, to exchange words with Brand, to call out the women and children. Slowly Shef, his mind still turning continually over the little boy who had died in his arms, realized that the mood at this farmstead was somehow different. The menfolk were not just uneasy or suspicious, they were amused. They had come to some kind of conclusion. Shef looked round more alertly. How many of them were there? Were there still as many as there had been at the start? How many in his own party?

A shriek came suddenly from behind the cow-byre. A voice calling out in English. Edith's voice, the youngest and prettiest of the women. Without words Cwicca, Osmod and the rest seized their crossbows and streamed towards it, Brand, Shef and the farm-folk following at a run.

As they came round the corner of the barn they saw two Norsemen holding Edith. One held her from behind, trying to clamp a hand over her mouth. The other had hold of one leg, was trying to grasp the other. As he heard feet behind him, the second man let go, turned.

"She's used to it," he said. "Look at her. Just a whore of a slave. Does it all the time. Why shouldn't we get a turn too?"

"She's no slave," snapped Osmod. "And she never was your slave."

"Who are you to say?" The other farm men, half a dozen of them, had come round now, were siding with him and the other man still clutching Edith. "She has no rights here. Nor have you. If I say you're a slave you'll soon be one."

Shef pushed his way forward, made the Norseman meet his eye. They were not in danger here, he knew, or at least no immediate danger. He had heard the crossbows click, and though the Norsemen had axes and knives to hand, they would be riddled before they had a chance to use them. But if they did that, even if they killed every man, even if they killed every woman and child as well, as Viking raiders would have done in England, still the news would go out and a hue and cry raised. These men had to be made to back down. But they had decided, in their unthinking way, that they were dealing with lesser beings.

"Just leave us this one," suggested the Norseman, "and the rest of you can ride on."

Edith screamed from behind the covering hand, thrashed violently. She thinks we might just do it, thought Shef.

Brand stepped from behind him, the axe he had taken from his saddle sliding through his massive palm. It was a mighty weapon, the haft a three-foot shaft of ash, the curved convex edge a foot long from horn to horn. The iron head was inlaid with serpent-patterns in silver, the welded steel blade flashing bright against the darker iron. A long spike jutted from the back of the head, for balance, and for the back-stroke. It was the weapon of a champion.

"Let her go," he said. "Unless you want to fight me. All of you, or one at a time. I don't care."

The Norseman who had spoken first looked up at him. He was not as big as Brand—no-one Shef had ever seen was—but once again Shef realized what giants the Norwegians were. The Norseman was a good four inches taller than Shef himself, far broader and heavier. He was considering the challenge, Shef realized. Was it worth it? What was the risk?

Brand flicked his axe into the air, let it twirl over and over, caught it without glancing up.

The Norwegian nodded slowly. "All right. Thorgeir, let her go. I don't think she's worth it. This time. But someone will catch you before you get out of the mountains, big man. Then we'll see why you're running slaves through the Buskerud. Slave-blood in you too, maybe."

Shef saw Brand's knuckles whiten on the axe-handle at the insult, but he made no move. Edith, released, ran instantly to the center of the group that faced her, crossbows cocked and leveled. Slowly, facing outwards, the women, the Englishmen and Brand retreated to their horses, silently gathered up their possessions. Two of the horses were missing, stolen during the brief confrontation.

"Don't fuss about it," muttered Brand. "Just get going and keep going." The column wound through the farm-buildings and middens. A child threw a clod of earth after them as they left, and then the rest joined in, mingling earth and stones with taunts and jeers that followed them half a mile on their way.

The party camped that night in more comfort than ever before, spreading out their meager supply of blankets and taking time to cook the salt meat and dried onions they had bought a day before. But they ate silently and anxiously. A sentry remained on his feet all the time, watching the trail before and behind them.

As the others rolled themselves up to sleep, Osmod and Cwicca came over to sit next to Shef and the still-silent Brand.

"We're not going to get very far like this," said Osmod. "The news will go ahead of us, along paths we don't know. We could have trouble at every farmstead. If there's a village or a town it could be worse."

"I told you," Brand replied. "Like taking a nest of mice through Catland."

"We were relying on our dog," said Cwicca.

Shef looked at Brand with instant alarm. He had seen Brand challenged or provoked several times during the campaigning winter, in the camps round York or East Anglia. Provoked a good deal more gently or carefully than this, and by men many times more formidable than Cwicca. The response every time had been the instant blow or grapple: a broken arm, a man knocked senseless. This time Brand sat motionless, seemingly deep within himself.

"Yes," said Brand finally. "You were relying on me. You still can rely on me. I gave my word to see you through to the Gula Fjord, and I will do my best to keep that word. But there's something you ought to know. I know it now, if I didn't before.

"I have been a warrior for twenty-five winters. If I were to count up the men I have killed or the battles I have seen—well, it would sound

like a saga of one of King Hrolf's champions, or of old Ragnar
Hairy-Breeks himself. In all that time no-one can say I ever turned tail,
or held back when the spears crossed.''

He looked round fiercely. ''You have seen that! I should not need to
boast here.

''But the fight with Ivar took something out of me. I have been
wounded many times, and left for dead more than once. I never felt in
my own heart that I was dead. When Ivar dodged my blow and got his
sword through me I felt the blade in my guts, and I knew, I knew that
even if I could get myself off it and live that day, then I would die
within two more. I knew. It took less time than a heartbeat, but I could
never forget it. Not even after Hund over there sewed up my torn guts
and my belly and nursed me through the fever and the draining pus. I
am as strong as ever I was now. But I cannot forget what I once knew.''

He looked round again at the others. ''And the trouble is, you see,
up here in the mountains, where every district has its champion, and
mannjafnathr is what they do all the time, comparing men to see
which they think is the deadliest, they can feel it. That man back there
knew he wasn't my match—knew I had killed a dozen farmhands like
him before my beard was fully grown. But he could tell as well that my
heart wasn't in it. Just a little more time to think about it, and he might
have taken the risk.''

''You are as strong as ever,'' said Osmod. ''You would have killed
him. Better for all of us if you had.''

''I expect I'd have killed him,'' Brand agreed. ''He was only the
cock of his own midden. But funny things happen when a man loses
heart. I have known great warriors stand still with the piss running
down their breeches till they were cut down. They freeze, and the
Valkyries, Othin's daughters, the Choosers of the Slain, throw their
fear-fetters over them.''

The Englishmen sat in silence. Finally Osmod spoke again. ''That's
it, then. We'd better go through every place we come to all closed up
and ready from now on. Halberds showing, crossbows cocked. I wish
these silly bastards up here had seen crossbows work. Then they'd be
more frightened. But we can't shoot somebody just to show them.''

''One other thing,'' he added. ''Edith didn't go off behind that barn
just because she's dumb, you know. She was called over. By a woman.
Woman speaking English, not Norse. She must have heard us talking
among ourselves. A slave-woman. Been here twenty years.''

Brand nodded heavily. ''They have been running slaves out of
England for fifty years now. I dare say every farmstead in the whole of
the North has its English grinding-slave, or half-a-dozen of them, and

men-thralls for the heavy work out in the fields as well. What did she want?''

''Wanted us to take her with us, of course. Spoke to Edith because she thought she'd be sympathetic. Then the men came round the corner, must have been watching.''

''Did you speak to the slave-woman?'' asked Shef, finally breaking out of his own internal struggles. ''What did you tell her?''

''Told her she couldn't come. Too much trouble for us. I should have said the same to Edith and the others, even if they were down to have their throats cut over some dead prince-brat's tomb. The woman back there was from Norfolk,'' Osmod added. ''They stole her out of Norwich twenty years ago, when she was a girl. Now she'll grow old and die up here.''

He and Cwicca got to their feet, walked away, began to spread out their blankets.

Shef looked at Brand, did not venture to speak. What the big man had said must have cost him as much grief and inner shame as breaking down in public tears might have done to someone lesser. Shef wondered what sort of man he would be in the future. Could they ever nurse him back to health in his mind, as Hund had done with his body? Long after the rest of the camp was asleep, except for the patrolling sentry, Brand sat restless, moodily breaking sticks and feeding them into the fire.

The next day, as they jogged along through the mountain pinewoods, moving now without the frantic haste of the rush from Halvdan's kingdom, Shef found Udd riding by his side. He looked down with some surprise. Udd normally had little or nothing to say except when there was forge-work to be done.

''I've been thinking about those millstones,'' said Udd. ''They're not very much use up here, because the water only flows half the year. And when it does it's like that.'' He pointed to the mountain-stream ahead of them, pouring down in a thin deep channel over a succession of six-foot drops in the hillside.

''What they need here is something more the same all the time.''

''Like what?''

Udd licked a finger, held it up in the air. ''No shortage of wind up here, is there?''

Shef laughed. The thought of wind, a thing no-one could see or measure or weigh or even catch, driving the most massive thing that men ever used, the great weight of the millstone, was impossible.

''Wind can drive a ship, though, can't it?'' said Udd, reading his leader's thought. "If it can drive a ship that weighs ten tons, why not a stone that only weighs one?"

"Wind's not like water," said Shef. "It comes from different directions."

"That doesn't stop the sailors, does it? No, what I was thinking was this . . ." As they rode on, Udd began to outline his idea of a sail-powered wind-mill, mounted on a rotating frame that could be turned to face the wind by a post like a ship's rudder. As he made objections, received answers, added his own notions, Shef found himself slowly drawn more and more into the deep incommunicable excitement of the inventor. Riding behind them, Cwicca nudged Karli.

"He's got him talking then. About time too. I was getting worried riding through this place with two leaders, both of them in some other world. I wish we could do the same for the other." He indicated the giant figure of Brand, slouching along at the head of the column with one arm over his over-burdened horse's saddle.

"He may be more of a problem," cut in Hund from behind them. "I wish we could just get him to his ship."

The challenge came not at any of the farmsteads they passed through that day, nor the next, though they rode through all of them greeted only by lowering faces and men standing silently by their barns and byres. Forewarned, Shef looked round keenly at every place they came to for signs of the others there, besides the men. Twice he caught sight of thin faces peeping from behind shutters: women hoping for a miracle, or maybe only for a friendly word in their own tongue. In his sleep he thought to hear the grinding noise of the querns, on and on for twenty years, thirty years, marking out a life of hopeless toil.

But at least the farmsteads spread only over a few yards, had in them never more than ten or a dozen men and boys, of all ages, not likely to test their strength against a well-armed body of their own number, even if the strangers came of slave-race and were headed by a doubtful champion. Where the road over the mountain passes finally dipped down into a dale, and the dale ran down to meet two more, the little cavalcade saw before them a cluster of houses spreading out where the streams intersected, and rising above them all a taller building, more than one story, its gables and side-posts fantastically carved into dragon shapes.

Brand reined in, turned to face the others. "That's Flaa," he said. "It's the main town of the Hallingdal district. They have a temple there. Just try to ride on through as if it was another farm-garth."

As they rode through the small square at the center of the

settlement, the bulk of the timber church to their left, men emerged from between the houses, blocking the path forward and on all sides. They were fully armed, spears and shields ready, bows in the hands of the youths and boys behind the warriors. Shef heard the click of the crossbows being cocked yet again. They might kill or cripple their own number, he was sure. After that they stood little chance against the thirty or forty men that would be left. Pick one direction and break out?

A man was coming forward to greet them, no weapon drawn, right hand up for parley. He and Brand stared at each other.

"Well, Vigdjarf," said Brand. "We haven't met since Hamburg. Or was it the raid on the Orkneys?"

"The Orkneys it was," said the other man. He was shorter than Brand by some way, but heavily-built, thick-necked and balding. Squat arms bulged with muscle over gold bracelets: a bad sign in both ways. This man had made heavy profits out of something, and here in the poor mountain lands it would not be from rearing cattle.

Vigdjarf looked pointedly at the hammer pendant on Brand's chest, then past him at the clump of horses, men and women behind him. "You are in strange company," he remarked. "Or maybe not so strange. Once people start wearing things round their necks I always think it's the next thing to turning Christian. And then what? They start talking to the other slaves, start helping them to run off. Start being one yourself. Are you that bad yet, Viga-Brand? Or is there a bit of your old self yet?"

Brand slid off the pony he had been riding, walked forward, axe in hand. "You can cut the talk, Vigdjarf," he said. "When we last met I never heard a peep out of you. Now you think you're something. Well, what's it to be? Are you and your cousins just going to try to jump us? Because if you do we'll kill a lot of you, that's for sure."

Behind him Osmod raised a crossbow, sighted on the thick oak of the temple door, squeezed the trigger with its carefully-ground sear. A flash too fast for sight, a thump echoing round the silent square. Osmod reloaded without haste, four easy movements, a click, another square iron bolt dropped home.

"Try digging that out," Brand went on. "Or have you got some other deal? Just you and me, maybe, man to man."

"Just you and me," Vigdjarf confirmed.

"And if I win?"

"Free passage through, for all of you."

"And if you win, Vigdjarf?"

"We take the lot. Horses, slaves, men, women. We can find a place for the women. Not the men. Thralls who've been allowed to run around thinking they're people get funny ideas. They'll go to the sacred tree, to hang for Othin's ravens. Maybe we'll keep some of them, if we think they're safe. But you know how we deal with runaways up here. If we don't kill them we geld and brand them. Only safe thing to do.

''But you've got another way out, Brand. You personal, I mean. Just walk away from them. They're not your folk. Join us, hand them over, no trouble for you or me, we'll even cut you in on the profits.''

''No deal,'' said Brand. He flipped his axe up, to grip it in both hands. ''Here and now?''

Vigdjarf shook his head. ''Too many people want to watch. I told them you'd say that. Now they're coming down from all the garths in three dales. We've marked out a duelling-ground down by the river. Tomorrow morning. Me against you.''

As Shef stood listening to the talk, the talk that might condemn him to the gelding-iron, the brand, and the iron collar, he felt the familiar pinch at the back of his neck which meant his vision was being directed. This time he did not struggle against the sight he was being shown. As had happened when he sat on the howe by Hedeby, his eye remained open, he still saw the small muddy square, the wooden temple, the armed men tensely waiting. But at the same time another picture swam across his vision, filling his brain, as if the eyeball they had taken from him were somewhere else, reporting on what it saw as well as the one still in his head.

He saw a great mill, like the one Udd had first shown him at the college in Kaupang, two horizontal stones, the one turning over the other, fed by a hopper from above. But no cog-wheels, no water running. Instead the mill-room was dry, like the middle of summer in a hot year, and the dust rose chokingly from the ground with never a drop of water to lay it.

Through the dust a man moved, a single figure thrusting slowly and steadily at a bar. The bar, thick as the steering-oar of a warship, was set into the upper millstone, and as the man pushed so the millstone moved round and round. And the man moved round and round, in the same weary circle, never resting, never coming to an end, never seeing anything but the same dusty room.

Yet in fact he could see nothing, Shef realized, for the man was blind, his eye-sockets empty. The man slacked his pace for a moment, trying to get better grip for his footing. Instantly a lash from somewhere, a red stripe springing up across the naked, filthy back. Though he was blind the man looked back, as if bothered by some fly he could not quite get to grips with. His hands were fettered to the bar he pushed with great gyves of iron. As he put his weight on the bar again, Shef saw the monstrous muscles stand out on arms and back and sides. There seemed to be nothing between them and the skin. The man was as strong as Brand, as tight-drawn muscularly as Shef himself. Long black hair curled down over his shoulders.

That is a way of milling Udd has not thought of, Shef reflected as the vision began to blur, he came to himself again. Use a man instead of an ox, or a horse, or a dozen grinding-slaves with hand-querns. But I do not think my protector in Asgarth has sent me this to tell me about milling, any more than he sent me the Völund-vision to warn me of open chests. Then he meant to tell me the boy had to die. And the slam of the chest closing was the crash of the catapult-stone, the mule-stone. Now the mill-stone . . . It means something more immediate than cog-wheels or gearing.

"Tomorrow morning," said Brand, repeating Vigdjarf's words. "Me against you."

Shef pushed his horse forward till it drew level with Brand's side. "Tomorrow morning," he said, looking down from horseback at the burly Vigdjarf. "But not you against him. Our champion against yours."

As the warrior eyed the crossbows and opened his mouth to protest, Shef cut in quickly. "Your champion may have choice of weapons." Vigdjarf looked thoughtful, suspicious, eyed the group behind Brand, then nodded agreement.

From somewhere, not too far away—or was it in his own head?—Shef could hear the dreary, slow creak of a millwheel turning.

CHAPTER SEVENTEEN

Shef realized a man was coming towards his little group bivouacked in a fenced yard on the edge of the village's common grazing land. He seemed uncertain rather than hostile or aggressive. Indeed, as he reached the group he paused, sketched what might have been a clumsy bow— performed by someone who had heard of the custom but never seen it done. His eyes were on the white priest-clothes of Hund, now badly soiled, and the Ithun-apple that hung round his neck.

"You are a leech," he said.

Hund nodded, remained seated.

"There are many in this village who are sick, or with wounds that have not healed. My son broke his leg, we bound it up but it is crooked, he can put no weight on it. My mother has the eye-sickness. There are others—women whose childbirth tore them, men who have had the jaw-ache for years, no matter what teeth we pull . . . Leeches never come up here. Will you look at them?"

"Why should I?" said Hund. The priests of the Way did not believe in humility, had never heard of Hippocrates. "If our champion loses tomorrow you are going to hang us, or maim us and enslave us. If you brand me tomorrow, why should I heal your sick today?"

The man looked uneasily at the others in the group. "Vigdjarf did not see that you were a leech. I'm sure . . . Whatever happens . . . He did not mean you."

Hund shrugged. "He meant my companions."

Shef got to his feet, looked down at Hund, winked his one eye barely perceptibly. Hund, who had known Shef since they were boys, caught the hint, looked away, his face unreadable.

"He will come," said Shef. "When he has unpacked his leech-tools. Wait for him over there."

As the man walked away Shef said to Hund, in an urgent undertone, "Treat the ones he shows you. Then demand to see the others. Even the thralls. Ask anyone you think you can trust about the mill. The mill we can hear creaking. Whatever happens, be back here at dusk."

The disk of the sun was already poised on the jagged mountain-tops as Hund walked back to the others, looking weary. The brown stains of dried blood showed on the sleeves of his tunic. From time to time during the afternoon, the listeners had heard faint cries of pain: a leech at work in a place where even poppy and henbane were unknown.

"Much to do up here," said Hund, sitting down and accepting the bowl of food Shef passed him. "I had to break that child's leg again to set it properly. So much pain in the world. And so much of it easy to cure. Warm water and lye for the midwives' hands would save half the women who die in childbirth."

"What about the mill?" demanded Shef.

"Late on they brought a thrall-woman to me. They did not want to, told me it was useless, and so was she. They were right. It was useless. She has a growth inside her and even in Kaupang with assistants and my best potions I doubt I could save her. But I tried to ease her pain. Her pain in the body, that is. There is no cure for what is in her mind. She was an Irish woman, stolen from her home when she was fifteen, forty years ago. They sold her to some man up here. She has never heard a word of her own tongue since, had five children by different masters, all taken away from her. Now her sons are Vikings, stealing women on their own. Never ask yourself why there are so many Vikings, so many Viking armies. Every man breeds as many sons from slave-women as he can. They do to fill the ranks."

"The mill," said Shef firmly.

"She told me there is a mill, as you said. It was set up only last year by a Way-priest who came up here, one of Valgrim's friends. Last year, too, they brought up a man to turn it. How can a man turn a mill?"

"I know," said Shef, remembering the god-vision he had seen. "Go on."

"She says the man is an Englishman. He is kept locked up there all the time. Twice he has broken free and run into the hills. Both times they ran him down. The first time they beat him with rawhide outside the temple. She said she saw that. She said he is a man of great strength. They lashed him for as long as it would take to plow an acre, and he never cried out except to curse them. The second time he ran, they . . . did another thing."

"What was that?" asked Brand, listening keenly.

"When they say slaves are gelded, it usually means they cut off their stones, like a bullock or a cut stallion. To make them tame and docile. They did not do that with him. Instead they cut off the other thing that makes you a man. They left him his stones. He is still as strong as a bull, and as fierce. He has the desires of a man. But he can never act like one again."

The men listening stared at each other, each one wondering what his fate might be in the morning.

"I'll tell you one thing," said Cwicca definitely. "I don't care what promises anyone makes. If Brand loses tomorrow—and Thor send he won't—the man who beats him gets my first bolt right through him. And then we're all going to start shooting. We may not be able to get out, but I'm not going to be a thrall here. These mountain-trolls are as bad as the black monks."

A rumble of assent came from the others, men and women together.

"She said one more thing," Hund went on. "She said he's mad."

Shef nodded, reflectively. "A mad Englishman," he said. "As strong as a bull and as fierce. We will loose him tonight. I know there are sentries watching us. But they will expect us to try to sneak off with the horses. All of us will go to the latrine separately once the sun is down, but three of us will hide the other side of it till full dark. Me. You, Karli. You, Udd. Put your smith-tools inside your tunic, Udd. And a flask of grease from the meat-pot. Now, Hund, show us as much as you can about how the village is laid out . . ."

Hours later, in deep darkness lit only by the stars, the three men clustered in shadow outside a rough hut on the outskirts of the village: the place of the mill.

Shef glanced round at the lightless houses not far away, waved Udd forward. A heavy door, barred, the bar clamped down and secured with a heavy iron bolt. No lock on the bolt. There only to prevent someone getting out. No need for Udd's skill yet. The little man slipped the bolt, raised the bar, stood ready to open the door.

Shef fumbled with lamp and strike-light, catching the sparks, blowing on the tinder, finally lighting the wick that floated in the whale-oil container, and sliding down the thin-shaved, transparent horn screen that let light out but shielded the wick from wind. A risk to show a light out here, however carefully shielded by tunic and body. But if what Hund said was right, a greater risk to plunge into the beast-den blind.

The light working at last, Shef signaled to Udd, who jerked the door open. Shef slid inside like a snake, Udd and Karli just behind him. He heard the door pulled softly shut as he looked inside at the great mill. At the huddled shape lying under sacking a few feet away, by the wall. He stepped forward one pace, two, his eye drawn to the massive bar jutting out from the center of the upper wheel, the thick chain leading from it to . . .

A flash of movement and something was lashing at his ankle. Shef leapt in the air, still holding the lamp incongruously upright, came down three feet back.

The hand missed his ankle by an inch. A bone-wrenching thud. Shef found himself staring down in the uncertain light of the lamp at a pair of glaring wide-set eyes. The thud had been a chain jerked to the very last fraction of its run by a collar round a thick neck. The eyes glaring up showed not a flicker of pain, only bitter rage at having failed.

Shef's eye went to the chain. Yes, from the bar to the collar. Another chain from the collar to a shackle set deep into the wall. The hands gyved together and chained also to the collar, so that they could not move further than from waist to mouth. Why had all this been done? Slowly Shef realized it was so that the chained man could be dragged from the wall to the bar, and from the bar back to the wall again, without anyone having to go within his reach. The room stank. A latrine bucket. It was doubtful if the man used it. A pot for water. He must use that. No food, no light, only sacking to cover himself with in the cold air of the mountain spring. How had he lived through the winter? The man wore only a single ragged tunic, torn till one could see the matted hair of his chest and body.

The chained man was still waiting, still watching, without so much as a blink. Waiting for the blow. Hoping the striker of it would come within range. Slowly he shuffled back, attempting with an imbecile cunning to look afraid. Trying to tempt Shef forward, within the reach of the chain.

Something stirred within Shef's memory. Disfigured as he was, hair and beard trimmed only where they fell to the length of the circling mill-bar, the man looked familiar. And, amazingly, something like recognition was dawning in his eyes as well.

Shef sat down, carefully out of reach. "We are Englishmen here," he said. "And I have seen you before."

"And I you," said the man. His voice creaked as if he had not used it for many days. "I saw you in York. I tried to kill you, one-eye. You were near the front of the men who broke in. Standing next to one of the Viking whoresons, a giant. I struck at him and you parried the blow. I would have killed him with the back-stroke and you a moment later. But the others got between us. And now you are in the Viking lands to make sport of me, traitor."

His face twisted. "But God will be good to me, as he was to my king Ella. At the end I can die. God send me a free hand before that!"

"I am no traitor," said Shef. "Not to your king Ella. I did him a favor before he died. I can do you one too. A favor for a favor. But tell me who you are, and where I have seen you."

The crazy twist of the face again, like a weeping man determined never to shed a tear. "Once I was Cuthred, captain of Ella's hearth-band, his picked champions. I was the best warrior from Humber to the Tyne. The Ragnarssons' men pinned me between shields after I had killed half a score of them. Gyved me and sold me for my strength."

The man laughed silently, throwing his head back like a wolf. "Yet there was something they never knew, that they would have paid gold to know."

"I know," said Shef. "You put their father in the worm-pit, to die of adder-bite. I was there. I saw it and that is where I saw you. I know something else too. It was not your doing, but that of Erkenbert the deacon. Ella would have set him free."

He leaned forward, not quite close enough. "I saw you throw Ragnar's thumb-nail on the table. I stood behind the chair of Wulfgar my stepfather, whom the Vikings made a *heimnar*. The man who brought Ragnar to York."

The mad eyes were wide with surprise and disbelief now. "I believe you are the devil," Cuthred muttered. "Sent as a last temptation."

"No. I am your good angel, if you still believe in the White Christ. We are going to set you free. If you promise to do one thing for us."

"What is that?"

"Fight Vigdjarf the champion tomorrow."

The head turned back like a wolf's again, on it a look of savage glee. "Ah, Vigdjarf," Cuthred husked. "He cut me while they held me. He has never come within my reach again. Yet he thinks he is a bold man. Maybe he will stand up to me. Once. Once is all I need."

"You must let us come close to get your shackle out. Get your collar off."

Shef waved Udd forward. The little man, a bundle of tools in his hand, stepped forward like a mouse towards a cat, one pace, two. Within range. And Cuthred had him, one great paw round his face, one gripping his neck, ready for the snap.

"A poor exchange for Vigdjarf," reminded Shef.

Slowly Cuthred released Udd, looking at his own hands as if he did not believe them. Karli lowered the point of his sword. Udd, shaking, stepped forward again, peered near-sightedly at the iron, began to try to work it loose. After a few moments he turned back to Cuthred, stared at the collar.

"Best to file the collar off, lord. It might make a noise. Can't help hurting him, too."

"Keep greasing the file. Do you hear, Cuthred? He may hurt you. Don't lash out. Save it for Vigdjarf."

The Yorkshireman's face twisted, he sat immobile while Udd slowly filed and greased and filed again. The lamp burned its oil, began to gutter. Finally Udd stood back. "It's through, lord. Needs pulling back."

Shef stepped forward, with caution, Karli standing just out of reach, sword poised again. Cuthred waved him away, grinned, put his hands up, seized the two ends of the thick collar still twisted round his neck. Pulled. Fascinated, Shef saw the muscles standing out like cables on his arms and chest. The stout, cold iron bent into a bow as if it were peeled greenwood. Cuthred stepped free, dropping collar and chains with a crash. He knelt, seized Shef's hands in both his own, pressed them to his head, pressed his head to Shef's knees.

"I am your man," he said.

The lamp went out finally. In the darkness the four men cautiously eased the door open, went out into the starlit night. Like shadows they crept back through the village, snaked back to their camp-site, keeping the hobbled horses between them and the Norwegians' sentry. The fire was still burning, tended by the watchful Edith.

As he saw the woman, Cuthred made a choking noise in his throat, seemed ready once again to pounce.

"She is English too," whispered Shef. "Edith, feed him with all we have. Talk to him quietly. Talk to him in English." As the others started to stir in their blankets, he crept over to Cwicca. "And you talk to him too, Cwicca. Give him a pint of ale, if there's any left. But first, quietly, cock your crossbow. If he lunges for anyone, shoot him. Now I'm going to sleep till dawn."

Shef stirred, not at first light, but as the sun first started to show over the mountain tops that hemmed in the valley on both sides. It was cold, and dew lay thick on the single blanket. For a few moments Shef was reluctant to stir, to break the little cocoon of warmth his body had created. Then he remembered the mad eyes of Cuthred, and sprang up.

Cuthred was still asleep, his mouth open. He lay with a blanket pulled over him and his head pillowed on the breast of Edtheow, oldest and most motherly of the slave-women. She lay awake but unmoving, one arm crooked round Cuthred's head.

And then he was awake. His eyes flicked open without a transition, took in Shef staring at him, took in the men beginning to light fires, roll blankets, head for the latrine. Fell on Brand, also on his feet, also studying Cuthred.

Shef never saw Cuthred move. He saw the blanket fly one way, behind it Cuthred must have sprung to his feet in one movement from a lying position, before his eyes could focus he heard the crash and grunt of knocked-out breath as Cuthred drove into Brand with his shoulder. Then they were both on the ground, rolling over and over. Shef saw Cuthred's thumbs drive at Brand's eyes, saw Brand's great quart-sized hands grip the Englishman's wrists, try to bend them back. Then the two were locked for an instant, Cuthred on top, neither able to force the other back. Cuthred twisted his hands free, jerked the knife from Brand's belt and leapt to his feet with the same uncanny speed. Brand too was struggling up, but Cuthred had the knife swinging forward for the killer stroke under the chin.

Osmod grabbed his forearm as he struck, pulled the knife aside. Then Osmod was rolling on the ground, knocked sideways by a backhand blow from the pommel. Cwicca had both hands on the knife-wrist. Shef ran in, seized Cuthred's left arm, twisted for a bone-breaker hold. It was like seizing the fetlock of a horse, too thick to manage. As Cwicca on one side and Shef on the other grappled with an arm each, Karli stepped forward, face alive with excitement.

"I'll quieten him," he yelled. His feet shuffled, his shoulder dropped, he swung with both hands, left-right-left, hooking into Cuthred's unguarded belly, driving upwards to go under the ribs and reach the liver.

Cuthred lifted Shef bodily off the ground one-handed, smashed an elbow into the side of his head, jerked an arm free. A fist like a bludgeon came down on Karli's head, he stamped violently on Cwicca's feet, failed to dislodge the desperate grip on his knife-wrist, reached across to seize the knife left-handed.

Staggering to his feet again, Shef saw Udd sighting deliberately with a crossbow, started to shout "Stop!", realized that in one instant either Cwicca would be disemboweled or Cuthred shot dead.

Brand stepped forward, between Cuthred and the crossbow. He said nothing, made no attempt to grip the other man. Instead he held out his axe, balanced across both palms.

Cuthred stared at it, ceased to reach for the knife, reached instead for the axe-helve. Paused. Cwicca, gasping, slowly let go, retreated out of range. Half-a-dozen crossbows were leveled now. Cuthred ignored them, staring only at the axe. Slowly he reached out and took it, felt the balance, swung it backwards and forwards.

"I remember now," he muttered hoarsely in his Northumbrian English. "You want me to kill Vigdjarf. Ha!" He hurled the axe upwards, twirling it so that it span in the air, the light flashing off its brilliant edge, caught it at its balance point as it came down. "Kill Vigdjarf!" He looked round as if expecting to find his enemy in sight already, began to move towards the village like a landslide.

Brand jumped in his way, arms spread, calling out in his primitive English. "Yes, yes, kill Vigdjarf. Not now. Today. Everyone watch. Now eat. Get ready. Choose weapon."

Cuthred grinned, showing a set of gums with a few sparse front teeth remaining. "Eat," he agreed. "Tried to kill you before, big man, in York. Try again later. Now, kill Vigdjarf. Eat first." He buried the axe-head with a chunk deep in a tree-stump stool, looked round, saw Edtheow coming towards him with a hunk of bread, took it from her and began to gnaw at it. She gentled him like an anxious horse, rubbing his arm through the filthy tunic.

"Oh yes," said Brand, looking at Shef still rubbing a buzzing ear. "Oh yes. I like this one. We've got a berserk here. Very useful people. But you do have to get them pointed the right way."

Under Brand's direction the entire camp got to work on Cuthred, scurrying round him like men with a champion race-horse. First, food. As he gnawed his way through the crust Edtheow brought him, the ex-slaves heated their staple oat porridge, passed him a bowl of it, began to warm over the stew they had made the night before from unwary chickens pecking too near the camp-site, diced onions and garlic into it. Cuthred ate continuously, supervised by Brand and Hund together. They gave him only small amounts at a time, seeing him scrape each bowl down to the wood before passing him the next one. "He needs the food for strength," muttered Brand. "But his belly's shrunk. Can't handle much at a time. Give him a pint of ale to slow him down. Now, get that tunic off him. I'm going to wash and oil him."

The catapult-crew prized hot stones out of the bed of the camp-fire, dropped them into a leather water-bucket, watched the steam rise. But when Shef stepped forward, making gestures to take off the tunic, Cuthred scowled, shook his head violently. Looked at the women.

Realizing he did not wish to show the shame of his mutilation, Shef waved the women away, stripped off his own tunic. Turned deliberately so that Cuthred could see the flogging-scars on his own back, scars his stepfather had put there, pulled the tunic back on. Fritha and Cwicca stretched out a blanket on the ground, made signs that Cuthred should lie on it face-down, then cut the tunic from his body with their seax-knives.

When they saw his back the ex-slaves looked at each other again. In places the flesh had been flogged off clear through to the spine, only thin scar-skin covering the vertebrae. With lye and warm water Fritha began to sponge off a winter's accumulation of filth and dead skin. When he had finished, Brand came forward with his own spare pair of breeches, signed to Cuthred to put them on. The men stared elaborately into the far distance while Cuthred donned them. Then they sat him on a tree-stump while Fritha worked on his arms, face and chest.

Shef observed him carefully as they did so. Cuthred was, indeed, a big man, far bigger than any of the ex-slaves, bigger by a long way than Shef himself. Not the size of Brand—the breeches were rolled up twice at the ankles, and hung so loose at the waist that Brand's belt would have gone round him twice. But he was different from almost any man Shef had ever seen, any of the warriors he had known from Brand's crew or from the Great Army. Someone like Brand had no paunch or beer-belly, but he was thick-set, he ate well every day, his muscles were covered with a thick coat of padding to keep out the cold. If you seized him over the ribs you could pull out a handful of flesh.

By comparison with Cuthred, Brand was shapeless. On the mill-slave, turning a great weight with arms and legs and back and belly hour after hour, day after day, week after week, fed on little more than bread and water, the muscles stood out as if they had been drawn on paper. Like those of the blind man Shef had seen in his fleeting vision. It was the combination of strength and thinness that made Cuthred so blindingly fast, Shef realized. That and his madness.

"Start work on his hands and feet," ordered Brand. "See, he's got toenails like a bear's claws. Trim them, or we'll never get shoes on him, and he needs them for grip. Let me see his hands."

Brand turned them over and over, testing to see if they flexed. "Hands like horn," he muttered. "Good for a sailor, bad for a swordsman. Give me some oil, I'll rub it in."

Cuthred sat as they worked on him, oblivious to the cold, seemingly taking the attention as his due. Perhaps he was used to it from his former life, Shef thought. He had been captain of the companions of the King of Northumbria, a rank you could reach only by fighting your way up. Cuthred must have fought more duels than he could remember. Besides the marks of torture, old scars of point and blade were showing up beneath the shaggy mat of hair. Like a horse, he must have grown his own pelt in the heatless hut through a mountain winter. They began to trim his hair and beard with the group's one pair of precious scissors. "Don't want anything blowing in his face," Brand explained.

He passed over his spare tunic to go with the breeches, a splendid one of dyed green wool. Cuthred shrugged into it, unfastened the breeches, tucked it in and tied the rope belt round himself once more. Washed, trimmed and dressed, did he look different from the wretched creature they had rescued, Shef asked himself.

No, he looked just the same. Any sane person, meeting Cuthred on a path or road, would have jumped off it and climbed a tree, as if he had met a bear or a wolf-pack. He was as crazy and as dangerous as—as Ivar the Boneless, or his father Ragnar Hairy-Breeks. He even looked like Ragnar, Shef remembered. Something in the stance, in the careless eyes.

Brand began to show Cuthred the weapons they had available. A poor selection. Cuthred looked at Karli's treasured sword, sniffed, bent it without words over his knee. Looked up at Karli's grunt of shock and protest, waited to see if it would come again, grinned as the stocky Ditmarsher fell silent. He tossed the seax-knives aside contemptuously. Osmod's halberd interested him, and he fenced for a few seconds with it, whipping its great weight round one-handed as if it had been a willow-wand. But the balance was wrong for a one-handed weapon. He put it aside, scrutinized Brand's precious silver-inlaid axe.

"What is its name?" he asked.

"*Rimmugygr*," said Brand. "That is, 'Battle-troll.'"

"Ah," said Cuthred, turning the weapon over and over. "Trolls. They come down from the mountains in the winter, peer through the shutters at chained men alone. This is not the weapon for me. You, chieftain," he said to Shef. "You wear gold on your arms. You must own a famous sword to lend me."

Shef shook his head. After the battle at Hastings his thanes had insisted that a king must have a great weapon, had picked out for him a sword of the finest Swedish steel, with a gold hilt and its name engraved on the blade: *Atlaneat*, it had been. He had left it behind in the treasury, carried only a plain sailor's cutlass. He had left the cutlass behind on the trip to Drottningsholm, taking only the 'Gungnir'-spear. But Cwicca had brought the cutlass with him when they rescued him, he had pushed it back in his belt. He unsheathed it, handed it over. Cuthred looked at it with much the same expression he had shown for Karli's. It was a single-edged sword with a heavy back, slightly curved, made of plain iron though with a good steel blade welded on by Shef himself. Not a weapon to fence with, just a slashing sword.

"No back-swing with this," muttered Cuthred. "But force in the first blow. I'll take it."

On impulse, Shef passed him also the shield that Udd had made, case-hardened steel pegged over plain wood. Cuthred looked at the thin metal with interest, scrutinized its odd color, tried to strap it on. Strap would not meet buckle over his forearm till they had punched an extra hole in it. He stood up, bare sword in hand, shield strapped on. His face grinned like the mask of a hungry wolf.

"Now," he said. "Vigdjarf."

CHAPTER EIGHTEEN

A man stood at the perimeter of the camp, fully armed, a short staff in his hand: a marshal, come to call them to the dueling ground. Shef rose to mask Cuthred from him, jerked a head to Brand to do the talking.

"Are you ready?" called the marshal.

"Ready. Let us repeat the terms of the duel."

As the others listened, Brand and the marshal went over the terms of the agreement: only hewing weapons, champion against champion, free passage staked against return of all those alleged to be thralls, at the disposal of the winner. As they heard that condition laid down, Shef felt the tension rising among the English, men and women.

"Win or lose, we aren't having none of that," Osmod muttered. "All of you, keep your bows and bills right handy. You women, hold all the horses' bridles. If our man goes down—which he won't, of course," Osmod added, glancing hastily at Cuthred, "we're going to try to bust our way out."

Shef saw Brand's shoulders tense with disapproval as he heard Osmod's unsporting orders, but he continued talking. The marshal, unable to speak any English, paid no attention. Cuthred grinned even more widely than before. He was behaving with a strange restraint for the moment, back on his stool, making no effort to show himself. Either the familiar ritual of a duel-morning had gripped him, or else he was relishing the surprise they had planned for Vigdjarf.

The marshal turned away and Brand walked back to the group, already prepared to move, horses loaded, packs strapped. At the last moment Cuthred's eye fell on the small hatchet they used for firewood. He twitched it from its strapping, passed it to Udd. "Put an edge on that with your file," he ordered.

The party led on through the short village street, already deserted. In the small square outside the temple clustered not only the entire population of the little town, but also scores more, men, women and children from the length of the dales, eager to see the clash of champions. They had left the one street clear for Brand's party to enter by, but as they passed through men with spears and shields moved to block further exit from it. Osmod looked round with calculating eye, trying to spot the weakest place in the circle surrounding them. Saw none.

Immediately facing them, outside the temple door itself, scarlet cloaks marked Vigdjarf and his two seconds. Brand looked round, eyed Cuthred carefully, nodded to Osmod and Cwicca either side of him. "Wait," he said, holding up a finger. "Wait for the call."

Cuthred took no notice. He had taken the sharpened hatchet and was holding it in his left hand, along with the shield-strap. With his other hand he had begun to flip Shef's cutlass into the air, letting it turn over and over in its unbalanced way, seizing it by its guardless hilt every time it came down. Murmurs were beginning to run round the crowd as some of them recognized him, realized it was the mill-thrall, speculated what it might mean.

With Shef at his side, Brand began to walk out to meet the others. "Should we have tried to get some armor on him," muttered Shef. "Your mail? A helmet? A leather jacket, even? Vigdjarf has everything."

"No point with a berserk," said Brand briefly. "You'll see."

He halted seven paces from the others, raised his voice for the watching crowd as well as the challengers.

"Ready to try your luck, Vigdjarf? You could have tried me years ago, you know. But you didn't feel like it then."

"And you don't feel like it now," replied Vigdjarf, grinning. "Have you decided who's going to try me? You? Or your one-eyed friend bare-handed here?"

Brand jerked a thumb over his shoulder. "We thought we'd try the one in the green tunic behind us there. He's very keen to fight you. He *really* feels like it."

Vigdjarf's grin faded as he peered across the square to where Cuthred stood, now clear of the others, standing out in plain sight, still tossing the sword up and down. He had started now to throw the hatchet from hand to hand as well, tossing it left to right and back again while the sword was still in the air.

"You can't send him out to fight me," said Vigdjarf. "He's a thrall. He's my own thrall. You must have stolen him in the night. I can't fight my own thrall. I appeal to the marshals." He looked across to the two armed and armored men waiting either side of the square.

"You're very quick to call people thralls," said Shef. "First you say some travelers are thralls, and they have to fight you to prove they're not. Then when someone wants to fight you, you say he's a thrall too. Maybe it would be simpler if you just said everyone was a thrall. Then all you'd have to do would be make them act like thralls. Because if they don't—they aren't."

"I won't fight him," said Vigdjarf positively. "He is my own property, stolen in the night, and you are all night-thieves." He turned to the marshals, began to protest again.

Brand looked over his shoulder. "If you won't fight him, that's up to you," he remarked. "But I can tell you one thing for sure. He's going to fight you. And anybody else who gets in his way."

With a hoarse bellow, Cuthred had stepped away from his handlers, was walking forward across the square. His eyes were set and unblinking, and as he came he began to sing. From his brief career as a minstrel, Shef recognized the song. It was the old Northumbrian lay of the Battle of Nechtans-mere, where the army of the Northern English had been wiped out by the Picts. Cuthred was singing the part where the valiant retainers refused to fly or surrender, but formed the shield-wall to fight to the last man. Hastily Brand and Shef moved out of his path, saw him go by, still walking slowly but braced for a pounce at every step.

Vigdjarf, facing him, grabbed at his second's cloak, waved again to the marshals, saw them all back away, leaving him face to face with the enraged man he had gelded.

At five paces range, Cuthred charged. No feinting, no feeling-out. No defense. The attack of an enraged churl, a swineherd or a plowboy, rather than a king's champion. The first blow started with the tip of the curved cutlass touching Cuthred's spine and came down in a sweeping arc at Vigdjarf's helmet. Reflex alone would have served to block it, for any but a joint-locked grandfather. Vigdjarf, still yelling protests to the marshals, had his shield up without thought, took the blow full on the shield-boss.

Dropped almost to his knees, driven down by the sheer weight of the blow. And the second one was already in the air, and the third after it. Making no attempt to guard, Cuthred danced round his enemy, slashing from every angle. Splinters flew from the iron-rimmed and bossed linden-shield at every blow, in instants Vigdjarf seemed to be holding only a hacked remnant. A furious clang echoed round the square as for the first time Vigdjarf managed to get his sword up for a parry.

"I don't think this is going to last very long," said Brand. "And it's going to be nasty when it finishes. Mount up, everyone. Shef, get some rope."

Cuthred's attack had not slowed at any moment, but Vigdjarf, a veteran, now seemed to have pulled himself together. He was using both sword and the fragment of battered half-moon of shield left to him to block strokes. He had also realized that Cuthred never parried, never got into a position to do so. The shield in his hand might as well have been there only for balance. Twice in quick succession he lunged out of a parry, stabbing for the face. Both times Cuthred had sprung sideways already, angling for another cut.

"He's going to get one home," muttered Brand, "and then . . ."

As if remembering his wits, Cuthred suddenly changed tactic, instead of hacking at the head and body, stooped, slashed backhand at the knee. Vigdjarf had seen that many times, far more often than the crazed attack he had just survived. He leapt over the stroke, came down crouching and swung in his turn.

With a groan of dismay the English watching saw the slash come down full across Cuthred's thigh. They waited for the spurt of arterial blood, the last agonized stroke, easily blocked, the sideways topple and the killing slash or stab. This was how it always ended. Vigdjarf's teeth showed across the square as he waited for Cuthred to crumple.

But not this time. Cuthred sprang, whirling the sword at his enemy's head and in the same clumsy movement lashing out with the hatchet in his shield-hand. There was a single meaty thud, and the hatchet was buried through helmet and skull.

Cuthred had let go of the hatchet and grasped Vigdjarf's sword-wrist with his shield-hand. As Vigdjarf clubbed desperately and unavailingly at him with his broken shield, he stepped in, drove the cutlass home under the mail, started sawing deliberately back and forward. Vigdjarf began to scream, dropped his sword, began to try to claw the cutlass away. Cuthred was talking to him, holding him up now, shouting words into the dying face.

Horror-stricken, not at death but at loss of dignity, the marshals and Vigdjarf's second rushed forward. In the circle Shef realized that prudent men were starting to hustle their wives and children away, back through the narrow streets or into doorways. Still bare-handed, he stepped forward, shouting to the marshals to stand back.

Cuthred dropped his still-bleeding enemy on the ground and without warning charged again. One of the marshals, still holding his staff out and trying to shout some warning, dropped, cut from neck to breastbone. As the sword jammed on bone, Cuthred swung his shield for the first time at the other, knocked him staggering backwards, seized the sword from the dying marshal's hand, and slashed the second's leg off at the knee. Then he was in motion again, charging without pause or hesitation at the crowd of Vigdjarf's supporters grouped outside the temple.

A spear flew to meet him, a heavy iron-shod battle-spear thrown with full force at ten feet range. Straight for the center of the body. Cuthred dropped the case-hardened shield across his heart. The spear met it full on, did not sink in, dragging down his shield-arm, bounced back as Gungnir had when Shef had first tried the metal.

A yell of surprise and alarm and suddenly all that could be seen were turned backs, Cuthred slashing at them, men falling or fleeing, the shout going up: "Berserker! Berserker!"

"Well, now," said Brand, looking round at the suddenly-deserted square, "I think if we just ride away very very quietly . . . Perhaps pick up some of these useful bits and pieces scattered around, like that sword there—you don't need it any more, do you, Vigdjarf? You were always a bit too hard on the thrall-women for a proper *drengr*, that was my opinion. And now it's been the death of you."

"Aren't we going to bring poor Cuthred along?" said Edtheow indignantly. "I mean, he's saved us all."

Brand shook a disgusted head. "I think we would all be better just having nothing to do with him."

Cuthred was lying motionless in the mud fifty yards down the street on their way out of the town, two heads lying by him, their long hair twisted in his grip. Shef was suddenly pushed aside by Hund who stared in fascination at the left thigh where Vigdjarf's full-blooded slash had gone home.

A deep, deep cut, six inches long, white bone glinting at the bottom of it. But like a cut in dead meat, only the barest trace of blood.

"How has that happened?" asked Hund. "How could a man not bleed from that? Keep walking with the muscles severed?"

"I don't know," said Brand, "but I've seen it before. That's what makes a berserk. People say that no steel bites on them. It bites all right. But they don't feel it. Not till later. What are you doing?"

Hund had produced needle and gut thread, was beginning to stitch the edges of the great gash together, stitching large at first, then turning and going back over with small precise movements like a tailor. Blood began to seep and then to well from the wound as he did so. He finished, wrapped lengths of bandage round and round, rolled his patient over, turned back his eyelids. Shook his head wonderingly.

"Put him over a horse," he ordered. "He ought to be dead. But I think he's just fast asleep."

He had to use his knife to saw through the hair of the severed heads to get them out of Cuthred's clench.

"Yes," said Brand judiciously. "There're lots of theories about berserks. I don't take much notice of most of them, myself."

They were riding along the crest of a ridge, as they had been for some days now, first winding up, then seemingly more or less on a level, now perhaps with the down-stretches lasting longer than the ups. To their right lay a long sweep of valleys with water glinting in them and here and there the bright green of fresh grass. To their left the land fell more sharply, into a waste of fir and pine, and they could see little ahead but the ridge rising and falling, with chain after chain of blue mountains lifting into the far distance. The air was cold and keen, but filled the lungs with life and the sharp smell of the pine-woods.

Behind Brand and Shef, and the interested Hund riding close beside them, a string of ponies stretched out for a hundred yards, with people walking here and there among the riders. More people than there had been when they left Flaa the week before. As the English had made their way through a now-deserted countryside, a countryside that emptied before them, figures had crept out to join them, emerging from the woods by the road, stalking softly into the firelight when they camped: runaway slaves with the collars still round their necks, most of them English-speaking. Drawn by the rumor of the free folk moving through the land, headed by a giant and a one-eyed king, and guarded by a mad berserk of their own race. Most of the ones who had come in were men, and not all of them thralls or churls by birth. It took determination and courage to break free from one's masters in an alien country: and when they could get them, the Vikings were very ready to enslave former thanes or warriors, valuing them for their strength. After brief debate, Shef had agreed to accept all those who could find their way to them, though he would not search farms or pursue their owners to liberate the countryside. Men who could break free, and women too, might be an increase in force. There was no hope any more of passing unnoticed.

"Some people say the word really means 'bare-sarks,'" Brand went on. "'Bare-shirts,' that is, because they'll fight in their shirts alone, with no armor. I mean, you saw our mad friend back there—" he jerked a thumb at Cuthred, who now, amazingly, was well enough recovered to sit on a pony. He was riding near the back of the cortege, well-surrounded and escorted by those he seemed able to tolerate. "No defense at all, and no interest in it. If we'd put armor on him it's my belief he'd have torn it off. So 'bare-shirt' makes a kind of sense.

"But there's others say it's really 'bear-sarks,' like 'bear-shirts.' Because they act like bears, that just come at you and can't be frightened off. What they mean is that they're really, you know—" Brand looked round cautiously and dropped his voice, "like Ivar, *not men of one skin*. They change into another shape, sort of, when the fit takes them."

"You mean they're werewolves," suggested Shef.

"Were-bears, yes," Brand agreed. "But that doesn't make sense, really. The were-shape runs in families, for one thing. But a berserk can be anybody."

"Can this condition be created by drugs?" asked Hund. "It seems to me that there are several things that can take a man out of himself, can make him think he is a bear, for one thing. In small quantities, the juice of the nightshade berry, though that is also a deadly poison. Some say you can make an ointment of it mixed with hog-lard, and smear it on. It makes people think they are flying out of their bodies. And there are other growths with similar effect."

"Maybe," Brand said. "But you know that wasn't the case with our madman. He'd had nothing but what we ate, and he was as mad as ever before we even fed him.

"No, I don't think it's really very hard to understand at all. Some men like fighting. I do myself—not as much as I used to, maybe. But when you like it, and you're used to it, and you're good at it, the noise and the excitement lifts you, you can feel it swelling inside you, and at its peak you feel you are twice as strong and twice as quick as you usually are, and you do things before you know you've done them. Being a berserk is like that, only much, much more. And I think you can only get to that if you have some special reason inside you. Because most men, even when they're caught up with the excitement, remember somewhere deep down what it feels like when you get hit, and how you don't want to go home with just a stump, or what your friends look like when you shovel them into a hole. So they keep using their shields and their armor. But a berserk's forgotten all that. To be a berserk, deep down, you have to not want to live. You have to hate yourself. I've known some men like that, born like that or made like that. We all know why Cuthred there hates himself and doesn't want to live. He can't bear the shame of what they did to him. He's only happy when he's wiping it out on someone else."

"So you think the other berserks you knew had something wrong with them too," said Shef thoughtfully. "But maybe not in their bodies."

"That was the case with Ivar Ragnarsson," Hund confirmed. "They called him the Boneless, from his impotence, and he hated women. But he was normal in body, I saw that for myself. He hated women for what he could not do, and he hated men for what they could do that he could not. Maybe the same is true with our Cuthred, only with him he was made like that, he did not make himself. I am amazed at the way he healed. That cut was all the way through the thigh and into the bone. But it did not bleed till I began to dress it, and it has healed like a surface scratch. I should have tried tasting his blood, to see if there was something strange in it," he added thoughtfully.

Brand and Shef looked at one another for a moment in alarm. Then their attention was distracted. The ridge-path made a sharp turn to the left, by a cairn of stones, and as they followed it round the land seemed to part before them.

There, down far below, was a deep valley with at the end of it a new and silver gleam. Too big for the mountain streams they could see everywhere, a gleam that led widening out to the horizon. On it, for those with the far-sight of seamen, little flecks of color.

"The sea," muttered Brand, reaching out and gripping Shef's shoulder. "The sea. And look, there are ships riding at anchor. That is the Gula-fjord, and where the ships are is the harbor for the great Gula-Thing. If we can reach there—maybe my *Walrus* will be there. If King Halvdan did not take her. I think—it's too far away—but I could almost think that one moored far out was her."

"You can't tell one ship from another ten miles away," said Hund.

"A skipper can tell his ship ten miles away in a fog," retorted Brand. He kicked heels into his weary pony's barrel sides and began to plunge forward down the slope. Shef followed more slowly, waving to the rest to close up.

They caught up with Brand as his overburdened pony flagged, and managed to persuade him to halt as night came on, still several miles from the site of the Gula-Thing and its harbor. When they finally rode or walked next morning into the half-mile wide cluster of tents, turf booths, and temporary shelters, all of them leaking smoke into the Atlantic breeze, a small knot of men stood to greet them: not warriors in their prime wearing armor, Shef was concerned to note, but older men, even greybeards. Spokesmen for the community, the counties served by the Thing, and the kinglets or jarls who guaranteed its peace.

"We hear that you are robbers and night-thieves," said one of them without preamble. "If you are such you may be hunted down and killed without penalty by all the free men who come to this Thing, and you have no share in its peace."

"We have stolen nothing," said Shef. It was not true—he knew his men stole chickens from every farmyard and butchered sheep for their stewpot without compunction—but he did not think that these petty thefts were the problem. As Osmod said, they would have paid for food if anyone had offered to sell it to them.

"You have stolen men."

"The men were stolen in the first place. They came to us of their own free will—we did not seek them out. If they have freed themselves, who can blame them?"

The Gula-men looked uncertain. Brand followed up in a more conciliating tone. "We will steal nothing within the circuit of the Thing, and will observe its peace in every respect. See, we have silver. Plenty of it, and gold as well." He slapped a clinking saddle-bag, pointed to the precious metal shining on Shef's accouterments and his own.

"You will promise to steal no thralls?"

"We will steal no thralls and harbor no thralls," said Brand firmly, waving Shef to silence. "But if any man following us or here already wishes to claim that any of our company is or ever was his thrall, then we will make counter-suit against him for enslaving a free man without right or justice, and claim against him for every injury, blow, insult or mutilation suffered in the course of that slavery. As also for each year spent in slavery, and for loss of rightful earnings during that time. Furthermore . . ."

Knowing the intense glee with which the Vikings pursued legalities of even the most trivial kind, Shef cut him off. "Adjudication to be settled by stated champions on the dueling ground," he added.

The Norwegian spokesmen looked at each other with some uncertainty.

"Furthermore we'll be out of here as soon as ever we can," offered Brand.

"All right. But don't forget. If any of you gets out of hand—" the old man looked over Shef's shoulder at the lowering figure of Cuthred, slouched on his pony with Martha and Edtheow gently patting an arm each ''—then you will all be responsible. There are five hundred men here. We can take you all if we have to.''

''All right,'' said Shef in his turn. ''Show us where to camp, show us the water place and let us buy food. And I need to hire a forge for the day.''

The spokesmen parted, let the little cavalcade pass through.

King Alfred's good silver pennies met with immediate approval inside the Thing-ground, and within hours Shef, stripped again to the waist and wearing a charred leather apron, was beating out metal at a hired forge with borrowed tools. Brand had headed straight off to the harbor a mile away, the rest had been told to establish a perimeter with stakes and rope and not stray outside it; Cuthred had been settled down with a carefully-organized team of minders. His likes and dislikes were well-known to everyone by now. He responded well to Udd, for some reason, probably because of the little man's total lack of any threat, and would listen for hours to Udd's boring monologues on the subject of metalworking. He liked the motherly comfort of the older and plainer women. Any sign of sexual display or intimacy from one of the younger women, even an accidental turn of hip or glimpse of calf, was likely to set his face in murderous lines. He tolerated the weakest of the thralls and freedmen, obeyed Shef, sneered at Brand, bristled at any sign of strength or competition from other men. If Karli, young, strong and popular with the women, so much as came into sight, Cuthred's eyes would follow him. Shef, noticing it, had told Karli to keep well away from him at all times. He had also told Cwicca and Osmod to set up a rota: two men with crossbows to watch Cuthred at all times, without being seen to do so. A tame berserk was valuable, especially for crossing hostile country. Unfortunately there were no tame berserks.

As some form of protection for their straggle of runaways, Shef had begun by beating out a dozen Wayman pendants. Only of iron, for the silver Waymen preferred had other uses at the moment. But at least they would be distinctive. To make them more so, Shef had made all of them his own emblem, the pole-ladder of Rig. None of the people they had rescued knew what it meant, but they would wear it as a talisman.

His next task was to see every man had at least some form of weapon: not for use, or at least he hoped not, but as a mark of status in a world where every free man carried at the very least spear and knife. Shef had bought a bundle of ten-inch spikes used to fix timber where doweling pegs would not do, and was beating each into a spearhead, to be sunk into ash-shafts and lashed tight with wetted rawhide. They would outfit their newest recruits. The catapulteers still had their halberds, knives and crossbows. Shef had taken back his cutlass from Cuthred, and straightened once more Karli's cheap and ineffective sword. The fight at Flaa had yielded a handful of other weapons, including Vigdjarf's sword, picked up and handed over to Cuthred.

The last of the spearheads done, Shef turned to his final job: converting the case-hardened shield into an offensive weapon for Cuthred. Although he seemed to have forgotten all his training in scientific fencing with shield and broadsword he kept the shield by him at all times. He was parted from it only with great difficulty and stood close and watched as Shef, remembering Muirtach and Ivar's Gaddgedill followers, decided to remove the double leather grips for hand and forearm and put a straight handhold across the shield's center on the inside. Cuthred grunted what might have been approval, then, with great reluctance, let Shef take the shield to the smithy where he fixed one of the ten-inch spikes to its middle on the outside. There was no way of driving a hole through the metal without ruining a dozen punches, so he would weld it on to the case-hardened surface. A tricky job, involving desperate efforts by relays of bellows-men to keep the metal glowing as near white-hot as they could manage.

Straightening, finally, Shef picked the shield up, rotated it from side to side in his left hand, and reflected that what was hard even for his smithy-trained muscle would be light work for Cuthred. He turned and walked out of the borrowed booth. Found himself face to face with a newcomer. He rubbed the smoke from his eyes, blinking in the sunlight, and recognized a grinning Thorvin, Brand just behind him.

"I see you are yourself again," said Thorvin, gripping his hand. "I told Brand that if you were well we need only head for the sound of the hammer."

CHAPTER NINETEEN

When King Halvdan knew that his son was dead," Thorvin explained an hour later, seated comfortably on a camp-stool with a mug of bought ale in his hand, "he went into a giant-rage. He told his mother that she had lived too long, put a rope round her neck, and told her to stab and hang herself at the same time as a sacrifice to Othin, so that little Harald might join the warriors in Valhalla. She did it willingly, or so I heard.

"Then he found that Brand was missing, and Shef's men as well, and decided to take it out on Brand's ship and crew. But they barricaded themselves in a hall in the college of the Way, and called on some of the rest of us to protect them. Valgrim sided with Halvdan, and many of his followers too, and for a while it seemed there might be civil war even within the college of the Way.

"But Halvdan did another thing. It could not be hidden from him that Shef had been on the island of Drottningsholm, and one of Stein's guardsmen confessed that he had been invited there. So Halvdan had Ragnhild to blame as well, and swore that she should follow his mother into the mound for her disloyalty and carelessness over his son."

"Well." Thorvin took another pull at his ale. "He was dead the next day. Dead in his bed. Died a straw-death, like a worn-out thrall."

"What symptoms did he show?" asked Hund, sitting close by on the ground.

"Ingulf said, henbane poisoning." Karli, also allowed to listen to the informal council, rolled his eyes, opened his mouth to say something, shut it again as he caught Thorvin's eye.

"So then there were men gathering everywhere, and oaths of vengeance on all sides. It was said that King Halvdan's conquests would seize the chance to break free of the Westfold rule, Queen Ragnhild was supposed to be going back to her people to raise an army to send after the killers of her son, the skippers of the coast guardships all came into port to protect their own interests, Brand's crew got back to the *Walrus* and asked me to take to flight along with them."

"But you didn't?" Shef guessed.

Thorvin shook his head. "There was Way business to settle first. Besides, everything quieted down suddenly. King Olaf then showed what was in his hand. Did you ever wonder," Thorvin inquired, "why they call King Olaf *Geirstatha-alfr*, Elf-of-Geirstath?

The listeners shook their heads mutely. After a moment Cwicca volunteered, "*Alfr* is what we call *alf*. Like in Alfred or Alfwyn. One of the Hidden Folk, but not ugly or vicious like a fen-thurs or a mountain-troll. Elf-women mate with men sometimes, and the other way round, or so they say. They are wise, but they have no souls."

"What happens to them when they die, then?" asked Thorvin. He looked round, observing the uncertain shrugs and headshakes of his listeners. "None of us knows, though some say they go to a world of their own, one of the nine worlds of which this is the midmost. But others say that they die. Die and then return again. And some say that the same may happen with men born of women. Now that is what King Olaf believed of himself. He said that he had been on this earth before, and that he would yet return in the person of one of his blood. Or if not—for now he has none of his blood or his brother's living—then his life would pass into some other keeping.

"He said, Shef, that he had set a test for you with Valgrim, and that you had passed it. He said that you had taken the luck of his lineage with you, and that from now on his luck and his spirit would flow through yours. And he told me to tell you that you had passed his test and Valgrim's, and he would now hold both Eastfold and Westfold for you. As your under-king."

Thorvin rose, walked over to where Shef sat, and carefully closed Shef's hands round his own. "King Olaf told me that I was to place my hands in yours on his behalf. He accepts you as the true king, the One who is to come from the North, and asks you to return to take your proper place in his kingdom and in the college of the Way."

Shef stared round at a ring of equally surprised faces. The very idea of an under-king did not come easily to the Norse or the English alike. A king was someone who acknowledged no superior, by definition. How could an under-king, who accepted an over-king, be a king, rather than a mere jarl or *hersir*?

"How did his men take this?" asked Shef tentatively. "Olaf has been supported by his brother for many years, has he not? Since they say he lost his luck to him. If the districts were thinking of revolt, Olaf would be able to do little against them. Especially if he declared himself under-king to a stranger."

Thorvin smiled. "No-one had any time to say anything. After all these years Olaf moved like—like a Ragnarsson. He burned Ragnhild's brother in his hall, before he could get his boots on. He had all the prominent men of the Eastfold who had spoken of revolt and independence brought to him in their shirts with ropes round their necks, and made them beg for their lives. He called a full meeting of all the priests of the Way, in conclave with the fire burning, and made Valgrim say in conclave how he had tested you, and made him admit that you had passed. There was no standing up to him. And now he is out, going from Thing to Thing in his own territory, making the men of each district accept his authority—and yours."

"And what about Ragnhild?" asked Shef. "How has Olaf dealt with her?"

Thorvin sighed. "She got away. Went back to her father's territory somewhere. I believe Valgrim went with her. His followers were convinced by Olaf, mostly, but his spite against you was too strong. He felt you had bested him."

"Still. The way is clear for us to go back. Back to Kaupang, and then back to England. How soon would you be ready to start, Brand?"

Brand scratched his head. "We have the two ships here, *Walrus* and Guthmund's *Seamew*. But you have picked up a lot of people coming across the country, the ships will need to be provisioned for so many passengers. Two days after next dawn."

"So be it," said Shef. "We return south two days after next dawn."

"When we first met," said Thorvin, "you said you came from the north. Now you are very quick to want to return to the south. Are you sure that you have come as far as you need to along the *northr vegr*, the North Way?"

"You mean there's places north of *here*," muttered an unidentifiable English voice from the circle of listeners. "I thought only trolls lived north of *here*."

*   *   *

Many hundreds of miles to the south, in the great palace of the Archbishop of Cologne, the plotters who had removed Pope Nicholas met again. Not all of those present at the first meeting had returned: Hincmar of Rheims was missing, delayed by his own affairs. But his absence was more than compensated by a throng of lesser prelates, bishops and abbots from the length of the German-speaking lands, all now ready and eager to be associated with the founders and rulers of the famous *Lanzenorden*. Archbishop Gunther looked round at them with both satisfaction and contempt. It was good to find so many supporters, a good sign too of the weakening of the power of the new Pope that so many were ready to attend a gathering that old Pope Nicholas, at least, would have denounced as treasonable. Yet as numbers increased, so strength of purpose was diluted. These men here were followers of success. Success would have to be provided for them. Fortunate that there was so much.

Gunther's chaplain and assistant Arno was coming to the end of the report he had been invited to deliver. "So," he concluded, "recruitment to the *Lanzenorden* continually increases. Teams of priests and guardians have entered all the northern lands. Many captives have been rescued or ransomed and sent home, among them many of our brothers in Christ enslaved over many years by the heathen. And while we move freely into the heathen lands, their assaults on us and on our Frankish brothers have ceased, or slackened."

Because they are afraid to come down the Channel, Gunther thought grimly. They fear the English apostates, not us. He let none of his doubts show on his face as he led the applause. As it died down another voice cut across Arno's smiling satisfaction. The voice of Rimbert, the ascetic, Archbishop of Hamburg-Bremen and the major force in the spread of the new Order.

"Yet for all this," he said. "For all the recruits and the money and the slaves rescued, we are no nearer the Order's true purpose. We have not found the Lance, the holy relic of Charlemagne. And without that all our success is as a tinkling cymbal. As vain as the ribbons on a strumpet's sleeve."

Gunther shut his eyes for a moment as the grim voice rasped on, opened them to note the alarm spreading across many faces. For if the saintly Rimbert did not believe in his own creation, who else should?

"Yes," replied Arno, shuffling his papers. "That is true. Yet I have reports here from the most daring of our teams sent into the heathen lands, a report sent by the English deacon Erkenbert, strong in the strength of the Lord, at the instructions of his commander Bruno son of Reginbald."

The very mention of Bruno's name, Gunther noted, created a wave of relief. Even Rimbert nodded acceptingly, not continuing with his denunciation.

"The learned Erkenbert reports that he and Bruno and their men penetrate ever deeper into heathendom, fearing no persecution. They test every king and kingdom for signs of the Lance at work, and have found nothing yet. Nevertheless, the learned Erkenbert says we must remember that it is a gain in knowledge every time one learns nothing."

Arno looked up, saw that this thought had proved too hard for all his audience, and tried again. He was speaking to an audience at least theoretically literate, and could afford an appeal to writing. "He means that if one has a list of names—like the list of witnesses to a charter, each one written below the other." Puzzled nods from most of the bishops and abbots, following so far. "Then every time one crosses such a name *off*, there are fewer names left to consider. If one crosses every name off but one, then that one must be the one you seek. So, you see, even a negative result—even finding a nothing—tells you something."

Silence greeted this exposition. Faces looked by no means convinced. Archbishop Rimbert finally broke it.

"The efforts of our brothers in heathendom are beyond praise," he said. "We must support them with every man and every mark we can raise." He looked round challengingly. "I say, every man and every mark! Yet for all that, I do not think the Lance of Longinus, the Lance of Charlemagne, the Lance of the Emperor-to-be: I do not think this will be brought to light by the hand of man alone."

While Brand and Guthmund sought out provisions for their sail south, Shef spent much of his time wandering round the great meeting, half way between a shire-court and a summer fair, watching how the Norse-folk did their business. Those of his band who could be allowed to wander freely did the same, but there were few of them—Cuthred remained under guard at all times, and the runaway slaves never left the perimeter that Shef had marked out except to visit communal latrines, in groups with Brand or Guthmund supervising.

The Thing was a strange custom, Shef concluded. Rightly speaking, it had not happened yet. Round about Midsummer's Day was the traditional time for the Gula-Thing, still some weeks off. At that time many law-cases would be decided by the thirty-six chosen wise men of the Thing-lands, the three *fylkir* of Sogn, Hord and the Fjords. These were the areas that provided so many of the horde of summer pirates that sailed south every year. It was therefore no easy business to summon a man for murder, for land-disputes or for a paternity case at midsummer, when they might be, or pretend to be, away. So a kind of reduced court met much of the time, trying usually to get some agreement without the matter going to the final decision of the wise. At the same time trade and business of many kinds never ceased, with ships continually coming and going.

Shef was amazed at the wealth on display. England was a rich country in land and in food, he had realized during the short period that he had ruled some of it. But the Viking lands had had coined silver and even gold flowing in to them for two generations or more. The well-off among them would pay high prices for luxuries, making it worth while for strongly-manned ships to come up from the south, past the pirates of Rogaland. And the flow of materials from the north included luxuries that Shef had never seen. He was, now, rich himself from the taxes of East Anglia, some portion of them held by Brand in the *Walrus* for his use. At Brand's urging Shef bought for himself a hooded coat of the best waterproof sealskin, the hood fringed with wolf hair on which a man's breath would never freeze, even in the coldest weather. A two-edged sword of the finest Swedish steel, its hilt cut from the twisted horn of some fabulous beast of the northern seas that Brand called a narwhal. A bag for sleeping in, sealskin again on the outside, wool on the inside, with between them a thick layer of down from the northern birds. Shef, reluctant to spend money which he never felt was his, had nevertheless spent enough nights shivering in thin clothes and blanket to be ready never to feel cold again. He had marveled at the patience with which these goods were assembled, wondering how long it would take to trap and pluck the rare eider-birds that gave the best and warmest down in the world. But Brand had laughed when he mentioned this.

"We don't catch them," he said. "We make the Finns do that."

"Finns?" Shef had never heard the word before.

"Up north," Brand pointed, "where Sweden and Norway run close together, beyond Halogaland where I live, the world turns into a place where no man can grow anything fit to eat, not rye, not barley, not even oats. Pigs die of cold, and cows have to be stall-fed all winter. There the Finns live, without houses, in skin tents, wandering from place to place with their herds of reindeer. We put tribute on them, the *Finn-skatt*, the Finn-tax. Every man of them has to pay so much a year, in skins, in furs, in down. They spend their time hunting and fishing, so it goes easily for them. What they catch beyond their tax, we buy off them and sell all together to the traders here or further south. The

kings of the world dress in furs caught by my Finns, and they pay
kings' prices too! But I buy the stuff in the first place for butter and
cheese. No Finn can milk a cow, and no Finn can walk past a bowl of
milk. It is a good trade."

Good for you, thought Shef. It must be a difficult tax to collect.

Trading done, he had walked over to the area where legal cases
were settled. Most of the time, just men standing in groups, fully
armed, leaning on their spears, but listening for the most part to what
their friends or their adversaries had to say, and to the advice of the
wise men of their district. The Gula-Thing had strict laws, but few
men knew what they were, since they had never been written down. It
was the task of the wise to learn as much law as they could, or all of it
if they wished ever to be law-speakers, and to announce it to
disputants. They might then wriggle or quibble, try to find other laws
more suitable for their case, or simply intimidate their opponents into
accepting a cheap settlement, but they would not simply deny the law
existed.

Yet there were some matters, often involving seduction, rape,
adultery or woman-theft, where the law might be clear but where
passions ran high. Several times during the two days Shef heard voices
suddenly raised and the clang of weapons. Twice Hund was called
away to patch and bandage, and once men rode away with set faces
and a corpse of their own slung over a horse.

"Someone will get burnt out over that one," Brand remarked.
"Hard men round here, they can get away with things for a fair while.
Then the neighbors get together, come down and torch the place. Kill
everyone who tries to get out. Works even on berserks, eventually. As
the poem says:

> Every wise man shall count himself warlike
>   With moderation.
> Or find, when he comes among the fierce ones,
>   No man has no match."

On the second afternoon, as Shef lounged in the sunshine watching
Guthmund bargain furiously for two barrels of salt pork—his bargaining tactics were much admired, even by the victims, who swore that
they could never believe a famous abbey-robber could express such
passion over a mere clipped penny. Then Shef noticed men's attention
start to waver, heads turn, and then a general drift begin up to the
stones of the doom-ring. Guthmund broke off, releasing the pork-

merchant's collar, slapped his money down, and began to follow the drift, Shef hastening after him.

"What's up?" he asked.

Guthmund had picked the story out of the crowd. "Two men agreed to settle their business Rogaland-style."

"Rogaland-style? What's that?"

"The Rogalanders are poor, couldn't afford proper swords till recently, just carried cutlasses like the one you had, or timber-axes. But they really mean business just the same. So if they decide to fight a duel, they don't square off inside an enclosure marked with hazel twigs, or fight a formal holmgang like you did once. No, they stretch out a bull's hide, and both men stand on it. Not allowed off. Then they fight with knives."

"That doesn't sound too dangerous," Shef ventured.

"First they tie their left wrists together."

The place for duels of this kind was in a hollow, so men could line the sides and watch. Shef and Guthmund found places high up. They saw the bull's hide carefully laid out, the contestants brought forward. A priest of the Way spoke words which they could not hear, and the two men slowly stripped off their shirts and stepped out in their breeches alone. Each held in his right hand a long, broad knife, like the seax-knife Shef's catapult-men carried, but with a straight blade and sharp point—a stabbing weapon as well as a chopping one. A leather rope was tied first to one wrist, then the other. Shef noted that there was maybe three feet of slack left. Each man took half the slack and held it in his bound left hand, so that the fight began with the backs of the left fists touching. One man was young, tall, with long fair hair braided down his back. The other twenty years older, burly and bald, an expression of grim anger on his face.

"What's it about?" Shef muttered.

"Young one got the other one's daughter pregnant. He says she consented, the father says he raped her in the field."

"What does she say?" Shef asked, remembering similar cases from his own time as a judge.

"I don't think anyone asked her."

Shef opened his mouth to ask further, realized it was too late. More words spoken, a ritual request to accept mediation, now impossible to take without shame. Two headshakes. The law-speaker stepped carefully off the bull's hide, made a signal.

Instantly the two men were in motion, springing round each other. The father had stabbed at the first flicker of the judge's hand, stabbed

low under the linked hands. But at the same moment the young man
had dropped his slack and sprung back to the full extent of the rope.

The father dropped his slack too, snatched forward at the rope
trailing from his enemy's wrist. If he got it he could hold the younger
man to him, keep him no more than one arm's length, perhaps pull
him close and stab him in the body. But to commit yourself to a mortal
stroke left you open to a mortal counter. In this kind of duel it was easy
to kill your enemy. If you cared to give him the chance to kill you.

The older man's snatch missed, the younger one was leaping away,
keeping near the edge of the hide. Suddenly he stretched forward,
slashed his enemy across the back of the arm. A shout as the blood
showed, a sneer in answer from the wounded man.

"Easy in this game to give a scratch," Guthmund remarked. "But a
scratch won't settle it. Loss of blood, if it goes on a long time—but it
never does."

The fight had reached a kind of pattern, one man trying to close,
stabbing always underneath the two arms, jerking and grabbing at the
rope that joined them. The other ignoring the rope, keeping away,
flicking quick slashes at arm or leg, but taking care not to let his knife
catch, to trap him for an instant.

He did it once too often. The bald father, bleeding from a dozen
minor wounds, took yet another slash high up on the left biceps.
Caught the retreating hand, the knife-hand, with his own tied left.
Started to twist it savagely, shouting something Shef could not catch
over the crowd noise. The seducer lashed out with his own left hand,
desperately trying to catch the other's knife-hand in his turn. But the
older man had twisted, holding the knife away behind his body out of
reach, feinting to thrust low, then high, twisting the caught wrist all
the time.

With no other hope left the trapped man kicked both feet off the
ground, tried to catch the other's thighs in a scissors grip, sent him
staggering. As the two fell locked to the ground Shef saw blood spurt,
heard the groan of released breath from the spectators close up. The
judge stepped forward, pulled the two men apart. Shef saw one knife
jutting from deep in the chest of the young man. As they rolled the
other over he saw a second hilt standing up from the older man's eye.

Women were shrieking, rushing forward. Shef turned to
Guthmund, ready to rebuke a system that lost a woman husband and
father in the same heartbeat, and a child father and grandfather. But
the words died in his throat.

Cuthred was striding down the hollow, spiked shield in one hand,
sword in the other. Behind him trailed Fritha and Osmod, Udd a pace

or two after them, all carrying crossbows but looking helpless. As Shef started to shove his way forward, he heard Cuthred's crazy voice lifted in pidgin Norse.

"Bunglers! Nithings! Have to be tied together not to run away. Hold a man to be cut. Fight an Englishman, why don't you, one with hands free. One hand tied, give you choice. Hornungs, sons of drabs! You, you there."

White spittle was flying from his mouth, and a circle was steadily widening round him, leaving him isolated with the two dead men at his feet. Staring down, Cuthred slashed suddenly at one of them, opening a great gash across the young man's dead face. He began to stamp his feet and breathe in great gasps, ready to charge the entire crowd.

Shef stepped in front of him, waited for recognition to show in the mad eyes. Reluctant recognition.

"They won't fight," said Shef slowly. 'We'll have to find a better time. And striking a corpse is foul play, Cuthred. Foul play for an *ordwiga*, a *herecempa*, a *frumgar* like yourself, a king's champion. Wait for the Ragnarssons, for the killers of your King Ella."

Cuthred's face worked at the string of honorifics, all of which he had earned in former life as captain of the King of Northumbria's guard. He looked at his bloody sword, at the corpse he had struck, threw his weapon down and burst into racking sobs. Udd and Osmod closed on either side, took his arm, started to lead him away.

Mopping sweat, Shef turned to meet the disapproving look of the duel-judge, the law-speaker.

"Mutilating a dead body," the Norseman said, "is punishable by a fine of . . ."

"We'll pay," said Shef. "We'll pay. But someone ought to pay for what has been done to that live one."

The next morning, Shef stood by the narrow gangplank leading to Brand's prized and cherished ship, the *Walrus*. Guthmund's *Seamew*, already loaded, rocked easily in the water twenty yards out, a row of faces looking over the low gunwale. Loading the ships had not been an easy business. Each rowed eighteen oars a side and carried a normal crew of forty. To this had had to be added Shef, Hund, Karli and Thorvin, the eight men of the catapult crew, the four women they had rescued from Drottningsholm, Cuthred, and the train of runaways they had attracted in their ride across Upland and Sogn—nearly thirty all told, a large number to add to the cramped quarters of two narrow ships.

But now they were not all there: Lulla, Fritha and Edwi of the catapult crew, all missing. Had they been cut off somehow? Were they being hidden somewhere in the Thing area, destined for slavery or revenge, or even sacrifice? At the thought of his men being strung up on the temple trees of some backwoods town, Shef's patience snapped.

"Get all the men off," he shouted to Brand. "You too Guthmund. We can muster a hundred men between us. We'll go through this place and turn every tent over till they hand our men over. Anyone doesn't like it, he'll get a bolt in his belly."

Shef became aware that Cwicca and the others were not reacting with the enthusiasm he would have expected. They had donned their glassy expressions, always a sign they knew something they did not dare to reveal.

"All right," Shef said. "What's up with those three?"

Osmod, usually the spokesman on difficult occasions, spoke up. "It's like this," he volunteered. "We've been walking round, some of us, looking at things. And all they're talking about here is catapults and crossbows and that. They've heard a lot about them, don't know how they work. So we said, naturally, that we knew all about catapults, and as for crossbows, well Udd here practically invented them. So they say—by this time they'd stood us all a drink or two—they say, 'very interesting, do you men know what's happening down south?' 'No,' says we, naturally enough, since we don't. So then they say . . ."

"Get on with it!" Shef bellowed.

"They're paying big money for experienced catapult men, men who know how to build and shoot them. Big money. We think Lulla and Edwi and Fritha have decided to go in for that."

Shef stared for a moment, uncertain how to react. He had freed those men. They were landholders back in England already. How could they go off and take service with anyone, leaving their lord? But then they were free men, because he had freed them . . .

"All right," he said. "Forget it, Brand. Osmod, the rest of you, thank you anyway for staying. I hope you won't lose by it. Let's get on board and get going. Back in England in two weeks, if Thor sends us a wind."

He did not, or not immediately. All the way down the long fjord from where the Gula met the Sogn to the open sea, the two boats pulled steadily into the teeth of a fresh breeze, low in the water from their weight of passengers and stores. Brand spelled the rowers, rotating the male passengers with his own men.

"Get round the ness," he remarked. "Wind'll be on our beam then, we can stop rowing and sail south. What's that ahead?"

Round the point of the promontory that guarded the Gula-fjord, little more than half a mile away, came a ship. A strange ship, not like the traders and fishing-boats they had passed half a dozen times already. Her blue and white striped sail bellied in the breeze behind her, a pennant flew from her mast, blowing towards them so they could see it only fitfully as a gust took it wide. Something wrong with her sail. Something wrong with her size.

"Thor aid us," said Brand at the steering-oar. "It's one of Halfdan's coastguard ships. But she's got two sails. She's even got two masts. I never saw such a thing in all my born days. What have they done all that for?"

Shef's one sharp eye caught sight of the banner, the Gripping Beast design on it.

"Turn," he said. "Get us out of here. It's Queen Ragnhild. And she means us no good."

"It's a big ship, but we're two to one, we can fight her . . ."

"Turn," shouted Shef, recognizing something about the motions of the men on deck.

Brand caught on in the same moment and sent the *Walrus* heeling round in a turn so violent that the rowers were sent skidding along their benches. "Back starboard," he shouted. "Pull backboard. Now pull together. Pull hard, get the stroke up. And drop the sail and sheet home, you in the waist there, help him, Narr, Ansgeir. Guthmund . . ." His voice carried over the water to their companion lagging a furlong behind. The *Walrus*, wind now behind her, began to scud back the way she had come.

Watching the pursuing ship, Shef, as he had expected, saw her yaw to bring her beam round. "On the word, swing her hard to starboard," he said quietly. "Now."

The *Walrus* swung briskly round. At the same moment Brand shouted to his crew to lift their oars, let the boat run freely under sail. The oars heaved smartly together out of the water. A hum in the air, three oarsmen together span out of their seats, landed in the belly of the ship, cursing or moaning. Shattered pieces of oar flew up in the air, splashed slowly into the sea. The mule-stone that had smashed through them just above head-height flew on, hit the water, bounced from wave to wave to wave before sinking.

"They were talking about fitting one of those," said Brand. "But they said she'd never take the recoil. Must have rerigged her internally along with the two masts."

"But who's crewing the mule?" asked Shef, still watching the ship behind them trying to make up lost distance, alert for any second swerve that would bring the mule round to bear. It was fortunate this was a stern chase and Ragnhild's men could not shoot over the bow. "Renegades of mine? But where would they have got them from?"

"The Way has been very interested in all that you did," put in Thorvin, standing close to Brand. "They built copies of all the machines you made. Valgrim could have built the mule and found a crew. Some of his friends are priests of Njörth, would know how to rebuild a ship. What are we going to do? Run back into the Gula-fjord and hope to fight them on land?"

Shef was once more staring intently at the activity in the bow of the pursuing ship. She had lost way by turning beam-on to shoot, and now both were under sail the *Walrus* and her consort were making ground with every wave. The ships had begun half a mile apart. Now they were certainly more than that. Even at that distance, though, Shef was certain that he could make out a tall figure, a tall female figure, standing in the very prow of the ship, long hair streaming disheveled. Ragnhild coming after him. Chasing him, however fast they sailed, into a long fjord with no other exit. And they were certainly doing something strange in the prow there. Could they have built a mule that did not need to be bedded low down and centrally in a ship?

Light showed behind Ragnhild, fire, a strong fire blazing brightly. At the same moment Shef's brain recognized the motions of the men round it. He had never seen a catapult being wound from in front of it before, but that was what they were doing—had been doing, for they had just jumped back to clear the view for the shooter, just like Cwicca's crew. Not a mule, one of the great dart-shooters he had used himself to release Ella and to break Ivar Ragnarsson's army.

As Shef turned to shout at Brand to swerve again, he saw the light suddenly coming straight at him with inconceivable speed, rising and falling slightly a bare six feet over the waves. Involuntarily, Shef cringed. Bent forward, arms over belly, sure the machine would send the great javelin-size bolt straight through body and spine.

A thump just below his feet, sending him staggering. Instant reek of burning tar, burning wood. Brand yelling hoarsely and a lurch as he abandoned the steering oar to look over the side. Then Shef was shoved aside by men running up from the waist of the ship with bailing buckets, trying furiously to lean over far enough to reach the water, scoop it up, throw it on to the great fire-arrow that had slammed into the *Walrus*, come clean through her rear planking three feet from Shef's leg, was now setting fire to planks and thwarts at once.

"Use the drinking water!" shouted Brand. The driblets of sea-water his crew were bailing up from the waves barely within reach were making no impact on the mass of pitch and tar on the bolt's head, jammed through the planks. And the fire was spreading. If it caught the sail . . . A man ran from the water-barrel by the base of the mast, lost his footing and fell, bucket going wide into the bilge. Others hesitated, torn between the sea just out of reach and the water-barrel too far away.

Cuthred slouched from his place near the bow. No-one had ventured to ask him to row. He had an axe in his hand. Standing over the fire-arrow, he smashed three strokes down through the *Walrus*'s frail planking, bent over the side, thrust the bolt further through till the blazing head stood well out from the ship's inner side. Swung the axe again, shearing through the thick wood with one blow. Picked up the severed head, ignoring the flames that ran up his arm, tossed it over the side. As Cuthred turned sneering to Brand, Shef realized that the ship behind them had yawed again.

Machine-war, he thought sickly. It comes too fast. Even a brave man wants to stop, to shout "Wait till I'm ready!" Helplessly, he saw the mule-stone come blurring towards him, again seeming to come directly at him, not the ship, him personally, aiming for his rib-cage, to shatter the thin bones and crush out the heart.

The stone hit the water thirty yards short, bounced like a child's skimming-stone, bounced again, and hit the *Walrus* like a hammer just forward of the steering-oar. Planks stove, a rowing-bench hurled from its socket, green water poured through. But only a hole, not the complete shattering and disintegration of a ship struck on keel or stem-post.

You were a king before, Shef told himself. Now they say you are an over-king. And what are you doing? Cringing. Waiting for help from a madman. This is not the way for a leader. You have destroyed men from a distance before. You never thought how you would behave when the other side had all the machines.

Shef stepped up to the stern again, leaving the others to deal with the leak. Ragnhild's ship was still coming on behind them, while men worked to wind their machines, prepare for their next shots. One or other would sink them, once they had learnt to hold their hand till they were in proper range. Meanwhile they had come back under full sail almost to their starting-place. Shef could see a crowd down by the Thing-harbor, watching them. And just in front lay the island, the Gula-ey, on which the Thing itself had been held in years gone by. Shef eyed the narrow channel between it and the shore, considered the size of Halvdan's warship, remembered the trick Sigurth Snake-eye had played on him. He did not think an experienced Viking skipper would fall for that one.

He caught Brand by the shoulder, pointed. "Take us through there."

Brand opened his mouth to argue, closed it as he caught the tone of utter certainty in Shef's voice. Silently he leant on the oar, steered between rocks, waved peremptorily to Guthmund to follow. After a few moments he ventured to say, "We'll lose the wind in a moment."

"All right." Shef was watching the ship behind. As he expected, she had shifted course. Not going to follow. Going to go round the island to the left as they had to the right. Take the wind on the beam, keep up speed, overhaul the two ships she was pursuing, destroy them at close range. Probably their skipper thought his enemies intended to beach and escape on foot. Ragnhild would have a plan for that too.

But for a few moments the island would be between them.

"On the word," said Shef quietly, "furl sail, turn, and row back as fast as ever you can. Once we're past it'll be a rowing match. With a ship that size and with that much extra weight, we're bound to win."

"Unless she just sits and waits for us. Then we're rowing back to face catapults at fifty yards."

Shef nodded. "Turn now."

The *Walrus* and *Seamew* turned together, began to row back, the men at the oars heaving in an intent silence. The only noise they could hear Shef realized, was the hum of voices on the shore a hundred yards away. He hoped pointing fingers would not give his plan away. What Brand said was right. This was like two children chasing each other round a kitchen table. If the chaser just stopped, the one who doubled back would run right into him. Shef did not think the chaser would stop. That ship there, however experienced the skipper, was commanded by Ragnhild, he knew. She would not stop to think. She wanted to run him down. Besides that, he had seen the men lining the bulwarks, waving weapons and shouting. They had acquired machines, but they did not think like machine-warriors yet. Their instinct and training was to close and overwhelm, to break the line by force and weight. Not to sit back and shoot from a distance, use their weapons' range.

As the *Walrus* scudded out from the channel and back the way they had come, Shef looked over the starboard quarter. Relief filled him. Halvdan's ship had raced round the island, realized too late what had happened, was only turning now in a flurry of flapping sails. Badly handled, too. The crew and skipper had evidently still not worked out the problems of their two-mast rig. Nearer a mile off than half a mile, and no chance of catching up. Brand's oarsmen were throwing their weight on the oars now, one of them singing and the rest giving the refrain each time they swayed their oar-handles forward. Three men were bending planks back into place, plugging gaps with sealskin and sailcloth. The way was clear to run out into the open sea and south again.

Karli caught Shef's arm and pointed ahead. A small skiff, rowed by one man, paddling out from the harbor to intercept them.

"It's Fritha," he said. "Must have changed his mind."

Shef frowned, stepped forward to the bow again, seizing a rope. As the *Walrus* came up on the small skiff he heaved the rope across, saw Fritha grasp it. He made no attempt to haul his boat alongside but abandoned it, dropping the oars and swinging himself waist-deep through the water till he could clutch the *Walrus*'s side. Shef seized his collar, heaved him over, stood looking down forbiddingly.

"What happened? Silver not paid on time?"

Fritha gasped, struggled dripping to his feet. "No, lord. I had to tell you. The Thing is full of the news. A ship came in ahead of that one there. We knew the queen Ragnhild was coming before you did. But the ship said another thing. As she sailed up the coast, she—the queen—told every harbor along the coast that if you escaped her she would pay a bounty for your head. A great bounty, all her inheritance. Every pirate in Rogaland is looking for you now. All along the coast. Two hundred miles of it.''

And Rogalanders are poor, Shef reflected, but they really mean business. He looked at Thorvin.

"It seems the way south is blocked. I will have to be the one who comes from the North after all."

"We say the words," said Thorvin. "But the gods put them there."

CHAPTER TWENTY

ure they'll come after us," said Brand. He held a seal's flipper in one hand, gnawed carefully along one of its long bones, sucked the blubber noisily from the skin, hurled the remains into the sea. As an afterthought he wiped both greasy hands carefully on his beard, rose to his feet, slouched off towards the boathouses of Hrafnsey, his island home. Over his shoulder he shouted, "But they won't find us. And if they do, we'll see them first."

Shef looked after his retreating figure. Brand worried him more and more. Shef had known him for almost two years now, and at no time could Brand ever have been taken as a model of courtly etiquette. Nevertheless, by the admittedly low standards of Viking armies his behavior had been normal enough: rough, violent and noisy, but capable of finer feeling and even of an element of show. Brand had cut a fine figure at the wedding of Alfred and Godive. When Shef had arrived at Kaupang, Brand had put up a very creditable impersonation of a courtier welcoming an honored king. He had always been clean and careful about the hygiene of the camp.

As the ships had run further and further north, racing up the seemingly endless coastline of Norway with the wind behind them, always the long jagged coast to starboard and a turmoil of reefs and islands and tidal skerries between them and the Atlantic on the backboard, Brand's behavior had steadily changed. So had his accent and that of his Halogaland crew. They had always spoken oddly compared to the other Norwegians. As they neared the everlasting ice their accents had thickened, their voices grown gruffer, they had begun to revel, it seemed, in oil and grease. They ate their bread ration soaked in seal-fat, scattering pinches of salt on it. They ate the fish they caught raw, and sometimes alive: Shef had seen a man pluck a herring from the sea on his line and sink his teeth into it immediately, the fish still flapping in his hands. One day Brand had reduced sail as if looking carefully for landmarks, and finally steered into a beach. His crew had piled out whooping before the boat had even come to the shore, run up the beach to a cairn, and started instantly to demolish it and dig into the sand beneath. The stench that came up sent Shef and his English crewmen reeling backward to a safe distance, where they were joined by Guthmund and his Swedes from the *Seamew*, for once in complete agreement with the English as against the Norwegians.

"What out of Hel have you got there?" Shef had shouted from the safe side of a wood fire, the smoke in his nostrils.

"Rotten shark liver," Brand had shouted back. "We buried it on the way down to age a bit. Like to try a bite?"

As one man the Swedes and English had moved another fifty yards down the beach, pursued by guffaws and shouts of "It's good for you! Keeps out the cold! Bite a shark and he can't bite you!"

Once they got to Hrafnsey things had got worse. The island itself was about five miles long and two wide, and relatively flat. Much of it could be grazed, some even plowed. It lay opposite the most desolate coastline Shef had ever seen in his life, far bleaker and more jagged than even the mountains of Norway running down to the Oslo fjord. Even past midsummer, snow could be seen everywhere. The mountains seemed to run straight and undeviating down into icy water, with only here and there the barest glimpses of green growth on little shelves and ledges, for all one could see inaccessible from the water or from the mountain-tops above them. For many days Shef continued to find it impossible that anyone could live and find food there. Yet Brand's crew had dispersed for the most part into the rocky wilderness like water into sand, pulling away in two- and four-oared rowboats, or in small sail cobles. In every fjord there seemed to be a farm, or at least a hut or cluster of stone-walled turf-roofed cabins.

The truth was, Shef had realized, that these people, though they grew some oats and barley in favored places, were essentially carnivores. The freezing water teemed with fish, easy to pickle in brine for the winter. Seals were everywhere also, competing with men for the fish and so doubly valuable to kill. There was enough grass to graze cows and sheep in the summer, and to make hay to feed them through the winter. Goats could be turned out to forage for themselves on the mountains. These Norsemen of the furthest North put an immense value on milk and butter, whey and curds and cheese, milking all their animals, sheep and goats as well, twice daily through the summer, and preserving all of it which they did not consume immediately. It was indeed a rich land that they lived in, though it seemed no more than rock. But it needed special qualities to survive in it. Some of Brand's men had taken Karli, the flatlander from the Ditmarsh, and a few of Guthmund's crew bird's nesting after eggs, to be found in vast quantities on every cliff and skerry during the breeding season. They had returned helpless with laughter after half a day, depositing the white-faced outlanders on the shore with exaggerated care. Only someone with no nerves at all and no slightest sense of vertigo could swing down the iron-bound cliffs on fingertips and toeholds alone. A man could not marry on Hrafnsey, Brand had told Shef, till he had gone to a certain stone two hundred feet above the jagged rocks of the shore, balanced on it—for it was a stone that moved in the wind—bent over the edge, touched his toes and then pissed into the surf below. It was his grandfather's time since any man had slipped: the fear of falling had been bred out of Brand's line and that of all his fellows.

None of this made the Halogalanders easier to live with. From the start Shef had worried about how they were to get away. Then he had worried about how, if they did not get away—and Brand seemed content to wait for pursuit rather than try to counter-attack or avoid it—they were to live through the winter with their great trail of useless mouths, Englishmen and Swedes who could not harpoon seals, climb cliffs or digest the buried livers of the enormous basking sharks. "Catch more fish," was all Brand would say. He seemed unworried about everything, content only to be back in his alien home, making plans only for the collection of the Finn-tax.

Shef had many things to worry about besides Brand. They crowded on him as he lay sleepless in the short twilights of the northern summer. For one thing, on the long voyage up the coast he had had time to talk to all his crew members, Cwicca, Hama, Udd, Osmod and the others, who had all occupied their time at the Gula Thing by collecting as much gossip as possible. The Norwegian Thing-goers were startlingly well informed—though it was not so startling when you reckoned the volume of trade and warfare that passed through their hands. Piecing together what they had said, Shef realized that his own actions had caused far more repercussions in the Scandinavian lands than he had ever imagined. The whole of the Norse-speaking world was alive with interest in the new weapons that had defeated the

Franks and the Ragnarssons. That was why high prices were on offer
to genuine experts. The sea-battle off the Elbe had also been reported
on in detail, and plans for fitting catapults to ships were far advanced.
There was no point in raiding to the south any more, some said, till the
Norse were on even terms once more, or better, against their English
prey.

Expectation was mounting, too, about the Ragnarssons' counter-
stroke. According to Osmod, the most accurate informer, there was
very definite feeling that the Ragnarssons would have to do something.
They had failed in Northumbria, failed to avenge their father properly.
Lost one of their number, failed to avenge him too. Failed at the start of
their great counter-raid in the spring, failed even to buy the man they
saw as the origin of their misfortunes when he stood for sale on the
slave-block. That story was well-known, Osmod said, and men were
laughing openly as they heard about it. Wiser men felt that the
Ragnarssons must do something. Only the year before it had been
common knowledge that Sigurth the Snake-eye meant to establish his
brothers on the thrones of England and Ireland, and then return with
their aid to unify all Denmark under his own rule, as had never been
done since the days of the mythical Skjöldungs. And now what did
they say of him? That he could not catch a man on a sandbank with
the tide coming in. Many laughed, Osmod repeated, but others said
that you could be sure of one thing: the Ragnarssons would return
from their forays in Scotland ready for some desperate stroke. Sensible
kings in Denmark had forbidden their subjects to raid abroad, and
were calling up their fleets and armies for home defense.

And then there were the Christians stirring. Here it was Thorvin
who had told Shef most, Thorvin who had been so exultant the year
before at the thought of Christian kings calling in Wayman missionaries. Now, he said, it began to look as if the boot were on the other foot.
Report after report had come in to him of strange behavior in the
markets and at the Things of the south Scandinavian lands: Christian
priests not just coming in to try to make converts, as they had for
decades, among the slaves and the poor folk and the women of the
country, usually finding themselves mocked and enslaved in their
turn. No, coming in with a swagger and a guard, returning insult with
insult and violence with violence, buying back their own. And asking
questions. Questions about the raid on Hamburg sixteen years before.
Questions about kings. Writing down the answers. Not trying to save
souls, no, looking for something. Thorvin had heard especially, and in
tones of deepest admiration, about the man they called Bruno.

But there Shef had been able to tell Thorvin of what he had seen in the market at Hedeby, and of the conversation he had had afterwards. What had surprised him was not that the Vikings were impressed by Bruno—anyone as fast and skillful as he was would naturally be a success in the Viking world—but that Bruno had continued on from Hedeby, into the country of the Swedes, the Smaaland counties and the two Gautaland provinces south of the great Swedish lakes.

Thorvin had told him one thing especially that he did not know before. "Do you know why so many of us are called Eirik?" Thorvin had asked. "It is because of the Eiriksgata, or better one should say the *Ein-riks-gata*. The road of the one ruler. No man can become king of all the Swedes, it is said, unless he has traveled that road. It goes round all the Things of all the provinces. The true king must go to each Thing, and declare himself king in each assembly, and overcome any and all challenge. Only once a king has done that is he king over all the Swedes."

"And who was the last king who ever did that?" Shef had asked, remembering what Hagbarth had told him months before about the way you became a king, though it might be no more than king of the Eastfold, or the Fjord-countries, or as Shef had said mockingly, of the Next Midden or the Further Cow-byre.

Thorvin had pursed his lips and shaken his head slowly, remembering history so old it was myth. "Maybe King Ali," he had said. "Ali the Mad, uncle of King Athils. The Swedes say he was king over all Sweden, including the Gautlands and Skaane. But he cannot have held those lands for long—his nephew was put to scorn by King Hrolf on Fyrisvellir Plain. You know. You saw that yourself," he added, reminding Shef of one of his own visions.

It seemed to Shef sometimes that the wide-shouldered Bruno was touring the Scandinavian lands as if he meant to follow the *Einriksgata* himself, to make them Christian by force from above rather than by conversion from below. If so, the Wayman victory in England with East Anglia and Alfred's kingdom would be canceled out, and more, by Christian victory in the North. He could not imagine it would be so. Still, it fretted him that he had no news, no further news once every last bit of nourishment had been chewed from what his men reported. It fretted him even more that he was up here at the very last edge of the inhabited world, while great matters were stirring in the center. Driven away to a land of birds' eggs and shark liver, while the armies marched in the south.

And indeed the armies marched and the fleets maneuvered. While Shef and his men twisted rope and shaped wood, setting up catapults, mules and dart-shooters to cover every seaward entrance to Hrafnsey for the attack of Ragnhild, the Ragnarssons came down like a cloud on the Ditmarsh and the islands of North Frisia, sending King Hrorik into a frenzy of recruiting and appealing and gathering stores for siege in Hedeby. The Archbishop of Hamburg-Bremen, the ascetic Rimbert, hearing stronger and stronger reports from his agents in the North, doubled the forces of the Knights of the Holy Lance and sent them in their own ships across the Baltic, with the enthusiastic support of his brothers in Cologne and Mainz and Trier and even beyond. The Frankish descendants of Charlemagne bickered and sparred for the succession to Charles the Bald, with the new Pope—the Popelet, men called him—lending his support now to one, now to the other. And in a season of unexpected peace Godive's child grew in her womb, while her husband received the deputations of many kingless English counties, anxious to join in what they saw as the new Golden Age without either Church or pagans.

But Shef waited on events, his whereabouts known to none, relieving his feelings only by constant work at the forge and among his fellow craftsmen.

Cwicca's gang were attempting to make winter wine in summer. They had been vastly impressed by the strong drink they had been given in Kaupang, and had managed to buy a small barrel between them at the Gula-Thing. It was gone now, but they had time on their hands, and Udd had explained his theory to them.

"What they do with winter wine," he lectured, "is freeze the water out of it, so that what remains is stronger."

Nods and general agreement.

"Now steam is water." There was more discussion about this point, but everyone had seen steam rising from damp ground, or sweat turning into steam when it hit a hot iron. "So if we heat beer up till the steam comes off it, we'll get the water out of it just as if it had been frozen. It won't be winter wine. It'll be kind of summer beer."

"But it'll be stronger," said Cwicca, wanting to get the main point straight.

"Right."

The men had got a tub of beer—most of the scanty barley production of Hrafnsey went into brewing rather than bread—put half of it into the largest copper pot they could borrow, and heated it over a gentle fire, careful not to burn the bottom of the pot out. Slowly the thick brew began to bubble, the steam rose off it in the thick-walled, low-roofed brewhouse. A score of men and half a dozen women were jammed in together, the catapult-team and with them the *kraki* wearers, as they were called, the rescues of the trek across the Upland.

Udd, presiding, watched carefully, superintending the fire-tenders, beating away attempts at preliminary tasting with his largest beechwood ladle. Finally, watching the level in the pot, he judged that almost half of the beer had been steamed away. Two men lifted it carefully away from the fire, waited for it to cool.

Udd had learnt some very elementary man-management over the months, enough for him to give the honor of first taste to someone else, and to someone who would value it. He passed over Cwicca and Osmod, the gang's natural leaders, called forward one of the recent rescues, a big silent man whom the freed but still class-conscious English suspected of having been a thane of King Burgred before the Vikings captured and enslaved him.

"Ceolwulf," he called out. "I expect you've been used to good stuff. Come and try this."

The former thane stepped forward, took the wooden mug held out to him, sniffed the liquid, drank deeply, rolling it round his mouth before swallowing.

"What does it taste like?" asked Karli anxiously. "Is it as good as the last barrel?"

Ceolwulf paused to give weight to his words. "What it tastes like," he said, "is water that's been used for washing old musty grain. Or maybe it's very very thin old porridge."

Cwicca seized the mug from him, drank deep in his turn, lowered the mug with an expression of complete disbelief. "You're wrong there, Ceolwulf," he said. "What this tastes like is gnat's piss."

As the other men dipped their mugs into the pot to confirm the judgment, Udd stared open-mouthed at the brew, the fire, the condensing steam on the membrane that covered the glassless window.

"The strength was there," he muttered. "It's not there now. It must have gone off in the steam. But it doesn't go off when you freeze drink. The ice and the steam are different. The ice is water. So the steam must be—something else." Experimentally he put out a finger, ran it along the steam-wet membrane, licked it.

"So don't keep the brew that's left," he concluded. "Keep the steam. But how to collect it?" He looked consideringly at the copper pot.

*   *   *

Weary and anxious, Shef decided to spend an afternoon in the
steam-bath. It was a small wooden hut built out on the end of a pier,
with a platform beside it overhanging the deep water of the fjord that
led down to the Hrafnsey harbor. Every day men lifted hot stones out
of the pit where they had been heating overnight and trundled them
along to the hut, where they lay glowing for hour after hour. It was a
common thing for those who had nothing to do, or who were weary
from some task or other, to stroll along and sit in the heat for an hour
or so, dropping water on to the stones, and from time to time going out
on to the platform for a plunge into the freezing water.

When Shef stepped in to the dark hut, he realized there was
someone already there, sitting on one of the benches. Peering into the
gloom, he saw from the light of the opened door that it was Cuthred,
sitting not naked, like every other man who went there, but in a pair of
ragged woolen drawers. Shef hesitated, went in. He did not know of
anyone else who would willingly sit in the dark with Cuthred, but
something told him he had nothing to fear. Cuthred did not forget,
even in his berserkergang, who had released him from the mill. He had
said, also, once he found out how Shef had recognized him, and that
Shef had been there at the start of the whole story, the capture of
Ragnar, that he knew their fates were twisted.

After they had sat together in the dark for a while, Shef realized that
Cuthred had started to talk, very quietly, and almost to himself. He
was talking, it appeared, about Brand.

"Big fellow, he is," Cuthred muttered. "But there's nothing special
about size. I've known some almost as big, and one or two who were
taller. That Scotty I killed, he was seven feet tall, I measured him.
Brittle-boned, though. No, it's not the size that gets me about that son
of a bitch, he's just not normal. His bones are wrong. Look at his
hands, they're twice the size of mine. And his eyes. Over his eyes."

A hand reached out, rubbed firmly across Shef's eyebrows, the
voice muttered on. "See. Normal people, they have nothing under
their eyebrows, just a socket. I haven't felt his eyebrows, can't get close
enough, but I've looked carefully. He has a bone ridge there, makes his
eyebrows stick out.

"And his teeth, now." Again the hand, peeling Shef's lower lip
down. "See, most people, nearly everyone, the top set of teeth goes
over the lower set. When you bite with your front teeth, it's like
scissors, the one sliding over the other. Now his teeth aren't like that.
I've watched for a long time, and I reckon his teeth fit edge to edge,
they don't slide over each other at all. When he bites, it's like an axe

on a block. And his back teeth, they must be real grinders. Something very strange about him. And not just him, quite a lot of them round here. His cousins have it too. But he's the worst.

"And there's another thing. He's hiding something round here. You know, lord—" for the first time Cuthred acknowledged that he knew who he was talking to. "You know that these days I spend a lot of time rowing round by myself."

Shef nodded in the darkness. Cuthred had indeed taken to rowing round in a little two-man dory he had borrowed, or commandeered. There was a general feeling of relief that he was out of the way for as long as he was.

"Well, I went right round the island first time, and then I went down the coast a bit to the south, and then I went up to the north, not very far, because I started late in the day. But when I got back from that one they were waiting for me at the dock. Brand, and about four of his cousins, all with spears and axes and their armor on, as if they were ready for trouble.

"Now, that got me mad right off. But I'm not as mad as they think I am. I reckon they'd have liked me to be, that day. But I got out of the boat, and got right up close to Brand where I could get my hands on him if anything started—he knew what I was doing.

" 'Now listen,' he said, talking very carefully. 'I mean you no harm, but I want to give you a warning. Go round in your boat. That's all right. Go anywhere you like—round the island, out to the seal-skerries, anywhere to the south. Not north.'

" 'I've just been north,' I said. 'No harm in that that I could see.'

" 'You can't have gone very far,' he said. 'You just went up to Naestifjorth, that's what they call the next big fjord north of here. That's all right. Most of the time. The next one is Midfjorth. You don't want to go in there.'

" 'And the one after that?' I asked him, pushing him a bit.

"Well, he shut his jaw like a wolf-trap. In the end he just said, 'You don't want to know about that at all. Stay away from it.' "

"That's strange," said Shef. "After all they go north often enough, all of them, to meet the Finns and collect the Finn-tax. They say no-one really lives north of here, not Norsemen anyway, just the Finns. But they seem to know their way north all right."

"But when the ships go north," Cuthred answered, "they go *outside* the line of the skerries. I've been asking round, as much as I can, and Martha, she asks the women-folk for me. North of here, on the real coast, inside the skerries—that's no-go country. I wonder why.

They're hiding something. When I walked off, after they'd warned me, I heard one of Brand's cousins say something to him, trying to calm him down. 'Let him go,' he said, 'he's no loss.' So he really was trying to warn me, of something they think really is dangerous. But they don't want it talked about just the same."

Cuthred's low voice slowly drifted off to a list of other insults and spites that had been put upon him, while he toiled at the mill. Men and women who had mocked him, the bitter cold of the mountain winter, the way he had tried to block the shutter with dirt, the way the shutter kept opening again, faces that had appeared at the window, the way they had rattled the door trying to reach him in the night . . .

Relaxing in the heat, Shef's mind slowly lost its incessant turning over of the problems of Bruno and Alfred and Sigurth and Olaf, of the dead Harald and Ragnhild, yes, and Godive too. His head sank back into the corner, against the pine-scented wooden walls, he dropped into an uneasy sleep.

He was still in the dark, but a different dark—not the warm, comfortably-scented, mildly companionable one he had left, but a place cold and still and smelling of earth and mold. Yet it was not an enclosed place. It was a road, and there was a mount beneath him, carrying him along at an unearthly pace, with a strong swarming movement, as if it had more legs than a horse should.

The horse was Sleipnir, Shef realized, the eight-legged steed of the father of the gods. But he, the rider whom Shef was accompanying in his dream, was not All-father. He could feel what sort of a person it was, and it was not a god, but a man. A madman, like Cuthred, but without Cuthred's reasons. The main emotion he felt—he felt it all the time—was a furious glee at meeting and overcoming obstacles. His memories were a blur of slashing and slicing and trampling, broken only by the oblivion of drink. Of Othin's mead. The rider of Sleipnir, something told Shef, was Hermoth. It was a name he had met before. The name the champions had shouted in celebration and praise at the end of the long day's fighting at Valhalla. The champion for the day, before the host of Othin, the Einheriar, returned to the hall, their death-wounds magically healed, for an evening of carouse before the next day's contests. Hermoth had won more often than any other hero, more often than Sigurth Fafnisbani, more often than Böthvar Bjarki. So they had chosen him for this exploit, the most vital Othin had ever dispatched a hero on.

To bring back Balder from the dead. The Shef-mind that observed all this knew a little of the dead god, Balder, had heard a story from Thorvin.

Now it came to him not as a story but as a series of flashes of sight. Balder, Othin's son, most beautiful of all the gods. Though he was a male god, he was too beautiful to be called handsome. Shef could see no picture of him, just a blur through Hermoth's mind of brilliant light, that seemed to blaze from the flesh of the god.

So beautiful was Balder that the gods, fearing ever to lose him, had made all created things take an oath not to harm him. Iron had sworn, and fire, and disease, and terrible old age, and the giant-brood even, unable to resist his beauty, and every fish and snake and animal in the world, and every tree in the wood. One thing had not sworn: the little, weak, sappy mistletoe plant that climbs up the oak-tree. It could do no harm if it wanted to—or so the gods reasoned.

And once the oath had been taken, Balder was invulnerable, and so the gods, amusing themselves in much the same way as their earthly followers, made sport out of setting up Balder the beautiful as a target and throwing at him every kind of edged and pointed weapon that came to hand. One god could not join in—Hoth, Balder's brother, who was blind. But one day a voice came to him in his blindness and said, would he not like to join in. Yes, he replied, but I am blind. And the voice said, I will set you in the right place and direct your arm. Throw this. And the voice put in his hand a spear made of the mistletoe plant, but hardened with magic arts.

The voice was Loki's, the trickster of the gods, enemy of gods and men, father of the monster-brood. Hoth took the spear and threw.

Hermoth's ears were still ringing with the great cry of lamentation that went up when the gods, and then all other created things, realized that Balder was dead, realized because of the way the light went instantly out of the universe, so that all things became mundane and dreary and dull, as they have stayed forever since. In his mind's eye he could still see the great pyre on which Othin had laid his son, in the funeral ship that would take him down to the Hel-world. Saw how even the giants had been bidden to the funeral and had come. Saw the giant-woman Hyrrokkin push the boat out, weeping—Hermoth had been one of the four champions chosen to hold her wolf-steed with viper-reins. Saw, just as the boat was pushed out along the slipway, Othin bend and whisper something in the ear of his dead son.

What had that word been? He did not know. It was his task, now, to ride to Hel and fetch Balder back.

The horse was out from its constricting walls now, clattering out on to a great bridge that sprang through the air—what air this could be in the world below, Hermoth did not know. He was passing ghosts now, shades that looked anxiously at him, aware of the clatter of the hooves, unlike their own silent passage. They were insignificant ghosts, pale men and women, children, not ghosts chosen for Valhalla or the groves of Frey. And at the bottom of the bridge there, there were gates.

As Sleipnir tore towards them they swung slowly shut. Hermoth stooped, whispered encouragement in the ear of his steed.

A clenching of muscles, a leap so high it seemed they would strike the lower surface of Hel itself. The gates were behind them, the baffled guardians gaping in their track.

This time it was a wall, a wall that ran up, or so it seemed, to the sky that was not there. Yet there was a crack, a tiny crack, at the top. Too small for Sleipnir, too small for Hermoth. Hermoth did not need to be told that this was magic. He drew rein, cantered up, stopped, dismounted. Beat with his massive knuckles on the stone wall, beat till his knuckles were bloody, ignoring the pain, as he always did.

A voice from the other side. "Who is that, that does not beat like a pale ghost from Hel?"

"Hermoth I am, Othin's boy, Othin's errand-rider. I come to speak to Balder."

Another voice, and this one Balder's, slow and dragging and weary, as if the mouth were filled with mold. "Go home, Hermoth, and tell them: I may not leave unless the whole world weeps for me. And I know. Just as there was one thing that would harm me, so there is one thing that will not weep. Tell them." And the voice trailed away as if being dragged down some long and dusty corridor.

Hermoth did not hesitate or falter, for such was not his nature. He knew certainty when he heard it. And he had no fear of returning with such a discouraging message. He mounted and turned again to ride back. Thought for a moment. Reached inside his tunic, where he had stowed a black cock from Asgarth, one of Othin's own breed.

He whipped the knife from his belt, slashed the head from the cockerel, threw first the head, and then the body, with the accuracy of the great ones through the crack between wall and sky.

A moment later he heard a sound through the stone wall, a sound so strong it seemed to make the wall reverberate. A cock crowing. Crowing for dawn, for new life, for resurrection.

Wondering, Hermoth turned to ride back through Helgate and over the Giallar-bridge that divides the Hel-world from the other eight. He did not know what this meant, but he did not think it would be a surprise to Othin.

What was it that Othin had whispered to his dead son on the pyre?

Shef's head jerked upright, conscious that something was going on outside. His body ran with sweat, he had slept too long. For an instant he thought the shouting must mean that at long last, Ragnhild had come. As she had done once before when he slept in the steam-room. Then his ears caught the sound of exultation, delight, not dismay. They were shouting something. What was it? "The wind, the wind?"

Cuthred was at the door, gripping the handle. The door had stuck, as they often did in the heat, and Shef's heart thumped for an instant—few worse fates than dying baked in the heat of a steam-bath, but it had been known to happen. Then the door snapped open, and the light and cold air streamed in.

Cuthred took two paces out and leapt over the railing into the water below. Shef followed him, gasping as the bitter-cold water closed over his head. After his experience on the ice Shef had thought he would never willingly enter cold water again, but steam-baths changed your mind. The two men swam together to the ladder that led out to the platform where they had hung their clothes, climbed out, gaping at the horde of running men who seemed to have appeared from nowhere.

They were running down to the boats, all of them. Not the sea-going boats, the *Walrus* and *Seamew*, but the dories, the rowboats. Hauling out boats Shef had never seen. And there were other boats, pulling into the harbor like demons, with the men of the fjords shouting. All shouting the same word. This time Shef caught it. Not the wind. "The grind! The grind!"

Shef and Cuthred stared at each other. Down below, at the harbor, Brand saw them slowly rubbing themselves dry. He made a trumpet of his hands, bellowed up to them.

"We are leaving your men behind. No room in the boats for idiots when the grind comes! You two follow if you want to see something."

Then he was off, in a boat, balancing on the thwart with a great lance in his hand.

Cuthred pointed to the little two-oar boat he had commandeered, tied up ten feet away on the shore. Shef nodded, looked round for his narwhal-hilted sword, remembered that as usual he had left it by his bunk. No time to go for it now, he had the eating-knife strapped to his belt. Cuthred stowed sword and spiked shield as ever in the bottom boards, grabbed the oars, began to pull out into the long fjord that led to the open sea. As they rowed out Shef saw the English catapulteers standing by the machines that now guarded entrance to the harbor. They were shouting "What? What is it?"

Shef could only shrug helplessly as Cuthred rowed on.

CHAPTER TWENTY-ONE

As Cuthred rowed the two-oared boat down the fjord, Shef saw a young man bounding down the rocky slope from one of the outlying farmsteads, waving desperately to be picked up. Shef signed to Cuthred to pull over.

"Maybe he can tell us what's going on."

The young man stepped out from one sharp-pointed rock to another, gauged the rise and fall of the boat on the waves, and dropped into the prow like a seal sliding on to a rock. He was smiling broadly.

"Thanks, mates," he said. "The grind comes every five years maybe. I don't want to miss it this time."

"What is the grind?" said Shef, waving down Cuthred's furious scowl.

"The grind?" The young man sounded as if he was unable to believe his ears. "The grind? Why—it's when the whales come, in a flock, a school. Come inside the skerries. Then, if we can get outside them, we drive them inshore, beach them. Kill them. Blubber. Oil. Whale-meat for the whole winter." His teeth showed in an ecstatic grin.

"Kill a school of whales?" Shef repeated. "How many will there be?"

"Maybe fifty, maybe sixty."

"Kill sixty whales," snarled Cuthred. "If you could do it, you lying Norse walrus-get, you could never eat them if you sat and ate till Doomsday."

"They're only the pilot whales," said the young man, sounding hurt. "Not the sperm whales or the big baleen whales. They're only ten, twelve ells long."

Fifteen to eighteen feet, thought Shef. Maybe it could be true.

"What do you kill them with?" he asked.

The young man grinned again. "Long lances," he said. "Or else this." He pulled a knife from his belt, long, broad, single-edged. Instead of a plain point it had a long sharpened hook, sharpened, Shef could see, on both its outside and inside edges.

"A grind-knife," the young man said. In his thick accent, the "f" became a "v", the long "i" an "oi." "*Grindar-knoivur.* Jump out of the boat in shallow water, straddle the whale, feel for its backbone, stab in to the side of it. Pull back. Cut the spine. Ha! Ha! Much meat, fat for the winter."

As the boat emerged from the mouth of the fjord, the young man looked round, saw the trail of dories all pulling rapidly away from them to the north, and without further words sat down on the thwart next to Cuthred, took an oar and began to row alongside him. Shef was surprised to see a sour grin on Cuthred's face, perhaps at the young Norseman's obvious assumption that Cuthred the mighty berserk needed assistance.

Ahead of them Shef saw the boats eventually ease to a halt, form a loose circle on the waves. And then, perhaps a half-mile beyond, Shef saw for the first time the school of whales they were pursuing: first a slow white spout against the gray sea, then another, then more of them all together. And beneath them, just a glimpse of black backs rolling easily in turn.

The men in the boats saw the rise as well, Shef could see them standing up, shaking their long-headed lances, and hear faint cries of excitement. Even from a distance, though, he could hear Brand's bull roar shouting them down, giving what sounded like a long string of explicit orders, boat by boat.

"You have to have a grind-captain," the young man explained between strokes. "If the boats do not work together, the whales will slip out. Everybody works together, and then we all share equally. One share for each man, one share for each boat, captain gets a double share."

Shef's boat came up with the main cluster just as they began to separate and move off. At the last moment the young man stood up, hailed a relative, and stepped from boat to boat with the same ease that he had joined them, pausing only to wave a cheerful farewell. Then all the Norse whaleboats, mostly four- or six-oared, moved off in a long unraveling string. Brand, positioned at the center of the line, turned to Shef as his boat moved off and shouted across the waves: "You two! Stay at the back, and don't do anything. Keep out of it!"

For a long time, Cuthred swung determinedly at the oars, maintaining station on the last boat in the long line. He seemed, Shef thought looking at his sweating frame, to have grown even stronger in the last few weeks, as solid food put a layer of fat over his tight-drawn mill-slave muscles. Yet it was hard work for one man to keep up even with the four-oared boats, all manned by skilled seamen. Cuthred stuck to it grimly. But in any case the whaleboats were not rowing at their maximum speed all the time. As the chase progressed, Shef realized there was a skill in it, a form of tactics.

Brand's first aim had been to get a line of boats outside the whale-pod, to the west, between them and the skerries that marked off the coastal channel from the open Atlantic. Once he had done that, he tried to move them inshore. Boats would swerve in close to the pod, and then stop, the crew leaning over and slapping the water with their oars. What this sounded like to whale-ears, who could tell? But the whales plainly did not like it, swerving away, trying to escape. Sometimes they tried to accelerate, to get round the far end of the line of boats. Then the lead dories would swing across, beat the water, force them to slow or turn back. Once it seemed as if the whale-leader had decided to turn round and swim back to the south, towards Shef and Cuthred bringing up the rear. For minutes the water was churned by black backs swarming close together, some swimming forward, some already turning back. Then all the boats moved in together, shouting and splashing, herding the whales towards the rocky shoals they feared.

Brand was relying also on panic, Shef realized as he got them moving again. And he had a particular place in mind. It was not enough to drive the whales on to the rock-bound coast. If it came to that they might turn and break through the line by sheer force. They had to be driven on to a killing-ground: a beach, for choice, but anyway an inlet or cove that they would be prepared to swim into but whose mouth could be firmly blocked. Best, too, if it could be done at high tide so that the ebb would leave the beasts stranded.

Slowly Brand jockeyed boats and whales till he had them where he wanted. The whales in a frothing mass just outside the entrance to the bay he had marked, the boats in a semi-circle from point to point of the bay. Then Brand waved his lance in one wide sweep and the boats moved in.

Brand himself made the first kill, his boat coming up alongside a slow-swimming cow-whale, while he leaned out, one foot on the gunwale, and drove home the long lance with its barbed head just forward of the low dorsal fin. From their position fifty yards behind Shef and Cuthred could see the instant flow of dark blood into the water—water whipped up instantly into a frenzy by lashing flukes.

The dying whale must have emitted some underwater bellow of agony, for the rest of the pod seemed to panic immediately, leaping forward away from the terror in their rear. Instantly they found themselves in the shallows, bellies grinding on gravel, tails rising out of the water as they fought for room. The other boats came in as one for the kill, a headsman in each prow looking for a place to plant his barb, the men shouting each other on.

As he watched Shef saw the first man leave his boat. It might have been the young man they had ferried, clutching his grind-knife, but he was followed by a dozen others, plunging recklessly into the turmoil of heaving bodies, seizing fins and trying to straddle their prey. Knives raised, plunged, plunged again as the men tried to find the vulnerable spot between vertebrae, where the hooked knife, hauled upwards, could sever the spinal cord and cause instant death. The whales twisted and thrashed, unable to fight back, unable to swim out, trying only to keep their tormentors from the kill.

"Looks risky," muttered Shef.

"But it isn't." Cuthred's voice had a note of disgust in it. "No more than killing sheep. Those things don't fight back, I don't think they have any teeth even. You could get squashed between two of them, but they're not even trying to hurt each other."

A group of men had hold of one whale and were running it up the beach as far as they could, seizing it by its fins and by the spears and blades protruding from it. They left it squirming weakly and ran down into the water for another. Already the whole surface of the bay had turned red from the streams of arterial blood pumping into it from the whales' punctured hearts. From the melee Shef saw a calf whale struggling free, having abandoned its dying mother. Barely six feet long, it floundered out of the shallows and made towards them for the open sea. A boat steered in front of it, a man leapt on to its back, grind-knife flailing. The spurt of blood that rose leapt into the boat, splashing his oar-mates. Shef heard them roar with laughter, saw another group on the shore already starting to flense the blubber from a dying whale, cramming handfuls into their mouths, and shouting with manic glee.

"I think we've seen enough of this," said Cuthred. "Nobody ever called me squeamish, but if I hurt people it's because I don't like them. I've got nothing against whales. I don't even like whalemeat."

He began to pull away from the cove of butchery, with Shef's silent agreement. The Norsemen, intent on their work, ignored them. By the time Brand thought to look up, they had gone.

Outside the cove, Shef was surprised to see how far the sun had gone down. At this time of year in a latitude as high as theirs, there could hardly be said to be a night-time. The sky remained pale continuously. Yet the sun did drop below the horizon for a short while every day. It was now close to it, the low red disc beneath the clouds sending long shadows across a placid sea. Cuthred bent to the oars and urged the boat along what would be a long trip back to a bed and fire. Shef became aware that it was hours since he had eaten or drunk; and he had begun the long boat-ride dehydrated from the steam-bath.

"Have you anything to eat in the boat?" he asked.

Cuthred grunted, "I always keep something in the cuddy there in the stern. Butter and cheese, a crock of milk, fresh water. Let me get us going and we can take turns to row and eat."

Shef found Cuthred's provision box in its compartment and hauled it out. It was well stocked, but for the moment Shef was content to drink water, chew on a wrinkled apple stored from the autumn before.

"You know," he remarked between bites. "This is the place Brand warned you away from. Inside the skerries, north of the island. I guess none of them come here much, from what he said. But with the grind out they wouldn't take any notice of where they were. And if there was anything dangerous it probably wouldn't want to mess with the grind boats. Not all of them together, all worked up."

"But it might just fancy two men on their own with the sun dropping," concluded Cuthred. His teeth showed in a snarl. "Well, just let it try."

Shef threw his apple-core overboard, squinted into the long shadows, reached forward and put a hand on Cuthred's brawny arm. He pointed silently.

Perhaps a quarter of a mile away, a giant fin showed above the water. It seemed almost man high, stuck straight up at right angles to the water. A black back showed beneath it, and then more of them, fins coming up out of the water, backs swirling and then dipping down like the top of enormous wheels.

"Killers," said Cuthred positively. They had seen several schools of them on the journey north in the *Walrus*, and each time Brand had gone to the side and regarded them speculatively. "Never heard of them attacking a ship," he had said. "Never heard of them attacking a boat either. But then, you wouldn't. If one of them decided to attack a boat there wouldn't be anyone left to tell about it. Seals are their meat. People must look pretty much like seals to them. I never go in the water if there's any of them about."

The lead fin suddenly changed course, angling sharply towards them. Without hesitation Cuthred swung the boat and headed for the rocky shore a hundred yards off. There was no chance of landing on it, it ran straight down into the water, but any kind of shoal or rock projection would keep the great beast off. It had certainly seen them, or sensed them. The fin was coming straight at them, a white wave cresting in front of it as it tore through the water.

The orcas had sensed the blood spilled in massive quantities into the water. They might have been following the pod of pilot whales themselves, intending to close in and make a kill. Could such a creature feel frustration at being forestalled? Resentment at the snatching of so many potential prey all at once? Anger against the land-apes, for so easily and ruthlessly destroying the whale-kind? It might just have been excitement from the blood, and a sportive urge to even the score against men moving so confidently out of their native element. The bull orca raced down on the small boat with menace in his very line. Shef felt instantly that he meant to toss the boat in the air, catch the men as they came down, and chop them to bits in the water with snaps of his great cone-toothed mouth.

"Head in," he called to Cuthred. "Right against the rock."

The boat glided along a sheer rock face, the two men reaching out for handholds to pull it closer in, uncomfortably aware of the deep water still only feet away. The fin lowered, rose up again till its tip was higher than Shef's head, sitting on the thwarts, and the whale surged alongside, almost rasping the boat's seaward gunwale. Shef saw the white markings under the black top, heard the sharp exhalation from the blowhole, saw its cold and careful eye on him. The tail slapped the water, the whale sounded, turning for another pass.

Shef seized an oar, thrust it against the rock, drove the boat a few yards along. Only feet away was the dark opening of a cove, a rocky inlet too small to call a fjord. Inside that the whale would be cramped, might turn away. The rest of the school were here now, sweeping past less closely than the bull-leader, filling the air with the spray from their blowholes.

Cuthred pushed too hard and the boat swerved away from shore. The bull was there instantly, boring in head first. Shef swung an oar, jerked the boat's bow back towards the inlet shore. As one man they thumped the oars into the rowlocks, heaved furiously, two strokes, three, rocketing into the quiet water of the inlet.

Something beneath them, lifting them irresistibly, the boat almost
out of the water, starting to tip. If he fell in the water, Shef knew, the
next thing he would feel would be great jaws about his middle. He
hurled himself sideways, kicking with all his strength, and landed with
one leg in the water and the other foot on a tiny rock ledge. A thrust, a
heave and he was scrambling on to a tiny flat place, a hearthrug-sized
patch of shingle on the rocky shore.

The boat turned over completely as the whale shook its body.
Cuthred was launched out like a diver, turned in the air, a shower of
objects coming down with him as the boat spilled its contents. His
spiked shield, the one made of case-hardened steel, landed a foot from
Shef's hand. He watched numbly as Cuthred splashed into the water
and the whale turned.

Cuthred trod water for an instant, then seemed to find footing
under him. He stepped backwards towards the land, only six feet from
where Shef crouched, still thigh deep. Somehow, his sword was in his
hand, he leveled it at the great black-and-white jaws boring in. The
whale swerved and as it did so Cuthred thrust forward in a classic
"long point," arm and body rigid.

A thump of contact, a sudden flurry, a slap of water from the tail.
Then the whale was gone, leaving a thin trail of blood in the sea, and
shattered planks where the boat had been.

Cuthred slowly straightened, wiping his sword on his wet sleeve.
The provision box floated a few feet from him. He stepped forward
again, up to his middle, and without haste gathered it in, turned and
waded over to the ledge where Shef still crouched motionless.

"How do we get off here, then?" he asked. "I don't fancy
swimming."

They crouched for a few minutes on the steep rock, looking across the
little inlet. The whales were still there, cruising in and out. Once one
of them rose to the stern of the boat, floating half-intact ten yards out
from shore, took it without haste in its jaws, crunched down.

The two men turned awkwardly to look behind them at the rocky
shore. The best that could be said was that it was not completely
vertical, rather a stiff slope, steeper than the roof of a house, but made
of a jumble of stone. There were handholds and footholds in plenty for
a scramble. But the mountain-side seemed to go on and on, up to the
pale sky with never a break. It could take hours to reach the top, hours
with never a place to rest. Yet there was no choice. Slowly and
carefully, aware of the deadly water a few feet away, the men gathered
their meager possessions together. Cuthred had his sword and spiked

targe. Impossible to carry them while scrambling up the mountain. After a moment Shef took the sword, cut a length from one leather shoelace, tied sword and shield together and showed Cuthred how to sling both on his back. The rope handles on the provision box could be extended, retied so as to make carrying straps. Shef fixed that on to his own back, made certain his short eating-knife was still in its sheath, the fire-flint he always carried next to it. He carried nothing else except the gold bracelets on his arms, was unarmed save for the belt-knife.

They began, carefully and slowly, to make their way up the mountain-side. For what seemed an age they crept from rock to rock, on all fours all the way, trying to angle round vertical precipices, never quite coming on the impassable, never finding a place to stop, to sit or even stand in safety. Shef's thigh muscles began to ache, then to jump spasmodically. At any moment, he felt, the cramp might strike. Then he would lose his grip and fall, or roll, all the way to the water. Looking down, he saw nothing but unforgiving stone all the way down to the metal-gray sea, still patrolled by the orca fins. He forced himself to thrust himself up another few feet. Brace a foot, push again, haul with all the failing strength of his arms.

A voice was talking to him. Cuthred's, just a few feet above. "Lord," it said. "Three more steps, two more steps. A place here to rest."

As if in reaction to what Cuthred said, Shef felt the searing pain of cramp in his right thigh. He knew he had to override it, but there was no strength left. He felt the leg give way, tightened his fingers despairingly on their last hold.

Fingers seized his hair, yanked mercilessly with terrible strength. Shef felt himself lifted off his feet like a puppy, hauled up and over a ledge. He lay belly down, gasping. Cuthred seized him by his breeches and hauled him the last few feet, rolled him over and began to knead his thigh.

After a score of deep indrawn breaths, Shef felt the pain ease. He knuckled involuntary tears from his eyes and sat up.

They were on what seemed for all the world like a narrow path, no more than a foot and a half wide, but luxury after the mountain-side. It ran along the side of the inlet, visible either way for only a few yards. Just on the seaward side of the place where they sat, it seemed to fork, one part continuing to run along horizontally, the other turning uphill.

Cuthred pointed to the second fork. "I reckon that might go up to the highest point of the ness," he said. "Good lookout point. I'll go along there, see what there is. Maybe we can find some wood, light a beacon. The whalers are bound to come back past here sometime."

Not for a while, Shef thought. And even then they may decide to keep outside the line of the skerries, as they do when they're not hot on the trail of the grind. But Cuthred had already slipped away, sword and shield now ready in his hands. What made this path anyway, Shef reflected. Goats? What else could live up here but mountain goats? Strange that they had worn such a clear track.

Suddenly aware again of his own hunger and thirst, he unslung the provision box, pulled out the milk crock, took a long slow draught of it. As he set it down again, he felt depression and despair settle round his shoulders like a heavy blanket.

The view in front of him was unutterably bleak: gray sea far below, tossing restlessly on gray stone. Above it, just rock and jumbled scree rising all the way to a ridge far above the level where Shef sat. And above that, another higher ridge, and another, rising up to the snow that never melted. White snow and gray stone merged into a sky from which every hint of color had been washed. No hint of green grass, no hint of blue sky, only the everlasting paleness of the high latitudes. Shef felt as if he were at the end of the world, and about to fall off it. The sweat of toil and pain was drying on him, turning him cold and clammy in the little bitter wind that whispered along the mountain-side.

If he died here, who would know? The gulls and the carnivorous skuas would eat his flesh, and then his bones would bleach for ever in the wind. Brand would wonder what had happened for a while. He might never bother to pass word to the south, to Godive and Alfred. They would forget him in a few seasons. His whole life seemed to Shef, in those moments, to be a remorseless pursuit from one disaster to another. The death of Ragnar and the beating he had got from his stepfather. The rescue of Godive, and his blinding. The battles he had fought, and the price he had paid for them. Then the stranding on the sandbank, the march to Hedeby, the way Hrorik had sold him to the Way in Kaupang, the disaster on the ice, his betrayal by Ragnhild, and the killing of little Harald. It all seemed of a piece: momentary success, bought by pain and loss. And now here, stranded beyond hope of rescue, in a place where no human foot had trod since the beginning of time. Maybe it would be better to let go now, fall down the hillside, and vanish from sight for ever.

Shef slumped back, shoulders against the stone, the provision box still open by his side. He felt the sight coming on him, taking over his mind and body in his exhausted, waking swoon.

*   *   *

I told you before, something told him. Remember the wolves in the sky and the serpents in the sea. That is what the pagans see when they look at the world. Now see another picture.

Shef found himself in the body of another man, like himself, exhausted, in pain, close to despair and even closer to death. The man was stumbling along a rocky slope, not as steep as the one Shef had just climbed. But the man was in worse shape. There was something heavy on his shoulder, grinding into it, but he could not put it down or move it to the other. It was rubbing grimly into his back too, and the back was afire—Shef's own back twinged with remembered sympathy, from the pain of a fresh flogging, the sort that tore open the skin and slashed deep into the flesh and bone beneath.

Yet in some way the man welcomed the pain and the exhaustion. Why? He knew, Shef felt, that the more exhausted he became, the shorter his sufferings would soon become.

They were there. Wherever there was. The man dropped the burden he had been carrying, a great wooden beam. Others took it, men in a strange kind of armor, not mail but metal strips. They fitted it to a still larger beam. Why, Shef realized, this is a cross. I am seeing the crucifixion. Of the White Christ? Why would my patron-god show that to me? We are not Christians. We are their enemies.

They had stretched him out and were driving home the nails, one through each wrist, not the palms where flesh would tear through as soon as full weight came on them, but between the bones of the forearm. Another through the feet, a tricky job to line them both up. Mercifully, by this stage the pain was not coming through to the Shef-mind observing. Instead, it looked hard at the men doing the grim task.

They were working quickly as if they had done this many times before, talking to each other in a language Shef did not understand. Yet as the moments went by he found he could catch a word or two: hamar, they said, nagal. But for "cross" they said, not rood as he expected, but something that sounded like crouchem. Roman soldiers, so Shef had always been told, but talking some kind of German dialect, with a garbled kitchen-Latin thrown in.

The man on the cross fainted as they hauled him up. Then his eyes opened again, and he was looking out, as Shef was doing now, as Shef had done years before after his blinding. Then he had seen the vision of Edmund, the martyred Christian king, coming to him with his backbone in his hand, and then passing on—elsewhere. So there was a place for Christians to go, as well as the Valhalla of the pagans.

The sun was already beginning to sink over Calvary. For a few brief *seconds, Shef saw it as the dying man, or man-god, saw it. Not the chariot drawn by terrified horses and pursued by ravening wolves of pagan belief, just as the earth and sea below were not the haunt of giant serpents seeking only to destroy mankind. Instead the man looking up saw, not chariot nor disk of gold, but a glowing bearded face looking down, full of both sternness and compassion. It looked down on a world of creatures that threw up their arms to him and begged for help, for forgiveness, for mercy.*

Eloi, eloi, cried the dying man, lama sabachthani. *My God, my God, why hast thou forsaken me.*

The glowing face shook in denial. Not a forsaking, a cure. A bitter potion for the sins of the world, an answer to the beseeching arms. And now a final mercy.

A man stepped forward from the ranks drawn up at the foot of the cross, red cloak above his armor, red hackle cresting his iron helmet. Inoh, *he said in the same half-German gabble that his soldiers had used.* Giba me thin lancea. *"Enough, give me your lance."*

The dying man found a sponge at his lips, sucked at it feverishly, tasting the thin sour wine that the soldiers had as a daily ration to mix into their water. As the blessed relief flowed down his parched throat, tasting better than anything he had drunk in the world before, the centurion below freed the lance from the sponge he had held up, dropped it two feet, poised it carefully, and then thrust home under the ribs to split the convict's heart.

Blood and water ran over his hand, and he gazed at the mixture with surprise. At the same moment he felt the world shift around him, as if something had forever altered. He looked up, and instead of the grim burning sun of this parched and desert land, he saw what seemed to be his own dead father's face smiling down at him. Around him a thrill of exultation seemed to rise from the sand, and beneath his feet a cry of relief came from the rocks, from under the rocks, from Hell itself where the prisoners saw their promised salvation.

The centurion swayed, caught himself, looked down again at the ordinary issue lance dripping blood and water down his hand and arm.

Now that is what the Christians see, said the voice of his guardian to Shef. They see a rescue from outside where the pagans see only a fight they cannot win and dare not lose. All well and good—if there is a rescuer.

The vision faded, left Shef sitting on the barren rock. He blinked, thinking about what he had seen. The trouble is, he saw in a moment of contrast, that the Christians put their trust in rescue, and so do not struggle for themselves, just put their faith in their Church. The pagans struggle for victory, but they have no hope. So they bury girls alive and roll men under their longships, for they feel there is no good in the world. The Way must be between these two. Something that offers hope, which the pagans do not have: even Othin could not bring back his son Balder from the dead. Something that depends on your own efforts, which the Christian Church rejects: to them salvation is a gift, a grace, not something mere humanity can earn.

He sat up, bothered by a sudden feeling of being watched, looked round for Cuthred, realized he had still not returned. He groped once more for the open provision box, hoping food and drink would put better heart into him. More milk, thick cheese and biscuit.

Seemingly sprung from out of the stone, a figure appeared before him. Shef found his mouth hanging open in mid-bite.

CHAPTER TWENTY-TWO

It took Shef a moment to realize that the figure was a little boy, a young child. Yet he was hardly little. He stood about five feet high, no shorter than Udd the metalworker, and a good deal broader. He could have been a small man. Yet something in the earnest innocence of his stance suggested youth.

And he did not look like any man at all. His arms hung low, his head slanted forward on an impossibly thick neck. Small eyes peered out under heavy eyebrows. He was dressed in—nothing. No, he had on a rough kilt made of some kind of skin. But it almost vanished against his own pelt. The child was covered from head to foot in long gray hair.

His eyes were fixed unmoving on the piece of cheese Shef was in the act of lifting to his mouth. His nostrils flared suddenly as he smelt it, and thin drool began to run from the side of his mouth. Slowly Shef took the cheese from the biscuit he had laid it on and passed it wordlessly to the strange boy.

Who hesitated, not wanting to come closer. Finally he came forward two paces, in a kind of awkward shamble, stretched out a long gray arm, and snatched the cheese from Shef's hand. He sniffed it, the nostrils flaring again, and then took it into his mouth with one sudden snap. He chewed, eyes closing in a kind of rapture, thin lips pulled back over what seemed to be massive canine teeth. His feet shuffled in an incongruous, involuntary dance of glee.

Finns can't turn down cheese or milk or butter, so Brand had said.

He did not think this creature was a Finn. But maybe it felt the same way about food. Still moving gently, Shef handed over the crock with the remains of Cuthred's milk in it. Again the careful exploration with the nostrils, the sudden decision and the instant draft. As he—or it—drank, it bent its knees oddly so as to tilt its body back. It could not throw its head back to drink like a proper person, Shef realized.

Finished, it dropped the crock. The noise as it shattered on the stone seemed to startle it, it looked down, looked across at Shef. Then, there was no doubt, it said something, and the something had all the tone of "I'm sorry." But Shef could understand not a syllable of what it said.

And then it was gone, whisking away down the path for a couple of paces, and then just gone, vanished, gray pelt merging with the gray stone. Shef scrambled to his feet and ran stiffly to the point where it had disappeared, but there was nothing to be seen. It had vanished like his own dream.

One of the Huldu-folk, Shef thought. You have seen one of the Hidden People, the people who live in the mountain. He remembered Brand's tales of the things that pulled people underwater, the long gray arms stretching out to seize boats. And the tales Cwicca and his gang told, of men caught in the mountains by female trolls and forced to serve them. They had been telling one only the other night: of a great wizard, a wise man, who had made it his task to free some island in the Northlands from the trolls and the Hidden People. He had gone all over the island, saying the words of power and driving the creatures out so they could harm men and women no more. In the end he had had himself lowered down the last cliff on the island to finish the job. But as they let out the rope from above, a voice had come from the cliff itself. "Manling," it had said, "you must leave some place for even the hidden folk to be." And with that a gray arm had come from the cliff and plucked the man from his hold and hurled him on to the rocks below. It didn't make sense, Shef had told them. Who could have heard the words but the man on the rope, the man hurled to his death a moment later? Suddenly the story seemed to make much better sense.

Cuthred was still nowhere to be seen. Shef opened his mouth to shout, closed it. Who could tell what might hear? He picked up a stone flake from the ground, scratched an arrow on the lichen-covered stone, pointing in the direction he was taking, inland. He left the provision box lying and began to sidle along the rocky narrow path as fast as he could.

It twisted on along the side of the inlet, but far above it, for perhaps half a mile, often narrowing to a bare foothold, never quite vanishing entirely. One of Brand's bird's-nesters would have followed it without hesitation. Karli the flatlander would have frozen with terror. Shef, a flatlander too, hobbled on carefully, sweating with fear and exertion, trying not to look down.

And then there was a clearing in front of him. In the dim half-light Shef looked round cautiously. A clearing? At least a flat place with a thin poor covering of grass and weeds in the everlasting stone. Why had they not seen the green from the sea? Because the whole place was hidden, in a dip in the ground between sea and mountain. On the other side of it, a chink of light. A fire? A cabin?

Stepping very cautiously forward, Shef realized it was indeed a cabin. Stone walled, turf roofed, set against the further hillside as if it had grown there. Even at fifty yards Shef could hardly be sure he was seeing it, though a dim glow came from some chink or other in its wall.

As he thought that, Shef realized that his left hand was actually resting on another wall, right by him. He had walked up to another building and still not seen it. Yet a building it was, and a big one, a lean-to of stone slabs running forty feet from the point where the path came out to what might be a door at the other end. He could smell something too. Smoke, and a faint flavor of food.

Hand on knife, and moving as gently as a fowler creeping up on a nest, Shef ghosted up to the door. Not a door, a leather curtain pegged across. He slipped the thongs off the pegs and eased inside.

For twenty heartbeats he was unable to see. Then his eye adjusted. Dim light was coming in from cracks in the wall, and from an opening in the roof, under which a low fire glowed. A carcass hung over it. It was a smokehouse, Shef saw. All along the far side stood rack after rack of split, smoked and dried fish. All along the near side, tubs of more fish, salted, fish and meat. In front of him, hanging from a peg, a seal carcass, with more in rows down the length of the building. He stretched a hand up to feel. The peg was of stone, the hook that supported the split seal of wood, not carved but bent and allowed to grow into the correct shape. Nothing he could see was of metal. Only wood, and stone.

The carcasses grew bigger as he walked fascinated down the row. Seal. A walrus, so large it stretched from roof to floor. And then a bear. Not the brown bear of the forests in the south, common in Norway, still to be found in the deep woods of England. No, a creature as much bigger than that as an orca was bigger than a porpoise, far bigger than

Shef as it hung there flitched and jointed. White fur still showed on it here and there. It was a great white bear like the one that had furnished Brand's best robe, an animal that had cost three lives to bring down, or so Brand said.

He was almost at the smoke now, where the fire glowed and the light came in from the roof. What was this creature that the mighty hunter of the mountains had brought down? Not a seal, not a walrus, not a porpoise nor a bear. Shef realized that there, turning gently in the smoke, hanging from a peg, was a man. Halved, stripped, gutted and chined, like a pig, but still certainly a man. Others too, racked behind him, men and women as well, hanging like so many flitches of bacon, some by the throat, some by the feet. The women's breasts drooped on their naked flanks.

Shef saw that there were other things piled carelessly in a corner. Clothes, mostly, thrown there in disorder. Glint of metal here and there, silver and enamel work and iron too. Whatever had caught and killed these people cared nothing for booty. It had all been tossed aside like horns or hooves or anything inedible. Was there a weapon there?

Two pegs on the wall supported between them a dozen long-shafted spears. Shef picked one up, realized immediately it was worm-eaten and bent from lying for years in the heat. He rummaged through them as silently as he could.

Junk, all of them. Split shafts, bent heads, metal thick with rust. He had to find something. He had only his tiny beltknife against a creature that could kill walruses and polar bears.

There. There was one. At the bottom of the pile Shef glimpsed a shaft that seemed to be sound. He picked it up, hefted it, felt relief sweep over him at the thought he was now not completely defenseless.

Somehow, as he hefted it, the idea of using it to strike and kill repelled him. It was as if a voice was telling him: "No. This is not the tool for such a purpose. It would be like trying to pick hot metal from the forge with a hammer, or beating out iron with the haft of your tongs."

Puzzled, Shef looked for a moment at what he held, his eye continually glancing in fear towards the entrance. A strange weapon. Not the sort anyone made nowadays. A leaf-shaped blade unlike the massive triangular head of Sigurth's 'Gungnir,' a long iron spike below it set into an ash shaft. Traces of ornamentation on it. Someone had even cut into the iron and then set gold into the tracery. Once there had been two gold crosses at the base of the blade. The gold was gone now, betrayed only by a fleck of color, but the chiseled crosses remained. A war weapon, from the iron spike, and a javelin from its weight. But who would put gold on a javelin which you hurled at your enemy?

Someone had valued it, at any rate. Some one of the carcasses now hanging in the smoke. Shef hefted the weapon uncertainly once more. It was madness not to take any weapon that would give him a chance of survival in this deadly place. Why had he already put it back, laying it gently once more across its pegs?

Alarmed suddenly by some faint stir of air behind him, Shef span round. Someone, or something, coming. He crouched, looking along the floor beneath the rows of human and animal bodies.

Someone was walking towards him. With a flush of relief Shef recognized the cross-tied breeches of Cuthred. He stepped out into plain sight, beckoned his companion over, pointed wordlessly to the hanging corpses.

Cuthred nodded. His sword was bare in one hand, his shield ready in the other.

"I told you," he whispered hoarsely. "Trolls. In the mountains. Peered at me through the windows of the hut. Rattled the door in the night to try to get in. They smelt meat. Thick bars they have on the doors in those mountain villages. Not that all of them need them."

"What do we do?"

"Get them before they get us. The cabin opposite, you saw it? Let's go. Have you no weapon?"

Shef shook his head mutely.

Cuthred stepped behind him, picked the spear he had just laid down from its pegs, held it out to him. "Here," he said, "take this. Go on," he urged, seeing Shef's reluctance, "it doesn't belong to anyone any more."

Shef stretched out a hand, hesitated, gripped the weapon firmly. In the warm, smoky dark there came a faint ringing sound, as if the metal head had struck stone. Shef felt a kind of relief again. Not relief from defenselessness, rather relief that the weapon had been handed to him. It had passed from its owner to the master of the smokehouse, and then to Cuthred, the man who was not a man. It was right for him to hold it now. Maybe not to keep it, maybe not to strike with it. But hold it, yes. For now.

The two men made their way out into the suddenly sweet-smelling air.

They moved across the small open space like two ghosts, treading carefully round the weeds to prevent the faintest brush or rattle. One mistake here, Shef thought, and they too would be hanging in the smoke. Had the little boy run ahead to warn his people? His father? He had seemed grateful rather than fearful or hostile. Shef did not want to have to kill him.

The door of the cabin, like that of the smokehouse, was covered with a pegged leather curtain, seemingly of horsehide. Should they try to lift it gently, or slash it down and charge through? Cuthred had no doubts. He waved Shef silently to hold the top of the curtain, then took his sword and applied its razor-sharp edge to each of the retaining loops in turn. The curtain hung loose, held only by Shef's hand. Cuthred nodded.

As Shef dropped the curtain, Cuthred whisked inside, sword poised. Then stood motionless. Shef moved in after him. The cabin was empty of life, but not bare. To their left stood what must be the main room, a rough table in the center with stools round it made of driftwood. The stools were of immense size. Shef would have had to climb up to sit on one. In the far corner a black entrance seemed to lead into the rock. The whole scene was lit by a wick burning in a stone bowl of oil.

Perhaps the inhabitants were all asleep. It was midnight, certainly, even though the sky remained light. But Shef had noted that in midsummer the Norse-folk lost most sense of time, sleeping when they needed to, and sleeping very little, as if they saved that up for the appalling winters. The Huldu-folk could be the same.

To their right, though, that must be the sleeping-chamber, reached through another narrow opening. Shef braced himself for what might have to be a killing thrust, and slid through the doorway, javelin poised. Two beds, yes, like shelves in the rock, to conserve warmth, heaped with skins and furs. Shef moved closer to check that the furs were all animal furs, not the gray pelt of a troll. No, nothing there.

As he turned to sign to Cuthred a great crash sent his heart into his mouth. He sprang forward to see what had happened. In the middle of the other room, by the overturned table, Cuthred was grappling savagely with a troll.

A female troll. She too wore a kind of kilt round her waist, but breasts swelled beneath her gray pelt, long hair hung down her back like a horse's mane. She had hidden inside the larder in the rock, leapt out as Cuthred closed on it. With one hand she grasped the spike on his round targe, with the other the wrist of his sword-hand. The two swayed backwards and forwards, Cuthred trying to free a weapon, she trying to wrest them away. Her teeth flashed in a sudden snap at Cuthred's face.

Shef gaped, amazed for a moment at the woman's strength. Cuthred was putting out every ounce of effort that he had, grunting furiously as he heaved at her, the immense muscles straining in his arms. Twice he had her off the ground, lifting her two hundred pounds easily, but she clung on.

Then suddenly she was moving forward, Cuthred pushed back, and as she gained momentum she thrust a heel behind his ankle and tripped him. The two went over together, the troll on top, and Cuthred's sword and shield went sprawling. An instant later and she had whipped a stone knife from her belt, was driving it at Cuthred's throat. Cuthred caught her wrist with one hand, and again they were frozen in a desperate test of strength.

The javelin was a hindrance in the narrow doorway. As Shef stepped sideways to try to angle through the door of the sleeping chamber, the dim light from outside was blocked. The master of the house, the hunter of the mountains, had returned. He stepped soundlessly through the outer door like a moving slab of rock, turned towards the struggle.

Even stooping, his skull brushed the ceiling. His arms hung almost to the floor. His shoulders were round and sloping, not square like a man's, but even so the space between his shoulder-blades was wide enough to fit a sword-blade lengthwise. His back was turned to Shef, whom he had not noticed, his attention fixed on Cuthred and the female.

Shef poised the spear. He had one chance for a completely unprotected strike, at spine or kidneys or angling up under the ribs for the heart. Not even a giant could survive that. In front of him, he knew, was the man-eater.

As he poised for the strike, a sense filled Shef suddenly of the utter dreariness of the place. He had felt it before, sitting on the ledge of the mountain path, a sense of colorlessness, harshness, hostility. Then in the passing vision he had seen and felt the world begging for a rescue, for a release, and the sun-face granting it; granting what had not been granted to Hermoth, or to Balder. The iron lance-shaft by his cheek seemed to exude both warmth, and a kind of weariness, an urge to desist from slaughter. The world had seen too much of it. Time for a pause, a change.

The female troll squatting on Cuthred's chest suddenly shot head-first across the room and crashed into the legs of the male, sending him staggering backwards almost on to Shef's spear-point. Cuthred had forced her back so that all her strength was pushing forwards, then dropped his hands, seized her ankles and hurled her clean over his head. He twisted and came to his feet, sword once again in hand, confronting the male troll with a grin of reckless fury. A snarl like a bear's came from the male troll as he thrust the female out of the way.

Shef slammed his spear-butt on to the stone floor and shouted at the top of his voice, "Stop!"

Both trolls jumped round to face him, eyes swiveling between the threat in front and the threat to their rear. Shef shouted again, this time to Cuthred gliding forward, "Stop!"

At the same moment the small male troll he had seen on the path ran through the outer door, clutched the large male round the legs and pattered out a long stream of syllables. Shef stepped through the narrow doorway of the sleeping-chamber, spread his arms wide and carefully propped his spear in a corner. He waved imperiously at Cuthred, who hesitated, doubtfully lowered his sword.

What of the trolls? Shef looked at them in the light of the lamp, looked again, looked a third time at the great male, standing staring down at him with a puzzled expression. A familiar puzzled expression. Gray pelt, round skull, strange undershot jaw and massive teeth. But something—something in the eyebrows, the cheekbones, the square set of head on pillared neck. Gently, Shef walked forward, took the male's enormous hand, turned it over in his own. Yes. Huge fingers, a fist that if doubled would be the size of a quart-pot.

"You look like someone I know," said Shef, almost to himself.

To his surprise the troll grinned broadly, showing huge canines, and replied in halting but recognizable Norse.

"I think you meet my good cousin Brand."

According to Echegorgun—much of the substance of what he had to say was passed on in the end to Shef by Cuthred over many days and many campfires—the Hidden People had once lived much further to the south, in Norway and in other countries below what Echegorgun called the Shallow Sea, the Baltic. But as time went by and the climate changed they had followed the ice north, harried all the way and all the time by the Chinned Ones, the Thin People, the Beaters of Iron—Echegorgun had many names for them. Humans were not, of course, formidable—Echegorgun laughed at the very thought that they might be, making a strange harsh noise deep in his throat. But there were a lot of them. They breed as fast as the seals, he said, or as fast as the salmon spawn. And in groups they were dangerous, more so as they acquired metal. It seemed that the memories of the Hidden People went back to the days before humans had metal, when all the Walking Creatures, humans and Hidden Ones, had only stone. But once the humans had metal, first bronze—Echegorgun called it the brown iron—and then true iron, gray iron itself, the old equality between the species, if species they were, began to break down. Echegorgun would not admit or concede it, but Shef thought sometimes that the fast-breeding which Echegorgun so much despised and thought less than fully sapient, had something to do with the metal. Beating iron out of ore does not come naturally, is the result of learning based on trial and error based on initial lucky accident. Short-lived creatures with little to lose and strong reasons for wanting to distinguish themselves among their too-many competitors, they would be much more likely to waste time on mere experimentation than the longer-lived, slow-maturing, slow-breeding True Folk (as they called themselves).

Whether that were true or not, over the centuries the True Folk had become the Hidden People, keeping to the inaccessible mountains, developing the skills of hiding themselves away. It was not so difficult, Echegorgun said. There were more True Folk around than most of the Thin Ones realized. They did not inhabit the same ranges, or even the same times. The Norse in Halogaland, Echegorgun said, being specific, were almost entirely coastal. They went up and down the sea road, the North Way from which the country got its name, they built their huts in the fjords, they pastured their animals in the bits of summer grazing they could reach. Rarely did one find any of them more than a few miles inland. Especially as those who did penetrate inland, exploring or hunting, were not at all likely to return.

The Finns were more of a nuisance, for they roamed widely with their reindeer herds, their sledges and bows and traps. Yet their roaming was mostly in the summer and in the day. In the winter they kept to their tents and their cabins and their regular trap rounds, all easy to avoid. The snow and the ice, the dark and the high places, Echegorgun said, they belong to us. We are the People of the Dark.

And what about the dead men you hang in your smokehouse, Shef asked him on the afternoon of their first meeting. Echegorgun took the question seriously. It was the seal-skerries that caused the trouble, he said. The Thin Ones had to be kept off them, or at least off those of them he regarded as his own. Shef slowly realized that Echegorgun, like the rest of his people, was as near amphibious as a polar bear, which are often found swimming contentedly well out of sight of land. His pelt kept the cold out, and was as waterproof as a seal's. Any of the adults would think little of swimming a couple of miles in the freezing water to a skerry, there to club seals or harpoon walruses. Sea-mammals were a great part of their diet. They did not like the Thin Ones to go there, and discouraged them by ambush. The stories about gray arms turning boats over were true. As for smoking and eating their prey—Echegorgun shrugged. He could see no harm in eating your kill. The Thin Ones might not eat the Hidden People, but they would kill them for any reason or for none, not because the Hidden People ate their food. So which was worse?

In any case, there was no real need for ambushes and killings, if everyone kept to their side of known lines. Trouble might arise in times of famine. If the grain crop failed—Echegorgun thought it was bound to fail three years in ten—then the Thin Ones started to come out and hunt the skerries in desperation. Don't eat grain, that was the answer, don't breed so fast you have to rely on chancy foods. But real northerners, the real northerners among the humans, Echegorgun said, emphasizing this distinction, they did not let things get so far. They knew their place, and they knew his. The humans he killed, they were always visitors who did not respect the slowly-evolved boundaries.

"Like the man who left this?" said Shef, holding up the spear he had taken.

Echegorgun took it, felt it, snuffed at the metal in a considering way with his great flaring nostrils. "Yes," he said. "I remember him. A jarl of the Tronds, from Trondhjem. Foolish people. Always want to take over the Finn-tax and the Finn-trade, take it from Brand and his family. He came up here in a longship. I followed it till they camped on an island, he and two others went to hunt birds' eggs. After he had gone—he and some more—the rest lost heart and went home.''

"How did you know he was a jarl?" asked Shef.

"The Huldu-folk know a lot. They are told some things. They see many more, in the dark, in the quiet."

Echegorgun would say no more at that point, but Shef was confident that he and Brand's family had ways of getting in touch with each other—sign left on a skerry maybe, rocks left a certain way till there was need of communication, and then altered to bring out an envoy. The Hidden Folk might have been an advantage to the Halogalanders, in getting rid of unwanted rivals from the south. Brand and his family in return kept pressure off certain fixed areas.

And besides, there was family feeling. Echegorgun smiled salaciously when Shef hinted at it. Years before, he said, the father of Brand's father Barn, a man named Bjarni, had been stranded on a skerry by a shipwreck. He had had food with him, good food, milk and whey, and had set it out as bait for the Hidden People. A girl of that race had seen it, taken the bait. He had not caught her, no, how could a Thin One catch even a girl of the True Folk? But he had shown her what he had got for her, and she had been enticed. You Thin Ones are thick in one place, Echegorgun said, his eyes rolling to Cuthred sitting close to the female he had wrestled.

Echegorgun went on to say that the girl, his own aunt, had kept the baby men called Barn till it was evident that it would be smooth-skinned, or too smooth-skinned to live like the True Folk. Then she had left it by its father's door. But first Bjarni, and then Barn, and then Brand, had remained conscious of their kinship at need.

Shef heard little of what was said then, for he had begun to worry about Cuthred. Thin Ones might be thick in one place, but Cuthred had no place at all. He had been behaving well up in the north, yet one thing Shef was sure of: any reminder of his mutilation, any sexual display by a male or provocation by a female, and Cuthred would revert to the berserker. And yet it was strange. He was sitting talking to the female Miltastaray, daughter of Echegorgun and sister of the little boy Ekwetargun, as if she were Martha or one of the least-challenging of the slave-women. Perhaps it was because he had overpowered her. Perhaps it was because she was female, but so different that there was no need or expectation of flirtatiousness between them. Either way, Cuthred seemed secure and safe, for the moment.

Shef turned his attention back to Echegorgun's story. By this time the five creatures—men and a woman? people? humans and not-humans?—had left the hut and were sitting out under a risen sun in the flat patch between hut and smokehouse. From where they were they could see a calm gray metallic sea, with islands rising from it, but were sheltered from closer observation. The Hidden Folk had a keen sense of "dead ground," Shef was to note. They kept always out of direct lines of sight, whatever else they seemed to be doing.

"So you see much, and are told more?" he said. "What do you know about me? About us?"

"About him," Echegorgun pointed with his underslung chin to Cuthred, "much. He was a thrall in the mountains south of here. Some of our people tried to get him out. Maybe they would have eaten him, maybe not. You people are hard on your own kind. I know what they did to him. It would not mean so much to us. We think of other things than mating.

"About you." Shef found deep brown eyes fixed on him. "There is no news of you. But people are following you."

Shef laughed. "That is no news to me."

"Other things are following you too. The killer whales that attacked you—sometimes they do that, I know, if they feel like sport or if something annoys them. But I have seen that school of them going up and down, and they are not from near here. They have come up from the south, like you. Maybe after you.

"Still, if you know people are following you, I need not tell you the rest."

Echegorgun stretched his enormous arms, over nine feet from finger-tip to finger-tip, with an air of complete indifference.

"What rest? Are other people following me now?"

"There is a ship hidden in the Vitazgjafi fjord half a day's swim south of Brand's farmsteads on Hrafnsey. I would have warned him but he is away with the grind—the grind, you understand, is within his rights. He was careful not to drive them ashore here or near here. But anyway, he is away, and the ship is down there waiting. A big ship. It has two . . . two sticks. Those things you put cloths on. A big fair-haired woman shouts orders at the menfolk." Echegorgun laughed. "She needs a winter with me to calm her."

Shef considered furiously. The woman was Ragnhild, the ship the one that had tried to sink them in the Gula-fjord. "What do you think they mean to do?"

Echegorgun looked at the sun. "If they did not attack last sunset, they will attack this one. The two ships Brand has will not be ready to fight. He will have taken them up to the grind-beach and loaded them up with oil and meat. The strangers will catch everyone else asleep or tired. The grind makes much work."

"Will you not warn them?"

Echegorgun looked surprised, as far as his flat hair-covered face would show it. "I would warn my cousin Brand. For the rest—the more Thin Ones kill each other, the better. I know you spared me when you could have struck me with the spear, so now I spare you, for True Folk keep their bargains, even if they have not been said. You fed my boy, my Ekwetargun as well. But I would be wiser to twist your head off your shoulders and hang you with the others."

Shef ignored the threat. "I can tell you one thing you do not know," he said. "I am a man who has authority. I am a king in my own land. Some say I am a sort of a king even here. And I speak for many people. Here is one sign of my authority." He showed the Rig-token, the *kraki*, round his neck, and pointed to the one he had made for Cuthred. "It may be I could do something for you. For you and your kind. Make the men stop hunting you. Let you live in a place less stony. But you would have to do something for me. Help me defeat those men from the south, and the woman with them, and their ship."

"Well, I could do that," said Echegorgun carefully. He rose to a strange squatting position, gripping his bare feet in his enormous hands.

"How? Would you warn Brand? Would you—fight on our side? You would be a mighty warrior if we gave you iron to use."

Echegorgun shook his massive head. "I will do neither of those. But I could speak to the whales for you. They are worked up already. If they thought I had killed you, they might feel like listening to me. And these are stranger whales, of course. If they were my own folk I would not deceive them."

CHAPTER TWENTY-THREE

Bruno, *Hauptritter* of the *Lanzenorden*, stood in front of a double rank of his armored knights, pikes sloped, standing immobile at attention as he had made their custom. All were looking at the ceremony taking place a hundred yards in front of them. They could have got a better view by marching closer, but one could not be sure how the natives would take interference in their sacred custom. Bruno had no objection to interfering with the barbaric customs of the natives, but this was not the time.

A roar came from the thousand throats of the men clustered at the center of the doom-ring of the Gautish peoples, a roar and a clashing of weapons on shields.

"What's that mean?" muttered a voice from the rear rank. "They've made a decision?"

"Silence in the ranks," said Bruno, though without heat. The *Lanzenorden* believed strongly in the theoretical equality of all its members, without the savage discipline that had to be imposed on armies of peasants. "Yes, look, they have a king. *Habeunt regem*," he added, parodying the formula for the election of a Pope.

A figure rose, swaying wildly, from the throng in front of them. A man lifted on a shield by a dozen eager supporters. Once he caught his balance, he looked round, drew his sword, shouted out his name and the traditional formula of proclamation. "I am the king of the Gauts. Who denies it?"

A moment's silence, then the clashing of weapons again. A week

before, and a dozen chieftains would have denied it. Fighting it out
hand to hand would have deprived the Gautish peoples of most of
their ruling class, the rich and the god-born together. So for days the
meeting, the *Gautalagathing*, the Thing of those bound by the Law of
the Gauts, had been abuzz with messengers, rumors, offers of support
and retractions, deals and promises. Now it was all settled. Till the
next shift of power.

The crowd began to disperse towards the smell of roasted oxen and
the great vats of beer which the new king would provide as part of the
price of his election. The German *Ritters* watched them with a certain
envy, a certain scorn. Bruno decided to hold them in their ranks a
little longer, to make certain no-one went down to the party, got into a
fight.

Another figure was coming towards them, the scrawny black-clad
Englishman, Erkenbert. As he came closer Bruno saw a slight flush of
excitement on his pale face, and felt his own heart thud in anticipation. The Englishman was holding one of his everlasting lists.

"Do you think you've found it?" said Bruno as soon as the other
was in earshot.

"Yes. Down at the tents I found an old man. Too old to attend the
election, but not so old that he had lost his memory. He was at the raid
on Hamburg. More than that, he was among the men who sacked the
cathedral. He remembers closely who was there—especially closely,
for he feels still that he was cheated of some share of the loot. He gave
me a complete list of the chieftains present, seven of them who led
more than a dozen ships' crews, he says. Now, and this is the
important thing. Six of those chieftains we have news of already, and
we know they do not fit."

"So it must be the seventh?"

"So it would seem. His name is Bolli. He is jarl of the Tronds."

"And who in Hell are the Tronds? I've been in this God-forsaken
country half a year, I've heard of more tribelets and kinglets than my
father has pigs in sties, and I never heard of the Tronds."

"They live far in the north," said Erkenbert. "Far up the North
Way, where they seek to control the fur-trade."

"Far in the north they may be," muttered Bruno, "but if there were
a new king there, an emperor-in-being, we would still have heard
about it. I begin to wonder if our method is wrong. Or could even the
holy Rimbert have made some mistake? Perhaps there is no Holy
Lance."

"Or perhaps it is lying in a treasury, unnoticed."

Bruno's face took on an expression quite unfamiliar to Erkenbert, one of depression and defeat. "I can't help thinking," he said, "you tell me the Lance is in Norway. We hear also that the great struggle for power in the North is going to take place where we left in the spring, at Hedeby in Denmark, everyone is full of it. And here we are, running round provincial gatherings in Sweden."

"Gautland," corrected Erkenbert.

"Same place. I have gone in the wrong direction."

Erkenbert reached up and patted the disconsolate knight on his enormous shoulder. "Whom God loves, he chastises," he said. "Think of King David in the wilderness. Think of Samson at the mill, and how in the end he brought down the great temple of the Philistines. God can bring forth a miracle at any time. Did He not deliver Joseph from Potiphar, and Daniel from the lions' den? I will tell you the holy text you must remember: *Qui perseravabit usque ad finem, ille salvabitur.* He who shall persevere to the end, he shall be saved. To the end, though. Not to near the end."

Bruno's face slowly cleared. He wrung Erkenbert's hand in a careful grip. "Thank you," he said. "Thank you. Wise words. We shall find out more about these Tronds. And meanwhile, I shall hope that God has some errand for me in sending me to these parts."

Hrorik, King in Hedeby, gnawed his beard as he listened to the reports of his scouts.

"Definitely the Ragnarssons?" he queried.

"Definitely. We got close enough to see the Raven Banner."

"Flown only when all the bastards are together. Well, at least there's one bastard fewer of them now. And him the worst bastard of them all. A hundred and twenty ships, you say, and harbored on the mainland opposite Sylt?" Hrorik calculated thoughtfully. "Well, the Ragnarssons are always bad news, but that could be worse. They have to get through the marsh first, and then they have to get over our good wooden walls. I know all about their rams and the tricks they learned from their father. I think we ought to be able to see them off."

One of the scouts cleared his throat. "More bad news, lord, I'm afraid. Catapults. We saw them unloading them. Big jobs, weighing a ton, I would say. Three or four of them."

Hrorik's face regained its concerned expression. "Catapults! What sort were they? Were they the stone-throwers we've heard about, or the dart-throwers, or what?"

"We don't know. Never seen one work. We've just heard these stories, same as you. They all come from men who've been defeated by them."

"Thor help us. This is where we need some men who know about these things."

Hrorik's port-warden, sitting in on the conference, broke in. "I can help you there, lord. I got a report from a skipper yesterday. He was up at the Gula Thing. He said there had been a lot of excitement up there—I'll tell you another time. But at the end of it he said that one of our ships had recruited two Englishmen and was bringing them south. Englishmen," he added with emphasis. "Those are the real experts. These are guys who were there when Ivar got his, and the Frankish king too. Ship should be in in a couple of days."

"So. While Sigurth Snake-arse crawls through the marsh, we can have these men building machines to fight his machines. That's good. But let's do the obvious things too. If the Ragnarssons are there on the west coast, the east coast's clear. So let's get ships out to King Arnodd, and King Gamli, and ask them to send every ship and man they can spare. Clean out the Ragnarssons, and we'll all sleep easier."

"Clean out the Ragnarssons," said the port-warden, "and maybe it'll be time to have just one king in Denmark."

"Just don't say that anywhere else," agreed Hrorik.

Many days' sail to the north, far from the gathering war-storms that would determine the fate of many kingdoms, Shef and Cuthred crouched immobile in the shadow of a rock. Twice they had got into what they thought was good cover. Both times Echegorgun had moved them out, muttering in his own strange language. "You Thin Ones," he said finally. "You don't know how to hide. Or how to look. I could walk through one of your towns in broad daylight and you would never see me." Shef did not believe him, but he had to acknowledge the uncanny skill of the Hidden People in vanishing, in the day, at night, or in the pale twilight that had come again after another long day of sleep and waiting.

In front of them, Echegorgun stood knee deep in the water at the edge of the inlet. He had led them down to it by barely manageable paths, the men slipping and scrambling on the rock, propped up by Echegorgun or Miltastaray, sometimes lowered from one place to the next. Finally, once they were concealed to his satisfaction, Echegorgun had told them to sit motionless, and watch. Watch what a True Person could do. They would see something no Hairless One had seen for many a lifetime. How the True Folk called their kinfolk, the whales.

Now Echegorgun stood facing out to the open sea. High above, Miltastaray kept watch for any boats that might appear, ferrying men or meat between the place of the grind and Brand's threatened home on Hrafnsey.

In one hand Echegorgun held a long paddle, its blade curiously rounded, cut laboriously with stone tools from the trunk of a mountain-aspen. Strange curlicues ran around its inside face. Echegorgun held it up, high above his head, the grotesque length of his arm suddenly clear. Then he brought it down with all his strength on the calm water. The sound of the slap seemed to run from horizon to horizon, as the ripples ran out into the Atlantic swell. Again Echegorgun brought it down. And again. The two men crouched, wondering how far the sound would run above water. And how far below it.

After a dozen blows, Echegorgun turned and put the paddle carefully on a rock on the steep shore. He took another implement, a long tapering tube, made out of layers of coiled and glued birch-bark, and took another cautious step further out, waist-deep now, standing on some unseen projection. He put the thinner end of the tube in his mouth, the trumpet end deep in the water.

From where they crouched, and even in the dim light, Shef could see the prodigious back widening as Echegorgun took a deep breath, a deep breath like the indraft of a bellows. Then he blew.

No sound reached the men on the shore, but after a few moments the air seemed to buzz, to vibrate noiselessly. Was the surface of the sea shivering in sympathy? Shef could not tell, though he strained his one eye to see. He had no doubt that beneath the water some immense disturbance was taking place.

The blowing went on and on, Echegorgun breathing in continually and somehow blasting out at the same time. Shef was not sure, but he felt dimly that the "notes" Echegorgun was playing altered now and then, according to some unknown code. He remained motionless, feeling the chill of the high latitudes creeping up on him, feeling his muscles stiffen, the cold stone strike through his breeches. He did not dare to move. Echegorgun had said that at any disturbance he would break off. "Just one pebble rolling," he had warned. "If the whale-folk were to think I was playing with them, even foreign whale-folk . . . I could never swim safely again."

Beside him Cuthred too sat like a rock image. But then, barely perceptibly even from two feet, his eyes moved, his chin rose a trifle, pointing. Between the shore and the skerries, a fin rose. The straight-up, right-angle fin of the killer-whale, the orca. It was coming towards them, not quickly, deliberately. From time to time the head too rose, and a spout went up, white against the gray islands. The orca was taking a good look. Behind it, well behind it, the rest of the school followed.

Slowly the fin came closer. As it closed, Echegorgun's breathing seemed to slacken, as if he were cutting down the underwater noise. He seemed to be blowing with a shorter, more varied rhythm. Finally the fin closed right up, the orca swimming along parallel with the shore, turning, cruising slowly back. Every time it turned it kept its eye on the strange gray creature standing waist-deep in the water. Shef felt his skin contracting at the thought of what might happen. A lunge of the jaws, a sweep of the tail, and Echegorgun would be off his feet and off the rock. Even his mighty frame would be no more than a bull-seal to the killer. Nothing was safe with them in the water, not the tusked walrus, nor the polar bear, not even the great whales which they tore to pieces while they were still alive.

Echegorgun put his tube carefully down on the rock behind him. Then, slowly, he sank down, submerging shoulders and head in the water, and began to swim out. The killer watched, giving him room. The men on shore could see little, only what showed above water. Yet it began to seem, after a while, as if Echegorgun was acting out some kind of pantomime. Sometimes he seemed to mimic a whale's motion, sometimes a man swimming. Once it seemed to Shef as if he kicked his heels above the water, and rolled over violently: a boat turned upside down? The killer's movements began to synchronize with his own, they swam up and down together, both moving at a fantastic speed for a human, a bare stroll for a whale.

And then the fin swung away, a great tail slapped the water twice, as if in farewell. The other fins cruising up and down offshore swung too, in unison. All together the school began to race down the sound at top speed, the whales arcing in and out of the water in a complex ballet, as if in exultation. They raced away to the south, towards Hrafnsey.

Echegorgun remained in the water till they were out of sight, cruising up and down with an easy overarm stroke, only skull and arms showing, with a faint flurry where his heels touched the surface. At a distance, just another seal. Finally he turned, swam into shore, heaved himself out, shook himself easily like a dog.

"Well," he said in Norse. "Come out now, Thin Ones. I told them the one who wounded their leader was dead. They asked, and the one they followed? Dead too, I said. They were disappointed. It was easy to tell them there were more whale-foes in the ship. The great ship going into Hrafnsey now. They said they would find sport with it."

"Going into Hrafnsey now?" said Shef. "How are we to get there?"

"There is a way," said Echegorgun. "No Thin One would find it, but I can show you. One thing I had better tell you, though. The whale-folk are not good at telling Thin Ones apart. Nor do they care much. Anyone on the water is at risk tonight."

"Show us how to get across," said Shef. "I swear to repay you for all this. Even if I have to become king of this land to do it."

The men of the two-masted ship moving under light sail towards Hrafnsey harbor had had a long voyage up the Norwegian coast in which to get used to their unfamiliar weapons and sail-rig. For the most part they were men of Agdir, Queen Ragnhild's homeland. In the turmoil following the sudden death of Halvdan and the seizure of power by Olaf, one of the skippers of King Halvdan's fleet had decided his best interests lay with Ragnhild, and had placed his ship at her service. Most of his crew had not stayed with him, but had deserted, their places taken by Ragnhild's own men. With them had come Valgrim the Wise, defeated in his plan to control the College of the Way, and eager to take revenge on the one who had thwarted him. Not only him—but also to set the Way and his misguided colleagues back on the true path of Othin, the path that would lead to victory, not defeat, at Ragnarök. He and his backers had built the catapults and trained their users. They were eager, too, to redeem their failure in the Gula Fjord.

Yet the driving force behind them all, skipper, crew and Valgrim as well, was the hatred of Queen Ragnhild for the man who had killed her son, or caused him to be killed. The man who had stolen the luck to which she had pledged her life. Ragnhild had seen her mother-in-law Queen Asa go to the gallows without blinking, had poisoned her husband King Halvdan without a tremor. One day, maybe, she would breed a new race of kings from her own loins. But before that the beggar-Englishman she had seduced, hidden, and thought to use to clear the path for her son: he must go to Hel to serve her son and her for all eternity.

As the great warship closed on Hrafnsey, its goal, its crew had ceased to follow the coastline and had moved offshore, into the Atlantic rollers but out of sight of land, coming in again only a few miles from where they reckoned their quarry to be. There they had lain upon a deserted inlet, one of the thousands on that jagged coast, seen by no-one. Or at least, no human.

Yet they had not lacked for close information. After the butchery was over at the grind, the real work had started for the men of

Halogaland. Vital to cut the carcasses up and salt as much meat as possible. Even more vital to rig the cauldrons on the beach itself, strip off the blubber, start the long job of rendering down the whale-oil, immensely valuable for lamps, for fuel and even for food through the long winter nights. Firing the cauldrons was not a problem. Once the oil had been cooked out of the blubber, the strips that were left became fuel for the next rendering. But every barrel the Halogaland coast possessed would hardly be enough for the sudden windfall of wealth that the grind brought. Boats were passing up and down in all directions, loading up barrels, towing strings of them, sending messages for urgent assistance. One whale-boat with two men in it passed by the fjord where Ragnhild's warship lay, to be snapped up immediately by its pinnace.

The Norsemen, mostly and with exceptions like Ivar the Boneless and his father Ragnar, were not torturers of each other, whatever they might do to slaves. Ragnhild had taken them on board and told them plainly that they had two choices: to be beheaded at once over the side of the ship, or to tell her the situation at Hrafnsey. The fishermen had decided to talk. Ragnhild knew the outline of the harbor, including its catapult defenses and its two longships. She knew, too, that half the men of the area were still boiling blubber at the grind-beach, and the rest were exhausted from hours of loading and unloading, making trip after trip between beach and harbor. What she did not know was that Shef and Cuthred were missing. Her prisoners had simply not noticed, preoccupied with other things.

What they had noticed and told her was that Brand, desperate for men, had taken the English catapulteers from their posts, and Guthmund's Swedes as well, and set them to work on the jetty, since they were all manifestly useless at anything to do with whales. Listening with half an ear to Cwicca and Osmod's protests, and their demands that something should be done to search for their master Shef, Brand had sent a sentry up to the harbor-point, with instructions to sound a horn for help if he saw any strange craft approaching. The sentry had sat down on the soft turf with his back against a stone and immediately fallen asleep.

Ragnhild's ship, the *Crane*, moved into Hrafnsey harbor a few moments before sunrise lit the pallid sky, meeting no challenge, its oversized crew of a hundred and twenty men ready for action. They nudged each other as they saw the bulks of the catapults against the sky, unmanned and untended.

Brand, down at the jetty supervising the unloading of another cargo of barrels from his own *Walrus*, saw nothing till the first catapult-stone whirred across the water.

It was aimed with deadly skill. The men of the *Crane* had had time to practice, and no shortage of good round rocks to practice with. Coming from a bare two hundred yards, the distance between jetty and harbor-point, it struck the *Walrus* full on the prow. The prow kicked back, the planks that fitted into it all sprang loose. If the ship had been running under sail she would have gone to the bottom like a stone. As it was, she merely sprang apart and settled gently on to the rock ten feet beneath her keel, mast still jutting upwards.

Brand stared, gaping, unable to realize what had happened. The second stone shattered the jetty a few feet from him, sending half a dozen men into the water. At the same moment, light flared on the dark decks of the *Crane*. The dart-shooter's crew, anxious to try their fire-arrows once more. As they sighted, Ragnhild stepped behind them.

"There," she snapped. "There. Aim for that big barrel. Surely you can hit that this time."

The crew trained their weapon round a trifle, sighted again, released the retaining toggle. The fire-dart shot across the water, its flight indicated by a line of fire. Slammed into the barrel of whale-oil just unloaded from the ruined *Walrus*. Instantly a tongue of flame shot into the sky, burning with a pure and brilliant light. The men on the shore stood out immediately as dark shadows, shrieking and running in confusion, some to put the fire out, some to fetch their weapons, the English catapulteers beginning the long run round the harbor and the point behind it to reach their abandoned weapons.

Ragnhild's skipper, observing, grinned with satisfaction. His name was Kormak, son of an Irishwoman, with long experience in the never-ending Irish wars. He knew when his enemy had lost the initiative.

"Close up to the jetty," he ordered. "You with the stone-thrower, sink that other big ship there, the Swedish one. Dart-thrower, set light to the barrels and then the houses. Boatswain, pick twenty men, furl sail, and take the ship back out a hundred yards under oars once the rest of us are ashore. I don't want anyone trying to take the *Crane* while we're busy. The rest of you, we'll land on the jetty and go straight through the village."

"And remember," shouted Ragnhild over him, "the one-eyed man. Six gold arm-rings for the one-eyed man."

Beside her, Valgrim hefted the 'Gungnir' spear he had taken from

Stein, and Stein from the shore where Shef had thrown it. A good weapon, he thought. To drink the blood of a heretic.

Not far away, but too far, Shef saw the flame suddenly light up the sky. He stood on the shore of the mainland a bare quarter of a mile from the edge of Hrafnsey island. But he had no boat. He would not have believed that they could even get so close so quickly. But Echegorgun, Miltastaray and Ekwetargun with him, had led them inland over paths not even a goat could find, and then over a surprisingly easy ridge-route to the coast close by where they stood. Though they had rowed for hours two days before, they must have walked only five miles, cutting across the base of a peninsula.

"How do we get across?" he asked.

"Swim?" suggested Echegorgun.

Shef hesitated. A quarter of a mile was not so far. But this water, he knew, was always bitter cold. And besides—he could not forget the threat of the whales.

Cuthred nudged him and pointed. Lit up now by the red glow in the sky, they could see the black dot of a whale-boat, with more behind it, pulling frantically down from the grind-beach. Men carrying a load down, or coming back for water.

"More Thin Ones," said Echegorgun. "We go now. Do not speak of us except to my cousin Brand. If you go on the water in a boat, you will speak to no-one again."

"Wait!" said Shef sharply. "Can you tell where the whales are?"

Echegorgun nodded. "Hear them in the water. I know already. They are outside the harbor, watch the strange ship. Unhappy. They want small boats to tip over, not big ship to ram. Don't go in boats."

"Can you tell us if they go into the harbor? If it's safe for a few minutes just to row across?"

Echegorgun sniffed doubtfully. "You hear a noise like a walrus sounding, you row across. Make it quick." An instant later he had vanished, his great bulk disappearing seemingly into a rock.

"Noise like a walrus sounding?" muttered Cuthred. "Might as well be an angel belching for all the good . . ."

Shef ignored him. He had stepped on to the highest point he could reach, waving the lance he had recovered in wide sweeps over his head. Moments later the leading whale-boat saw him, hesitated, pulled over.

"Stop the other boats," said Shef. "No, do as I say. I know the place is under attack. We have to go in together, not a few at a time."

Slowly the dories gathered, nine or ten of them, maybe forty or fifty men, fierce and skilled seamen, but unarmored and unarmed except for the long whale-lances some of them carried, their flensing-axes and grind-knives.

"You're going to have to listen very carefully to what I say," said Shef. "First, there is a school of killer whales out by the harbor, and we don't want to row into them. Second, we will know when they have gone into the harbor . . ."

As a buzz of incredulity greeted his words, he thumped his lance-butt on the rock and raised his voice commandingly over it.

Kormak was doing to the men of Hrafnsey much as they had done to the whales. Deliberately, he kept up the pressure to make them panic, though he knew their form of panic would be a headlong assault. As the *Crane* moved up to the jetty, stones whirred from her mule, each one smashing a house. Fire-arrows thumped into wood and oil, turning the whole settlement into a conflagration. Few were killed, few were hurt, the fighting strength of the defenders was hardly diminished. But they had no time to think. Besides, as Brand saw his beloved *Walrus* a wreck, saw his winter store and his warehouses going up in flames, his heart swelled till it seemed to burst his jerkin. No time to fetch his mail, no time to array the men. Between the flames he stood, his face working, clutching his axe 'Battle-troll' and waiting for the despoilers to set foot on land.

As the side of the *Crane* touched the jetty, the men Kormak had detailed off sprang ashore, forming an immediate armored front six wide. At the same time Kormak bent, said a quiet word to his boatswain. Two men slipped ashore, walking along the jetty's side struts, one each side. At the right place they heaved a rope across, made fast.

Kormak pushed forward to the center of the front rank, stepped on two more paces, arranged the men in the Viking wedge. Then they began to move forward, shouting in unison. Kormak waited for the furious charge he expected.

It came. Seeing the confident figure striding towards him, Brand, the doubts and fears that had afflicted him since the duel with Ivar entirely wiped out by fury and loss, ran forward, axe raised. Behind him, in a ragged wave, came the men of Hrafnsey with what weapons they could snatch up.

"A big fellow," remarked Kormak to his nearest shield-companions. He raised his shield to guard and shouted a taunt, unheard in the roar of flame.

As Brand charged forward, the boatswain, crouched in shadow, raised the rope. Brand's feet went from under him and he hurtled sprawling forward, full-length, his weight shaking the jetty. 'Battle-troll' skidded out of his hand. With a roar, Brand started to scramble to his feet, but at the same moment Kormak slammed him mercilessly, with every ounce of force he could summon, on the side of the head. Brand shook his head, continued to struggle upwards. Disbelievingly, Kormak swung his lead-shot loaded sandbag again. This time the giant went down on all fours.

The charging men behind him hesitated, some also brought down by the rope. Two ran on, were met by a concentrated volley of javelins, fell bristling. The rest wavered, then ran in ones and twos back into the blazing village.

"Tie him up," said Kormak briefly. He waved his troop forward, aiming to drive out the stragglers, establish a perimeter, and take control of boats, food and weapons. Hunting down the fugitives would be the job after that. He wished the one-eyed man had charged with Brand. It would have kept Ragnhild off his back.

The English catapulteers being employed as unskilled labor down at the jetty had run at the first stone. They had no weapons, and no impulse to fight in defense of the settlement. In the dark beyond the firelight, they rallied, gasping, round Cwicca.

"Shouldn't never have taken us away from the mule," said a voice in the darkness. "We knew they were coming, we told him, but no, he would have . . ."

"Shut up," said Cwicca. "Thing is, if we get up there now we can train round and shoot up that ship of theirs, no bother. That'll get them back aboard her in a hurry."

"No good," said Osmod. "Look."

He pointed to the *Crane*'s pinnace, loaded with armed men, now pulling across the harbor in the direction of the two untended catapults. Kormak had thought of that too.

Kormak had not thought of the whales. The orcas had been shadowing the *Crane* all the way in, eager to attack. Yet the bull leader had held off. He had an accurate sense of the *Crane*'s bulk, knew she was the biggest man-thing he had ever come across. Maybe if he rammed her head on, she would fill and sink. Maybe not. The scratch he had received from Cuthred irritated him, but at the same time gave him caution. The sport he wanted was to tip a boat like an ice-floe, to snap up the men inside like unwary seals. So he hesitated, and his school with him, cruising up and down at the harbor-mouth, half an eye on the *Crane* and the commotion, half an eye on the interesting but shore-sheltered whale-boats he had sensed lying under cover of the mainland a quarter of a mile away.

Then he heard the regular thumping oars of the pinnace, and hesitated no longer. Filled with the cruel urge, more than hunger, of the fox in the hen-roost, he swept down the harbor channel, with his school behind him.

"No good," said Osmod again. "Great holy suffering Christ." Driven back to childhood, he made instinctively the sign of the Cross to ward him from evil, over the hammer still slung round his neck. No-one corrected him. Staring at the pinnace, they saw all together the great fin that rose man-height behind the boat, the black-and-white body that reared beneath it.

Boat and men went over with hardly a cry. For an instant, bobbing heads. Then fin after fin cutting through the water as the killers went into their established ritual for striking at a great whale, a blue or a sperm or a finner, swinging in in turn, snapping with the great jaws and swinging out of the way of the next. But where a bite from a full-grown orca would merely wound a sixty-foot blue, it snapped a man in half. The flurry was over in seconds, the whales sounding again to hide their presence.

"I met one of those things out on the water," muttered Karli, his face white. "I told you it could have turned me over as easy as winking. The fin's as tall as I am. What are its teeth like?"

Cwicca roused the others from their paralysis. "Well, Thor help them, but look. The road's clear to the mules. Let's get up there."

Still gaping at the threatening fire-lit water, the catapulteers started to run round the harbor to their machines.

On board the *Crane*, all attention was concentrated on the charge and fall of Brand. No-one saw the pinnace go under except the two fishermen, still prisoner and lashed to the outer gunwale. They looked down at the water under them, trying to estimate its depth. Slowly, looking over their shoulders, they started with new determination to work their hands free.

On the mainland coast, Shef saw the flames leaping again. The men in the boats were grumbling, reluctant to believe in a threat from orcas, desperate to see what was happening at their homes. Behind him came a strange sound, a kind of long violent blowing snuffle, followed by a slap like a tail striking water.

"What was that?" he asked.

"Sounded like a walrus going down," said one of the men in the boats. "But it can't be, not . . ."

"All right," snapped Shef. He raised his lance high and called out to all the boats. "It's safe now, maybe just for a few moments. Row right across as fast as you can go, beach on the shore right opposite and get out. Don't go into the harbor. Do you hear, don't go into the harbor. Now row."

He sat down in the prow of the lead boat, Cuthred in the stern. The whale-men bent to their oars, sent the boat skimming over the calm sea. Shef twisted from side to side, fearing at any moment to see the fins racing again towards him. The boats reached the mid-point of their passage, raced on. As they closed on the island shore, outside the harbor entrance, maybe half a mile still from the main settlement and hidden from it by a hill, Shef felt the speed slacken.

"Why don't we just push on in?" called one of the oarsmen.

"Believe me," said Shef. "You wouldn't like it."

His boat grounded her prow on shingle, followed by most of the others. The men scrambled out, heaving their boats higher, snatching out their makeshift weapons. One boat ignored Shef's shouts, skimmed on towards the harbor entrance, disappeared from sight round the point. Shef shook his head in disgust.

"I still don't see why . . ." began another dissident. Cuthred, patience exhausted, clubbed him on the side of the head with a sword-pommel, seized him by the throat, dragged him again on to his feet.

"Do what he says and obey your orders," he snarled. "Got it?"

Shef waved the fifty men he had into a double extended line and led them off in a broad arrow formation. He kept them at a swift walk, curbing any impulse to run. They would need their breath if they had to fight armored men. His plan was to swing wide round the hill at the harbor mouth, and come out of its cover down the stream on which the main settlement stood, to drive the invaders back into the water. Maybe by then they would have dispersed to rape and loot. He hoped so. Surprise was his only chance now.

The catapulteers reached the first mule and paused for a moment. Man one, or man them both? Even with Karli added, they had less than two full teams.

"Just the first one for now," Cwicca decided briefly. "Get winding."

They had slacked the twisted ropes off before leaving. It was never good to keep them under torsion for too long. The winding levers were still stacked in their place, though, and the men sprang to it. At the same time Cwicca called Karli to assist him. One improvement they had made in the weeks of waiting. They had never before been able to train their machine round more than a few inches. On a ship, one had to aim the ship rather than the mule. However, by trial and error Udd had solved the problem. They had put the heavy machine on small iron-rimmed wheels of its own, not so that it could be drawn overland like the lighter dart-throwers, but so that those small wheels could rest on a larger one, placed flat on the ground and flanged to keep the smaller ones in place. Two strong men could tip the whole ton-and-a-quarter forward on its unmoving axle and train it round by a balancing trail.

Straining, Karli and Cwicca lifted the trail, walked the machine round from its first position covering the harbor entrance to bear on the *Crane* now slowly sweeping away from the jetty.

"Round half a pace more," grunted Cwicca. "Back a hand's breadth. Right. Tip her forward, hammer in two wedges, no, three."

They tipped the machine forward so it pointed, now, down at the water. The ropes were wound, the throwing bar straining at its retaining bolt. Cwicca fitted a thirty-pound rock into the sling, drooping from the bar, checked the very precise angle of the hook from which the sling's catch had, at the right moment, to fly free.

"Ready. Stand clear. Shoot."

The bolt was pulled back, the bar shot up with inconceivable force, the sling whirred round, adding its own vector to the force of the twisted ropes. The boulder shot across the water in a flat hard line.

And missed. The crew had wedged the machine down as far as it would go. But it was a hard business altering for range downwards. The rock skimmed narrowly over the decks of the *Crane* and splashed into the water in the center of the widening gap between ship and jetty. The plume it threw up hurled spray into Kormak's face, as he turned back from the won skirmish on the jetty.

"Thor aid me," he said. "What happened to the pinnace? They were supposed to secure that machine." Then he began to bark orders. A threat to his ship was the most serious thing, everything else trivial, winning the battle, securing prisoners, even appeasing Ragnhild.

As the queen realised Kormak meant to turn back from sacking the settlement, the settlement she was sure contained her son's bane, skulking somewhere away from the fighting, she flew at him with teeth and nails. He shook her off as she clung to his arm, shrieking her demands.

The important thing to do, he saw straight away, was to get the

Crane over on the other side of the harbor, where the catapults could not train down far enough to shoot. The ship needed more men, and in a hurry. There were still a dozen skiffs and dories lying round the jetty and the shingle by it. Quickly Kormak detached fifty men to hold the foot of the jetty, ordered the rest into the boats, jamming in as many as they could carry. At the last moment he stopped, ordered two men out of the nearest, replaced them with the still groggy Brand, hands lashed firmly behind his back.

"Let's get him safely stowed," he remarked, stepping into the same boat. He thrust a furious Ragnhild away from him again. "Lady, we'll come back for you. If the man you want is anywhere, he's on the shore. I suggest you go look for him yourself. Give way," he added to the oarsmen.

As a second stone thumped into the sea, aimed this time at the first boats creeping out, and missing once more, fifty men set out to cross the intervening hundred yards of water.

Shef brought his group hurdling over the stream and into the blazing village by the landward end of its one muddy street. As they moved down it, jogging now, men moved out of the flames and shadows to join him, adding themselves to the line, eager to support the first sign of concerted resistance. Shef felt the wolfish force of their anger sweeping him along. There was no way to halt them now. They were going to hurl themselves on the invaders whatever he said or did.

Yet the Halogalanders had no armor, and the only shield in the party was Cuthred's. The enemy were fully equipped, Shef could see them standing in a solid rank across the base of the jetty, unshaken and unafraid. In seconds he would have to lead the charge. What chance had he of surviving it? Standing in the center of the front rank, a target for every spear? This was the way of the world. Shef poised his lance. There was no way he could see of altering it. He tried to call up within himself the fighting urge he had felt when he killed Hrani the Viking on the sandbank. There was no response. The lance in his hand seemed to drink it, to send out an urge instead to delay. To pity, not to strike. The men on his right and left were looking sideways at him, expecting the word to charge. Something made Shef sweep the lance out sideways, holding them back.

Behind the shield-wall on the jetty, the rising sun cleared the surrounding hills and shone for the first time that day full on the water. It caught the fins and bodies of the killers as they swept in for the second time from the deep water, confident of what they had to do, emboldened by their first success. A great cry went up from the water as the men in the dories realized what was coming towards them.

Brave men, some of them struck out with spears and swords as the black-and-white bodies rushed in. Valgrim the Wise, standing disbelieving in the prow of his boat, swung back the 'Gungnir' lance to use as a harpoon. Too weak, too slow. The boats were taken from underneath. A blow from a snout, propelled at thirty miles an hour by a body tons in weight, and each boat disintegrated. The heavily-armed men splashed or sank in the water, and as they did so the jaws tore at them, into them, the killers sweeping backwards and forwards in the pattern they used for hunting seals or porpoise. In seconds the bay ran as red as the cove of the grind. But this time with man-blood, not with whale's, crewmen's mixed with that of their skipper, and that of Valgrim the Wise, priest of Othin, now sacrificed to Othin's own creatures. Unnoticed by any, the spear with the 'Gungnir' runes drifted gently to the bottom: it had brought its last owner no luck.

Shef's charging line faltered as the men took in what was happening, a thing no-one had ever seen before. Seeing their enemies stare and hesitate, Kormak's detachment turned as well. Both sides stood, struck with horror. There was no way for anyone to intervene.

After a time, Shef stepped forward, spoke to what seemed to be the leader of the men on the jetty. "Put your weapons down," he said. "We will give you life and limb, and passage home when we can. There is no way for you to escape now. And there has been bloodshed enough."

Lips pale, the leader looked at his men, saw their shaken and horrified expressions, the fight drained out of them. He nodded, slowly laid down sword and shield. Cuthred moved forward, shouldered a path through the others for Shef, walked with him to the end of the jetty to see the end of the story.

As he did so, a figure rose from the planking, shrieking recognition. Ragnhild, knife in hand, unmoved by the slaughter, desperate for revenge. She came at Shef like a fury, knife low for the thrust. Shef saw her come, recognized the green eyes he had kissed, the hair he had clenched in climax. The lance drooped disregarded in his hand, he groped for words of apology. She was shrieking something as she ran in, he caught only the words ". . . killed my son!" He stood, arms wide, paralyzed, hoping for a word of explanation, another miracle.

Cuthred stepped between them, the knife-thrust screeching off the hard surface of his shield. Automatically he lifted it to thrust her off. Ragnhild's eyes widened with sudden shock. Then she fell backwards, dragging Cuthred's targe with her. The targe with the foot-long spike

Shef had welded on himself. It had driven through her heart below her breasts.

"As God's my judge," said Cuthred, "that was an accident. I never killed a woman in my life."

"Too many killings," said Shef. He stooped, searching for signs of life. Her lips were still moving, still cursing him. Then they ceased, and he saw her eyes roll upwards. As he stepped away, Cuthred walked forward, put a foot on Ragnhild's outstretched arm, and jerked his shield free. He shook his head in self-reproach, looked to see if his leader had noticed what he had done.

But Shef's eyes had turned from the corpse on the jetty to the bloodstained, fin-slashed water. Then, disbelievingly, he looked again across the bay. There, in the shallows opposite, two figures were sitting, visible in the growing daylight. Behind him a murmur of amazement arose as more and more men saw the astonishing sight. The second thing they had seen that morning that no living man had ever seen before. One of the Hidden People.

Echegorgun, gauging the whales' mood exactly, had swum easily and confidently across the narrow strait after the whale-boats. He had seen Shef take the men on shore, had seen the one over-confident boat sweep on into the harbor, to be met and butchered by the whales. He had kept well back, but had followed the whales on into the harbor, sure that he would hear if they turned towards him. He had cruised along the shore, only the tip of his skull showing, and that looking like yet another gray rock. He had watched the doings of the men with interest, but without concern—till he had seen two men load an unmistakable figure into a boat. Brand son of Barn son of Bjarni. His own aunt's grandson.

Echegorgun knew exactly what would happen next. He had a couple of minutes only in which to avert it, alter it. Like a seal he had launched himself across the water, clung for a moment to the stern of the *Crane*, gauged the distance between himself and the lead boat with Kormak in it, felt the swarm and flurry of whale-flukes only yards away. He submerged, striking out like an otter.

Brand, bound helpless in the bottom of the boat, Kormak's foot resting firmly on his chest, saw only a great gray hand seize the gunwale. Then the boat tipped. Tipped towards Echegorgun, tipped a fraction before the first whale struck. As the men shouted and raised their weapons, an irresistible clutch seized his tunic, dragged him over the side and down deep, deep, away from the splintering planks and thrashing limbs on the surface.

For a second Brand felt all the superstitious horror of his race. Seized by the marbendill, dragged down to the monster's dinner at the bottom of the sea. And yet, in that flash, he had half-recognized the hand. He lay motionless, not resisting, holding his one deep-drawn breath.

Slowly the grip dragged him through the water, powered by the great muscles of the not-man. Under the *Crane*'s keel. Across the bay. Into the shallows. As they both came up, releasing their breath in a final gasp, Brand stared into the face next his own. The face staring back. As Echegorgun produced a flint knife and began to cut free the ropes that held Brand's arms, they explored each other silently, for similarity, for family resemblance.

Finally Brand spoke, sitting in the shallow water. "I have left messages for you and your folk in our secret place," he said, "and I have always kept to our compact. Yet I never expected to see you here in the daylight. You are of the race that grandfather Bjarni met."

Echegorgun smiled, showing his massive teeth. "And you must be my good cousin Brand."

CHAPTER TWENTY-FOUR

I t is an expensive business finding you shelter," said Brand wearily.

Shef said nothing. He might have replied that it had sometimes been profitable too, but allowances had to be made for Brand's state of mind. He was not sure how many days had gone by since the battle—in the high latitudes it was hard to tell. Everyone seemed to have been furiously at work for longer than they could bear, stopping only when they fell asleep. And yet—it was an ominous sign—dark was returning to the sky. Summer was past, winter coming on. It came on very fast in Halogaland.

However many days it had been, the settlement still looked barely survivable. All three of the ships in the harbor were sunk or unserviceable. By sheer bad luck Cwicca and his crew had found the range and managed to depress their machine just as the battle was won, and put a rock neatly through the base of the *Crane*'s mast. Driven by terror of the whales her crew had managed to pole her over and beach her, but she would never sail again. The *Walrus* still sat at the bottom of the harbor, her mast poking forlornly above the surface. The *Seamew* had caught fire and burnt. Though there were small craft of all kinds available, there was no ship big enough to sail south for Trondhjem, the nearest port, and return with provisions. In time, one would be made from the salvaged planks and timbers—for of course there was little large wood readily available on the barren coast or the wind-swept islands. For the same reason rebuilding the burnt huts would be hard, for all the local skill in using stone and turf. Much of the precious windfall of the grind had gone up in flame, and with it the storehouses and warehouses where Brand kept not only the furs and feathers and skins of the Finn-tax, which he traded, but also the meat and cheese and butter on which he lived.

And besides Shef's train, and Guthmund's crew, there were maybe seventy survivors off the *Crane*. They had been promised their lives, and no-one had suggested breaking the promise. But they all ate. There was no way everyone on the island could live through the coming winter, however hard they fished and sealed. Many of the Halogalanders had quietly slipped back to their homesteads, making it clear they wanted no part of Brand's problem. They would live. It would be the strangers, and their hosts, if they were fool enough to share, who would die.

"At least we have gold and silver," Brand went on. "That doesn't burn. The best thing we can do is put a boat together, a makeshift, load it with every man we can squeeze in, and send it off south. If it hugs the shore it might get to somewhere with food to spare. Then turn Ragnhild's Westfolders out, buy as much as we can, and head north again."

Again Shef forbore to say anything. If Brand were not so tired he would have seen the faults in the scheme. The Westfolders would be many enough to overpower their guards, take the money, and leave the settlement as foodless as ever. As it was, guarding them was taking far too much of everyone's resources. They would have to be sent off on their own. If they could be brought ever to venture out to sea again, with their new terror of the whales.

"I am sorry," said Brand, shaking his massive head. "I have experienced too much to make any sensible plan. A marbendill for a cousin! I knew, but now everyone does. What will folk say?"

"They will say you are fortunate," broke in Thorvin. "There is a priest of the Way in Sweden, whose special devotion is to the goddess Freyja. His craft is the breeding of animals, the way you must cross-breed or in-breed to get the best-yielding cows or the woolliest sheep. He has spoken to me often of mules, and the breeding of dog and wolf, and such things. As soon as he knows, he will come here. For it seems to me that we and the sea-men are more like dog and wolf than we are horse and donkey. For your grandfather Bjarni bred with one of their females, and she had a child, your father Barn. But Barn too had a child, and that was you, and your ancestry is plain if we see you together. If Barn had been a mule, a human mule, that could not have happened. So we and the marbendills are not so far apart. Maybe there is more marbendill blood in the race than we knew before."

Shef nodded. The thought had come to him before as he looked at
the northerners, with their massive frames, their eyebrow-ridges, their
hairy skins and bushy beards. But he had not aired the thought. He
noticed that the word "troll" was being used more sparingly around
the settlement, replaced by "sea-folk" or "marbendill," as if others
were also reckoning their ancestry.

"Well, be that as it may," said Brand, looking slightly more
cheerful. "I do not know what we are to do. I wish, I don't mind
saying it, I wish I had the good advice of my cousin."

But Echegorgun had slipped away very soon after dragging Brand to
the shore. He had seemed for a short time pleased with the attention
he received, and certainly pleased by Brand's gratitude. Then the noise
seemed to irk him, and he had vanished as only the Hidden Folk
could. He had also taken Cuthred with him, both of them apparently
swimming the firth back to the mainland. Echegorgun was impressed
by Cuthred.

"Not quite a Thin One," he had said. "Stronger than Miltastaray,
anyway. And look at the hair on his back! Grease him well, he could
swim with the seals too. Miltastaray likes him. He could be a good
mate for her."

Shef had gaped at the last thought, and then said cautiously, unsure
how to put it. "I thought you said, Echegorgun, that you knew what
had happened to him. Well, what happened was that some of the
other Thin Ones, they cut off, well, not what makes him a man, but
what . . ."

Echegorgun cut him off. "I know. It means less to us than to you.
You know why you live such short lives? Because you mate all the time,
not just in season. Every time you do it, more of your life gone. A
thousand times for every child, I have listened at many windows! Hah.
Miltastaray would look for something else in a man."

And with that they had gone. Shef had had time only to speak to
Cuthred and ask him to ask Echegorgun to bury his human kills, like a
civilized person, instead of smoking them like a—like a marbendill.
"Tell him we'll pay him in pigs," he had said.

"You haven't got any pigs," Cuthred had replied. "Anyway, I prefer
pigs to people."

Perhaps they would all have larders like Echegorgun's before the
winter was out, Shef thought. As the circular discussion between
Thorvin, Brand, Guthmund and the others continued, he got up,
brooding, and walked away. He carried with him the lance he had
taken from the smokehouse: it felt more comfortable than the

'Gungnir' spear, or the expensive swords he had acquired and lost. The best thing to do when you were faced with an insoluble problem, he had found, was to ask everyone about it till you met the one who knew the answer.

He found Cwicca and the gang sharing a scanty meal in a break from their work of trying to recover planking from the wrecked ships. As he approached, they stood up respectfully. Shef wondered for a moment. They did that sometimes. Sometimes, misled by his accent when he was speaking English, they forgot and treated him as one of themselves. They seemed to be doing that less often.

"Sit," he said, but remained standing himself, leaning on the lance. "Not much to eat, I see."

"And there's going to be less," agreed Cwicca.

"There's talk of sending the prisoners away in a ship, when we've built it. If we could build two we could trust someone to go south for food."

"If we could build two," demurred Wilfi.

"If we can get anyone to sail it," added Osmod. "Right now everyone's so scared of whales they'd run aground if they saw a spout."

"Dead right too," put in Karli fervently. "I mean to say one thing, lord. You know I saw one of those things when I poled across from Drottningsholm? Right out on the water, close up? Well, one of those here was the same one. I saw a bite-mark on his fin. Same thing here. It looks as if—well, as if they followed us up."

Or followed you up, he thought but did not say. The English ex-slaves had told him many strange stories of their master, whom they both venerated and felt at home with. He had believed few of them. Now, he was beginning to wonder. Was there a penalty, he thought, for a man who had greeted the son of a god by knocking him down. There had not seemed to be one so far.

"Well, if we don't do something we'll all starve to death," said Shef.

The ex-slaves considered the prospect. Not an unfamiliar one. Many slaves, and as many poor folk, died in the winter, from cold or hunger or both. They had all known it to happen.

"I had an idea," said Udd, and then stopped, with his usual shyness in front of a group.

"Was it about iron?" asked Shef.

Udd nodded vigorously, recovering his nerve. "Yes, lord. You know that ore we saw down at the College at Kaupang? The sort that took so little working, because there's so much metal in the stone? It comes from Jarnberaland. Iron-bearing Land."

Shef nodded encouragingly, with no idea where this thought was leading. They couldn't eat iron, but sarcasm would cut Udd off completely.

"There's a place called Kopparberg too. Copper Mountain. Well, the thing is, they're both over there." Udd pointed across the harbor to the mountainous shore opposite. "On the other side of the mountains, I mean. I thought, if we can't sail, we could walk. It's not as if there's nowhere the other side."

Shef looked at the jagged forbidding shore, thought of the terrible cramping struggle up the side of Echegorgun's inlet. The path they had come upon. The easy ridge route Echegorgun had taken to bring them out opposite the island.

"Thank you, Udd," he said. "I'll think about that."

He walked on till he found Guthmund the Swede. Guthmund was in unexpectedly good spirits. He had lost his ship, and there was every chance of dying of starvation. On the other hand, the loot from the *Crane* had been surprisingly good. Ragnhild had taken half her ancestral treasure with her, to buy men and revenge, and it had been recovered from the wreck. Deaths in the attack had meant fewer people to share it with, too. Guthmund greeted his young leader with a smile. They called him Guthmund the Greedy. His ambition was to become Gull-Guthmund, or Gold-Guthmund in English.

The smile vanished as Shef asked him about what Udd had said. "Oh, it's up there somewhere all right," he agreed. "But I wouldn't know where exactly. You folk don't realize. Sweden is a thousand miles long from end to end, all the way from Skaane to the Lapp-mark. If Skaane is Swedish," he added. "I am from Sodermanland myself, I am a true Swede. But I guess, I guess this is about as far north as Jarnberaland."

"How can you tell?"

"By the way the shadows fall. If you measure a shadow at noon, and you know how far it is from midsummer, you can tell how far north you are. It is one of the crafts of the Way, Skaldfinn Njörth's priest once showed me."

"So if we went up there and walked due east we would come to Jarnberaland in the country of the Swedes."

"You might not have to walk all the way," said Guthmund. "I have heard it said that there are lakes up there in the Keel, the central range, and they run east and west. Brand told me that when the Finns on this side raid the Finns on the other—Kvens they call them—they take bark boats and paddle along them.''

"Thank you, Guthmund,'' said Shef, and walked on again.

Brand looked incredulous when Shef reported the results of his conversations to him and Thorvin, still sitting together. "Can't be done,'' he said flatly.

"Why not?''

"It's too late in the year.''

"A month after midsummer?''

Brand sighed. "You don't realize. Up here summer doesn't last long. On the coast, all right, the sea seems to keep the snow and ice off for a while. But just think. Remember what it was like in Hedeby, like spring, you said. Get to Kaupang and it's still ice-bound. And how far is that? Three hundred miles north? Here you're another six hundred. A few miles in from the coast—and that's as far as I've ever been, even chasing Finns—and there's snow on the ground more than half the year. The higher you go, the worse it gets. The high mountains never melt at all.''

"So cold is the problem. But Udd's right, is he, it is Jarnberaland on the other side, maybe two hundred miles off? Ten days' travel.''

"Twenty days' travel. If you're very very lucky. In some of the country I've seen three miles is a hard day. If you don't get turned round and die walking in a circle.''

"Still,'' Thorvin put in, pulling at his beard, "there is something few people know. And that is that the Way is strong in Jarnberaland. Naturally, for we are craftsmen and smiths. And smiths go to iron. There are priests of the Way there, working with the folk who mine the iron. Some say it is as good as a second College. Valgrim was against it. He said there could only be one College.''

And he the head of it, Shef thought. Valgrim's errors had finally caught up with him. He had been in the boats that rowed back to the *Crane*, and only two of the men in them had survived, Brand and a young man who had remained hunched into a ball ever since they pulled him on shore, making small noises of fear. Ragnhild could have died that way too, Shef told himself. Just an accident. Another of the ones that surrounded him. Part of his luck, Olaf Elf-of-Geirstath would say, and King Alfred with him.

"So if we crossed the mountains,'' Shef went on, "we might even find help the other side.''

"But you can't cross the mountains," Brand repeated, exasperated. "The mountains are full of Finns and—"

"And the Hidden Folk," Shef completed for him. "Thank you, Brand." He rose to his feet and walked off yet again, the lance marking his paces.

The final word came from a man whose name he did not know, one of the *Crane*'s crew, sweating in the pale sunlight as he and his mates heaved rocks on to a sled, to drag to the settlement to make a few more winter shelters. Halogalanders watched them from a distance, carrying bundles of seal-harpoons. Shef, still unsure of his proper course, paused to watch them for a moment.

One of them looked up. A relative of Kormak, he spoke bitterly. "Today we sweat, you watch. We were defeated—but not by men, by whales! That cannot happen twice. Next time you will find no protectors. The Rogalanders are still looking out for you, and Ragnhild's kin will pay her bounty. And behind them, the Ragnarssons. Sigurth Snake-eye will pay as much for you as Ragnhild would have. If you go south, you will meet someone. You will never see England again, one-eye. The only man who could get through what waits for you would need an iron skin. Like Sigurth Fafnirsbane. And even he left a weak spot!"

Shef looked down reflectively. He knew the story of Sigurth who killed the dragon Fafnir—he had seen a part of it himself, in vision, seen the dragon-mask. He knew too that Sigurth had been betrayed by his lover, and killed by her husband and his kin, once they found out that the dragon's blood that had made his skin impenetrable had been checked at one spot by a leaf that stuck to it, and left him vulnerable only in the back. He, Shef, had had an angry lover as well, though she was dead, and her husband too. And he had killed a dragon, if Ivar Boneless might be considered as such.

The parallels were too close for comfort. And it was true enough that the North Way down the coast was also the one way south, and all too easily blocked.

"I hear what you say," he answered. "And I thank you for your warning. But you meant it in malice. If you have nothing better to say, do not speak next time." He reached out, carefully, and tapped the angry Viking on the very throat-ball with the point of his lance.

The human mind is strange. Nose-bleeds start from fear. A stammer is cured by a shock, feeble old women start from their beds in a crisis and lift great timbers from their sons' bodies. Kormak's relative knew he had spoken too freely. Knew that if the one-eyed man ran him through with the lance, there would be no complaint against him. As the point touched his throat, his gullet froze with fear. And remained frozen.

As Shef walked away one of his mates said to him in an undertone, "You chanced it there, Svipdag."

Svipdag turned to him, eyes wide. Tried to speak. Tried again, and again. Nothing came out but a low gargling. Men saw the terror in Svipdag's eyes as he realized that he meant to speak, but had been robbed of the ability as if a cord had been tied round his windpipe.

The other prisoners looked after Shef's retreating back. They had heard stories of him, of the death of Ivar, of Halvdan, of how King Olaf had handed over all his luck and his family's into this man's keeping. They knew he bore the sign of some unknown god round his neck, his father, some had heard.

"He said, 'do not speak,' " one of the Vikings muttered. "And now he can't!"

"I'm telling you, he called the whales in too," said another.

"And the Hidden Folk come to his help."

"If I'd known all that, Ragnhild could have whistled herself hoarse before I came on this gods-forsaken trip."

"You don't have to do this, you know," said Brand when Shef told him of his decision. "We'll think of something. Get those greedy louts from the *Crane* out of the way, things'll look better. We can send some lads south in the dories, maybe buy a boatload of food in Trondhjem, and a boat to put it in. *You* don't have to walk off into the snow, even if someone else does."

"That's what I'm going to do anyway," said Shef.

Brand hesitated, embarrassed. He felt he had spoken too gloomily earlier, provoked this insane decision. He remembered when he had first taken Shef under his protection, after they had put his eye out. He had taught him Norse, taught him how to use a sword properly, taught him the way of the *drengr*, the professional marching warrior. And Shef had taught him much too. Raised him to glory, and to riches—for the crisis now was one of food and fuel and ships, not of money.

"Look, no-one I know of has ever been deep into those mountains and come back, let alone come out the other side. Maybe the Finns do, but they're different. It's wolves and bears and cold. And where are you if you get through? Sweden! Or Swedish Finnmark, or somewhere. I can't see why you're doing this."

Shef thought for a few moments before replying. "I think I have two reasons," he said. "One is this. Ever since I went to the cathedral this spring, saw Alfred and—and Godive marry, I've felt that things were getting out of my hand. People pushed me, and I went along. I did what I had to. From the sandbank to the slave-market to Kaupang to the queen. Across the Upland and up to here. Chased by the Ragnarssons and Ragnhild and even by the whales. Now I think I've retreated as far as I mean to. From now on I'm going to go back. I have been deep into the darkness, into the smokehouse of the Hidden Folk, even. Now I have to get into the light. And I don't mean to go back the way I came."

Brand waited. Like most of the men of the North, he believed deeply in luck. What Shef was saying was that he meant to change his luck. Or maybe that his luck had turned. Some people would say that the young man had luck and to spare. But no man could judge of another's luck, that was clear.

"The other reason?" he prompted.

Shef pulled his pole-ladder pendant forward from his chest. "I don't know if you think this means anything," he said. "Do you think I have a god for a father?"

Brand did not reply. "Well," Shef went on, "I keep seeing things, as you know. Sometimes asleep, sometimes awake. I know someone is trying to tell me things. Sometimes it's very easy. When we found Cuthred, I had been shown to look for a man turning a great mill. Or had I heard the mill-wheel creaking already? I don't know. But then, and the time when Cwicca broke down the wall of the queen's house to get me out, I had a warning. A warning about something that was happening right then.

"All that's easy enough. But I have seen other things that are not so easy. I saw a hero dying, and an old woman. I saw the sun turn into a chariot pursued by wolves, and into a father-god's face. I saw a hero ride to rescue Balder from Hel, and I saw the White Christ killed by soldiers of the Rome-folk who spoke our own tongue. I saw the heroes in Valhalla, and I saw how those who are not heroes are received there.

"Now all those sights were trying to tell me something. Not something easy. Not only from one side, from the pagans or the Christians. What I think they were trying to tell me—or maybe I am telling myself—is that there is something wrong. Something wrong with the way we all live. We are sliding into the Skuld-world, Thorvin would say. Virtue has gone out of us, out of us all, Christians and pagans. If this pendant means anything, it means that I must try to put it back. One step at a time, as you mount a ladder."

Brand sighed. "I see your mind is made up. Who will go with you?"

"You?"

Brand shook his head. "I have too much to do here. I cannot leave my own kin unfed and unsheltered."

"Cwicca and his gang will come, I think, and Karli. He came with me for adventures. If he gets back to the Ditmarsh he will be the greatest story-teller they ever had. Udd for sure, maybe Hund, maybe Thorvin. I have to speak again to Cuthred, and to your cousin."

"There is a skerry where I can leave a message," Brand conceded reluctantly. "Your chances would go up a great deal if he would accompany you. But maybe he thinks he has done enough."

"What about provisions? What can you spare us?"

"Not much. But you will have the best of what we still own." Brand pointed. "One thing. Why are you still carrying that old weapon? All right, you picked it up in the smokehouse when you had nothing else, but look at it. It's old, the gold inlay is worn off, the blade is thin, it has no cross-piece. Not half the weapon Sigurth's 'Gungnir' was. Give it to me, I'll find you a better one."

Shef hefted the weapon thoughtfully. "I call it a good spear that conquers," he said. "I'll keep it."

CHAPTER TWENTY-FIVE

In the end the group that Shef led to the foot of the mountains numbered twenty-three, all but three of them English speakers by birth. Cwicca, Osmod, Udd and their three remaining mates Fritha, Hama and Wilfi had joined him without question, as had Karli. So had Hund, saying that he had a feeling they would have need of a leech. More to Shef's surprise, Thorvin had agreed to make the trip, giving as his excuse that as a smith he wanted to see Jarnberaland and the College's outpost there. Once the news of the attempt spread, Shef had been much more surprised to find a deputation come to him, headed by Martha, the woman from Frisia, once a slave of Queen Ragnhild, and by Ceolwulf, the rescued slave whom the others suspected of having been a thane.

"We don't want to be left here," they said. "We have been too much among the Norse-folk, and want to find our way home. Our best chance is with you."

"Not a good chance," Shef told them.

"Better than the one we had a while ago," said Ceolwulf grimly.

So the party was expanded by four women and eight men. Shef had wondered whether to argue that the women would not have the strength to make the journey, but the words died as he thought them. He had traveled from Kaupang to the Gula with them, and they kept up as well as the men, certainly better than the puny Udd or the short-legged Osmod. As for the male ex-slaves, all of them wearing still their Rig pendants, Shef had not the heart to leave them. They might be an asset. Certainly some of them, like the formidable

Ceolwulf, had talents of their own. They had fought well if briefly in the skirmishes against the crew of the *Crane*: some had died, over-anxious to get in a blow against the race that had enslaved and tormented them.

The last member of the party was Cuthred. Brand had gone off one evening in the growing dark, making it clear that he was not to be watched or followed. As had been the custom of his family, he had left a message in a secret spot that his Hidden Folk relations knew. In some private code he had passed the news that he needed a meeting. But Echegorgun had not replied, or appeared. Instead Cuthred had walked in two mornings later. His clothes were dry and he was carrying his sword and shield, so he had not swum the narrow firth from the mainland. Echegorgun must have had some kind of boat or water-craft, but Cuthred was as close-mouthed about that as if he had already become a Hidden One himself.

Told what was intended, he listened, nodded, sat silent during the day, and disappeared again in the dark. When he returned a second time he brought discouraging word.

"Echegorgun won't accompany you," he said. "He says he has been seen too often already. He says I am to come with you instead."

Shef raised an eyebrow. Cuthred spoke as if he had a better alternative—maybe to join the Hidden Folk for good, as a kind of exchange for the child Barn many years ago.

"He says he will keep an eye on you, or on us," Cuthred went on. "And he will pass the word to his relatives not to interfere with us. That is a great threat removed. You know why most hunters from here have never come back. They ended up smoked like stock-fish. But that still leaves the bears and the wolves. And cold and hunger. And the Finns. We will have to take our chances with them."

Shef had agreed, having no choice, and turned to his preparations. In the end Brand had paraded every single member of the party in front of him, and gone through their equipment minutely. All had stout and well-greased boots that reached up to the calf. Thick leggings and thick wool trousers over them, for women as well as men. Wool tunics, skin mantles, hemp shirts. "Sweat is a danger," Brand told them. "Freezes on you. Hemp soaks up the sweat better than wool. Better not to sweat. Just do everything at an even pace, but never stop unless you have a fire. That is the way to keep warm, but not too warm." He had made sure that everyone had a bag to sleep in. Not, alas, the magnificent model Shef had bought at the Gula, which had burnt with so much else. But a store of feathers had survived the fire, and everyone had a two-layer bag of some material, wool or skin, padded with the down of the seabirds. Mittens and hats, scrims to go round the neck and pull across the face in a blizzard. For each person, in a back-pack, ten day's food, mostly dried fish and seal-meat, or the strong cheese made from sheep or goat's milk. Not enough, but a person walking all day in the cold needs four pounds' weight of food a day. Carry more, travel less. "If you see anything living, eat it," Brand said. "Spin out what you carry as long as you can. You will be hungry before you reach the other side."

The party's weapons had been carefully selected as well, and not for war. The catapulteers carried their crossbows and their knives. Even Osmod had been made to abandon his halberd, too heavy and cumbersome. Thorvin had his smith's hammer, Hund was empty-handed. The others carried either wood-axes or spears, stout-shafted ones with cross-pieces, not javelins or harpoons. "For bear," Brand explained. "You don't want one of them walking up the shaft at you." Four short hunting bows were spread among the group as well, given to those who considered themselves good shots. Cuthred carried the sword they had taken from Vigdjarf, and his spiked shield. Shef had his lance as well as a broad sharp-pointed Rogaland knife taken from the *Crane*.

Finally, Brand had insisted on pressing upon them six pairs of the strange sticks the Norwegians slid on, the skis. "None of us can use them," Shef protested.

"Thorvin can," Brand replied.

"I learned too," added Ceolwulf. "Learned the first winter."

"You might need to send scouts out," Brand urged. What he thought was that some might survive, even if all did not.

At dawn, some fourteen days after the battle and the burning, the party set out. They were carried over the first stretch in the first ship Brand's folk had managed to make from salvaged parts: planks from both the wrecked ships, keel made from one half of the *Crane*'s originally riveted main timber. The ship was short, wide, and lacking in proportion, named by Brand in disgust the *Duckling*. Nevertheless she moved reasonably enough under sail, the party packed into her roomy waist with the six-man crew working round them. There had been some argument about where they should all be set down, Brand opting for a fjord which ran furthest into the tangled mass of mountains, and so cut down their marching distance as much as possible. But Cuthred vetoed the choice with total confidence. "Echegorgun said not," he reported. "He said, go to the fjord that leads to the triple-horned mountain. Then head due east. That way we will strike a line that may lead us down to the great lake that runs across Kjolen, the Keel."

"A line, or a path," queried Shef.

"A line. There are no paths. Not even Hidden Folk paths. In the deep mountains, they need no paths."

He had almost said "we," Shef noted.

So, in a chill wind, twenty-three laden figures stood at the very end of a deep fjord. The sun had climbed high up the sky. Even so, it was only just high enough to clear the mountain-tops, and half the fjord still lay in deep shadow. On the other side the snow-capped peaks lay reflected in deep still water, stirred only by the faint ripples of the *Duckling* being poled out from shore. The humans seemed a mere scattering of forked twigs under the impassive gray bulks, their path a mere slash in the rock down which bright water bounded.

Brand called out across the water, "Thor aid you."

Thorvin made the sign of the Hammer in reply.

"Lead on," said Shef to Cuthred.

Twelve days later, Shef knew he had calculated wrong. He was cutting a twelfth notch in a stick he had carried tucked in his belt since the first few days, and the rest were watching him. They were watching him because he had a dry stick.

That was part of the miscalculation. The first day had been as bad as Shef had thought it would be, remembering the agony of the climb up the shore, where he had met Ekwetargun. The mountain-side had never been a vertical wall, to be scaled. Yet it had never flattened out enough to become a place where a person could walk, either. First the thigh muscles ached. Then the arms began to join in, as the weary climbers pulled themselves up more and more, pushed with their legs less and less. The breaks for rest became longer, more frequent, the pain worse at each restart.

All that Shef had predicted. After all, it was only a matter of climbing, say, five thousand feet. Five thousand steps would do it. We must have done three already, he told the others. Two thousand steps! We can count them. And though he had been wrong about the number, he had been right that there would be an end.

So, then, for a few days, high spirits. Cooped up in slave-quarters or on ship-board for so long, the English had revelled in the air, the sunlight, the immense distances they could see, the exhilarating bareness. The bareness. That was the trouble. Even Thorvin had confided to Shef that he had expected to meet what the Norwegians called *barrskog*, thickets of scrub. But they were far above the tree-line here. Each night, each fireless night—for they had carried no wood—the cold seemed to clamp down more fiercely. Food was rationed strictly. It never seemed enough. Maybe if they had had a fire to boil their meat in, they began to mutter to each other, the dried seal-meat might have felt as if it filled a belly. As it was, it seemed to be like chewing leather. An age to choke down, and only cramp in the guts once it was there. Night after night, Shef woke from his cold sleep, even in the down-lined bag, dreaming of bread. Bread with thick yellow butter on it. And honey! With beer, thick brown beer. His body cried out for it. None of them had had much fat on their bones to begin with, and their bodies were beginning to break down muscle for want of anything else to use.

So they stared at his stick, wanting him to shave it down, use it for tinder, light a fire and burn—burn the sere brown grass and moss that covered the rolling upland plateau. It was impossible. But they thought it.

At least they had made some distance, Shef reflected. Neither hills nor woods had detained them, though swamp and bog had. Yet they had not come upon the lake he had hoped for, and all Cuthred would say was that it must be further on. A lake, he said, with trees round it, with bark that would make light boats. So Echegorgun had assured him. Pity Echegorgun won't come and show us, Shef had felt like saying again and again, keeping silent in view of Cuthred's doubtful loyalties.

A few days ago he would have told himself that at least the party was staying united. The ability of the ex-slaves to endure hardship had been a great asset. Where proud warriors would have argued and fought and blamed each other, making something out of every blister or bellyache, Shef's party had behaved to each other like—well, like women, Shef had to say. When Martha got the gripes one morning and might have delayed their start, it was Wilfi who acted the fool and distracted attention. When Udd, the weakest of the party, began to limp and go whiter and whiter in the face trying to disguise it, afraid that he would be abandoned, it was Ceolwulf who halted the march, dressed Udd's sore heel with his own ration of sealfat, and walked by his side to encourage him.

Yet the strain was starting to tell, showing in bickerings. Cuthred, especially, was getting worse again. The day before Karli, still irrepressible when it came to women, had caught up with Edith as she walked ahead, and fondled her buttock for a moment. He and Edith had been bed-partners since Drottningsholm, when the chance came, and she had not protested. But Cuthred, walking behind, had said nothing, merely caught Karli a great sweeping blow on the ear. For a second Karli had squared off to him. Then he saw Cuthred's ostentatious openness to the punch, knew that the counter would be lethal, dropped his shoulders and turned away. Now Karli was humiliated. Not as much as Cuthred had been, but there was enmity there now, and spreading as people took sides.

Shef tucked the stick back in his belt, looked up at the stars coming out in the frosty air. "Sleep now," he said. "March at dawn. We've nothing better to do. We'll find wood tomorrow, and Cuthred's lake."

When the leader weakens, then the army is hindered, so goes the proverb. When the leader has to joke, then the army is weak already.

Somewhere above, a mind was watching. Looking down at the little comfortless party, nipped by the cold and by the belly-pinch, one of them at least sobbing silently with an internal pain. It watched with satisfaction, tempered only by caution.

He survived my whales, it thought. He survived my disciple's test. He carried my spear and he still bears my mark, but he does me no honor. Has never done me honor. But what is honor? The important thing is, he weakens me and mine for the day of Ragnarök.

Yes, thought the Othin-mind, I have slept little since the death of my son. Since they took Balder from me, and the best of my men, my Einheriar, failed to bring him back from Hel. Since then the world has been gray and dull, and so it will stay till the day of Ragnarök. And if we do not conquer on that day, what hope is there? But this creature, this manling born in a bed, wants to make the world better as it is, to give men happy lives before Ragnarök comes. If that belief spreads, where will my Einheriar come from?

He must die here and his thoughts die with him. And his followers too. And yet there is a loss there, a loss there as well. For the creature with my one-eye has a kind of wisdom—I wonder who put it there? Sometimes he reminds me of one of my other sons. In any case, he sent me a great champion for the day of Ragnarök, Ivar Slayer-of-Kings, who now fights daily in Valhalla with his fellows. And the one he takes with him, he is a great champion too, the mutilated one. There are no women in Valhalla to irk him, he would be welcome. Baptized to the White Christ he may have been, but there is no belief there now, he could be mine, come to me for my collection. But to do that he must die with weapon in hand.

It would be a pity to lose him. Even the one-eye, he has a kind of cunning, and that is scarce enough in the fields round Valhalla. What shall I send them? Shall I send my wolves?

No. If the wolves ate them, that might be well enough. But just now they would eat the wolves and find them tasty. No, the whales failed and Valgrim failed, and the old iötunn was never mine but rather the brood of Loki. The wolves would fail too. So I will send them snow. And in the snow, my Finns.

The flakes began to whisper down out of the sky shortly after dusk, at first just one or two, seeming to crystallize rather than fall. Then bigger flakes, and bigger, and a wind rising out of the north to drive them on. Around midnight the two sentries, seeing the snow starting to drift around and over the humped sleeping bags on the bare ground, decided to wake people up and make them shake themselves clear. The camp turned into a slow shuffle of exhausted men and women struggling out into the cold air, shaking their bags down, moving to a new spot, lying down, feeling the hard ground beneath them turn to slush under their own escaped body heat. They began to shuffle unconsciously to get into the lee of each other, the camp moving slowly piece by piece downwind.

Some time before dawn Shef, realizing what was happening, made a line of backpacks and raked snow over them to create a makeshift wall, putting the party behind that in ranks, the weakest in the middle and the strongest on the edges. Few people slept much for all that. Dawn broke on people tired, hungry, and still fireless.

There was no moving till the snow stopped, as it did after a few hours. They looked out then on a featureless white plain, the sun hidden behind clouds. Shef felt a momentary stab of doubt. During the night he had lost all sense of direction. With the sun hidden . . . He had heard that there was a kind of clear rock that so concentrated the rays that you could see the sun even through cloud, but there was none of it in this group.

He controlled his fear. Which way they went was no longer material. They had to find wood and shelter, and any way that led to that was good. Salvaging the skis from under the snow, he told Thorvin and Ceolwulf, their only skilled users, to go in different directions as far as was visible, to look for a break in the plateau.

Only after they had left did he think to count heads. They were one short. The missing woman was Godsibb, a fair, silent, sad girl, who had trudged along without complaint ever since they had taken her from Drottningsholm. Even Karli had not bothered to try his luck with her. She had never responded even to his good cheer. They found her body, a hump in the snow surprisingly far away, showing how much they had moved in the night.

"What did she die of?" asked Shef after they had swept the snow off the body with their hands.

"Cold. Exhaustion. Hunger," said Hund. "People have different levels of resistance. She was a thin girl. Maybe her bag got damp. Nobody noticed her in the night and she fell into the snow-sleep. It is a peaceful way to go—better than the fate Queen Asa would have given her," he added, trying to deflect Shef's self-criticism.

Shef looked at the worn face, too tired for a young girl's. "She came a long way to die here," he said.

And in dying she had caused him a problem, too. Impossible to bury her in the frozen ground. Could they leave her in the snow, under the snow? It would look all right as they marched away, but no-one could avoid thinking of what would happen when the snow melted and left her exposed.

Hund touched Shef's arm and pointed silently. On a knoll a hundred yards away, a four-legged shape looked at them, then sat down to wait, tongue lolling. Others drifted up behind it, took in the situation, and sat or lay down.

There were different views about wolves. Some of the English were quite used to them, said they were hardly dangerous at all. Brand had contradicted that with his usual finality. "They'll pull you down," he said. "Not frightened of people at all. Of course they won't attack a score of you, armed and together. Two men off in the forest, that's another story."

The wolves meant they could not possibly leave Godsibb, not till they could find earth to lay her in, fire to soften it, and stones to pile on her grave. Carrying her would just weaken the carriers further. If they ended up with another corpse to carry, and another . . .

Shef called two men over, told them to tie her in her bag, attach ropes to it and drag her through the snow when they moved on. He waved aside Fritha's eager offer to shoot a wolf with his crossbow. Waste of a bolt. There would come a time when their need would be greater. Meanwhile the hunting bows had been lost in the night, put down on the ground and buried in the snow. Shef organized the party into a line and made them move back over the whole area they had covered in the night, back to where he thought was their original campsite, probing with feet and gloved hands. They found two of the four bows but only one quiver of arrows, also a set of skis and someone's discarded backpack. By then it might have been noon, and not a step advanced on their journey. A poor start for the first day of bad weather. Shef scowled at the man who had lost his pack, and rubbed the lesson home with harsh words.

"Keep everything by you. Or on you. Don't leave anything ever till the morning. Or there won't be a morning. And remember, your mother isn't with us!"

Thorvin and Ceolwulf were back, looking annoyingly warm and cheerful from hours of positive action.

"Head that way," said Ceolwulf, pointing. "There's a dip, a valley going down, and what looks like trees a few miles off."

Shef reflected. "All right," he said. "Look. Just two of you might not be safe, with our new escorts. Pick four of the youngest and show them how to use these skis. Then take them forward, ahead of us. Even your beginners will be faster than people floundering in snow. When you get to the trees, break wood and bring back as much as you can carry. A fire will put heart into people, and make it easier for them to walk on. I will bring everyone on as fast as I can. Take care not to lose sight of us, and come back at once if the snow begins again."

The skiers went ahead of them, Thorvin and Ceolwulf calling advice and helping fallers to their feet. Shef and the rest, sixteen of them towing one body, kept on trudging forward, occasionally stumbling into drifts. The snow crept down boots and inside mittens.

Piruusi the Finn reveled in the snow, the first fall of the year, early and welcome. He had left his snug skin tent at dawn, watered the bone runners of his sleigh and left them to ice, wiped his face and his skis with yellow reindeer-fat, and skimmed away, bow in hand. He hoped for ptarmigan or Arctic hare, but anything would be welcome, even nothing. Winter was the time of release for the Finns, and if it came early, then their ancestral spirits looked kindly on them.

As he swept up to and past the tent of old Pehto, the shaman, Pehto came out and hailed him. Piruusi stopped, frowning. Pehto was too powerful with the spirits to vex, but he called always for attention, respect, food and fermented milk.

Not this time. Capering professionally and shaking his rattle, Pehto nevertheless for once spoke sense. "To the west, Piruusi great hunter, lord of the reindeer. To the west, something comes. Something with power, Piruusi, and a god's disfavor. Aiiee!" And he began a manic stamping dance, which Piruusi ignored.

Nevertheless he swung out of the low birch wood, its leaves already turning brown from the first frost, and pushed up the gentle slope to the west. His skis hissed smoothly across the snow, Piruusi moving without thought and without effort. Ski-poles were slung across his back, but on anything less than a full slope he had no need of them.

More important to hold the bow and arrow, ready for a shot at any moment. One lived in the winter wild by preying on every opportunity. Never turning down a chance.

There was something there, sure enough. Had the old fraud really seen them with his mystic vision? Perhaps he had risen early to look, for they were plain enough, a straggle across the snow. First, men on skis. Men! They fell over every hundred paces, worse than boys, as if they were babies. And behind those, clear enough to Piruusi's long-sighted eyes, a herd of them, moving like oxen, floundering along, kicking up snow with every step. They dragged a makeshift sled or travois with them.

Piruusi had never paid a Finn-tax, but those of his cousins who lived nearer the shore did so. It was worth it not to have their summer fisheries and fowling-trips cut short by the murderous seamen. Time, Piruusi thought, for someone to pay a Norse-tax in return. He skimmed back to the cluster of tents, men and women inside the flaps cooking over their hot fires of dried reindeer dung, called the menfolk to their skis and bows.

Shef's party regained their strength as they reached the first clump of trees, mere dwarf birch, but desperately welcome. Shef called the skiers back to join the marchers, anxious that no-one should be lost sight of.

"We'll get into the trees, find shelter," he called. "Then we can have a fire and cook. At least we'll be off the moor."

As if in answer, an arrow from behind a tree struck Wiferth, struggling with his skis, in the base of the skull. He fell instantly, dead as a herring before he struck ground. Moments later the air was full of the zip of arrows, the trees full of figures flitting from one trunk to another, never showing for more than an instant, calling encouragement to each other in some unknown language.

Many of Shef's party were veterans. They crouched immediately, shook out into a rough circle, moved behind what cover there was. But the arrows came from all sides. Not shot with much force—Shef saw Ceolwulf grimace and pull an arrow from the brawn of his thigh, seemingly with little effort—but deadly to throat or eye. The shooters were quite close in.

"Fritha," Shef called, "use your crossbow. The rest of you with bows, shoot if you're sure, not otherwise. If you don't have a bow, lie down."

The crossbow clicked as Fritha cocked it. Cuthred, using his initiative, stepped over to behind Fritha, batted an arrow away with his shield, stood over him to guard his back. Fritha sighted on a tree-trunk with a Finn behind it, waited for the man to bob out for his shot. As the Finn emerged, Fritha squeezed the trigger.

Hit in the center of the chest at thirty yards, the Finn flew backwards, the bolt buried up to its feathers. Piruusi, ten yards away, looked over in surprise. The Norse were not bowmen! Nor had he seen a bow. He had no martial tradition, no urge for glory. He fought like a wolf, like a predator. If the prey offered resistance, withdraw, wait. The Finns drew back, still shouting and releasing arrows.

"Well, that seemed easy enough," muttered Shef, rising to his feet.

"Wait till we try and move," answered Cuthred.

A few hours later, with still time left before the dark came down, the position was clear enough. Shef's party had lost two dead—they now had three corpses to drag—and half a dozen with minor arrow wounds. Crossbows or the threat of them kept the Finns at a distance, but Shef believed only a couple of the dozen bolts shot had taken effect. They had not too many left, and the Finns were growing adept at creeping up, shooting, and skimming away in the trees. They were deep in the wood now, and the shelter they had looked forward to so eagerly was proving a menace. On the open moor they had left, their longer-range weapons would have been decisive. It was a bad prospect for the night. Time to fell trees, make a barricade. At least they could have their promised fire.

As the first axeman struck at a birch tree, Shef noticed a bundle wedged in its branches. He stared up. A long bundle. An ominous long bundle.

He pointed it out to Thorvin, both men crouching for fear of the flying arrow. "What is that?"

Thorvin pulled his beard. "I have heard that up here, where the ground is often frozen too hard to bury their dead, they place them in trees instead."

"We are in the Finns' churchyard?"

"Hardly a church. But a burial place, yes."

Shef waved the axeman on, looked round for other tree-bundles. "Get a fire lit," he called. "A big one. Maybe they will pay a ransom for their dead."

Piruusi, watching, scowled again. The fire the Norse-folk had lit silhouetted them, would make them good targets in the night. But that was his own grandmother they had cut from her rest! What might they do? Not burn her? A burnt ghost lost its body in the other world, would come back to haunt its careless relatives. His grandmother had been trouble enough while she was alive.

Time, Piruusi thought, for trickery. He skied away from the reindeer sleigh they had brought up to carry off their dead, broke off a branch with leaves still on it, waved it in token of parley, alert all the time for any sign of one of the strange weapons being brought to bear on him.

Shef saw the man in the skin coat and trousers waving a bough, noting with envy even at that moment the beautifully supple leather—Piruusi's wives had spent many a day chewing the skin to that grade of softness. He saw his alert readiness to dodge, pushed aside Fritha's crossbow, broke off a bough himself and walked forward a little way.

The Finn stopped maybe ten yards off. As Shef wondered what language he might speak, the Finn solved matters for him by calling out in fair if fractured Norse.

"You," he shouted. "Why fire? Why cut down trees, take down old people? You burn them? They do you no harm."

"Why you shoot arrows at us?" retorted Shef in the same style. "We do you no harm. You kill my friends."

"You kill my friends," replied the Finn. Shef noted a flicker of motion out of the corner of one eye, something moving from tree to tree to his left. And to his right. The Finn was calling out again, trying to fix his attention—while the others came in on him from either side. He was trying to take a prisoner, not make a parley. It might be a good idea if they did try. If Shef could embroil two or three of them Cuthred would charge to his rescue. And that might frighten them enough to ensure free passage. Of course he, Shef, might not survive it.

There was something else moving in the forest. Not to either side, but behind the parleying Finn. He had left his sleigh and the two reindeer that pulled it behind him. The animals were standing quietly trying to grub lichen of some kind off the ground. But there was something definitely there behind them.

With incredulity Shef saw the towering bulk of Echegorgun step out from behind a dwarf birch tree. He could not have been behind the tree. The tree's bole was at most a foot thick, barely thicker than one of Echegorgun's arms. Yet there he was in plain sight, looking at Shef, evidently meaning to be seen. A moment before he had not been there. In any case Shef pondered, baffled, they had just spent days and weeks crossing an open moor where you could see every bird and blade of grass. How could Echegorgun have tracked them? Even the reindeer did not seem to have noticed him. They ate on, unalarmed.

The Finn had noticed Shef's fixed stare. "Ho, ho," he hooted. "That old game. 'See behind you, Piruusi, something there.' Then I look, your men shoot, shoot."

Echegorgun stepped carefully up to one of the grazing reindeer, took its head in his massive hands, turned it with a kind of delicacy. The reindeer's legs crumpled immediately, it fell forward, held up for an instant by Echegorgun. He moved to the other, still unmoving, snapped its neck with the same care and lack of haste.

And then he had gone, faded into the birch-shade as if he had never been, leaving only two dead animals to mark his passing.

Piruusi realized suddenly that Shef was ignoring him, whipped round like an adder. Saw his dead beasts unmoving on the ground. His eyes widened, his jaw dropped, he turned back to Shef with fear and disbelief on his face.

Shef turned and looked deliberately at the Finns creeping up from each side, yelled back to Fritha and his mates to mark them. Pointed warningly at the crossbows coming up. Then walked over to where Piruusi now stood by his dead reindeer.

"How you do that?" asked Piruusi. Could Pehto have been right, old fraud or no? Was there some kind of power in this odd man with the one eye and the old spear?

He felt the broken necks of his darlings, his treasured speed beasts, and asked again, "How you do that?"

"I did not do that," said Shef. "But you see, I have friends in these woods. Friends you cannot see, friends you do not want to meet. Have you heard of such things?"

Evidently the Finn had, for he was looking round nervously now as if at any moment some creature might appear behind him and put fingers round his neck. Shef reached over and tapped him with the butt of his lance.

"No more shooting," he said. "No more tricks. We want fire, food. Give gold, silver. Go on to Jarnberaland. You know Jarnberaland?"

There was recognition in the man's eyes, as well as doubt. "I show you Jarnberaland," he agreed. "First we drink together. Drink of . . ." he seemed to have trouble finding a word. "Drink seeing-drink together. You, me, Pehto."

Not understanding, Shef nodded agreement.

CHAPTER TWENTY-SIX

On the evening of the next day, Piruusi took to Pehto the traditional offerings: the block of salt, the sack of strong-smelling half-rancid butter made from reindeer milk, the blood sausage stuffed with lumps of thick fat, the chewed and dressed reindeer hide. As the traditional extra gift he added a pair of soft boots with red thread to draw the tops tight. Pehto inspected the gifts with the expected lack of interest, and refused them twice. The third time he swept them to the side of his tent and called to his aged crone of a wife, more than forty years old already, to come and take them.

"For how many?" he asked.

"For myself and for you. For the stranger with the one eye, and for his companion."

Pehto considered. It was a brief moment for him, not of power—for there could be no question of refusal—but at least of attention. He decided not to make the most of it. The gifts Piruusi had brought were in fact generous—so generous Pehto knew something must have made him so.

"Come when the sky is dark," said the shaman.

Piruusi left without further ceremony. What he knew, and what the shaman did not, for all his claims of being able to look far afield and see what was hidden, was that the one-eye, when Piruusi had claimed compensation for his slaughtered reindeer, had stripped a gold ring from his arm and handed it over without further ado. It was true he had taken the reindeer, but he had returned the valuable hides again without argument. Piruusi had hardly ever seen gold before, the yellow iron as his tribe called it, but he was well aware of the value placed on it by the Norse-folk with whom he sometimes traded. For a ring of that weight he could buy everything the tribe owned, except for their reindeer herds.

Yet the stranger was not completely insane. When Piruusi had demanded further compensation for the two men killed by crossbow bolts, the stranger had waved at his own dead and said no more. Piruusi had noticed, too, the savage glare on the face of the very big man with the spiked shield and sword. Wiser not to provoke such, touched by the spirits. In any case, there was the matter of the dead reindeer. Piruusi had decided, tentatively, that the stranger was a mighty shaman of the Norsemen, of a kind he had not met before. He must be able to send himself out in a different shape, and that shape, probably a bear, had killed the reindeer while the man-shape stood in front of him.

They would know more after the seeing-drink. Eagerly, Piruusi went to his tent, called in the youngest of his wives, prepared to pass the time as well as possible till dark.

Shef was making a tour of their makeshift camp, with Hund. The two dead reindeer had vanished within a few hours as the starving men and women first built a fire, then eagerly began to toast strips of the fresh meat over it. Then they recovered themselves enough to heat stones, place them in their wooden pans and start more of the meat stewing its way towards tenderness. In the beginning they had been devouring the meat all but raw. Shef remembered the first rush of intoxication, almost like the effect of the winter wine, as he gulped down the first slice of fresh liver. But then, he reflected, not only had he been dreaming of thick bread and butter the day before, he had begun to wonder why he had not taken the chance of rotten shark while it was on offer.

"How do you think the people are?" asked Shef.

"It is surprising how quickly they recover," Hund said. "A day and a half ago I was afraid for Udd. He has little strength. I thought we might lose him the way we lost Godsibb, just too weak for a cold night. Now, with three heavy meals inside him, and a night spent by a good fire, he is fit for another few days' travel. One thing I worry about, though. Some of the men are showing old cuts that are opening again—cuts that had healed years before."

"What causes that?"

"No-one knows. But it comes at the end of the spring, when people have been living on stored food for the longest. All leeches of Ithun know that if you give people fresh green stuff, cabbage or kale, they recover immediately. Garlic and onions are good too. Bread is useless."

"We are not at the end of spring now, only the start of winter, and that early."

"True. But for how long were we living on shipboard rations? And what did we eat on Hrafnsey? Much dried meat, dried fish. It is fresh stuff we must have, eaten raw. I think the raw meat, or the half-cooked meat we ate yesterday may have done good. We can try and get some more meat, till we reach the Wayman mines. They will have some store of cabbage or onions there, even if it is pickled."

Shef nodded. There was something strange in this, as if food were something more than fuel you burnt, the only concern being to get enough of it. Yet he had never heard of cows or sheep or horses, or dogs or wolves come to that, sickening because they had only one thing to eat. He changed the subject.

"Do you know what it is we are to drink with the headman of the Finns tonight?"

"I will know when we see it, or sniff it or taste it. But if it is a seeing-drink, there are not so many things it could be. It might be a weak draught of the henbane that Ragnhild used on her husband, or of the deadly nightshade berry. But I doubt they grow up here in the waste. Most likely—well, we will see. One thing I will say, Shef."

Hund turned and faced Shef with unusual gravity. "We have known each other a long time, and I know you well. You are a stiff man, who has grown stiffer. Let me tell you, you are in a strange country now, stranger than Hedeby, or Kaupang, or Hrafnsey. They may ask you to do things that you would find demeaning. They mean no harm. If the headman does it, you do it."

"How about you?"

"I am a leech. It is my place to sit and observe, and see you come to no harm. Take another man to drink with you if that is what they expect. But do what they expect."

Shef remembered a proverb from their shared youth, that Father Andreas had been accustomed to say. "If you're in Rome, do as the Romans do, you mean?"

"The other way to say it is, 'if you are with the wolves you must learn to howl.'"

A short while later Shef, lance in hand, led Hund and Karli towards the Finn encampment a short quarter-mile from their own. He felt a

certain release and anticipation, as if he were going to a drinking-party
in Emneth in his youth, not to some strange ritual among people who
had just tried to kill him. Examining his feelings, he realized why. It
was freedom from the overpowering presence of Cuthred. Obviously
there could be no question of taking him among strangers who might
provoke him by accident. Karli seemed relieved as well. He stared at
each of the Finns who occasionally swept by over the light snow on
their skis.

"Some of them must be women," he remarked finally.

Shef led them to the tent he had heard described, the tent of the
sorcerer. The flap was open, a withered old man beckoned them in to
where Piruusi the headman already sat. Piruusi seemed irritated at the
sight of three men.

"Only two," he said, holding up two fingers. "Not enough for
more."

"I shall not drink," said Hund carefully. "I watch only."

Piruusi did not seem mollified, but he remained silent as the old
man waved the others to sit on the skin floor, handed each of them a
birchwood frame to support their backs. He began to sing a monotonous chanting song, from time to time shaking a rattle. From
somewhere outside the tent a small drum thumped in accompani-
ment.

"He is calling the spirits to guide us," said Piruusi. "How many
reindeer do you want for that gold ring on other arm? I can give you
two, fat ones, though no other man would give you more than one."

Shef grinned and made a counter-offer of three entire silver pennies
for three reindeer, one penny to be returned in exchange for their
hides. Realizing with some relief that his guest was not completely
insane, Piruusi cackled professionally and tried again.

As they reached a final agreement—ten silver pennies and a gold
finger-ring for five reindeer, hides to be returned, and twenty pounds
of bird feathers for sleeping bags—Pehto ended his song. With the
lack of ceremony which the Finns seemed to use, he reached out of the
tent and took a large steaming vessel passed in by the unknown hands
that had beat the drum. He dippered out of it in turn four large mugs
of hollowed pine and handed one each to Piruusi, Karli and Shef, kept
the fourth himself.

"Drink," he said, in Norse.

Shef passed his mug without words to Hund, who sniffed it
carefully, dipped a finger in and licked it. As he did so Piruusi's brow
cleared. At last he had realized the function of the third man. He was a

taster. Certainly the one-eye was a man of great importance, to have such a functionary.

"It is water in which the fly killer mushroom has been boiled."

"Is it safe to drink?"

"Safe for you, I think. You are used to these things. I dare say it will do Karli no harm."

Shef raised the mug politely to his host, and drank deep. Round him the others did the same. Shef observed that it seemed to be the polite thing to drink a third, pause, drink some more, pause again, and finish the draught. The liquid tasted hot, musty, with a faint bitterness: not pleasant, but better than many things Hund had made him swallow. The men sat in silence for a while, drifting into their own thoughts.

Shef felt his soul rise through his mouth and out, through the tent as if it were impalpable, out into the wide air and wheeling like a bird over the dark wood and the great expanse of white moorland that lay all around it. He noted with interest the lake, part-frozen, that lay on the other side of the wood, not far away: Ceolwulf had been right. But while his mind was interested, his soul was not. It darted away, like a flash, winging westwards. As it shot across land and sea, as fast as thought, the light came back into the world. At the place where it hovered, it was still evening, not night. Still autumn, not winter.

It was Hedeby. Shef recognized the mound where he had sat outside the walls and seen the terrible defeat and sacrifice that took place long ago. But the air of peace that hung over the countryside then, when he had sat there, was gone now. No contented plowman, no smoking chimneys. Instead a great camp of tents outside the wall, and lining the walls hundreds of men. It was like the siege of York that Shef had seen, and ended, two years before.

Except for two things. The walls were wood, not the stone of the Rome-folk. And the defenders had no mind to let the walls do all the work for them. Many were outside, skirmishing with the besiegers, fighting it out with sword and spear and battle-axe, exiting from sally-ports and wickets, making their raids, and returning hastily or triumphantly to the stockade.

Yet there was a pattern to the confusion, Shef slowly saw. And as he saw it, the conviction grew on him that he was not seeing the past, or some mythical story, or something that might have been. What he saw was taking place at the same moment as he sat in the Finn's tent. It was a vision, but a vision of the real, one that needed no interpretation.

The besiegers were fighting to set up catapults, mules, by the knoll where Shef had sat. The besieged were trying to hinder them. Not successfully. But then they had only been playing for time. The skirmishers heard a horn blast, drew back. On the walls nearest to the three mules that the besiegers had set up were six, ten, a dozen of the simple stone-lobbing machines that Shef had himself invented, the pull-throwers. They were set up now on platforms broadening the stockade's fighting gangways.

Pull-teams clustered round each one, eight men to a machine, holding the ropes. The long arms were lowered, the thrower-captains loaded rocks into the slings, tugged the arms down. The pullers heaved in unison—not quite in unison, Shef noted professionally, the fault of the unbiddable Norsemen—the arms swept up, the slings lashed round.

A rain of stones landing round the mules, each one ten pounds' weight, coming from the top of a two-hundred-yard arc, enough to batter a helmet in on a skull and the skull into the neck. But only landing round the mules. The trouble with the pull-throwers, as Shef remembered clearly, was that they were easy to aim for line but very hard to adjust for range. The missiles were lobbed, not flung. Fine against a static army, especially one caught in a long line. Against a point target, like trying to lob stones into a bucket thirty yards off.

Shef's vision seemed to sharpen as he watched. He recognized, on the wall, shouting exhortations, the fat but formidable figure of King Hrorik, who had sold him on to the Way. He was wearing a silver helmet and carried a painted shield. And he was shouting at—in the far-off tent in the birch-woods the Shef-body grunted with surprise—shouting at Lulla, who had deserted at the Gula-Thing. So that was who had been paying the high wages for experts.

Lulla, Shef could see, was trying to set up a mule, and Edwi, the other deserter, another one ten yards away. They were having trouble. Unlike the relatively light pull-throwers, their force given by muscle-power, the mules were made of the heaviest timber to take the shock of the throwing-arm's strike. Difficult to get up high on to a fighting-platform, and not easy once you did it. But they had swayed the machines up on sheer-legs, and both the Englishmen were running round, each one trying to do, or to check, what would normally take a full catapult-team of eight.

They were going to be too late. The besiegers . . . Who were the besiegers? With a feeling of growing doom Shef saw the Raven Banner advancing across the battle-plain, the three Ragnarssons clustered about it. Even at a distance the strange white-surrounded pupils of the Snake-eye seemed to pierce the walls and the defenses, and Shef flinched as the gaze seemed to pass through him. They were calling their men on, rallying them for a charge, because they knew . . .

Their own mules shot first. Two of them. One had taken a rock from a pull-thrower right on its retainer bolt, and the crew, casualties lying around them, were struggling frantically to free the bent metal. But two was almost enough. One shot low, sent its ball skimming along into the earth-wall at the base of the stockade, where it bounced and flew just over the stockade. The second struck square on, in an instant beat flat a gap three tree-trunks wide. The Ragnarsson stormers surged forward, were stopped and heaved back.

Lulla had got his machine ready, was yelling at King Hrorik, who shouted back and hit him over the shoulders with his sword-flat. Lulla crouched behind the machine, shrieking directions—his crew seemed baffled by them—trying to get line and elevation correct. Then, battered again by the sweating Hrorik, he pulled the release.

And a hit! Shef heard voices cheering, wondered if one was his own. One of the Ragnarsson mules had disintegrated, hit square on by the much more powerful mule-ball, its crew scattered round it, laid low by splinters or the lashing twisted ropes suddenly released.

Edwi's mule shot an instant later. For a moment Shef could not follow the flight, then he realized, seeing the Ragnarsson crews duck their heads in automatic reflex, that it had shot a foot too high, skimming over the crewmen's heads and speeding on to land half a mile over.

And now the Ragnarssons had the range, had got their third mule repaired as well. Shef saw the mule-captains glance at each other, lift arms to show they were ready, drop them together as the signal to shoot. They had learnt that well. Who had taught them? More deserters? Many men had learnt how the machines worked, in Shef's army or Ivar's, or maybe even from their first makers, the black monks of York.

Shef's soul in the sky saw the flying stones trundle through the air as if they flew through treacle. He had time to project their flight, to see where they would strike, to try to gasp out warning. Then time was at the right speed again. He saw the stones smash through the logs, hurl aside the machines they had been aimed at, sweep the whole pile of wood and rope and stones and men off the wall in a shrieking pile. There was Lulla on the ground, looking up, trying to struggle up, his arm broken, while down on top of him, brushed from its base, came the ton-and-a-quarter of his machine.

Shef flicked his gaze away as he heard the thud, the snap of shattered ribs. He could not see Edwi. The Ragnarssons were streaming straight for the gap in the wall. King Hrorik was in the center of it, sword drawn, calling to his men to come on. Behind him others tried to rig up a makeshift barricade, the battle was not yet lost . . .

Shef sprang to his feet in the tent, shouting, "The warriors round Hedeby!" Realized where he was, realized the others were all conscious and watching him. He wiped cold sweat from his brow, muttered, "I saw . . . I saw a siege. In Denmark."

Piruusi caught the word "Denmark," a place he knew was far away, and grinned. Clearly this man was a great shaman of the Norse-folk. His spirit flew wide.

"What did you see?" Shef asked Karli.

His face was full of unusual dismay. He looked down, said in a low voice, "Oh. A girl."

The Finnish headman caught the word, slapped him on the back, grinning cheerfully. He said something Shef could not catch, said it again. Shef turned inquiringly to Hund.

"He says, do you need to piss?"

Shef realized he did indeed feel a pressure from his bladder. The mug had held at least a pint of the strange drink, and he must have sat in his vision for most of an hour.

"Yes," he said. "Er, where?"

The old man had brought out another vessel, a larger one, again of hollowed pine. He put it on the ground, made inviting gestures, passed another to Piruusi, who began to struggle out of his laced breeches—no easy job, in cold-weather clothes. Shef looked round, wondered if it was not possible at least to go outside. Perhaps they didn't do that here. Perhaps you could get frostbite leaving the tent much of the year. Untroubled by inhibitions, he followed the lead of his hosts, as did Karli.

The old Finn picked up Piruusi's chamber pot and Shef's mug, dipped the steaming fluid out, held it out to Shef. He recoiled, pulling his hand away. An outburst of angry Finnish from both the Finns. Then old Pehto took Shef's pot and Piruusi's mug, and did the same action for him. Piruusi took it, held it up, and deliberately drank a third.

"Remember what I told you," said Hund quietly. " 'Among the wolves . . .' I think this is to show trust. You drink what went through him, he drinks what went through you, you share your visions." Piruusi clearly caught the sense of what the little leech had said, nodded vigorously.

Shef saw Karli and Pehto exchanging mugs, realized he was committed. Deliberately, he lifted the mug, controlled a reflex to gag at the strong animal smell, drained a third of it. Sat down again, drained another third. Paused ritually, drained it to the dregs.

This time his soul left faster, as if it knew what to do. But though it sped away, the journey this time did not take it to a different climate and a higher sun. It went into the dark. The dark of some poor village; Shef had seen them many times, in Norway, in England, in the Ditmarsh. All much the same, one miry street, a huddle of buildings, houses in the center, on the outskirts, on the edge of the surrounding forest, barns and byres and sties.

He was inside a barn. People there, kneeling in a row on the bare ground. Shef realized from his own upbringing what they were doing. They were taking the Christian communion, the body and blood of their god, who had once been his god. Yet Father Andreas would never have countenanced this miserable procedure, in a barn piled with sacks, only two candles burning. Nor would Shef's stepfather Wulfgar. To him, the Mass was an occasion to count your tenants, be sure all were in place, and woe betide the villager who was not! It was public. This seemed almost secret.

The priest was a thin man whose face seemed to have known much hardship, and Shef did not recognize him. But following him, holding the vessel of wine to follow the makeshift dish of wafers—that was Erkenbert the deacon. Only a deacon, and so not fit to celebrate the Mass. Nevertheless participating. And that was wrong too, for his masters, the monks of York, would also not have let one of theirs participate in such a huddled and tawdry ceremony.

The celebrants were slaves, Shef realized. Or more strictly, thralls. They had the collars round their necks, most of them. All those who did not were women. Poor women, old women. That was the way the Christian church had begun, Shef seemed to remember. Among the slaves of Rome, and the outcasts.

Some of the communionists looked up in fear, hearing heavy feet and loud voices outside. Shef's view shifted. Out there, in the village street, a dozen angry men were approaching, talking loudly to each other. They had thick Swedish accents, like Guthmund's. True Swedes then, from the Swedish heartland.

"Taking my thralls from their work!" shouted one of them.

"Getting the women in there, and who's to know what happens next with their love-feast!"

"We'll teach them their place. And the priestling with them! He should have a collar on by rights."

The one in the lead rolled a sleeve above a brawny arm. He carried a heavy leather strap. Shef's own back twinged in memory.

As the Swedes came to the door of the temporary church, two shapes moved out from the door-posts. Armored men, with helmets, cheek-flaps. In their hands they carried short pikes, though they had swords belted on as well.

"Have you come to the church to pray?" said one of them.

"*If you have, you will not need that strap,*" *said the other.*

The Swedes hesitated, began to spread out. They were not armed except for knives, obviously not expecting resistance, but they were big men, angry, used to command, twelve of them, six to one. They might just try a rush.

From somewhere in the night a voice barked an order and round the corner of the barn came a double file of armored men, marching along, to Shef's surprise, with their feet all moving at the same time, a thing he had never seen. The voice barked again and they stopped all at once, again, and they turned to face the Swedes. A pause, no further order, and the front rank stepped forward, one-two-three, halting with their pike-points almost touching the leading Swede's breast. They stood, impassive.

From the rear strolled Bruno, the German Shef had met at Hedeby. As usual he seemed amused, affable. He carried a sheathed sword in one hand, drew it out a few inches, thrust it back.

"*You can come into the church, you know,*" *he said.* "*We would like you to. But you have to behave, mind. And if you thought you could see who was there and maybe take it out on them later—*" *His voice hardened.* "*I wouldn't like that. Someone called Thorgisl did that, not so far away.*"

"*He was burnt in his house,*" *said one of the Swedes.*

"*Yes. Burnt to ashes. But, you know, not one of his household was harmed and all his thralls escaped. It must have been the hand of God.*"

Bruno's good cheer vanished suddenly. He threw the sheathed sword on the ground, stepped forward to the leading man, the one still holding the strap.

"*When you go home, pig, you will say, 'Oh, they had weapons and we had not.' Well, you have a knife, pig, and I have one too.*" *A flicker, and Bruno was holding a long straight single-edge with a brass hilt.* "*Oh, and look, you have a strap. So why don't we just strap our wrists together, and I'll teach you to dance!*"

Bruno stared up at the big man, started to reach for his arm, face working like Cuthred's. But the big Swede had had enough. He said something no-one could catch, backed away, away down the dark street. The others trailed after him, their voices raised in defiance only at a safe distance. Behind them song pealed suddenly from the barn that was now a church. Shef did not recognize the mangled Latin words or the tune, but the German Ritters straightened even tauter, began to sing as well. Vexilla regis prodeunt . . . "The battle-standards of the King advance . . ."

And in a room, not so very far away, an earthly king, with a golden coronet on his long fair plaited hair, listening to a crew of men, richly dressed but carrying strange things, rattles and dried horse penises and polished skulls.

"*. . . no respect for the gods,*" *they were shouting.* "*Bad luck for the* *country. Christians wandering free and never put down. The herring gone and a poor harvest and now the snow earlier than any man has ever known. Act or go the way of foolish King Orm!"*

The king raised a hand. "What must I do?"

"Make the great sacrifice. The true sacrifice at Uppsala. Not nine oxen and nine horses and nine dogs, but all the worst of your realm. All the poison. Ninety men and ninety women you must hang on the sacred tree, and more to bleed on the plain outside. And not old broken slaves bought cheap, but the evildoers. Christians, and witches, and warlocks, and Finns, and the cheating priests of the Asgarth Way! Hang them high and earn the gods' favor. Leave them, and we will look again along the Eiriksgata." The Way of the One King, Shef remembered from Hagbarth. The road every would-be king of the Swedes had to travel, to expose himself to challenge. This one must have traveled it.

"Very well," the king's voice rumbled. "Now here is what I will do . . ."

Outside his palace again, Shef saw the bulk of the great heathen temple at Uppsala, rising in jagged layer above layer, dragon-heads at every corner, fantastic carvings from the age of the mythic kings on its door. And outside that, the holy oak tree where the Swedes had come to sacrifice for a thousand years. Things swayed creaking on the branches. Men, women, dogs, even horses. They hung there till they rotted and dropped, eye-sockets empty, bared teeth grinning. Over the whole place lay the holy stench.

And Shef was back in the tent, eye clearing. This time he did not jump up, for the weariness and horror on him.

"What you saw?" asked Piruusi. He too looked drawn, as if he had seen something he did not want to, but he was intent as well.

"Death and danger. To me, to you. From the Swedes."

Piruusi spat on Pehto's floor. "Always danger from the Swedes. If they find us. Maybe you see that too?"

"If I see it close, I will tell you."

"You need piss again?"

"Not again."

"Yes again. You great—great *spamathr*. Drink what went through our *spamathr*."

What was that in English, Shef wondered vaguely. A man would be a *wicca*, a woman a *wicce*. A cunning one. It rhymed with pitch and flitch, a flitch of bacon. Like a halved human hanging in a smoke-house.

He struggled to his feet again, stood over the bowl.

* * *

The last two things he had seen had been "now," he knew. Not "here" in the sense of by the Finnish wizard's tent, but "here" in the world. His spirit had traveled only in place.

Where he was this time was neither "here" nor "now," not in the same way. He was in a different world. It felt as if he was underground in some lightless place, but there was glimmering light from somewhere. He seemed to be walking over an immense arching bridge, with a noisy river running below. Walking down the arch now, to something blocking the way. Not a wall. A lattice, really. It was the Grind-wall that blocked the road to Hel. Strange, that "grind" should mean that and also the death of the whales.

There were faces pushed up against the lattice, watching him, faces he did not wish to see. He walked on. As he had feared, the first one was Ragnhild's, twisted and hating, spitting out bitter words at him, shaking the lattice as if to get at him. That lattice would not be moved by any human hand, of dead person or alive. Her breast dripped thick blood.

Beside her was the little boy, eyes wondering. He did not seem to hate or to recognize Shef. He twisted away suddenly from a third figure, reaching out to grasp him, hold him to a skinny bosom. The old queen Asa, a rope round her neck.

What have these to tell me, Shef wondered. That I killed them? I know that.

The ghosts were backing away from the grille, reluctantly and angrily, as if compelled. Someone else was coming, another woman. Shef recognized a worn face from which he had brushed snow two mornings before, Godsibb, who had died unnoticed. Her face was tired still, but less lined than he remembered, more peaceful. She wanted to speak. Her voice was like a bat's squeak, and he bent forward to listen.

"Go on," it said. "Go on. I am here, in Hel, from following you. I would have been anyway. If I had not followed you I would have been a slave here—a slave to those." She nodded at the retreating ghosts of the two queens. "I am spared that."

The voice faded, and the wall, and the bridge, and the darkness. Shef found himself once more sitting in the tent, tears rolling down his cheeks. Though the vision had seemed to take no time to him, he was the last to wake again. The others looked at him, Hund with concern and Karli with fellow-feeling. The two Finns seemed pleased, satisfied, as if his emotion proved him human, of the same flesh as themselves.

Slowly Shef rose, muttered a few words, picked up his lance from by the tent-flap. Frost glinted on its tip, yet the weight of it seemed to steady his nerves. The three walked out into the freezing night and the dark birchwoods.

As they crunched through the snow towards the fire and the sentry's challenge, Shef said to the others, "We must bury Godsibb and the others properly, not burn them or hang them in a tree. We will dig beneath the fires where the ground has been warmed. Take stones from the stream-bed and make a cairn."

"Does that do the dead any good?" asked Hund.

"I think so."

CHAPTER TWENTY-SEVEN

Two nights and a day later, the party stood ready to move on, on a bright windless day, in light snow. Shef would willingly have assembled them all and set off the day before, but Hund had vetoed it.

"Some of us are too weak," he said sharply. "Hurry them on and you will find more of them not waking up in the morning, like Godsibb."

Shef, haunted by the memory of her peering through the lattice of Hel-gate, gave way unwillingly. Yet even as he hauled stones out of the freezing stream-bed for her cairn, watched by interested but disbelieving Finns, he thought to himself, she said "Go on."

"I have to get out of this wasteland," he had told Hund, trying to get some urgency into him. "I told you, I saw the warriors round Hedeby. It may have fallen by now, and the Ragnarssons will be richer and stronger. At the rate we're going, Sigurth will be King of all Denmark by the time we are there."

"And is it your duty to stop him?" Hund looked at his friend and reconsidered. "Well, maybe it is. But you cannot stop him from here. We will just have to move on as fast as we can."

"Do you think these visions of mine are true?" Shef asked him. "Or is it just the drink that does it, as beer and mead make men think they are mightier than they are? Maybe all my visions—maybe Vigleik's visions and all the things the Way sees, maybe they are just some kind of delusion, some kind of drunkenness."

Hund hesitated for a while before replying. "That could be," he admitted. "I will tell you one thing, Shef. That fly killer mushroom, the red one with the white spots on it, that men crush and put on the walls to keep insects off, you would not eat that by accident. But there are other things like it that sometimes grow in the corn, get reaped with it. Maybe find their way into the bread. Or the porridge. Especially if the corn has been left damp in store."

"It's always damp in store in England," said Shef. "So why doesn't everybody have these visions all the time?"

"Maybe they do, but dare not speak. But more likely you are especially sensitive to such things. You drank no more than Karli or the Finns last night, but it seemed to affect you for much longer. And then, maybe because you are affected by such things, the gods send themselves to you. Or maybe the gods have given you this weakness for their own purpose."

Shef, always impatient with speculation which could not be settled one way or the other, shook the thought off. Concentrated on hustling everyone into action, even on the rest day Hund had decreed.

So, their dead buried, a supply of cooked meat in every pack, they mustered to travel onwards. Remembering what he had seen on his soul-flight, Shef led them confidently to the lake through the birches. It was where he thought, stretching away as far as the eye could see, long and narrow, a natural water-road. Still unfrozen—but not for long as the chill of autumn gave way to winter.

Yet they had no boats. Shef had had the idea of making light boats from bark, as Brand had said the Finns did. A little experiment proved that none of Shef's party had the faintest idea how it was done. The Finns who sometimes skied by, keeping an eye on the visitors, shrugged uncomprehendingly if appealed to. Many in Shef's party were skilled craftsmen, who could—given time—have built anything up to a complete ship from trunks and planks. By the time that was done, they would all have starved.

They plodded on on foot, keeping to the birches as long as they could, for shelter from the wind and the drifting snow. Another day's travel and the wood came to an end with the lake, leaving only the immense level moor stretching out before them, now covered in snow. Nineteen pairs of eyes turned to Shef as he contemplated the prospect. All but Cuthred's showed doubt and hesitation.

Silently Shef gave orders to camp again in the kindly woods, light fires and cook their already-dwindled supplies. He waved at the Finn who seemed never to be too far away, like the wolves, and said to him firmly, "Piruusi. Bring Piruusi."

The headman skied eventually out of the dark, as untroubled by the snow and wind as if it had been a spring day in Hampshire, and settled down enjoyably to a long night of bargaining.

The real solution was to turn everyone in Shef's party into expert skiers, make skis, and set off to the Way-College mining station which, if Piruusi could be trusted—and on this he probably could—was maybe sixty, maybe a hundred miles downstream. Again, they would all have starved long before that could be achieved. In the end, and after arguing himself hoarse, Shef settled for as many pairs of spare skis as the Finn camp could provide, together with four reindeer sleighs and their drivers to take the rest. It cost Shef his second gold arm-ring, another twenty silver pennies, and four good iron wood-axes. It might have cost more if not for an intervention from Cuthred.

"Make iron yourself?" Shef asked, as they haggled over axes.

Piruusi signed a vehement no.

"What you cut with before the Norse-folk come, then?" Shef went on.

"They cut with these," said Cuthred from his place by the fire. From inside his jacket he produced a stone axe, a worked flint too big even for Cuthred's powerful hands. An axe to be used by a giant, a gift, seemingly, from Echegorgun.

Fear showed in Piruusi's eyes as he looked at it, and remembered the strange powers these pathetic foreigners were in league with. He ceased to haggle, came quickly to an agreement. The next morning, sleighs and skis arrived, and Shef began the still-laborious process of deciding who should do what, who was the strongest, the likeliest to learn. He was careful not to let only his weakest ride in the sleighs, for those carried his reserves of cash, gold and silver. He had been careful also never to let the Finns see how much he had. Drink-brother he might be to Piruusi, even piss-brother if there were such a term: none of that, he was sure, would shield Piruusi from giving in to temptation.

The early coming of winter had surprised but not particularly alarmed the Way-College's mining station deep inside Swedish Finnmark. There were a dozen men there and half that number of women, four priests of the Way, apprentices and hired workers. They had good supplies and plenty to keep them occupied. During the summer they dug the ore, during the winter smelted it and made it into trade products, pigs of iron or such things as half-finished axe-heads, which could be threaded on bars and moved in bulk. They had built their work-station at a point where they had good communications at all times, by water down the river when it was unfrozen. After that they shipped metal down, by ski and sleigh over a plain road once the ice came. They were well-stocked for the winter in food and fuel. Indeed, they spent much of their time in winter burning charcoal in the birch and pinewoods that began to grow out of the moor as it sloped down towards the sea.

When apprentice Egil first called out to him that strangers were coming from the west, Herjolf the senior of the priests was, again, surprised but not alarmed. They must be Finns, he assumed. There was no-one else there. He would soon find out what they wanted. Meanwhile he ordered work to cease and the men to arm themselves quietly, many with the new crossbows that had come out of England the year before. The Swedish steel made these, he was sure, the best weapons known in the world. Far better than the English example his friend Hagbarth priest of Njörth had given him as a model.

His men covered him, most of them keeping out of sight, as he watched the black dots sweeping across the snow. Not Finns, after all. Some of the skiers were passable, some astonishingly inept, but even the best of them did not have the easy grace of the Finns. Yet the sleighs must belong to Finns, and they were being driven well, if as sedately as if they were taking a crowd of old grandmothers to a funeral.

Herjolf's expression of doubt turned to incredulity as the leading skier put on speed, away from the others, and hissed up to him. Eyes red-rimmed from the snow glare looked at him out of a wilderness of untrimmed beard.

"Good day, Herjolf," said the apparition. "We have met. I am Thorvin priest of Thor, like yourself. I would show you my pendant if I could get it out, and my white tunic if it were not deep under my skins. But I call on you as a Way-fellow to help us. We have done the Way good service, and come a hard journey to find you."

As the sleighs and the slower skiers swept in, or crept in, Herjolf called to his men to put their weapons down and come to help. The wayfarers climbed stiffly out of the sledges where they had been loaded, took out packs, looked round in relief. One of the skiers seemed to chaffer with the Finnish sleigh-drivers, in the end paid them off and walked hobbling over as they swung away, cracking their whips and racing off in the wild style Shef had forbidden for the last three vexing days of travel.

"This is Shef Sigvarthsson," said Thorvin, introducing the one-eyed man. "You have heard many stories of him."

"Indeed I have. Now tell me, Thorvin. What are you all doing here?

And where have you come from? And what do you expect me to do now?"

"We have come from the coast of Norway," said Shef. "We are going down to the coast of Sweden, where we mean to take ship for England. Or, it may be, for Denmark. It depends on what news you can give us."

Hagbarth the Njörth priest appeared at Herjolf's elbow. Shef looked at him with weary surprise. They had not met since Shef had fled from Kaupang. Yet if Hagbarth could appear at Hedeby on the business of the Way, it was natural to find him somewhere else, even here a hundred miles inland. Njörth-priests were favoured errand-runners. Shef wondered what had happened to Hagbarth's ship, the *Aurvendill* which had carried him from Hedeby to Kaupang.

"There is no shortage of news," he said. "Whether you will want to go on to Denmark, or to England, once you have heard it is another matter. It seems to me that your arriving in Hedeby, and then in Kaupang, started a turmoil that has never ceased since. I hope you have not brought more with you."

"We will go on as soon as we can," said Shef. "And you will remember, Hagbarth, that it was not my wish to go to Kaupang, turmoil or no. It was you who took me there. If you had followed my wishes you would have let me take passage home."

Hagbarth nodded in acknowledgement of the truth of what Shef said, and Thorvin spoke up again. "You will give us shelter for a while, then, Herjolf? We are all followers of the Way, as you will see when we are indoors."

Herjolf nodded also. "One or two of you I could have recognized under any circumstances." He pointed a finger at Udd, who had crawled out of a sledge, looked around him, recognized the chimneys of the iron-working shop and was now standing entranced, staring in at the red glow of the banked fires in the biggest forge he had ever seen.

"That is the one who invented those crossbows you are carrying," said Shef. "A *Skraeling*, he seems, yet some would say he is the man who defeated the king of the Franks and all his lancers."

Herjolf looked at Udd's unimpressive form with a new surprise and respect. "Be welcome, then," he said. "But from the look of you I doubt whether many of you will be fit to travel on soon. Here, look at that one!"

Cuthred, who had skied awkwardly but uncomplainingly for the last three days, was tugging at his woollen breeches and leggings, trying to roll them down. As he did so he swayed, holding himself up only by the effort of his will. Moving to help him Shef suddenly saw a splotch of dark blood soaking through the thick layers of wool.

"It is the disease I told you of," said Hund, stripping away the wool as Shef and Thorvin held the big man up. "See, the cut he got from Vigdjarf. It healed as if it were magic, but now it has broken out again. Come, get him indoors. He will not be fit to move for many days. Not ever, if this place has no store of greenstuffs."

The poor condition Shef's people were in became obvious once they had been taken indoors and the clothes they had worn for weeks on end stripped from them. It was the disease a later age would call scurvy: a disease of long voyages and dried food. The symptoms were obvious. Long-healed wounds opening of their own accord, teeth loosening in the jaws, fetid breath, and over it all a general weakness, lassitude and gloom. It was not unfamiliar to anyone in the North, but they expected to find it in the late spring, when folk had been cooped up in their cabins for months, eating salt herring and stored grain. The cure was light and sun, some said. Fresh food, said others. The two went together, usually. This time, Hund pointed out, there was a chance to know for sure, since there was no chance of light and sun—but leeks, onions, garlic, peas and beans to hand. If the sufferers improved, then food was the cure. Which showed, reasonably enough, that there was something in some kinds of food that there was not in others. One day a true priest of the Way might be able to extract it, dry it and store it, for the benefit of all.

But not this year, as Herjolf pointed out. There was no chance of moving on. When Herjolf, Hagbarth, Thorvin and Hund came to Shef in a body to confront him with the fact, he sat silent for a while. Ever since the first meeting with Echegorgun he had felt a fierce urge to turn, to attack his pursuers, to act instead of reacting. For weeks he had been driven on by desire to get back to the main cogwheels of the action, instead of lurking out on the edges. The desire had been sharpened by the vision he had seen in the shaman's tent, of the Ragnarssons round Hedeby and King Hrorik in the breach of the stockade.

Yet at the same time there was something very tempting in the idea of staying where they were, in the wilds yet under cover, unknown yet not lost. Patiently the priests explained things to him. They had supplies, they could get more. The road was easy to drive in any but the worst weather, or one could take sleigh down the river, once it was firmly frozen. Cultivated farmlands lay not impossibly far away, with surplus of grain and meat and all kinds of stores. No great suspicion would be aroused by the priests of the Way buying more. It might be thought they had miscalculated, or needed the food to trade with the Finns.

"And you can make yourselves useful," added Herjolf. "Your little man Udd is never out of the forge even now, and he knows a great deal. Has learnt it for himself too. Have you seen how he has found to harden steel? He should be a priest of the Way—" Herjolf barked with amusement at the thought of the scrawny Englishman reaching that dignity, then said more soberly, "No, if he were to think of that I would be willing to stand his sponsor. He is talking already of millwheels and devices, of great hammers to pound out the iron by machinery rather than by muscle. If a tenth of what he says is true, his stay will be worth all the supplies it costs us. So stay. Thorvin tells me you are a smith too, and a seeker of new knowledge. You and Udd can think, the rest can burn charcoal or blow the bellows. In the spring, then you can seek your destiny. Hagbarth's ship is laid up here in the boathouse till spring. It will take you on your way faster than any other."

Shef nodded. Beneath the relief, a kind of excitement was growing. Time to think. Time to try things out without the frantic, driving, battle-in-the-morning haste that had always been his fate so far. Time to plan. A chance to move when he was ready and the other side was not, instead of the other way round. Of course they would have a winter to prepare and grow strong too. But then they might not know he was coming.

He remembered the words of Svipdag the prisoner. What were they? "The only man who could get through what waits for you would need an iron skin." They had been spoken in malice and to frighten him, he knew, but there was a proverb in Norse that Thorvin often quoted. "The words of fate will be spoken by someone." Maybe Svipdag had been the emissary of fate. An iron skin. He would see.

Chewing carefully with loose teeth on the whole green pea-pods that Hund had forced upon him, Shef swallowed, nodded again. "We will stay, Herjolf, and I thank you for your offer. And I promise you, no-one here will be idle. Many things will be different in the spring."

Soon chimneys smoked, clangor rang out over the snow, men skied out to cut wood and raise new huts, sledged out iron to pay for food and beer. The passing Finns, wondering, saw unceasing activity when the Norse-folk usually slept.

Far in the south the Ragnarssons, with the head of King Hrorik on a pole as a reminder, marched their army from kingdom to kingdom, demanding the surrender of all the little kings of Denmark, Gamli of Fyn and Arnodd of Aalborg, Kolfinn of Sjaelland and Kari of Skaane.

In Sweden King Kjallak the Strong, brought to the throne by discontent with his peaceful predecessor Orm, consulted with his priests and heard continual reports of the insolence of the German missionaries and their protectors. We cannot defeat them, said village after village. What do we pay our herring-tax for? Come and defend us! And Kjallak agreed, but found it hard to pick a champion who was prepared to meet the Germans' awe-inspiring leader. The time would come to crush them in battle, and also in the spirit, so he told the impatient priests of the great temple at Uppsala.

And in Hamburg the fierce and saintly Archbishop Rimbert heard the same reports with pleasure, and circulated them to his brother prelates, the archbishops of the German lands, sure that destiny lay in the West, not as the fool Pope Adrian thought through some accommodation with the Greekling Emperor and his Popelet. In all the German lands the stories of the bold *Ritters* of the *Lanzenorden* spread among the landless younger sons of aristocratic families, and the recruiting tables were never free of applicants.

In Norway King Olaf Elf-of-Geirstath, whom men were now beginning to call ''the Victorious,'' as they had never done all the days his brother was alive, looked at his retinue of under-kings, of Ringeriki and Ranriki, Hedemark and Uppland and Agdir, and at the newly-cautious embassies from the West, the fierce Rogalanders and the men of the fjords, and wondered where the man was whose luck had so changed his own.

And Godive, now swollen with child, wondered occasionally what had become of the boy she had once known, her first man and her foster-brother.

But far in the North the land lay hidden and peaceful under snow.

CHAPTER TWENTY-EIGHT

The scurvy lifted quickly as Hund forced his patients to eat onions and leeks, peas and beans, some dried, some still relatively fresh from the recent harvest. Hund made careful notes in runic script, saying that he would give the answers to other Ithun-priests. Certainly the answer to this disease lay in food, not in air or light.

With the disappearance of the scurvy went the feelings of gloom and weariness which had beset so many of the party, replaced as if by contrast by a mood of energy and excitement: all necessarily turned inwards, for the wind and the cold increasingly contrived to isolate the little community, except for the muffled sleigh-drivers trading for supplies or bringing back wood from the forest.

When he looked back on the events and the progress of that winter, Shef sometimes found it hard to believe. Sometimes easy. He had noticed already during his brief term of office as jarl of Norfolk, and even briefer term as co-king with Alfred, how little of a busy person's time was spent doing what that person wanted to do. Most time, for most people, was wasted on irrelevancies, on trivialities, on confusion and conflict, all seemingly inseparable from daily life. "It is like," Shef had said to Hagbarth the seaman-priest, "it is like sailing along with a sail tied to the back of the boat, in the water, dragging you back."

"You mean a sea-anchor," said Hagbarth. "Very useful sometimes. In a storm at night when you fear you may be running on shore."

"I dare say," said Shef impatiently. "But think, Hagbarth, think what it's like when you cast the drag off!"

In the little community of perhaps forty souls, the drag was removed. Many of them were simply glad to be alive. Those who had once lived as slaves were disinclined to quarreling or self-assertion. And of the forty a high proportion—perhaps the highest proportion ever assembled in the history of the world under such circumstances—were curious, inquisitive and skilled. The forty included seven priests of the Way, all committed by faith and temperament to the quest for new knowledge. They had ten apprentices between them, all eager young men with their way to make, a way that would be much eased if they could show contributions to new knowledge. There was Shef himself, inventor and builder of the machines that had set the Northern world on a new course. And there was Udd, perhaps the most creative and persistent of all, in spite of his shyness and life's history of low regard.

Even the others made a contribution, Cwicca and Osmod, Fritha, Hama and Wilfi. What they all shared, Shef eventually realized, was belief. They were men who had been raised from the dirt by machinery, who owed everything they had to it. Furthermore, they had seen the pride of the Vikings and of the Frankish lancers fall before them. One might almost say they did not have belief, or faith, but something even stronger, impossible for any skeptic to argue with. They *knew* new machines could be made for new purposes, they were certain that novelty would work. It was impossible in their presence to shrug one's shoulders and say, "that's how it's always been done."

Yet it was something like that which triggered the first major project and innovation of the winter. Large supplies of grain had been brought back from the farms towards the coast, and the bread-starved travelers were eager to have it baked. First it had to be ground. The task was handed over without thought and as a matter of course to the women in the community. Women ground flour. Many slave-women did nothing else.

However, in the spirit of fellowship which joint travel had brought, it was argued that men should take their turn too. In the end Udd was given a pestle, mortar and sack of grain, and told to take his turn at grinding. He ground ineffectively for half an hour, stared at the sack remaining, put his pestle down and went to find Shef.

"Why isn't there a mill to do this?" he protested.

Shef jerked a thumb out at the frozen ground beyond the wooden shutters. "Because the river's frozen, Udd."

"There are other ways to run a mill."

"I know," said Shef carefully, "but are you going to suggest it to Cuthred? Maybe he'd like to take a turn at his old trade? If we had an ox I'd say we could use that for power, but we only have the cows for milking, and no-one will let you use those."

"I told you," said Udd. "We could make a wind-mill."

In other circumstances a busy ruler would have been distracted from the detailed consideration needed by some task or other. In the winter waste, there was nothing else to do. Shef and Udd walked across to the water-mill which the Way-priests had set up, and which they used for half the year, to see what could be done.

Much of what was needed was there already: the two great stone wheels that did the grinding. The thick axle that turned the upper stone and the system of cog-wheels that transmitted power from the river to the wheels. That changed it from horizontal to vertical rotation, following the very latest developments. All that was needed was a new motive force. "Like a big sail, on four arms," said Udd. "There's sail-cloth in the boat-house."

"It won't work," said Herjolf, listening. "The river always flows in the same place. Wind can come from anywhere. I grant you, here it comes mostly from the mountains, the north-west. But if you set it up and the wind changed, it could tear your wheel off its supports."

"I know how to fix that," said Udd with the confidence that came to him when faced with a technical problem. "Think of the way we made the catapults rotate. We put them on small wheels and turned those on a larger wheel. We can do the same thing here. Make the whole mill rotate. It can be trained round by a beam, as we turn the trail of the new mules."

In other circumstances, again, some scoffer would have laughed the matter off. There were no scoffers here. Herjolf hesitated, then said, "Well, let's try it."

Soon most of the community was outside, dismantling the old mill, helping to build the shell of the new one, sent off to the main forge to make the heavy nails and bolts that were needed. Shef, thinking back over the event in later times, noted again how many valuable skills were present among the people there. Many were perfectly familiar with heavy weights, not daunted at all by the process of lifting the mill-wheels and taking them to the new site. Hagbarth, who had lifted and laid many a ship's keel made all of one timber, directed operations. For several days all energies were directed to the mill, even the grinding of the grain put aside by common consent till there was a better way of doing it.

Finally all was in place, and Udd was allowed to slip the retainer catch that had held the wheels from turning. He did so. The wind blew, filled the sails, they turned the vertical wheel that was to turn the horizontal one that was to turn the mill-wheel. Nothing happened except a great straining of timber. Udd slipped the catch back again.

"We need bigger sails," he said.

A day later the process was in full stream, Herjolf rubbing his hands as he thought of the profits that might be made by setting up mills of this kind all over Scandinavia. Nearly all of it country unsuited to water-power, but a ready market for a mill that would grind all year. Priests of the Way, it was their boast, supported themselves by working rather than by claiming tithes and landholdings like the priests and monks of the Christians. There was no objection, furthermore, to priests becoming rich by their knowledge—as long as they shared it.

Yet the success of the first windmill seemed only to whet Udd's appetite. As soon as the first one was working, he was at Herjolf's ear with plans for another: this time, to drive the trip-hammer that he had sketched out for Shef the year before in Kaupang. Herjolf listened dubiously, at first, not hostile, but not able to understand what Udd was proposing.

The appeal was clear enough. Iron, though well-known and well understood everywhere in the Western world, remained if not a precious metal, a valuable one. One reason for the dominance of the Franks' and Germans' armored lancers was the weight of metal they carried. This was a great investment in a world where the peasant's spade characteristically had only an iron tip over a wooden blade, and where many plows as well were little more than iron-shod scratching-sticks. Iron was expensive not because it was hard to find, like gold or silver, but because it took so many man-hours to work. The ore had to be heated again and again and beaten by hand with hammers until the slag was worked out of it, then being smelted in the crude charcoal-burning ovens. The iron of Jarnberaland was the best in the world. Still, it needed working, as did every grade of iron except the very rare pieces taken from fallen thunder-stones. Herjolf had fuel, he had ore. If the hammering time could be cut he would have the more trade-goods in the spring. But how could a turning wheel make a hammer go up and down?

Udd drew his pictures in the snow again, while Shef, called into service as the argument grew heated, translated from English to Norse—Udd's Norse had never reached the technical stage. Finally Herjolf sighed, and agreed to let Udd try. "It's a blessing," he remarked, "that this time he only wants something half the size of the last one."

"A hammer is easier to lift than a mill-wheel," Shef explained. "Udd says he is willing to start with only a light hammer."

"How light?"

"A hundredweight."

Herjolf shook his head and turned away. "Tell him to see Narfi Tyr's priest, the chronicler, and ask him for vellum and a pen. His sketches will be easier to follow if they are in pen and ink, not drawn in the snow. Besides, if what he says is true, in time to come men will fight for a page of them."

Soon, when the wind blew, the trip-hammer pounded, beating out metal at unheard of rates like the never-ceasing hammer of Völund, the lame smith of the gods.

It was Cwicca who was responsible for the next step. Not having a skilled trade, other than playing on the bagpipe and shooting a catapult, he was usually assigned to some repetitive task. One day, struggling with the leather bellows which provided forced draught to the forge, yelled at continually by the smiths not to stop or everything would be ruined, he stepped off the upper handle he had been working with his leg and shouted, "We need a machine to do this as well!"

Converting a trip-hammer to pump a bellows was almost easy. And yet the alteration brought about more change, as if one change was feeding off another. The very much improved flow of air through the ovens which smelted the finished ore raised the temperature very markedly. The smiths said iron went first blue-hot, when it was dangerous because you might put a hand on it without realizing, to red-hot, when it was soft enough to work. Only rarely had they seen iron white-hot, beginning to melt. Though cast-iron had been made, usually by accident and under especially lucky circumstances, the forced-draught bellows made molten iron for castings a possibility.

Underlying all the activity was the threat and fear, or certainty, of war. Shef had consulted Hagbarth and Narfi the priest of Tyr, and following his custom, tried to make a map of where he and his fellows had been. From all that they said, and from his own experience, he was in what looked very much like a trap, more of a trap even than the coast of Norway. From there, if he had had a ship, he could have sailed out into the open sea and tried to make the long passage to the Scottish shore, and then down the east coast to England. Where he was, even if he had free passage in Hagbarth's *Aurvendill*, he would have to make his way out of the gulf between Sweden and the far shore of the Eastern Sea, where the Balts lived, then round Skaane and through the narrows between it and Danish Sjaelland to make his way home.

"How wide is the gap there?" he asked.

"Three miles," said Hagbarth. "That's how old King Kolfinn got rich. Levying tolls. Last I heard, he wasn't likely to be there much longer. If you're right about the Ragnarssons getting rid of Hrorik, there wouldn't be too much left to stop them."

"And where is their famous Braethraborg, the Stronghold of the Brothers?"

"There," said Hagbarth, tapping the map at a spot on the north shore of Sjaelland maybe fifty miles from the narrows. Half a day's sail.

The only other way back to England that Shef could see was to go back to Hedeby and walk across the marshes to the Ditmarsh, and so be back where he started. He would be once more without a ship. And anyway, if his vision was true, and it was confirmed by Hagbarth's definite knowledge that the siege had started, then Hedeby was in enemy hands. Ragnarsson hands. Nothing anyone could imagine was worse than falling into Sigurth Ragnarsson's hands. Shef would rather have died and been hung up in Echegorgun's smokehouse.

So the iron-workers made not only ingots of pig-iron and easily-traded goods like axe-heads. They also, following Udd's direction, made bow after bow of spring-steel, cocking-handles, iron quarrels. Men and women carved wooden parts, set them in piles. Every few days they would turn from that task and assemble them. Shef noted how much quicker it was, say, to make a dozen sets of parts and then assemble them all the same way, instead of following the time-honored procedure of working on one implement till it was done, and then starting the next one. The pile of crossbows grew, well beyond the numbers they had to use them.

"We can always sell them," said Herjolf cheerfully.

"That is looking on the bright side," said Shef.

Of all the innovations Udd had brought, though, none interested Thorvin and the other smiths more than the case-hardened steel. They had borrowed Cuthred's shield repeatedly, testing its powers, and been amazed. Ideas sprang up quickly. Make mail of the strange hard metal. It proved impossible to work, too hard to bend, too hard to fit together. An attempt to take a mail-shirt and case-harden it as one unit produced only an extremely expensive lump of rings half-welded together, the waste of a month's work for a skilled smith, as Herjolf pointed out. Flat plates were relatively easy to make, but useless once made. People did not have flat surfaces to fit them over. The metal seemed to have no use in war except for shields, and even then it had disadvantages. Shields were convex both because missiles tended to fly off such a surface, and—no trivial consideration—because a rounded shield could be carried on the shoulder. No-one, not even Brand or Cuthred, could march all day holding a shield up on his arm alone. Most deaths in battle went to the side whose shield-arms tired first.

The hardened metal, while fascinating, seemed to be practically useless in war. Yet Shef could not shake off the words that Svipdag the prisoner had hurled at him. "The only man who could get through what waits for you would need an iron skin." He knew who would be waiting for him at the Braethraborg. Where was his iron skin? And how to carry it?

Shef found himself talking, often, to Hagbarth. Hagbarth was interested especially in the details of the various new types of ship that Shef had sailed or had encountered. He had nodded consideringly over Ordlaf's design for the English mule-armed "battleships," and pressed Shef again and again for details of the short action with the *Frani Ormr*, a famous craft in her own right, the greatest warship of the North, of the traditional ocean-going type.

"It's no wonder you were outsailed by her," he remarked. "I am not sure even my own *Aurvendill* would have done better. Faster by sail, I dare say. But the more oars you have for foot of keel, the faster you are rowing. In enclosed waters, *Frani Ormr* might be better."

He was interested also in the design of the two-masted *Crane*, about which Shef could tell him a good deal, having helped to dismantle her for planks and parts. King Halvdan's coastal patrol ships were familiar to Hagbarth in any event. He could make a good guess at how one would have been strengthened to take catapult shock. It was the sailing qualities of the two masts that puzzled him. Yet, Shef assured him, the *Crane* had sailed, and sailed well. The *Norfolk*, on the other hand, had been something of a tub.

"Now we've got the idea of putting the mules on wheels, to rotate them," Cwicca said one meal-time. "What we'd really like would be a mule at each end, front and back, high up. But I suppose all that weight high up would make the boat tip over, like, if the wind came from one side. Even the *Norfolk* wasn't very high out of the water."

Hagbarth, listening, snorted beer through his nostrils. " 'Make the boat tip over, like,' " he gasped. " 'Each end, front and back.' It's well for you you're not at sea and the sea-trolls listening. They punish sailors who do not use the proper *haf* words, the words to be said at sea."

"So how would you make a boat like Cwicca said?" asked Shef, ignoring the complaint about sea-language.

"I've been thinking," said Hagbarth, scratching lines in the table with his dagger. "What you want, I think—it's what they did with the *Crane*, but they only did it half way—is a rigid frame for the ship, much more solid than the way we build."

Remembering the way the *Aurvendill* had flexed on her passage from Hedeby to Kaupang, both Shef and Karli nodded.

"Then you would want to build up the sides, like this." Hagbarth drew on.

Studying the plan on the table, Shef said thoughtfully, "What you have there looks to me, in a way, like one of your own ships with a second one built over it."

Hagbarth nodded. "Yes, you could do that. A conversion."

"So we could convert, for instance, your *Aurvendill*, out there in the boathouse. Extend the keel and rivet it—we have plenty of hard steel—put in a frame, build up the freeboard, as you call it, ballast her heavy and put mules on fighting platforms bow and stern."

Hagbarth cried out in honest pain. "Not the *Aurvendill*! The most beautiful sailer in the north!"

"Though not as fast as the *Frani Ormr*," Shef pointed out.

"If you did all that," said the unnoticed Edtheow, who had been staring grimly at Hagbarth's dagger marks on the polished table, "you could put iron plates all over it and really weigh it down."

Shef stared at her open-mouthed.

"The words of fate will be spoken by someone," remarked Thorvin, yet again.

In the end Hagbarth was sent out on skis while work started on *Aurvendill*. He had been reconciled to the idea, and confessed that he would have been fascinated to see it tried on anyone else's ship. He could not bear, though, to watch them slice into his own. After the main sawing was done, he promised, he would watch and assist. Till then, he would stay away.

Cuthred volunteered to escort him. Of all the men and women there he had played least part: refusing even to look at the mills being erected, taking little interest in the forge. He lay abed a long time with his leg-wound open, as if his body were taking revenge for the way he had overridden its demands during the berserk fit. When it healed, he took to skiing alone, quickly becoming expert, often staying out all day. When Shef asked him once whether he felt hungry or thirsty out in the waste, he replied, "There is food out there, if you know how to get it."

Shef wondered. Echegorgun had trailed them across the mountains to Piruusi's camp. Could he have followed further? The Hidden Folk seemed to be able to go where they pleased in the wastelands. Cuthred had said once that there were more of them than true people realized. Maybe he was meeting Echegorgun, or even Miltastaray, in the wasteland. The Hidden Folk liked him. Hardly anyone else did, though some among the women were sorry for him. At least he was a good protector for Hagbarth, and Hagbarth was not one of the men who were likeliest to offend him, unlike Karli, now paired with Edith, or Ceolwulf, who seemed to remind Cuthred of what he had once been.

Yule came, with roast pork and blood sausage to add to their usual fare, with tale-telling and songs from the Way-priests of their mythical stories. The deep winter came after it, with such howling winds that the mill-sails had to be taken down and stored for a while, and thick snow drifting. The small community, with ample food and fuel, blankets and down-lined bags, ignored it. Shef wondered again at the good cheer on every face, but not for long.

"It's cold up here, right enough," said Cwicca. "But if you think what it was like back in Crowland in the fens, slaving for the black monks! Lucky to have a blanket at all, no food but porridge and not much of that, living in a hut with an earth floor and that soaked through from Michaelmas to Easter. And nothing to look forward to but Lent! No, I've never passed a happier winter."

One thing that added to the gaiety was yet another of Udd's experiments. He had never forgotten the total failure of his attempt to make winter ale by steaming water off rather than freezing it off. Winter ale could be had now for the trouble of putting a bucket outside, but Udd persevered. If the strength in the drink was not left in the heated ale, he reasoned, it must have flown off with the steam. Slowly he experimented. Catching the steam. Enclosing the heated pot. Running a pipe, a copper pipe for its ductility, out from the heat into the cold, to liquefy the steam more quickly. Catching the end product. Repeating the process with ever tighter seals and more careful catchment. In the end, Udd had something which he was prepared to offer to the others. They tasted gingerly, curiously, appreciatively.

"A good drink for a cold day," said Osmod. "Not as good as mulled winter ale, I reckon, but that's more natural, isn't it. This has still some of the reek of the forge about it. 'Burnt ale,' we'll call it."

"It might be better to use wine," said Udd, though he had tasted wine no more than twice in his life.

Cuthred said nothing, but took a flask with him next time he skied alone into the snow.

* * *

The day came at last when they were ready to roll the remade *Aurvendill* out of the boathouse into a backwater of the river, now beginning to flow stronger under the ice, and to show signs of break-up.

"Should we not put something on the rollers, for luck?" asked Shef.

Hagbarth looked at him sharply. "There are some who do that," he said. "Blood usually, a sacrifice to Ran, the troll-goddess in the deeps."

"I don't mean that. Udd, have you a small keg of burnt ale? Put that under the keel. As she rolls forward, she'll crush it."

Hagbarth nodded. "And then you must give her a new name." He patted the stem-post. "She is my *Aurvendill* no longer. That is a star, you know. Made from the frostbitten toe of a giant which Thor flung into the sky. A good name for a fast ship. She is that no more. What will you call her?"

Shef said nothing till the men were at the drag-ropes, ready to pull her out of the shed in which they had worked for so long. Then, as they heaved together and the strong brown liquid splashed on the keel, he called out, "I name you *Fearnought!*"

Fearnought slid slowly down the runway and crunched through the thinning ice, to lie at rest on her ropes.

She seemed a strange craft. They had cut, spliced and riveted her keel with the stoutest wood and steel they could contrive. On the extended keel they had fitted frames every few yards, and to these frames, against the usual practice, which was to use sinew, they had nailed the planking. The *Aurvendill's* original planks now formed only the upper part of her sides. Stouter ones, split from pine-trunks, held her lower down. At prow and stern fighting platforms disfigured her previously clean lines, copies of the ones Shef had seen on Hedeby walls. Two new-built mules squatted on each. To balance their cumbrous weight the *Fearnought* was built deep and round, with heavy ballast in what was now a capacious hold. The fighting platforms had been extended to half-decking, giving some shelter for the crew underneath them, more than the skin awnings which were all Viking crews normally had, even for the Atlantic.

On two matters Hagbarth had had his way. The *Fearnought* remained a one-master, though with her greater bulk the sail had been extended outwards, though not upwards, giving her almost half as much sail area again. And the iron plates that were to armor her sides and the rotating mules were stored in the hold, to be fitted only as needed.

"I wouldn't like to try the long open-sea passage to England in her," said Hagbarth, careful to speak well away from the ship in case his words brought bad luck. "She makes the tubbiest knorr look graceful, and once you put the plates on she's worse."

"She's not designed to reach England," said Shef. "If she gets us through the narrows and round to the Frisian shore, she'll have done her job."

Just past the Braethraborg will do, thought Hagbarth, but did not say the words. He himself had no intention of risking that dangerous passage. He had a draft on Shef and Alfred's treasury for the price of the *Aurvendill*, and hoped only to collect it.

Shef wondered, indeed, who he had the right to ask to share his dangers. The English men and women who had come so far with him would continue, hoping to reach home, as would Karli, eager to tell his tales of travel in the Ditmarsh. So would Hund. Thorvin too insisted on going. Hagbarth and his small crew would travel as far as Smaaland in the south of Sweden, showing the landlubbers how to sail the boat as they did so.

As the snow melted and people thought of departure, Cuthred came to see his master.

"Do you want me to travel south with you?" he asked.

Shef stared at him. "I thought we would take you home. To Northumbria."

"There's no-one in Northumbria for me. My king is dead. I do not know if my wife is alive, but even if she is—I am no good to her now. I would rather live here in the waste. There are people here who would take me as I am. People who do not measure a man in only one way."

The terrible bitterness was in his voice again, Shef heard. And yet—he did not dare to let Cuthred go. He was worth a catapult on his own, or a case-hardened breastplate. He would be needed before they won south, of that Shef was sure.

"Do you remember the mill?" he asked. "When I released you from that, you said you were my man."

Cuthred had been a king's champion for much of his life. He understood loyalty and service, and accepted both as lasting to the death.

"See me through the Skagerrak and I will free you to return, to live in the waste, however you wish," said Shef.

Cuthred stared down at the slush. "I will see you through the Skagerrak," he agreed. "And past the Braethraborg. There will be someone waiting for me here."

CHAPTER TWENTY-NINE

The new king of the Swedes, Kjallak, knew well that he had been chosen to succeed his murdered predecessor Orm for one thing only: to cope with the menace of the German Christians, and to a lesser degree the Way-folk now spreading through the country. To return the land of the Swedes, *Sveariki,* to the old ways and the old customs of the priests. Failure, and the priests of Uppsala-temple would choose again.

He laid his plans carefully. A sacrifice had been demanded. A sacrifice he would give them. And it would consist of men and women from all the groups that the Swedes hated and feared: Christians, Wayfolk, Finns and even the *skogarmenn,* the small scattered communities of borderers who lived in the forests or on the moors and paid no taxes.

Chasing Finns in the winter was useless. In the summer it was hard also, because they retired with their reindeer to the deep tundra. There was a time to strike, a time when the Swedes had a natural advantage. In the deep mud of the melting season, when no-one moved if they could avoid it, but when the matchless horses of the Swedish horse-breeders could make their way. Kjallak sent sleigh-loads of forage during the winter to selected places. Picked his men and instructed them carefully. Sent them out, a week before the equinox, in wind and driving sleet.

Shef too had laid his plans. At the equinox, he thought, the ice might have gone from the fast-running river, and conditions would be good to take the *Fearnought* down-stream, on the first stage of the voyage home. His men were arming the ship carefully, stowing her dragon-plates of steel in the hold where they could be unshipped quickly, fitting beckets to the gunwales to hold crossbows and quarrels, chipping rocks for the mules.

As he watched, Shef realized that a group of Finns was heading towards them. They moved clumsily without their skis. There was still some snow on the ground, but much of it had churned to slush or mud. The Finns looked graceless, like birds with clipped wings. Yet they were often enough about the station, coming in to trade or to examine what went on. One of Herjolf's priest-companions was a devotee of the goddess Skathi, the ski-goddess of the mountains. He spoke the Finnish tongue and often traveled with them, learning their lore. Shef saw him go to meet them and turned back to the loading.

A while later, he found Ottar, Skathi's-priest, at his shoulder, and with him the Finn, Piruusi, a look of sullen anger on his face. Shef looked from face to face, wondering.

"He says the Swedes attacked his encampment two days ago," said Ottar. "Many men on horses. They had not seen them come because the snow was melting. Many Finns were killed. Some taken."

"Taken," repeated Piruusi. "One Swede got drunk, fell from horse. We catch him. He tell us, Finns to go to the temple. Temple at Uppsala. Hang there on a tree in honor of Swedish gods."

Shef nodded, still wondering why he was being told. "He wants you to rescue them," said Ottar.

"Me! I know nothing of Uppsala." But then Shef fell silent. He remembered the three visions he had had in Piruusi's tent. Of them all, he had thought most about the first, his old enemies the Ragnarssons seizing power and blocking his path. Yet he had seen the king too, the new king, threatened by his priests into promising a proper sacrifice, not the cheap disposal of surplus slaves that the Swedes had carried out for many years. And the Christians, they had been in it too.

"Did he say anything about Christians, your Swede?"

Piruusi's face lightened, he said something in Finnish. "He says he knew you were led by the spirits," said Ottar, translating. "Christians too are to go to the great oak. And the men of the Way, or so Piruusi says."

"We've had no trouble," said Shef.

"We live far up-stream. And in any case, we aren't all here."

Shef felt his heart lurch at the correction. Thorvin had gone to the farm-town thirty miles off, while the snow was still good for sleighs, taking with him Cwicca, Hama and Udd, to trade iron for food. They had not returned. If they had been taken too . . . Shef realized with surprise that of them all, Cwicca who had saved his life by pulling him from Ivar's drowning embrace, Thorvin who had taken him in as a wandering nobody, of them all, the one whose fate most concerned him was Udd. If he went, no-one could replace him. Many plans would die at birth without his inspiration.

"Do you think the Swedes might have got them?" he asked.

Ottar waved at the road from the east, from downstream. Riders were visible on it, spurring as fast as they could through the heavy mud. "I think someone is coming to tell us," he said grimly.

The news was as they had expected. The town lay in ashes, surprised at dawn and burnt to the ground. The raiders had killed every man, woman or child they met, but seized some to herd away with them on spare horses. For capture they had selected those with the pendants of the Way, or youths, or maidens. In the confusion little had been made out as to why the Swedes had attacked the town. But some said they had called out "*skogarmenn! skogarmenn!*" as they had killed. Woodmen, men of the forest, outlaws. All the same thing. Thorvin the priest had certainly been taken, been seen led away. A gap-toothed man had also been recognized, who must be Cwicca. No-one could remember seeing anyone who might have been Udd. But that was entirely probable, Shef reflected. Even people in the same room as Udd often did not see him. Till it came to iron and steel, to metal and contrivances, the little man was made to be ignored.

"What is the day of the sacrifice?" Shef asked.

Gnawing his beard, Herjolf replied, "The day the Holy Oak, the Kingdom Oak as they call it, the day its buds first show green. In ten days. Maybe twelve."

"Well," said Shef, "we shall have to get our men back. Or try at least."

"I agree with you," said Herjolf. "And so would every priest of the way, even Valgrim, if he were still alive! What the Swedes have sent us is a challenge. If they hang up our priests in their sacred clothes, with the rowan-berries at their belts and the pendants round their necks, then we will lose every convert we have ever made among the Swedes. And further afield, when the news spreads."

"Ask Piruusi what he will do," Shef said to Ottar. All that a man can, came the reply. The Swedes had taken his youngest and favorite wife. Piruusi's account of her charms was vivid, made it plain that he found her, like Udd, irreplaceable.

"Good. I need Hagbarth too. Tell him, Herjolf. This is Way business now. And another thing. I am going to fly a banner."

"With what device?"

Shef hesitated. He had seen many banners now, and knew the power they had on the imagination. There was the dreaded Raven Banner of the Ragnarssons, had been the Coiling Worm of Ivar. Alfred flew the Gold Dragon of Wessex, left over from the Rome-folk. Ragnhild's device had been the Gripping Beast. He himself had marched to Hastings under the Hammer and Cross, to unite Way-folk and English Christians against the army of the Pope. What should he choose this time? The device of Rig, the ladder he wore round his neck? No-one would recognize it. A hammer and a broken shackle, for freedom? This time he was not coming to free slaves, but to rally border-people and outlaws.

"You will fly the Hammer, surely," pressed Herjolf. "Not the Hammer and Cross, as you once did. There are no Christians here. Only the Germans and their converts, no friends of ours."

Shef decided. He still held the lance he had taken from Echegorgun, the lance that the troll-man had taken from Jarl Bolli of the Tronds. "I will have an upright lance as my own device," he said. "With a hammer across it, for the Way."

Herjolf pursed his lips. "That will look too much like a cross, for my liking."

Shef stared at him. "If I am to fight a king," he said, "I will be a king. You heard the king's order. Send me all our needlewomen, and do it at once."

As Herjolf walked away, Shef spoke quietly to Cuthred. "We will not leave till tomorrow morning. Go out tonight. No chance of help from the Huldu-folk at Uppsala, I suppose? Too far from the moors and mountains. Just the same, word can be passed. Maybe there are other half-troll families in the north besides Brand's. See to it. Make your farewells."

Shef thought to add, "and see you return," but curbed the words. If Cuthred wanted to desert, he would. All that held him now was pride, and that was not to be insulted.

Cuthred stood unspeaking in the prow of the *Fearnought* next morning, in full mail, with sword, shield, spear and helmet. He looked like a king's champion again, except for his eyes, weary, red-rimmed.

The ship was crowded with men, and women too. Only half a dozen had been left at the mining station. Priests, apprentices, Englishmen, Englishwomen and Finns were all crowded in together, fifty and more. They could never have managed to do so if the ship had needed to be rowed or sailed. But the snow-melt whirled her away without human effort, fast as a racing horse. Hagbarth at the tiller had only a lookout on the yard for ice, and men at the prow with oars to boom off floating debris.

All the way down the stream they saw the signs of devastation, burnt farms, burnt villages. Men called from the banks as they saw the standard flying, were hailed, told to rig their boats and follow. By the time the *Fearnought* reached the sea, a small armada of four- and six-oared boats trailed in her wake. At the sea itself, the fishing villages of Finnmark yielded larger craft. Shef reorganized, commandeering the largest boats, filling them with men from the smallest.

"You can't take them very far like this," protested Hagbarth. "They can't carry enough water for one thing. No, don't tell me, I know. Obey orders. You have a plan."

As the *Fearnought* and her tail of small craft nosed down the Finnish Bight, as the Swedes called the deep gulf between Swedish Finnmark and the land opposite, they sighted a cluster of small islands. Piruusi, hitherto silent, came to Shef and pointed.

"Finns on those islands," he said. "I cross sometimes, on ice. Sea-Finns."

Shef motioned to Ottar, put him, Piruusi and a clutch of his Finnish followers into a boat, told them to bring on every boat and man they could. They pressed on under light sail, waiting for the challenge that must come from King Kjallak's coastguards.

Ali the Red, skipper of the *Sea-bear*, patrolling the seas towards the Finnish Aland Isles, saw the strange sail bearing down on him, and approached cautiously. He had heard tales of strange and strangely-armed vessels, and had no mind to take needless risks. The rag-tag of sails behind, he scanned and dismissed. Fishing boats of the broken men, scavengers only. In any case, as they saw his striped sail and that of his consort, he saw them wear in unison and scud away. But what were they doing on the strange ship? The knorr miscegenated with a Frankish cog? Trying to flee as well?

"She's in range for a long shot," snarled Osmod. The former captain of halberdiers was in a state of barely-controlled rage, had been ever since he realized his long-time friend and comrade Cwicca was facing a Swedish noose, as sacrifice to Frey and Othin.

"Stand away from the mule," Shef ordered. "Get down in the hold, all of you. Hagbarth, you too. Now, Osmod, you're in charge. Turn this ship around and sail away, in flight."

Osmod gaped. "But I can't sail a ship."

"Yes you can, you've seen them do it often enough. Now you do it. Karli, Wilfi, and me, we're your sail-crew. Cuthred, take the steering oar."

"Well," said Osmod uncertainly. "Which way's the wind. Cuthred, turn the front bit away from the wind, um, to the left. Karli, you take that end of the yard, and Wilfi, that end, and turn it round so the wind is behind it. Christ, Thor, I mean, what happens next?"

While Hagbarth held his hands over his eyes, the *Fearnought* lumbered into flight, the very image of an undermanned trader on a maiden voyage. Watching, Ali grinned into his red beard and brought his two ships slanting expertly across to intercept.

"Get your heads down," ordered Shef. "Forget the mules. One crossbow each and another to hand."

He waited till the *Sea-bear* was almost alongside, her gunwales lined with fierce bearded faces, spears poised to board, before he gave the word to rise. Anyone can wind a crossbow, as Udd had said two years before. Even easier when they had only to be cocked. At ten yards' range even the most inexpert could not miss, and at ten yards' range the stout iron quarrels went through wood and mail, flesh and bone as if they were so much canvas. As Shef's archers dropped their first crossbows and reached for the second, it was already clear there would be no need for another volley.

Hagbarth stepped from ship to ship trailing a rope, looked at the few instantly demoralized survivors and ordered them to make fast alongside.

"Now the mule," said Shef, looking at the desperately turning consort vessel. "One rock over their heads, Osmod, and tell them to throw their weapons overboard."

A short time later, his fleet now consisting of three strongly manned large craft with dinghies and pinnaces in tow, Shef's armada moved on for the Swedish shore. Behind them, in small boats so loaded their gunwales were within inches of the water, the disconsolate coast-guards surviving argued whether to try for the Aland Islands and the Finns, or the Swedish shore, to face their king's vengeance.

The men of the *Lanzenorden*, for all their prowess, had made few converts among the Swedes, at least among the men and the native-born. The congregations they protected had mostly been drawn from the slaves, Christians when they were brought to the land. Some were Germans, some Frisians or Franks, the majority English and Irish.

The *Ritters* felt little kinship with them. They enjoyed the experience of imposing their will on the Norse who had persecuted them for so long, enjoyed realizing that power was largely a matter of concentration. When a Viking army thousands strong came down on some town or village in the West, of course they seemed superior. When fifty armed and trained Germans appeared in the middle of a Swedish village with a population of two hundred, it was the same story. If the natives ever concentrated against them, it would be a different matter. But there was no loot to be won, it was no-one's responsibility. The *Lanzenorden* wintered in peace, but not in content. The rank and file were bored, forbidden to get drunk or lord it over the handsome Swedish women. Erkenbert the deacon feared his chances of promotion were vanishing, stuck here far from the center of affairs. Bruno the leader fretted alone in his quarters. He had not found the lance of Charlemagne. If it was anywhere it was far away in the north in another country. The God in whom he trusted seemed to have deserted him.

When the frantic knocking sounded on the door of the knights' quarters, they sprang out of their torpor, chessboards flung to the ground. Weapons were seized from walls, men struggled into their armor. Someone opened the door cautiously. A thin shabby figure scrambled in.

"They've taken them," he babbled.

"Taken who?" snapped Bruno, alerted by the uproar. "Who's taken who?"

The fugitive's wits seemed to desert him, faced by hostile looks and bared weapons. Erkenbert stepped forward, spoke in English to the frightened man.

"He is from Hadding," he reported. "The town ten miles off, where we have held Mass. He says that this morning soldiers of King Kjallak came, rounded up all the Christians who have attended our services—they had a list—and took them away under guard. It is said by the Swedes, with great satisfaction, that they are to be sacrificed to pagan idols at the great temple, maybe in five days' time."

"A challenge for us," said Bruno, looking round and grinning. "Isn't that right, boys?"

"A challenge to the holy God," said Erkenbert. "We shall meet it as did the holy Boniface, who smote the great pillar Irminsul of the Saxons unharmed, and converted the pagan Saxons from their unbelief."

"I heard a different story," muttered one of the knights. "I'm a

Saxon myself. But anyway, how are fifty of us going to get a bunch of sacrifices away from the whole assembly of the Swedes? There'll be thousands of them there. And the king, with his housecarls.''

Bruno slapped him violently across the back. ''That's why it's a challenge,'' he shouted. More soberly, he added, ''And don't forget, they believe that things must be done in certain ways. A challenge must be answered. If I challenge the king, he'll have to fight, or put in a champion. This isn't going to be a battle. It will be a show of our strength—of God's will. We'll face them down. Like we've done before.''

His men looked uncertain, but discipline was strong, and faith in their leader even stronger. They began to collect their weapons, packs and bedrolls and horses, working out the march in their heads. Five days. Fifty miles to pagan Uppsala. No trouble, even over muddy roads. But it would be difficult to come at the assembly of the Swedes with any element of surprise. Suspicious, too, that they had been left unharmed, when one might have expected firebrands in the thatch and men outside at dawn. Maybe King Kjallak of the Swedes had thought ahead of them. Was expecting their coming. Had prepared a welcome. The two priests of the mission found a queue at their doors of men waiting to make a confession, and ask for shrift.

CHAPTER THIRTY

As they drew nearer and nearer to Uppsala, Shef felt a mood of foreboding come over him. It should not have. Everything was going as well as anyone could possibly have expected. No resistance on the shore, the fighting men of the Swedes already marched for the assembly and the sacrifice, or so they were told. Guided by boats with lanterns sent out off shore, Piruusi had appeared with a heavy reinforcement of Finns, eager to strike a blow for once at the stronghold of their hereditary enemies. Scores of spare crossbows had been distributed and every man who received one given a short course of instruction and five practice shots—all that were needed to enable a man to load and fire a crossbow of the newest pattern, and hit his target at fifty yards' range. With the Finnish bowmen as a screen and two hundred crossbows behind them, Shef knew he had a force which was at least to be reckoned with, one that would defeat any casual or careless attack. He had had to detach only a dozen men and women to guard the boats and moor the *Fearnought* especially beyond casual reach.

Morale was high, too, borne up by resentment. Also by the cautious welcome they received as they pressed forward—too much of a straggle to be called a march—through the villages of heathen Sweden. Those who were left behind in the villages were women and slaves and the low-born. Many of those, seeing the banner with lance and hammer, took it for some kind of a cross, as Herjolf had feared, and if they were of Christian origin saw it as a liberation. Others saw the Wayman pendants and cautiously joined the party, or volunteered information. Yet others had had friends or relatives snatched for the great sacrifice, and willingly asked for weapons, to help free them. There was a sense of support, of the army growing, not shrinking as so many did on approach to battle.

So why did he feel the foreboding, Shef asked himself. It was because of Cuthred. Shef had some inner presentiment that this matter was not to be decided by pitched battle: that in the end it would come down to a test of champions. Till this time he had relied implicitly on Cuthred, on his strength and skill, but most especially on his uncompromising spirit. Cuthred never had to be encouraged, always restrained. Never till now. But now he was silent, gloomy, without the aura of lurking menace that had always surrounded him.

Jogging along on a commandeered pony, Shef found Hund riding alongside him. As usual, he did not bother to speak, merely waited for Shef's opening.

Speaking quietly, Shef glanced at Cuthred's back ten yards away and muttered, "I fear I have lost my berserk."

Hund nodded. "I had thought so too. Do you think you will have need of one?"

"Yes."

"I remember Brand talking of what makes a berserk. He said they were not men possessed by other spirits, but men who hated themselves. Maybe our berserk—" Hund avoided using his name in case Cuthred heard it "—maybe he has been given some reason not to hate himself."

Shef thought of Miltastaray and the strange remarks Echegorgun had made about the Hidden Folk, their disabilities, and their rare matings. He could see that Cuthred, if he did not think himself a man again, might have been able to think himself a troll.

"I don't want to give him that reason back," he said, "but I would prefer him a bit more like his older self."

Hund produced something from under the long cloak most of the men were now wearing, against the wind and squalls of rain. "It came to me that there might be another thing that makes the berserk. Just as your visions might be caused by something in you, or something in the grain, or something in the Finn's drink, so the berserkergang could be caused by something in the soul—or something in the body. I have talked to the Finns, with Ottar's help. The fly-killer mushroom is not the only one they use. There is this potion too." He showed Shef a flask.

"What is in it?"

"A decoction. Boiling water poured onto another mushroom. Not the red one with the white spots this time, the one that makes the seeing-drink. Nor the other one I know of, the death-cap mushroom, the one—" Hund lowered his voice again "—that looks like a prick.

"There is a third. The Finns call it the tuft-ear mushroom, after the big cat that lives in the forests. It sends men into frenzy, makes berserkers of the mildest." He handed over the flask. "If you need it, take it. Give it to Cuth— to our friend."

Shef took it thoughtfully.

Outside the great temple at Uppsala was a yard, roofed over with thatch but earth-floored, wattle-walled, the rain driving in through every chink. Nine score men and women crowded into it, hands tied into iron rings set into long bars. Given time and effort, a man could break free, untie others. But guards patrolled up and down, clubbing savagely at anyone who shifted, made anything that looked like an attempt at escape. The guards were having more trouble than usual, as they remarked to each other. Not only were there far more for the sacrifice than in living memory. They were not the usual bone-bags, dying by noose or blade only days ahead of death from cold or starvation. That was as it should be, the guards said, aiming blows to break fingers or collar-bones. The gods would have fresh meat for a change. Perhaps the Swedes' ill-luck was caused by the gods having to boil their victims down for soup.

Cwicca, nursing a fractured arm gained when a guard saw him trying to pull the iron ring out of its bar, whispered out of the corner of his mouth to Thorvin next to him. "I don't like the look of Udd."

The little man indeed seemed almost on the point of tears: natural enough, but neither Englishman nor Wayman wanted to give their enemies a chance to mock. He was staring at one of the Swedes, a priest, who had come into the slave pen. It was the custom of the Swedish priests of the temple, of the Kingdom Oak, to taunt and jeer at their captives, believing that their fear and despair were acceptable to the gods. Some said it was a custom set by their ancient king Angantyr. Others said the bastards enjoyed it. Udd's lower lip was trembling as he listened to the Swede's shouts.

"Don't think it will be quick! Don't think you'll get off easy. I have made the sacrifice at this assembly for twenty years. When I was young, then I made mistakes. I let men slide to the gods not knowing they'd gone. Not now! Those I hang, they'll still be awake with their eyes open when the ravens of Othin come to peck them out. How will you feel then, when the raven sits on your head and reaches out its

beak. I've seen them! You'll try to lift your hands, won't you? But I'll
have tied them down.

"And that's not all. Even after you've gone to death, gone to the
gods, what do you think will happen then. You'll sit on clouds with
harps in your hands, you Christians, eh? No! You are slaves here and
you'll be slaves there."

The priest began to sing a sacred song, his voice and rhythm
strangely like Thorvin's. This was where the Way had come from,
Cwicca realized with a flash of insight. From beliefs like this one. But
changed, not made gentle exactly—the Way-followers were as fierce
as any—but without the undercurrent of desperate anxiety that made
the true pagans, the hard-core, so addicted to pain.

> "The thurs who shall have thee is called Hrimgrimnir,
>   Behind Hel's gate your home;
> There the wretched slaves beneath roots of trees
>   Get dogs' piss for drink.
> No other draught shalt thou ever drain . . ."

Udd's head dropped, his face twisted, the pagan priest saw and
broke off his chant with a crow of victorious laughter. As he did so
Thorvin too began to sing, his deep voice carrying on the very tune of
the pagan's, but to a different rhythm:

> "I saw a hall standing, sun-bright it shone,
> Thatched with gold, on Gimli plain,
> There shall the trusty dwell in troops,
> Live for ever in love unfading . . ."

The pagan shrieked with fury, ran down the rows of chained
prisoners towards his rival, shouting curses, a weighted club in his
hand. As he raced past Hama, chained with the others, stuck out a
foot. The priest tripped over it, landed sprawling almost at Thorvin's
feet. Thorvin eyed the club regretfully, his hands chained above his
shoulders. He stepped forward at full stretch, brought a booted heel
down. A crunch, a snoring sound from the pagan, deep in his throat,
then a choking.

"Snapped windpipe," remarked the guards, removing the body
and clubbing Thorvin dispassionately senseless.

"In Thruthvangar, when we reach it," Thorvin gasped between the
blows, "he will be my servant. Our servant. And we are not dead yet,
though he is."

Unnoticed now, Udd began to weep again. He had traveled far, endured much, done his best to counterfeit the warrior. Now his nerve had gone, his reserve of courage drained empty.

As Shef's army closed on Uppsala, the last night before their informers insisted the sacrifice was due, the rain came down harder. The muddy tracks began to be thronged with worshipers, sightseers, adherents of King Kjallak and devotees of Othin and Frey, all mixed in hopeless confusion. Rather than trying to fight a way through all at once, Shef simply told his men to put their unfamiliar weapons under their cloaks and press on as if they were just another group, an unusually large one, heading for the ritual. In better weather the Finns, at least, would have been recognized. With all heads bent in the streaming rain, and the Finns kept in the center, no remark was made, no opposition organized. Shef heard many voices say that the gods had not relented. They would demand blood in torrents before the Swedes would see good harvests again.

In the dark hour before dawn, Shef saw the dragon-gables of the temple rear against the clouds. Even more unmistakable, the great bulk of the oak-tree itself, the Kingdom Oak, around which the Swedes had worshiped their gods and elected their kings since before they were a nation. Forty men with hands outstretched would not span the trunk, it was said. Even in the growing crowds, no-one ventured under its branches. Some of the offerings of last year still swung there, human and animal. A charnel of uncleared bones lay beneath it.

As they halted Shef sent word along to Herjolf, Osmod and the others, to try to get the men into a deep line unblocked by Swedes, and prepare them for whatever might come. He himself moved up to Cuthred's shoulder. The big man stood unspeaking, weapons hidden.

"I may need you at my shoulder soon," said Shef.

Cuthred nodded. "I will be there when you need me, lord."

"Maybe you should drink this. It— it makes a man readier, or so Hund tells me."

Cuthred took the flask, unstoppered it, and sniffed it gingerly. He snorted with sudden contempt, threw it onto the sodden ground. "I know what that is. They give it to the striplings they do not trust before battle. Offer it to me, Ella's champion! I am your man. I would have killed any man else who gave me that."

Cuthred turned his back, stood angrily aside. Shef looked at him, bent and picked the flask up, sniffed it himself. Perhaps a third of the

draught remained. They gave it to the striplings before battle? He was a stripling, or so people kept telling him. On impulse he lifted the flask, drained it, threw it back to the ground. Karli, a few feet away—he took care not to get too close to Cuthred—watched anxiously.

Horns had started to blow somewhere, low and heavy in the damp. Was it dawn? Hard to tell. Hard to tell, too, whether the Kingdom Oak was budding. But the priests of the temple seemed to have decided to begin. Doors opened as the sky slowly paled, priests filed out chanting, circled the oak. Another blare of horns, and a gate swung slowly open. Guards began to herd a double line of shuffling figures out into the chill. Shef undid his cloak, let it fall into the mud, stood breathing heavily and deeply. He was ready now to act. He waited only for his target.

Not very far away, behind a low ridge that fringed the temple-plain, Bruno had mustered his riders. He had decided to keep his men mounted, for the shock effect. It was true that the mounts were only Swedish horses, not the highly-trained chargers of Frankland or

Germany, but his men were all horsemen, true *Ritters*. They would squeeze a charge out of any animal.

"I think they're getting ready to start," said Bruno to Erkenbert. The little deacon could hardly ride at all, but refused like the mission's priests to be left behind. Bruno had swung him up onto his own saddle-bow. Erkenbert was shivering with cold. Bruno refused to consider that it might be fear. Perhaps it was excitement at the thought of striking a blow for the faith. Erkenbert had read to them all, the day before, the legends of the holy saints, the holy *English* saints Willebald and Wynfrith, who had taken the name Boniface. They had attacked the pagan Saxons in their own sanctuaries, cut down their holy pillars, gained eternal salvation in Heaven and also everlasting glory among men. Martyrdom, Erkenbert had said, was nothing in comparison. It was certainly true that the little Englishman was eager himself to be the hero of story. Bruno had other intentions, not involving martyrdom.

"There!" said the deacon. "They are leading out the martyrs to their doom. When will you strike? Ride forward now in the strength of the Lord."

Bruno tensed, rose in his stirrups to give the order, settled slowly back. "I think someone is there before us," he said in surprise.

As the captives were led slowly forward, Shef realized that someone had come to take charge. The growing light revealed a block of gray stone in the center of the plain between the temple and the oak, a flat square platform maybe four feet high and ten across. A man stepped out from the group near the temple doors, swinging a spear. He vaulted suddenly and powerfully onto the platform, heaving himself up on the spear, and raised his hands high. A concerted shout came from his supporters, drowning out the buzz of comment from the rest of the crowd. "Kjallak!" they shouted. "Kjallak king, favored of the gods!"

Shef began to walk forward, lance in hand. He knew, but did not care, that Cuthred was behind him. His body seemed buoyed up on a cushion of air, as if something inside him were lifting him, as if his breath were too great for his lungs.

"Kjallak!" he called out harshly. "You have my men there. I want them back."

The king stared down at him, a warrior in his prime, thirty-five years old, veteran of many wars and many single combats.

"Who are you, manling, that disturbs the assembly of the Swedes?" he asked.

Shef, within range, swung the lance-butt at his legs. Kjallak leapt nimbly over it, came down on wet stone, slipped and fell. Shef vaulted onto the stone to stand over him. His voice lifted and rang across the plain, shouting out words he had never thought to say.

"You are no king! A king is to guard his people. Not hang them on trees for a crowd of old tricksters. Get off the stone! I am the king of the Swedes."

Weapons clashed in the background, but Shef ignored them. Half a dozen of Kjallak's men had run forward as soon as their king was threatened. Three met crossbow quarrels humming from the crowd. Cuthred, stepping forward, coldly cut the legs from under one, slashed furiously at the others, driving them back.

"Is this a challenge?" called Kjallak. "This is not the place or the time for it."

Shef responded with a kick that caught Kjallak rising to his feet, tumbled him off the stone. A groan rose from the watchers. Kjallak got to his feet again, face paling.

"Whatever place or time, I will kill you for that," he said. "I will make a *heimnar* of you and give what is left to the priests. You are the first sacrifice to the gods this day. But you have neither sword nor shield. How can you fight me with that old pigsticker?"

Shef looked round. He had not planned this. It was the recklessness born from Hund's potion that had done this: left him facing a fully-armed hero himself, instead of sending forward his champion Cuthred. Impossible to ask for a substitution. The day was up now, he saw, and by some chance the rain had stopped. All eyes were on him, up there on the stone, at the center of a natural amphitheater. The priests of the temple had ceased their chanting, stood there in a grisly group, next to their herded captives. Round him in a great ring of spears stood the assembly of the Swedish nation. But they made no move to interfere. They stood, waiting for the judgment of the gods. He could never expect a better chance than this. And the potion was still strong within him.

Shef threw his head back and laughed, lifted the lance and threw it point-first into the wet turf. He raised his voice so that it would carry not to Kjallak but to the rearmost row of the spectators.

"I have no sword and shield," he shouted. "But I have this!" He pulled from his belt the long single-edged knife he carried. "I will fight you Rogaland style! We need no bull's hide. We have the holy stone. I will fight you here, wrist tied to wrist, and he who steps down from the stone, he is king of the Swedes."

A slow rumble came from the crowd as they caught the words, and

Kjallak, hearing it, tightened his lips. He had seen duels like that before. They took away the advantage of skill. But the crowd would not let anyone back out now. He still had strength and reach. He reached down, unbuckled his sword-belt, threw it from the stone, hearing the Swedes begin to cheer and clash spear on shield as they realized he had taken the dare.

"Dunghill cock!" he said, keeping his voice low. "You should have stuck to your own midden."

Cwicca, holding his broken arm up by the sleeve, muttered to the battered and bleeding Thorvin, "There's something funny going on. He would never have planned this. Nor he hasn't been levered into it either. This isn't like him."

"Maybe the gods have taken control of him," said Thorvin.

"Let's hope they keep it up," said Hama.

Bruno, still watching the arrangements being made from his unnoticed vantage-point, looked round thoughtfully. All eyes were on the center, where men were helping Kjallak out of his mail as Shef stripped to his tunic as well. A rope had appeared, cut from the hangman's coil, and they were preparing to lash the two men together, each man with two seconds now to see fair play. One of the temple priests had insisted on singing an invocation to Othin, and Herjolf, pushing out of the crowd, had begun a counter to it.

"We can't even get at them now," said Bruno. "The crowd's too close-packed. See here, what we'll do is this." He pointed out to his men a circuit they could make. To the right, round behind the temple and the slave-yard, to appear between the temple and the oak, where a gap had been left for the prisoners. "Come out there behind them," he concluded. "Ride forward and make a wedge. That way we'll get our people away at least."

"What's that banner they've broken out down there?" asked one of his men.

"It is a cross," cried the weak-eyed Erkenbert. "God has sent a sign!"

"Not a cross," said Bruno slowly. "It is a lance. Like the one the young man just threw down. A lance with something I can't see across it. I don't deny it may be a sign for all that."

Breathing deeply and slowly, Shef waited for the signal to begin. He wore only his breeches, shoes kicked off as well for a surer grip on the wet stone. He had no idea what to do. It did not seem to matter.

Hund's potion filled him with rage and ecstasy. The calculating part of
him that lived on somewhere below the potion had given up its
protests, was telling him instead to keep his eye on his enemy, not just
luxuriate in feelings of power.

A sudden silence as the rival chantings stopped, a blare of horns,
and Kjallak stepped forward over the stone platform like a panther and
slashed. Shef leapt away almost too late, felt a line of fire across his
ribs, heard from some far distance the roar of acclaim. He began to
move, pulling with one hand on the rope both men held, feinting to
thrust with the other. Kjallak ignored the feints, waited for the real
stab. When it came, the one-eye would have to step close. When he
missed, Kjallak would strike again for the body. He circled always to
the right, crowding the knife-hand, making his opponent back away to
keep him off his blind side. Every few seconds he slashed quickly,
professionally, at Shef's exposed left arm, enough to make the blood
run, the strength go.

"How's it going?" asked Thorvin, his left eye swollen shut.

"He's cutting our man to bits," answered Cwicca.

He's cutting me to bits, thought Shef. He felt no pain, no physical
fear, but there was an undercurrent of panic rising, as if he were out on
a stage in front of thousands of people, and had forgotten what he was
supposed to say. He tried a sudden sweep with one leg, a wrestling
trick. Kjallak evaded it economically, and sliced him across the knee.
Shef slashed back at Kjallak's rope-arm, drawing blood for the first
time. Kjallak grinned and thrust suddenly over their joined arms,
forcing Shef to jerk his head aside and leap back, dropping the rope, to
avoid the instant second thrust for the heart.

"Learning, eh?" panted Kjallak. "But not fast enough. You should
have stayed with your mother."

The thought of his mother, her life destroyed by the Vikings,
stabbed Shef into a flurry of thrusts, coming forward recklessly.
Kjallak dodged them, caught a couple with his own knife in a clang of
metal, waited for the surge to die down. Like a berserker, he thought.
Don't take them head on. Keep out of their way and wait for them to
tire. He could feel it already, the spasmodic strength draining.

"Stayed with your mother," he repeated. "Maybe had a nice game
of knucklebones."

Knucklebones, thought Shef. He remembered the lessons from
Karli in the marsh, remembered Hedeby market. Seizing the trailing
rope again, he jerked it taut, slashed it suddenly through. A groan from
the crowd, a look of surprise, disgust in Kjallak's eyes.

Shef threw his knife high in the air, spinning end over end. Kjallak, whose eyes had never left it, looked up, followed it automatically for an instant, his head rising.

Shef stepped forward, pivoting from the waist as Karli had taught him, and threw a clenched left fist in a sweeping hook. He felt the blow run up his arm, felt the crunch of fist on beard and bone. Kjallak staggered. But he was a man with a neck like a bull's, knocked off balance but not down.

The spinning knife came down. As if he had practiced the catch for a dozen years, Shef caught it left-handed by the hilt, thrust upwards at the raised chin. The blade skewered through beard and chin, mouth and palate, drove on till the point wedged hard in the roof of the skull.

Shef felt the dead weight fall forward, twisted the blade, jerked it free. He turned in a slow semi-circle towards the crowd, raising the bloody knife. A roar of applause from his own men, confused cries from the rest.

"Foul!" cried one of Kjallak's seconds, stepping towards the stone. "He cut the rope! That's against the rules."

"What rules?" said Cuthred. Without further words he slashed at the second, half-severing his head. From the stone Shef saw spears poised, crossbows leveled.

A ray of sunshine broke through the clouds, fell on the bloody stone. This time a groan from the crowd, of awe. And in the same moment, a clash of metal. Shef looked up, saw between the oak and the temple a solid line of armored horsemen, driving between the prisoners and their guards, hustling the temple priests towards him. He did not know who they were, but they gave him a chance. The potion filled him with one more inspiration, a surge of fury.

"Swedes!" he called out. "You are here for good harvests and prosperity. They grow from blood. I have given you blood already, king's blood. Follow me and I will give you more."

Voices from the crowd, shouting about the oak and the sacrifices.

"You have sacrificed for years and what good has it done? You sacrificed the wrong things. You must sacrifice what is dearest to you. Start again. I will give you a better sacrifice."

Shef pointed across the clearing. "Sacrifice your oak. Cut it down now, and set free the souls that hang from it. And if the gods want blood, send it to them. Send the gods their servants, the priests of the temple."

Across the clearing, a small black-clad figure had scrambled from a horse, was running under the ghastly swaying boughs. He had an axe in his hand, snatched from a gaping priest. He reached the oak, raised the axe and swung. A groan again from the crowd at the sacrilege.

Chips flew, men stared upwards for the avenging thunder. Nothing. Just the hard noise of metal on wood as Erkenbert swung like a man possessed. Slowly eyes turned towards the priests. Bruno's men rode forward, herding them towards the stone. Herjolf turned towards Shef's followers, seizing the moment.

"Right," he shouted. "Crossbows, down here and make a ring. Ottar, get your Finns organized. The rest of you, seize those men. And you," he called to Bruno, "stop your little fellow before he does himself an injury. Make a ring round the oak and get four men at it who know their business."

The Swedes watched in amazement and acquiescence as Herjolf made his grisly preparations. Before the morning was over the Kingdom Oak would be in flames, and tossed onto it as a pyre, the bodies of its servants.

"Does that make the one-eye king of the Swedes?" they asked each other.

"Who knows?" went the answers. "But he has brought back the sun."

CHAPTER THIRTY-ONE

The Ragnarsson brothers heard the news in their quarters at the Braethraborg, the Stronghold of the Brothers, their city-barracks on the island of Sjaelland in the heart of Denmark. After they had rewarded and dismissed the messenger—it was a settled policy with them always to pay for news, however unwelcome—they sat alone to consider it. Wine was on the table between them, wine from the south in a jar. It had been a profitable year for them, after a poor start. Ever since they took Hedeby they had marched or sailed from one small kingdom to another, forcing submission on the petty kings, each victory bringing them allies and troops for the next. The trade between north and south was now entirely in their hands, every load of furs or amber from the north paying toll to them, every load of wine or slaves from the south. Yet they had not succeeded in one thing, were left uneasy in their minds.

"Killed Kjallak," ruminated Halvdan Ragnarsson. "I always said he was a good boy. We should have kept him on our side. It was that business with Ivar's girl that spoiled it. Pity we couldn't get Ivar to see sense." Halvdan felt the most strongly of the brothers about the code of *drengskapr*, had taken a liking to Shef ever since his victory over the Hebrideans at the holmgang outside York. His feelings, as his brothers knew, made no difference to his loyalty. He was merely expressing an opinion.

"And now they say he's rowing south. There's only one place he could be aiming at," said Ubbi Ragnarsson. "That's here. I wonder what force he can raise."

"The reports say he has not raised anything like the full force of the Swedes," said their brother Sigurth, the Snake-eye. "That's a good thing. I know we laugh at the Swedes, they're old-fashioned, haven't had the campaigning in the West to teach them their trade. But there's a lot of them, if they got themselves together.

"Still, they haven't. Volunteers, they say, and a force he brought with him from the far North, Finns and *skogarmenn*. I doubt there's much to worry about there. What makes me think a bit harder are the Norwegians."

Olaf Elf-of-Geirstath, once he heard from the emissaries of the Way what had happened at Uppsala, had responded by calling out his full levies from all the kingdoms he had dominated since the death of his brother, and rowing south as soon as the ice would let him, to meet the man he considered to be his over-king.

"Norwegians!" said Ubbi. "And led by that fool Olaf. They'll start to fight among themselves before long, and he has sat at home for forty years. He is no threat."

"He was no threat," said Sigurth. "What bothers me is the way he's changed. Or been changed."

He sat silent, sipping the wine and pondering. His brothers exchanged glances, sat silent also. Of them all, Sigurth was the one who best read the future. He was sensitive to every change of fortune, every shift of luck and reputation.

What Sigurth was thinking was that he smelled trouble. In his experience, trouble came always from the quarter least expected, and was worst when you had had a chance to settle it and had failed to take it. He and his brothers had neglected this man Skjef, or Shef to begin with. He himself had let him off with the loss of one eye when he was entirely in his power. Then, alerted to his ability to make trouble for them, they had tried once and twice to deal with him. The first attempt had cost them their brother. The second had almost cost him and his two remaining brothers their reputation. And the man had got away from them again. Maybe he should not have restrained Halvdan when he wanted to plunge through the water and attack him. He might have lost another brother. If it had finished their enemy off once and for all, it might have been worth it.

Behind it all, Sigurth wondered, was there some suggestion, some hint, of a shift of favor from the gods? Sigurth was a skeptic in most ways, not above frightening priests or buying good omens. Yet beneath it all there had always been a bedrock certainty that the old gods did exist, and that he was their favorite, the favorite of Othin especially. Had he not sent him thousands of victims? Yet Othin might turn against a favorite in the end.

"We will send out the war-arrow," he said. "To every land we control. To turn out with full force or feel our retribution.

"You know what else worries me?" he went on. "Think of this table as the Scandinavian lands, Denmark here, Norway here, Sweden here." With flasks and mugs he began to trace a primitive map on the table. "Look at the way he's been traveling round. Here in the south, where we met his fleet at sea. Then up at Hedeby. Then off to Kaupang. Then up to the far North. And then he reappears where no-one would expect him, on the other side of the Keel mountains. He's making a circle. Or should I say a circuit?"

The circuit was the road the king rode on, to collect his taxes, expose himself to challenge, impose his authority. The *Eiriksgata* in Sweden was one. Shef's road could be seen as a greater one, a circuit of all the circuits.

"Well," said Halvdan, looking at the pattern of the mugs. "He has one step yet to take before he has completed the circuit. Or the circle. And that is here, at the Braethraborg."

Very far away, four others met in conclave. Not three brothers this time, but three brothers and their father. If he was their father, if they were really brothers. Such things become uncertain among the gods.

They stood at the Hlithskjalf, the lookout place of Asgarth, stronghold of the gods. To their eyes nothing was invisible, nothing at least on Middle-earth, centermost of the nine worlds. They saw the fleets crawling across the sea, the fish swarming beneath it, saw the corn growing and the seed springing.

"I have held him in my hand," said Othin All-father, "and let him go. And he has denied me, refused me sacrifice, slain my followers. I sent the snow and the Finns to kill him, and he escaped me. And what saved him? A troll, a iötunn, one of the brood of Loki the accursed."

The others exchanged looks. Heimdall, watchman of the gods, his great horn slung round his neck, ready to blow on the day that the iötnar should rise to bring Ragnarök to gods and men, spoke carefully. "One of the Huldu-folk saved him, All-Father. We do not know that such are the brood of Loki. But something stirred up the whales, the killers who obey nothing but their sport and their hunger. It was not I, it was not you. If it was the Chained One, as I believe, then he is the Chained One's enemy. And the enemy of our enemy is our friend."

"He burned the great oak. He burned the temple. He released those

dedicated to me and to your brother Frey. Even now he sails with Christians at his side."

This time Thor tried his skills of persuasion, never very great. "The ones dedicated to you were a poor lot. He sent you others—your own priests. They were a poor lot too, but it was a fair exchange. He has Christians with him, but he has done more to weaken them than any of your favorites. What did Hermoth do against them, or Ivar whom this man killed? Kill a few, I dare say, but that only encourages the rest. This one has taken kingdoms away from them. They fear him more than you do."

A careless word, and the glare of Othin's one eye shot like a dagger at the red-bearded god, who looked down and fingered his hammer awkwardly.

"Not fear, of course," he went on. "He is a smith, though, and a friend of smiths. He is that first and last. I am for him."

"If what you say is true," said Othin eventually, "then maybe I could find a place for him in my army at Valhalla, place him among the Einheriar. Is that not reward and honor enough for any mortal?"

Only for the crazy ones, thought the god who had not spoken. Heimdall looked at him in warning, for Heimdall could hear the thoughts in a man's head, or a god's. It was true, though. Only the crazy ones saw reward in fighting to the death every day and then coming to life to talk it over every evening.

"The Einheriar are there," said the silent god, "to win the day at Ragnarök."

"Of course," said Othin. He glared at Rig with his one eye. Rig was crafty, skilled with words beyond any of his other sons. Sometimes wondered if Rig might not be a son. Certainly Rig had cuckolded many husbands, made many men bring up cuckoos. Could he do the same to gods?

"And the purpose of Ragnarök is to destroy evil and make the world anew? To repair the great maim that we and it suffered when Balder died? When the Accursed One did his greatest evil, and became for us the Chained One."

The other gods stiffened a little. The name of Balder was no longer spoken among them, or not in Othin's hearing. It was ill to stir old wounds.

Rig went on, his voice cool and ironic, as always. "But are we sure that Ragnarök will be a victory? No. That is why Othin strengthens always his army in Valhalla. If it is a victory, are we sure that there will be a better world on the other side? No. For there are prophecies to say that all of us—or all of you—will perish on that day. You, Thor, from the poison of Iörmungand the World-Serpent. You, Heimdall, facing your brother Loki.

For me I have heard no prophecy. But Othin All-father—it is said that for him the jaws of Fenris-Wolf lie ever in wait.

"So why are we so eager to run to Ragnarök? Why has none of us asked himself: what if the world could be made anew without the destruction?"

Othin's fingers tightened on the shaft of his spear, and the knuckles showed white.

"One last question. We know that we tried to have Balder return from the dead, and Othin sent his hero Hermoth to try to bring him back. It failed. Yet there are stories that men have been released from Hel, though not by us."

"Christian stories," growled Thor.

"Even they may bring some hope. I know All-father shares that hope. Those who were there, they may remember. When Balder lay on his pyre, and we prepared to light it, to push it out onto the Shoreless Sea to send him down to Hel, then at that last moment Othin All-father bent and whispered words in Balder's ear. Words none heard, not even you, Heimdall. What did Othin whisper in dead Balder's ear?

"It comes to me that I know. May I speak those words, All-father?"

"If you have thought them, Heimdall has heard them now. Two may keep a secret, but not once it is known to three. Speak, then. What did I whisper in my dead son's ear?"

"You whispered: 'Would that some god would send you back to me, my son.'"

After a long silence, Othin spoke again. "It is true. I confessed my own weakness then, as I have never done before or since."

"Confess it again. Let this play itself out without your intervention. Let my son have his chance. Let me see if I can use him to bring about a better world without the fire of Ragnarök. To cure the maim of Balder dead."

Othin stared once more at the crawling fleets below. "Very well," he said in the end. "But I will find recruits still for my Einheriar. Soon my daughters will be busy, the Valkyriar, Choosers of the Slain."

Rig made no answer, his thoughts veiled even from Heimdall.

The battle council Shef called on the deck of the *Fearnought* looked as if the battle had already taken place. Cwicca, there as captain of the catapult squads, had an arm splinted and bandaged. Thorvin's face was still covered in bruises, one eye swollen shut and just beginning to work its way open. Shef himself looked white, propped up with cushions in a chair: the gashes on his arm and leg had received more than a hundred stitches from Hund, and according to the leech what blood he had left at the end of the duel would barely have filled a wine-glass.

Others looked more warlike. At the foot of the long table Shef had commissioned sat Olaf Elf-of-Geirstath, newly and respectfully called by his Norwegian subjects, "the Victorious." Flanking him was Brand, who had made his way south at the end of the winter to buy a new *Walrus*. Looking at him, Shef thought the troll blood more and more obvious. His eyebrows beetled out like ledges over a cliff, his hands and knuckles seemed even too large for the rest of him. Guthmund sat next to him, newly named on Shef's authority jarl of Sodermanland, in succession to the dead Kjallak. The other Swedish jarls had taken the designation better on learning that the new jarl was indeed a countryman and even a kinsman. They had also listened with deep interest to Guthmund's emphatic opinions on the potential wealth to be gained in the new king's service.

Herjolf too was at the council, and Ottar to carry its decisions to Piruusi and the Finns. So too, lounging back in his seat with an air of unconcern, was the broad-shouldered figure of the German Bruno. His men's intervention at Uppsala had won him a place at the table. There was no doubt, at least, of his opposition to the Ragnarssons, now that they controlled Hedeby and had abandoned Hrorik's trade-for-all policy, a standing threat to the northern borders of Germany.

Brand, who three years ago had carried the news of Ragnar Lothbrok's death into the Braethraborg itself—a story now continually retold—had been asked to describe its defenses to the commanders of Shef's allied fleet, more than a hundred warships. He had drawn the shape of the bay it stood in, in a great tray of sand on the table, and was now sticking pieces of wood into the sand to show the position of the main buildings.

"A tough nut to crack," he concluded. "When I went in there was a standing patrol of half-a-dozen warships of the largest size. We hear that has been doubled, since the Ragnarssons know we are close. Each ship must hold at least a long hundred of men, six score, proven champions, and they stand higher out of the water than any of our vessels—except for the coastal patrol ships brought down by King Olaf, of which we have only four. Of course, since the Ragnarssons' ships never leave the bay, they have no problems with water storage and can remain fully-manned at all times, returning for rest and food one at a time.

"And then there are the catapults. Everyone agrees that the first success of the Ragnarssons against Hedeby was caused by their use of the new machines. Since then they have continued to build them and train men in their use, all directed, so they say, by a renegade monk or lay-brother from the Minster at York."

Eyes turned with a certain reproach to the small black figure of Erkenbert sitting at Bruno's side. Erkenbert took no notice. Since his attack on the Kingdom Oak he had lived in a perpetual daydream, in which he continually rewrote the *legendum* of Erkenbert *arithmeticus*, smiter of the pagans, in the form of a saint's life. He was unsure still about the role that should be given in it to the one-eyed apostate who had smitten the pagan king: perhaps it would be best to omit all mention of him, to ascribe the victory to a Christian champion. In the Christian world only the Church recorded history.

"The catapults are here," Brand went on, driving a handful of pegs into the promontory that guarded access to the inner bay. "They can wreck any ships that approach and get past the standing patrol, at a range of close on a mile.

"And finally, there is the Ragnarsson main force. Armed longships, beached here—" another handful of pegs, "—at least as many of them as we have, and again without problems of water storage or provisioning."

"Tell us, Brand," said Shef. "Is there any good news?"

Brand grinned. "Well, lord, I could say 'it isn't raining,' but it probably will be soon. But yes, there is. When it comes to it, many of the Ragnarsson allies are there under coercion. They're there because the Ragnarssons came against them one at a time and forced them to surrender and contribute forces. But if they thought they could get away with it they'd desert like a shot. If the Ragnarssons are winning, they'll fight for them. If it once looks as if they're losing . . . Support will crumble very fast. To be honest, I think we would stand a good chance—if, if we could get past the hard core. But the catapults are a problem, and so are the big ships."

Brand hesitated, unsure whether he was explaining the obvious. But the council contained so many non-Norsemen it was best to be explicit. "You see, in a sea-fight the size of your ship is like, like being behind stone walls. These big ships would go to the bottom in an hour in an Atlantic storm, and their keels are always weak. But if one of them comes alongside you in enclosed water, all they have to do is throw a couple of rocks down from behind their scantlings, and you'll be swimming. They're feet higher than an ordinary ship. The men in it are protected from anything you can do, but your decks are wide open to their bows or spears. If they board you they're coming downhill. You'd have to climb a rope on a grapnel to board them, and as long as there's anyone alive on board them, that's impossible. One of King Olaf's ships could fight one of them on even terms, but they outnumber us three to one in that class. And they'll be manned, I repeat, by the Ragnarssons' best. Only Danes, I dare say, not Norwegians," Brand added with a bristle of national pride. "But not beardless boys for all that."

"Alas," said Bruno in the silence, his Norse strongly accented. "I fear we shall all have to go home."

Brand flushed angrily and started to reach over the table to grip Bruno's hand in his own, meaning to crush it till he screamed for release. Bruno evaded the grasp easily, the smile never leaving his face.

Shef rapped the table. "Enough. Thank you, Brand, for your report. Count Bruno, if you wish to go home we will continue without you." Shef held Bruno's gaze for a moment, forcing him to drop his eyes. "The Count intended a mere pleasantry. He is as determined as the rest of us to put an end to these mad dogs and restore law to the Northlands."

"Yes," said Herjolf, "but how are we to do it?"

Shef held a hand out, palm flat. "That is paper." He made it into a fist. "That is stone." He extended two fingers only. "Those are scissors. Now, who will play this game with me? Count Bruno, you."

Shef's voice was strong and certain, coming strangely from the pallid face. He was sure that he could carry them with him, sure even that he could read his man's mind well enough to win the game. What would Bruno do? He would not choose paper, that was sure. Stone or scissors? His own nature would be for the sharp cut. So he would choose stone, thinking others like himself.

"One, two, three," Shef counted. Both men thrust their hands out together, Bruno's a fist, Shef's a flat palm. "Paper wraps stone, I win."

Again, and this time Bruno would reject the scissors, which would have won last time, reject the stone which he had tried last. "One, two, three." Bruno's flat palm met Shef's two fingers. "Scissors cut paper, I win again. But enough—" Bruno's face was beginning to darken at the guffaws from Brand. "You see my point. They have big ships, and catapults, and ordinary ships. And big ships beat ordinary ships, as Brand has told us. Now what beats big ships? Catapults. And what beats catapults? Our plan must be always to oppose our strength to their weakness. Listen while I explain . . ."

As the council broke up, Shef sat back, hoarse from talking and tired still from loss of blood. Bruno, rising, performed a courteous bow in the direction of the scowling Brand, and then made his way to the head of the table.

"You have come a long way since they tried to sell you as a slave in

Hedeby," he remarked. He nodded to Karli behind Shef's chair. "I see you still have your young Ditmarsher with you. But the weapon you have, that is not the one you were carrying then. May I examine it?"

Oddly reluctant, Shef reached behind him, took the lance from its place against the gunwale, passed it over. Bruno turned it over in his hands, examining its head.

"May I ask where you found this strange piece."

Shef laughed. "It would take too long to tell the full story. In a smokehouse. I am told it belonged once to a jarl of the Tronds, one Bolli. But I never met him. Or not to speak to," he added, remembering the long row of swinging carcasses. "You can see that at one time it was in the hands of Christians. Look, there are crosses on the cheek-pieces, inlaid once with gold. But that had been scraped out long before I came by it."

Bruno turned the weapon in his hands, staring at the cross-marks on the blade. He handled it gently, reverently. After a moment he said, his voice quiet, "May I ask how the weapon came to you, if you never met its owner? This jarl Bolli of the Tronds. You found it somewhere? You took it from someone?"

Shef remembered the scene in Echegorgun's smokehouse: how he had laid the weapon down, how Cuthred had picked it up and pressed it on him. There was something odd in the way Bruno was pursuing this. He was reluctant to tell him the full story.

"Let's say it passed into my hands. It belonged to no-one at the time."

"Some man had kept it, though? Some man gave it to you?"

Echegorgun kept it, thought Shef. A marbendill, not a man. And it was Cuthred who handed it to me. "Not exactly a man," he replied.

Archbishop Rimbert's words had been reported to Bruno: how he had said that the Holy Lance of Longinus and of Charlemagne would not come to light through the hand of man. His doubts vanished. He held the holy relic of Empire, at long last, in his hands. God had favored him for all his trials. Yet he was on the deck of a heathen warship, surrounded by potential foes. What was it the little deacon had said to him? "He who perseveres to the end, he shall be saved." To the end. Not just to near the end.

His voice as casual as he could make it, Bruno grounded the lance-butt gently on the deck. "It is clearly a Christian weapon," he said. "No offense, but I would rather not leave it in the hands of one who is no longer a Christian. Perhaps I can ransom it from you, as we ransom Christian slaves."

Brand tried to persuade me to get rid of it too, thought Shef.

Strange. "No," he said, repeating what he had said to Brand. "I call it a good weapon that conquers, and it has brought me good luck. I have taken a fancy to it. I will keep it."

Bruno handed it back, straightened and bowed in the stiff German fashion. "*Uf widersehn, herra, bis uf die schlacht.* Farewell, lord. Till we meet in the battle."

"Awkward bastard," muttered Cuthred to Cwicca in English, watching him go.

CHAPTER THIRTY-TWO

*S*hef lay in sleep, conscious at some level of his mind that tomorrow would be the day of battle. The fleet lay beached some dozen miles from the entry to the bay of the Braethraborg, strongly guarded against any surprise sortie.

In his sleep he was in the bay of the Braethraborg itself, down at the far end, looking out in the direction that he knew he, Shef, must come in the morning. And indeed it was morning, and the man looking out of a just-unshuttered window could see ships creeping down the fjord towards him. Those ships, he knew, would bring his death.

The man watching swung the shutters fully open, stood facing the oncoming navy, and began to sing. The song he sang was one Shef had heard often before, a famous song among the Vikings, a favorite of Brand's. It was called "The Song of Bjarki," or "The Old Song of Bjarki." But this man was not repeating it. he was making it up for the first time. He sang:

> *"The day is come up, the cocks whir their wings.*
> *Time for the wretches, to rise to their work.*
> *Wake now, awake, you warriors, my friends,*
> *All the best of you, beaters of Athils,*
> *Har with the hard grip, Hrolf the archer,*
> *Men of good stock, who scorn to flee.*
> *I do not wake you to wine nor whispers of women,*
> *I wake you for the sharp showers of battle."*

The voice of Shef's frequent mentor cut in above the voice of the singing man, amused and ironic as usual.

"Now you will not fight like that," it said. "You want to win, not to gain glory. Remember though: I have done my best for you, but you must take every advantage you can. There is no room for weakness . . ."

The voices faded, both the impassioned singer and the cold voice of the god. As he woke—or perhaps they were what woke him—Shef heard the horns of the sentries blowing to signal dawn and battle-morning. Shef lay where he was, aware that now he was a king he could at least wait for someone else to light the fires and make the breakfast. No question of fighting on an empty stomach, not in the heavy manual labor of hand-to-hand battle. He was reflecting on the vision, and on the song.

"Men of good stock," the singer had said, "who scorn to flee." Was he a man of good stock? He supposed so. Whether his father was a god or a jarl, or even if he had been Wulfgar the thane, there was no churl-blood there. Did that mean that he, Shef, would scorn to flee? That those who fled were always of bad stock? Perhaps the singer thought that not fleeing and being noble were always the same thing. If he did, he was wrong.

And the god had said he must take every advantage. Something told Shef that was wrong too. That was it, there was something that had been bothering him. He sat up, called to his attendant. "Pass the word for the Englishman Udd."

By the time Shef had his shoes on, Udd was there. Shef looked at him critically. He was trying to hold himself together, but his face was white and strained. He had been looking like that for days. No wonder. He had spent weeks waiting for a painful death, and been rescued only at the last moment. Before that he had gone through more danger and hardship than he would have done in six lifetimes as a smith's helper, which is what he had been once. He had been overtaxed. Yet he would not wish to desert now.

"Udd," Shef said, "I have a special assignment for you."

Udd's lower lip quivered, the look of fear became more pronounced.

"I want you to leave the *Fearnought* and stay with the rearguard."

"Why, lord?"

Shef thought quickly. "So you can pass a message for me, if—if the day goes badly. Here, take this money. It will buy you a passage back to England one day, if that is what it comes to. If that happens, you are to greet King Alfred for me, and say I am sorry we could not work together for longer. And greet his queen from me as well."

Udd was looking surprised, relieved, slightly ashamed. "And what is the message for her, lord?"

"Nothing. Nothing. Just greetings, and the memory of old times. And listen, Udd. I wouldn't trust anyone to do this for me. I'm relying on you. Don't let me down."

The little man went out, still looking relieved. But less ashamed. Pointless, thought Shef. And directly against what the god said. We might need Udd during the day. But I could not bear to see those terrified eyes any more. Taking Udd out of the battle was an act of kindness. Also of defiance against the cynic-god Rig, his father and mentor.

Shef came out of the tent whistling, startling the sentries, who were used at least to reflective silence on mornings like this one. He hailed Cwicca, listening to Udd's explanation a few feet away. "Have you got that bagpipe you made over the winter, Cwicca? Well, play it today. If that doesn't scare the Ragnarssons, nothing will."

Hours later, on a calm sea, the fleet crawled towards the bay behind which lay the long-inviolate Braethraborg. To the left of it, as the fleet approached from the north, a spit of land jutted out. On it, just visible, the hulks of the Ragnarssons' four-mule catapult battery, flanked by the twist-shooters or torsion dart-throwers, and flanked again by the cheap, simple, inaccurate stone-lobbers. Out from the spit, almost blocking the entrance to the bay, lay the dozen shapes of the Ragnarssons' largest warships, the coastal patrol that never put out to sea. Behind them clustered the mass of conventional longships, the main body of their fleet, headed by Shef's old enemy, the *Frani Ormr*.

In the *Fearnought* Shef could hear the rowers grunting as they heaved on the oars—less oars now than sweeps. They were twice the size of ordinary oars and manned by two men each, the strongest in the fleet, carefully selected by Brand and Hagbarth. They had made their approach under sail, to save the rowers' strength, but now the time had come to strike the mast and yard. Close by, on the same course as the *Fearnought*, King Olaf's four large craft, each the size of the wrecked *Crane*, kept pace. Kept pace easily, at a paddling stroke, the rowers looking sideways at the strange ship they convoyed.

Shef had finally given orders to fit the plates of case-hardened steel. The two fighting platforms with the rotating mules on them were armored up to waist height, the plates slanting outwards. It would have

been impossible to armor the rest of the ship and still have her float and move, but Shef had rigged a frame that bolted onto each gunwale. On this plates were fitted, overlapping like the shingles on a roof, or like dragon-scales. They too sloped from bottom to top, beginning just above the height of the oarsmen's heads and running up till they almost met six feet above.

"You keep your shield up in battle," Shef had explained to a doubtful Hagbarth. "At least if you're expecting spears and arrows from a distance. And you keep it slanted so they'll skid off. That's what we're going to try."

Behind the laboring *Fearnought* and the large ships, as with the Ragnarsson fleet, came the mass of the attackers in the eighteen-oar-a-side craft that were the backbone of all Viking navies. Each towed behind it, hard to see in the sun-dazzle off the water, a smaller boat, fishermen's skiffs like the grind-boats of the far north, all that the local fishing villages could raise. Each held four to eight rowers and two pairs of extra men jammed in. The rowers had again been carefully selected from the best of the Swedes and Norwegians. In each boat two men clutched crossbows, two more were Bruno's German *Ritters*.

Watching from his place in the center, Sigurth Ragnarsson remarked, "Masts stepped, I see."

"Does that mean there'll be no funny business this time?" asked Ubbi.

"I doubt it very much," answered Sigurth. "But we know some tricks ourselves now. Let's hope they're good ones."

Shef stood on top of the forward mule, almost the only place left on the *Fearnought* from which one could now see anything. With his one eye he watched the Ragnarsson catapult battery. He was sharp-sighted, but not enough to see what he needed to. There had to be a way to look closer! He needed to know if they were ready to shoot. If they were cunning, they might hold their first volley till Olaf's ships were in range, conceivably sink all four of them with their first rocks. If that happened the battle would be lost before it started, Shef's "scissors"—for so he had mentally labeled the big vessels in his plan—blunted by the catapults' "stone." Yet he did not want to stop the ships too far out. The less distance that had to be covered by the small boats, the "paper" in his plan, the better.

They were close to being in range, he decided. He turned and waved to King Olaf, standing next to Brand on the forecastle of his heavy ship fifty yards off, three sweeps from side to side. Olaf waved in reply, called an order. As the rowers tossed their oars and the ship lost way, a thirty-pound boulder came sighing out of the sky, at extreme range. It plumped into the water ten feet from the prow of Olaf's *Heron*, the splash throwing spray over the king. Shef grimaced. A little too closely calculated. Would they try again?

The four big ships had lost way, were being left behind as the *Fearnought* ground slowly on into catapult range. Behind them the mass of the fleet had tossed oars as well, were drifting gently forward. As they did so they dropped their tows. The dead silence of the approach was broken suddenly by harsh cheering. The skiffs had cast off, their fresh rowers straining at their oars, each boat making the best pace it could, treating the last mile as a race. As they swept past first their tow-ships and then the leading line of large craft, the oarsmen lined the side, cheering in unison as their boatswains called the time.

The first of the skiffs shot past the *Fearnought*, its helmsman one of Brand's Halogalanders. Shef could hear him shouting, "Put your backs into it, will you, before some Swedish prick gets past us." Shef waved to him, to the two *skogarmenn* crossbows crouched on the rear thwart, to Bruno in one of the pursuing boats, and to the rest of them pouring past, sixty of them spread out like hounds on the scent of a stag. His oarsmen were breathing too deep to cheer, driving their immensely heavy ship on at a quarter the speed of the racing skiffs.

How would the catapults take that? Shef saw spouts of water rise suddenly, two of them, then a third, and felt his heart leap. Every plume was a miss, every miss was one fewer chance to shoot, and a minute gained before they could rewind their clumsy machines. Yet there must have been a hit, yes, there, near the leading skiffs, men struggling in the water by shattered planks. No-one was stopping or slowing to pick them up. Shef had rubbed that in hard. No survivors will be rescued. Keep rowing and leave them. Some of the mailed men would drown, some, he hoped, keep themselves afloat on planks and swim to the nearer shore. The skiffs swept on like so many water-beetles, oars skimming. The *Fearnought* was perhaps a furlong closer to the grim, banner-waving line of the Ragnarsson fleet.

"Give me a hundred strokes," shouted Shef to the rowers. "A hundred strokes and you can rest easy. Hagbarth, call the time. Cwicca, play them along."

The big men began to heave harder, using up the last of their hoarded strength, something they would never do at the start of a normal battle, to be decided by hard hand-strokes. The screeching music urged them on. Cuthred, grinning sourly, looked up from the shadow of the armor plating. "Ogvind here says he'll row harder without the bagpipe, can you shut him up?" Shef waved back and shouted something no-one heard. As the count ran down, Shef looked again at the scene in front of him, estimating distances, looking at the enemy catapults, the racing skiffs, the Ragnarsson front line, suddenly seeming much nearer. Lucky that that at least had not moved. If they had broken their formation instantly, their "scissors" might have cut his "paper," large ships riding down small ones. But now his "paper" would wrap their "stone," his "stone" blunt their "scissors."

"Ten last strokes," Shef shouted, "and steer to starboard. Put us broadside on. Cwicca, shoot for the one with the Raven Banner. Osmod—" he raised his voice even more to reach the aft catapult, "—shoot for the one to the left of the Raven and then work left, *left*, you hear?"

The ship swung, with a final gasp the rowers completed the stroke, slumped sweating over their oars. Shef jumped from his place and ran to another vantage-point clear of the catapults. As the *Fearnought* drifted to a stop, Cwicca and Osmod stared along the trails of their mules, through the gaps left in the plating.

Cwicca dropped his hand, Hama pulled the retainer bolt, the whole ship shuddered to the thwack of the throwing arm striking its padded bar. Shuddered again a moment later as Osmod followed suit. Shef watched the skimming black dots of boulders tensely. Cwicca and Osmod had had to train most of their crews. They had missed the *Crane* at a critical moment. Would they do better this time?

Both dots came to an abrupt end in the center of the Ragnarsson line, Shef was almost sure he could see splinters fly. He waited for the sudden collapse, the disappearance of a ship opened up like a flower, as he had seen happen at the battle off the Elbe. Nothing. The line was still there, dragon-heads glaring. What had the Ragnarssons done? Had they armored their ships?

"Two hits," Shef shouted. "Work out to left and right, as ordered." He did not know what was happening. But in machine-war, as in the old kind, once battle was joined you just had to put your head down and keep doing your job.

The winders whirled their levers, the oarsmen backed water gently to Hagbarth's directions, trying to keep the ship broadside onto the enemy line. Again the double shudder as the stones released, again the black streaks of boulders flying into the line of ships. Still no gaps, no sagging prows. But he could see men running, leaping from ship to ship. Something was taking effect.

As he stared out, the *Fearnought* was suddenly battered down in the water. A great clang made Shef cringe, something whirred over his head in pieces. He looked round, realized that the catapults up on the spit of land had changed their aim, were shooting now not at the skiffs closing on them, but at the ship destroying their battle-line. If the *Fearnought* had not been armored she would have sunk then and there. The boulder had hit dead center, in line with the stepped mast, had shattered on impact with the case-hardened plates, the fragments whistling overhead. Shef stepped through the rowers to join Hagbarth looking at the damage. The plates were unharmed, but the wooden frame that held them had cracked clean through, leaving the outer shell sagging.

Again the *Fearnought* quivered to her own discharges, and again and again came the violent clangs of boulders striking. One struck forward of center, again shattering the frame, the other on the aft catapult platform. Osmod stepped up, pushing sagging plates out of the way, shoving winders back to their places. "Some rope," he called, "tie these timbers back, we can shoot again." The whole platform was out of line, Shef saw, something broken deep in its mounting. They could not take very much more of this battering. A steel plate slid free of its broken frame, fell into the sea, leaving a gap of sunlight.

"Turn the ship while they're winding," Shef shouted. "Turn the undamaged side towards them. Three more volleys and we're done."

The leading skiffs had reached the shore, on the spit a hundred yards short of the battery. As they closed they had been engaged first by the dart-shooters, then the quick-shooting stone lobbing devices Shef's men called pull-throwers. The former were no danger to boats, but demoralizing as they drove their huge darts through man and mail. The latter could sink a boat, but only by random shooting, unaimable. The boats pressed on, clumping at the last moment to make a concerted charge onto the shore.

Two hundred picked men faced them, knee-deep in the water, ready to beat them back, protect their own catapults, give them more time to destroy the ship that was destroying their own front line. In the boats the crossbowmen cocked their weapons, prepared to shoot them down. In machine-war all the parts had to fit together, each part doing its job. If the parts separated, they were useless. If they fitted together, battle turned into butchery. The air filled with the zip of crossbow quarrels shot at short range through shield and mail. As the Ragnarsson champions fell, shot down by unarmored *skogarmenn*, the heavily-armed Germans stumbled from the boats, formed a line in the water, locked shields and marched forward, Bruno in the center. The Swedish and Norwegian oarsmen grabbed swords and axes and followed. For a few moments there was the traditional melee of battle, the clang of blade on blade. Then the Ragnarsson line, already shot full of holes, disintegrated completely, became a scatter of men fighting back to back or trying to struggle to safety. Bruno called his men together, dressed their ranks, took them up the slope at a steady trot. Some catapulteers ran at once, others tried for a last shot or groped for sword and shield.

How the Ragnarsson ships stayed afloat Shef could not tell, but someone seemed to have had enough. Behind the front line he could see their smaller craft beginning to sweep out, to come forward in a charge. And the front line might not be sinking, but they were lower in the water, he could see a dragon-head tip sideways. The *Fearnought* had almost done her duty. She had battered the Ragnarssons' twelve largest into unmaneuverable hulks, though they were grapneled together so that the one held the other up. Now the smaller craft would have to take over.

But as they swept forward King Olaf, also reading the battle from half a mile behind, ordered his horns to blow and his rowers to pull. The *Heron* and her three consorts drove forward to engage the enemy, horns blaring relentlessly across the shivering water. Paper had wrapped stone—small boats against catapults. Stone had blunted scissors—the *Fearnought*'s catapults against the large craft. Now, as King Olaf's giant warships swept towards the Ragnarssons' conventional longships, it was scissors to cut paper.

Shef watched as the *Heron* swept past, seeing Olaf and Brand on the forecastle directing the course, watching the two leading Ragnarsson ships boldly steer to take her on each side, like mastiffs trying to pull down a bull. They were met by a volley of crossbows, a shower of javelins hurled downwards, great rocks as heavy as a man could lift flung over the side to shatter the bottom-boards. One smaller ship hurled grapnels, managed to pull herself alongside though already starting to sink. Her crew scrambled up the sides of the larger ship, met spear-thrusts and sword-blows before they could free a hand. The *Heron* brushed them aside, steered to run down another. Behind her and her consorts the main body of Shef's fleet poured on, aiming for gaps in the enemy ranks, picking their targets.

Shef leaned on the gunwale, looking round. That was it, he thought. The battle was over, except for finishing off. He could see the Ragnarsson catapults had been captured, could see the row of abandoned skiffs drawn up on the shore. King Olaf's late but well-timed charge had broken the back of the enemy fleet. The biggest Ragnarsson ships had never come into action at all, been battered down by the *Fearnought*.

How easily it could have gone the other way! Without the crossbows the skiffs might not have made their landing. Then the *Fearnought* would have been battered to pieces, and King Olaf's ships as soon as they moved forward. If the *Fearnought* had not been there, then even if the Ragnarsson catapults had not done the business, their twelve great dragon-boats would have come out and engaged Olaf three to one. But paper wraps stone, stone blunts scissors, scissors cut paper. Every time. That is how it is with machine-war.

"She's going to the bottom," Hagbarth said briefly. "I think one of those boulders broke her back, finally. Look." He pointed to the water swilling round the open hold.

"Cwicca, Osmod," shouted Shef. "Get your crews bailing. All right, Hagbarth, see if you can beach her. Over there, on the spit below the catapults."

The crippled *Fearnought* crept across the water, while the battle both in the bay and on land moved rapidly away from her, leaving her limping across an empty sea dotted with wreckage and the heads of exhausted swimmers.

CHAPTER THIRTY-THREE

The *Fearnought* beached, or sank, but either way touched bottom a few yards from the sandy shore. Dead and wounded men lay stretched out in a scatter not far away. Here and there in the water, hands waved feebly for rescue. Shef pointed them out to Hagbarth. "Get a couple of men into the row-boat and pick up as many as you can. Send some more along the shore to do what they can for the wounded. Hund will direct them."

Hagbarth nodded. "I'll get the rest working to shed the plates and lighten the ship. I think we can refloat her in the end."

"All right." Shef looked up the slope to where the Ragnarssons had mounted their catapults. No-one there. The battle had moved on, the catapulteers fled, the men from Shef's small-boat flotilla pursuing them and heading for the loot to be found in the now-undefended Braethraborg itself. Shef felt weariness descending on him with the relief of tension, felt he could bear to make no more decisions. Now that the noise of battle had gone by, a lark was singing, high in the air above the grassy slope, reminding him of days in the Emneth meadows years ago. Maybe those days would come back. Days of peace.

He decided to walk up the gentle slope to look over the other side into the bay, see the end of the battle and what must follow it, the sack of the Braethraborg. As he started off up the slope, lance in hand, Cuthred followed him. Karli followed also, a few paces behind.

Hagbarth watched them go, felt a moment's concern. On any battlefield there were likely to be men who had feigned death, enemies who might suddenly get to their feet again. It was Viking routine to police a battlefield before ceasing precautions, going over it in teams to strip bodies, finish enemy wounded and look for those worth ransom. This time it had not been done. Still, the king had two bodyguards with him, and there was much to be done on shore. Hagbarth put aside his concern, began to detail the others to their tasks.

At the top of the slope Shef saw again the scattering of dead, not many of them—the catapulteers had mostly run as they saw the drilled German line come up the hill at them. From the highest point he looked out over the scene he had seen in his vision, from the other end of the fjord. A long, green, peaceful bay. Clustered together maybe a mile off, the row on row of longhouses, barracks, shipyards, slipways, slave-pens that had been for so long the center of the Ragnarssons' power, the most feared place in the north. Now the core of that power was sinking in the bay, smashed by King Olaf's ships now making their stately way towards the main dock. The survivors were being hunted down by the smaller craft following up. Some ships, manned by Sigurth's reluctant levies, were steering widely round in an attempt to make their escape. At the center of the whole scene, battered into hulks by the *Fearnought*'s artillery, the twelve great dragon-boats lay holed, awash, their crews clinging to timbers, waiting to be rescued or to drown. All over the bay small boats, makeshift rafts or strong swimmers made for the shore.

"Not much for me to do today," said Cuthred behind Shef. "I might as well have stayed behind."

Shef did not reply. His eye had been caught by three bedraggled warriors beaching a small boat below him, on the side of the spit away from the grounded *Fearnought*. They had seen him too, were walking briskly up the slope.

"Maybe this could be a good day after all," said Sigurth Ragnarsson, in the lead. He had begun the battle in the center ship of the line of the great warships. It had been struck and all but split open by the first stone that came flying from the strange metal-plated boat the Sigvarthsson had deployed. The grapnels which held ship to ship all along the line had kept his own afloat. But still the stones had come flying, flying, while he waited in a fury of impatience for his own artillery to find the range, smash the interloper. In the end he had torn the Raven Banner from the mast, and transferred it, himself and his brothers to his beloved *Frani Ormr*, leading the main fleet behind the

shelter of the great patrol craft. Then, with the metal boat at last
sinking and out of action, he had led the charge of the smaller ships
against King Olaf's *Heron*.

That had failed too, the *Frani Ormr* sunk under him, her bottom
smashed open by a boulder heaved from a higher deck. He and his
brothers had had to kill several of their own men in the melee that
followed to get off the sinking ship. His fleet and army had disintegrated behind him. In a bare hour, without the chance to strike a blow,
he had been cast down from power and kingship to being once again a
mere warrior, owning only his clothes and his weapons and what he
carried on his person. Sigurth had heard that Othin betrayed his
followers. But only, so the stories said, to glorious death, sword in
hand. Not to ignominious defeat without a chance to strike.

Yet now, Sigurth thought, it might be that Othin stood his friend
after all. For there, in front of him, was the source of all their troubles.
With two men only by him, to match Sigurth and his two mighty
brothers. Three against three.

Shef looked round, recognizing from fifty yards the strange eyes of
the Snake-eye. Sigurth, Halvdan and Ubbi, every one of them a
champion, and all of them fully armed for the hand-to-hand battle
that had not taken place. Against them himself, carrying only his old
and fragile lance, with neither armor nor shield, Karli, still clutching
his cheap sword, and Cuthred. Could even Cuthred fight three
champions at once, with only the doubtful help Shef and Karli could
give him? This was what Shef had always hoped and schemed to avoid:
the fair fight on even ground against better and more experienced
men. The sensible thing to do was run at once, down to the shore and
the cover of the *Fearnought*'s crossbows. Shef turned to the others,
starting to signal to them, point the way back over the little hill.

Too late. Cuthred's eyes had gone wide, he was breathing in with
great gasps, slaver beginning to run from the corners of his mouth. He
too had recognized the Snake-eye.

Shef shook him by the arm, was shrugged aside with a careless
sweep from the shield, its spike missing his face by a fraction.
"Cuthred," he shouted. "We must run, for now. Kill them later."

"Kill them now," came a hoarse inhuman answer.

"Remember, you are my man! I released you from the mill. You
swore allegiance."

Cuthred turned to look Shef full in the eye, some fragment of
intelligence still under his control despite the coming berserkergang.
"I was someone's man before you, king. Those are the men who killed

King Ella." He struggled to form words, his face twisting. Shef thought he caught the word "sorry." And then the berserk had thrust past him, running gleefully over the grass at the oncoming trio.

He stopped feet short of them, called out tauntingly, his voice clear and high, full of delight.

"Sons of Ragnar," he shouted. "I killed your father. I tore out his fingernails to make him talk. Then I bound him and put him in the snake-pit, the *ormgarthr*. He died blue in the face with his hands tied. You will not meet *him* in Valhalla."

He threw his head back, with a crow of triumphant laughter. Quick as a snake came the javelin from Sigurth. As quick the parry from the hardened shield that sent it flying high overhead. Then Cuthred had charged.

Sigurth stepped deftly away from him, dodging the first slash and ducking the back-stroke. Then Ubbi and Halvdan closed in, one from each side, swords swinging. The air was full of the clang of metal as Cuthred beat blows aside, swung and stabbed himself, pressing both men instantly back.

Yet he could not pursue three at once. Sigurth looked for a moment at the melee he had evaded, then turned from it, came on, sword drawn, shield up. Shef looked round. Karli stood by him, face pale, still clutching the reforged sword Shef had given him, taken from the unlucky Hrani. Shef had his lance. Neither had shields. Sigurth outnumbered them one to two. Yet he could not run now and leave Cuthred alone.

"No water between us this time, clever boy," said Sigurth. As he jumped forward Shef stabbed at him with the lance, the first time he had ever tried to wield it in earnest. Sigurth slashed head from wooden shaft with one forehand blow, swung the backhand instantly at Shef's neck. He ducked, sprang back, dropping the useless shaft and pulling out the belt-knife with which he had killed Kjallak. He still felt numb, useless, unprepared. Now was the time he needed Hund's potion. But Hund was on the other side of the hill.

Karli stepped forward to protect his master, swung with the sword he had carried proudly since the day Shef gave it to him. With sick recognition Shef saw that he had forgotten once more everything that had ever been told him about how to wield it. He struck like a plowboy, like a churl, like a webfoot from the fen. Sigurth took the first blow easily on his blade, waited with something like disbelief for the slow second, caught it on his shield and swung with an adder's speed before Karli could recover. Karli had no shield, no helmet. Shef heard the butcher's chunk of cleaver into bone as sword bit deep into skull. The stocky man from the Ditmarsh dropped his weapon, sprawled at the Snake-eye's feet.

Downslope Cuthred was beating Halvdan to his knees with a furious assault. Ubbi, head slashed from shoulders, lay a few yards from him. Sigurth saw the scene out of the corner of his eye and turned again to Shef.

"I'd better make sure of you, then," he said, stepping round Karli's body. Shef faced the veteran warrior with knife alone, too close to turn his back and run.

From far above Othin the one-eyed god looked down on his devotee, Sigurth son of Ragnar. "He is a great warrior," he said ruefully.

"But he has lost the battle," came the reply from the clever-faced god beside him.

"If it had been a fair match he would have won."

"Take him for your Einheriar *then."*

Othin paused in thought. Should he allow his worshiper one last victory? The words of his son Rig came back to him, and his own words too, the words he had whispered in the ear of his beloved son Balder on the funeral pyre. "Would that some god would bring you back to me, my son." No god had, no hero had, not even his trusted Hermoth. Maybe they were right. Blood was not the cure, but tears. He would never draw tears from the Snake-eye. Regretfully, he made his decision. "Not for nothing do they call me Bölverk, doer of evil, betrayer of warriors," he muttered, heard only by Rig and the all-hearing ears of Heimdall.

He whistled a call to his Valkyriar, who fly unseen over every battlefield, choosing the slain and throwing over them their nets of weakness, paralysis, making weapons turn in the hand and eyes miss the flight of spear or arrow. With his great spear he pointed out the Snake-eye.

Sigurth came up the slight slope like a hunting beast, sword-point low, shield high, his white-rimmed eyes never leaving Shef's face. Shef backed away from him, short knife in hand, open to slash or thrust as soon as Sigurth could close the six bare feet between them. As he backed he felt, suddenly, the ground beneath him at a different angle. They had reached the top of the slope, were starting to cross it. In a few moments they would be among the abandoned catapults, in sight from the *Fearnought*. If he could delay a hundred heartbeats longer . . . The same thought came to Sigurth. He came on faster, determined to make sure work before anyone could intervene.

All day the lace on his rawhide shoe had worked looser and looser. Now it trailed in the short grass. As he took the pace forward that would set up the killing thrust, Sigurth trod on the lace, tried to step forward with the foot that was trapped, slipped and stumbled off balance. He dropped his shield-arm, bracing himself for a moment with his left hand on the grass.

Shef, backing away, stepped forward on pure reflex and stabbed forward with the Rogaland knife. It drove home through the beard and under the chin, exactly as it had done with Kjallak. For an instant Sigurth stared up at him, the strange eyes widening in shock. Then they seemed to see something behind Shef's back, a look of mingled recognition and disgust crossed the dying face. The sword lifted as if to stab at some shape, some betrayer in the sky.

Shef twisted the knife savagely once and leaped back, as Sigurth fell face down.

Cuthred was limping up the slope towards him. His face was gashed open, a long unbleeding split, like the wound a butcher makes in long-dead meat. His mail was hacked and torn in a dozen places. It seemed impossible that he could walk, one thigh seemingly half-severed again, the one slashed open by Vigdjarf.

"You got one, I got two," he remarked. "I avenged King Ella. I will speak well of you to him." As he stood swaying the crazy light died in his eyes. In a more normal voice he added, "I wish you could bury me whole. Send word to the trolls for me, to Miltastaray. I would have been her man."

Suddenly blood began to flow from his wounds, as the strange auto-control of berserkergang left him. He sank down, rolled on to his back. When Shef felt for a pulse, there was none. He walked across the blood-stained grass to look to Karli, but without hope. Warriors like the Snake-eye did not miss their stroke. Not unless they were prevented. His guess was right. Karli was stone-dead as well, brains mixed with the blood around him, his cheerful expression faded for ever to one of surprise and dismay. Bad news for Edith, and a score of others. Bad news for Miltastaray.

Shef mechanically retrieved Cuthred's sword, started to trudge back to the ship, shoulders bowed. As he reached the abandoned catapults, to his surprise he saw Bruno the German standing in front of him. Behind him, Shef saw that Hagbarth had noticed as well, was calling men from their work on the *Fearnought* and directing them over the side. But for the moment they were alone.

"I saw your duel," said Bruno. "Now you have killed two

Ragnarssons. But I don't know how you do it. It seemed that he should kill you easily. Any one of my men could have done it. I doubt you would be any match for me."

"Why should we be a match?"

"You have something I want. Where is your lance?"

Shef waved over one shoulder. "Back there. What is it to you?"

As if in answer Bruno aimed a blow at him with his long horseman's sword. Shef parried automatically with the sword he had taken from Cuthred, parried again and again, found the sword spinning from his hand and the point of Bruno's resting in the hollow of his throat, exactly where he had stabbed Sigurth the Snake-eye.

"What is it to me?" repeated Bruno. "It is the Holy Lance with which Jesus Christ was slain. By a German centurion. The Lance that shed the Holy Blood."

Shef remembered the vision he had seen of a crucifixion, the man in the red-crested helmet speaking German words. "Yes," he said, speaking carefully with the cold point pricking his skin. "I believe you."

"He who holds it will be the Emperor. True Emperor of the West, successor of Charlemagne, uniter once more of the Roman Empire. The German Roman Empire."

Shef felt immense pressure bearing down on him, pressure greater than the fear of the sharp steel point at his throat. Twice men had tried to make him release the lance, twice he had resisted them. If he handed it over now he might be condemning the whole world to a new domination, a new tyranny from a new Rome, stronger than the old Rome and the old Pope. If he refused he would die. Had he the right to save his life at such a price? With Karli and Cuthred dead in the grass beside him?

And yet the Lance was not his. So much was clear. It belonged to the Christians. What they would do with it, only their God knew. But they had the right to follow their vision, as he and the Way, he and Thorvin and Vigleik and all the others had the right to follow theirs. Remembering his own vision of the dying Christ, remembering King Edmund of the East Angles and the old woman he and Alfred had met lamenting in the forest-clearing, he felt there was something yet to come from the Cross. If not from the Church. Yet Bruno was no Churchman.

"If the Lance is to make a German Empire," said Shef stiffly, "it had better be a German who holds it, then. You will find the lance-head by my companion's body there, where Sigurth cut it from its shaft. Only the head is ancient work. The shaft has been many times renewed."

Bruno seemed, for a moment, nonplused. "You are prepared to give it up? I would not do so, even with a point at my throat." He thought a moment longer, ignoring the men now running up the hill towards them. "It is true. Your emblem is not the spear, whether of Othin or of the centurion Longinus. What you wear round your neck, as I have told you, is the *graduale*. It is your destiny to pursue that, as mine was to retrieve the Lance."

He twitched his blade back, raised it in salute. "I ought to kill you just the same," he said. "I fear you are a dangerous man, though no swordsman. But it would not be knightly, in cold blood. Farewell, then, King of the North. Remember I was the first to hail you so."

He ran down the slope, picked something from the bloody grass, kissed it, and sped away towards a line of horses being led towards him from the Braethraborg corrals.

Shef took a crossbow from one of the lightly-armed *skogarmenn* who came panting up the hill, cocked it, dropped in a quarrel, looked at the broad back running away sixty, eighty, a hundred yards off.

I ought to kill you too, he reflected. But it would not be knightly, in cold blood, to return ill for good. Farewell, then, Emperor-to-be. Or as you say, *auf wiedersehen*.

JARNBERA-
Land

hrafnsey•

•trondheím

•the gula-thing

the
Rogaland westfold